Cosmopolitan

'A heartless hero for the millennial generation'
Standpoint

'The most original unreliable narrator and anti-hero
you'll encounter this year, maybe even this decade.
Crime book, literary fiction, contemporary tragedy;
it doesn't matter what pot you put it in, just read it.'
Crime Fiction Lover

'Jonathan Lyon has written the best
gay debut novel in YEARS'
Johann Hari, author of *Lost Connections*

'A compelling debut. Suspend all rational thought
and enjoy the - rather unsettling - ride'
Belfast Telegraph

'Echoes of the narratives of Irvine Welsh… a com-
pulsive psychoneurotic take on the crime thriller.'
G Scene

Jonathan Lyon was born in 1991 in London. He studied at Oxford University, graduating in 2013. He moved to Berlin the same year where he now works as a musician and writer. He has had a chronic illness for over a decade. *Carnivore* is his debut novel.

CARNIVORE

Jonathan Lyon

ONE PLACE. MANY STORIES

HQ
An imprint of HarperCollins*Publishers* Ltd
1 London Bridge Street
London SE1 9GF

This paperback edition 2018

1
First published in Great Britain by
HQ, an imprint of HarperCollins*Publishers* Ltd 2017

ISBN: 987-0-00-823261-0

Printed and bound by
CPI Group (UK) Ltd, Croydon, CR0 4YY

For anyone who's been ill too long.

ACT I

The ordinary world

1.

'What's your fantasy?'

All sex and storytelling starts with this, of course. Sometimes the question's self-directed, sometimes it's only implied. But here, obviously, I was supposed to reply 'being dominated,' so that's what I said.

I was actually fantasising about eating a satsuma, slowly, slice by slice, on the edge of a rooftop, or perhaps on a hilltop, watching a building below me burn in a fire I'd started. But this would be too long to say aloud, and probably wouldn't arouse a man in the prime of his mid-life crisis as easily as a boy begging for a beating.

So now that my victim thought that I was his victim, he could breathe more heavily, and began struggling to unbutton his shirt.

'No, no you should be doing this,' he said, fluttering his fingers. 'I mean, undress me, boy!'

Unsuited to the dominant role, he recoiled at his own orders. Clearly, he was a submissive – if I'd had the energy, I could've had him on all fours in a few minutes. But energy is not one of my vices.

'Of course, sir,' I said instead, my mouth twitching into a smile I had to hide by lowering my head.

Beneath his shirt was a paunch of greying hairs. As I removed the rest of his clothes, he hovered awkwardly between sitting and standing, his hands just above my back, not yet confident enough to touch me.

'Now, now… you!'

I took off my tracksuit – the uniform he'd requested – delivered my finest doe-eyed simper, and knelt down. But he rejected this arrangement and instead dragged me upwards onto the bed.

'No time for that… boy. Let's get to the point.'

He forced my face into the pillow and I began to moan in a way that would make him hard. Perhaps he hoped I'd feel a kind of shame in this, but 'this' meant nothing.

'This' was merely boring, but it was worth a thousand pounds. And he wouldn't last long. I was simply a blank page onto which he could write his desires. And what banal desires! There was no ambition in them, no real yearning, not even any real sadness. His mind was shut to himself – all he was semi-aware of were a few anxieties, a few humiliations, a few petulant disappointments. Perhaps he fancied himself a deviant for fucking a boy he believed to be nineteen while his wife wandered somewhere around the Mediterranean. But he was ordinary. To a true deviant, sex is much too straightforward.

I was aroused by making him think that I was afraid of him – extracting his desires like a vampire of fantasy, while giving him only falsehood in return.

My fiction was of the orphan desperate for money, slightly stupid, pleasingly unsophisticated beside the powerful newspaper-owner. I made him feel like his life – on the fifteenth floor of some glass and steel erection in central London – was beyond my understanding, and therefore more meaningful than it was.

He finished in about ten minutes. As he got off me, I assumed he was leaving for the bathroom – so I'd begun turning over, when he struck me with his belt. My body spasmed in delight – here, at least, at last, was a little more excitement, even if there was still no creativity in his lust. The pain made me laugh, but I hid it with a howl.

'No, no, please,' I begged, rolling my eyes at myself.

I could act more convincingly than this, but he wouldn't want me to. Part of my charm was my innocence. I needed to seem out of my depth, ineptly play-acting at being a seasoned sexual plaything. He needed me to be a bad actor, so he could see through to the lost boy behind the performance.

Of course, the lost boy was the performance, and the bad acting was excellent acting. His metal buckle bit into my flesh with an eroticism his body could never have communicated. With each hit, a hunger in my muscles was being satisfied. And soon, my trembling was not an act – I was aroused. My senses began to mix: a blue the colour of a kingfisher's back blurred the edges of my vision, and in my gums I tasted the squeezed juice of a lime.

He whipped me twenty or so times, until my pleading reached a satisfactory intensity, and he threw aside the belt – and left. As soon as he was in the bathroom, I sat up, rubbing my eyes so it would look like I'd been crying. Outside, October was white. I walked to the balcony and slid open its door.

Yesterday, I'd posed as an undergraduate for a calmer client – and quoted Nietzsche's desire for music 'to be as cheerful and profound as an October afternoon'. That had meant little then – but, following this violence, perhaps it could mean more to me. Nietzsche's philosophy had, after all, come out of chronic illness – and so maybe mine could too. I'd call for a different music, though, since my illness was dominated by pain – a constant, meaningless, incurable pain at the core of my muscles, that weakened me into a fog without memories or focus – a pain that confined me to a parallel word, the world of the sick – where being whipped until my blood spilled out seemed like pleasure, or even like music.

So perhaps this October afternoon was cheerful and profound. Though now its music was the sound of a man washing off his semen in a hotel shower, transitioning from delight to shame at how he'd got there. The sky had a clarity that I could almost forget my body in – to be purely mind, racing into a new weather. But I had to put on my clothes before he returned, and resume the posture of a wounded adolescent – to maximise his regret, and so increase my price.

With my phone I photographed the credit cards and driving license in his wallet. He should have kicked me out before he showered, but his embarrassment had made him careless.

When he did return, he paid me £1,500 in £50 notes. My posture combined fear with gratitude. He couldn't look me in the eye. I left him slumped on a chair in a towel, drained of his pedestrian ecstasy, shocked by himself and what he imagined I'd suffered.

The door closed slowly as I left along the corridor. By the time I'd got to the lift, I'd forgotten his face.

2.

'Life is about to happen to us babyboyyy
   Ring me cunt
   This is yr mother btw
   Luvvvv u'
These texts were from an unknown number, which I saved in my contacts as 'Dawn, Mother Errant' before ringing back.

'You fucking done yet?' she shouted. 'I told you he was easy. He was easy weren't he? I'm coming where you are. Wait — where the fuck are you again? You're at the Waire, yeah?'

'What? Yeah. How are you coming to me? Are you drunk?'

'Shut up. I'm amazing,' she laughed. 'I'm a woman of the world again. I'm a fucking miracle! I told you I still have my ways, don't I? I'm a goddess! Give me your perjury!'

'Perjury? What you talking about? Are you in a car?'

'Perjury, homage, whatever it's called. Gifts for goddesses. You know what I mean. And fuck yeah I'm in a car. The fastest car in the Milky Way, sweetheart, you've got a chauffeur today. I'm nearly there so don't move. Don't you move! You can't run off from me now anyway. It's got the worst art you ever seen, don't it? I told you.'

'You mean like a religious offering?' I asked, trying to address the first of her non-sequiturs.

The lobby I was passing through was indeed decorated with

7

bland attempts at pop art, which, despite their garish colours, somehow all seemed beige.

'No it's a fancier word than that, you fuckwit. One of your posh words. I only want your poshest words. The fanciest fucking words you've got, for the fanciest woman you know.'

'A libation?'

'That's the fucking one, beautiful!' she said. 'You're a gorgeous boy! Libation, invective, perjury – you know the words – only give me the good shit now.'

'How did you get a car?'

'No spoilers, bitch, you're waiting for me. Don't move!' She hung up.

I stepped onto the pavement. Kensington was tensing itself for rush hour. Bicycles flirted past wing-mirrors towards the calmer cobbled side streets. The clouds above us were tensed too, as if plotting violence against the autumn.

London seemed to grow out of its weather, not out of the ground – the mood came first and then the body – and this mood followed the whims of the surrounding sea, which was as changeable as a child – and had a child's fury and a child's persistence.

In a precaution I'd been taught by Dawn, I redistributed the stack of fifties across my two pockets, my boxers-briefs, and my right sock. The pain dizzied me pleasantly. And as I replaced my shoe, a white car drove up beside me – blasting one of Bach's Brandenburg Concertos through an open window.

'Oi, your highness!' Dawn shouted. 'Get the fuck in, we're going to the guillotine!'

'Have you had your hair done?' I asked, getting in.

It had been dyed the colour of honeycomb, and her skin seemed to have been pulled tighter over her face too – so that it was sharp and handsome in an untrusting way. She wore a black leather jacket over a black lace dress, on a petite frame thinned by years of addiction.

'I done everything. I look like a hundred years younger, don't I? I don't even remember what age is after thirty-four. I shaved my legs above the knee. I'm even wearing heels.'

'You're not,' I said, and tried to bend to see her feet under the dashboard, but she pushed my head away.

'Maybe I'm not wearing heels, you cheeky shit, you're not allowed to check. A woman is wearing heels if she tells you she's wearing heels. Wait, what's wrong with you?'

'Just drive.'

'You're flinching, what's wrong with you? Why can't you sit right? What he do?'

'What? Nothing, it was fine.'

I adopted a tone of alluring evasion – to make her think that I wanted her to ask further, and was only pretending to be brave – since I played the lost boy for her just as much as I did for the clients she sometimes sent my way. This was partly because I took pleasure in manipulating for its own sake – and partly because it was the role Dawn wanted me to play anyway – as it let her be a more caring, protective mother to me, and so let her atone for failing her other son, from whom she was estranged.

She turned off the radio and gripped my wrist.

'You're telling me this fucking minute what just happened up there.'

'I'm fine. He. I'm fine.'

Still gripping my wrist, she unzipped my tracksuit top. I twitched at her touch. She pulled the jacket over my shoulder, exposing the edge of a welt from the tongue of the belt.

'What the fuck?' She pushed me forwards to pull it down further, exposing the rest of his lashes.

I pretended to shiver, carefully, so as not to overplay it – and didn't reply. I wanted her mind to spread multiple narratives across my silence.

'Why'd he do this? That was never his game.'

'It's his game now,' I said, attempting a half-laugh.

'Fuck, babe, how'd I let this happen?'

But there was something so insincere about the way she said this that I began to wonder whether she was role-playing too. Dawn was as clever and as bored as me, after all – her other son refused to see her for a reason. Maybe she'd known her client would whip me, and wanted him to. He had acted as though it had been pre-arranged. Maybe she was playing a new game with me, then, a violent game – born of love and cruelty and love of cruelty, and love of games themselves – and in it we had to hurt each other, using people as our instruments. Or maybe I was being paranoid.

'This had nothing to do with you, it's not about you,' I said, now hopeful that the opposite of this was true.

'You need Savlon. It's ok I've got Savlon in my bag – mummy can get you some painkillers – oh shit, you need some painkilling, I was wondering why you weren't sitting right – look at you!' There was no sympathy in her voice. 'This is fucked up. How was you even standing out there? Who uses the belt end? You're bleeding! Fuck. Lean over, let me fix this.'

'Can we drive somewhere else first?'

'No, lean over.'

She reached behind her seat for her handbag, rummaged awhile, and found the antiseptic cream. Her fingers drew its ointment across my wounds with a tenderness that seemed almost admiring of – or excited by – the violence she'd arranged for me.

'Fuck men, fuck men, fuck men like that,' she said, enjoying her own performance. 'He better of given you extra for this. What the fuck? How much you get?'

'Eight hundred.'

'What? No! It was supposed to be a grand.'

'No, it was supposed to be five hundred. Then he gave me a three hundred pound tip for this.'

'Oh my god, baby, this is not how we start our new life. Life is about to happen to us, I've been telling you, we've got to be looking our best. Thank fuck he didn't touch your beautiful face! You been crying?'

She kissed my shoulder. I shrugged her off and pulled my top back up. I wanted to believe she'd had me wounded on purpose. And if this was a game, then it was my turn to play.

'I'm fine,' I said. 'Some painkilling would be good if we can get some though.'

'Course we can darling, I've got you. I got you. We're going to do something fun.' Bored of her fake dismay, she'd become enthusiastic again. She jerked the car forward, away from the main road, towards the backstreets. 'Mummy's going to give you a driving lesson. We got to act like rich people now. So we got to drive where they drive. And I've got so much to say, you've been gone so fucking long.'

'It's been like ten days.'

'Yeah and I made some changes. Cos I —'

There was a smack on the windscreen – we flinched. A bleeding lump rolled down the glass and slumped onto the bonnet. We peered forwards. It was an injured squirrel, perhaps fallen from a tree. It lay on its back, twitching, trying to right itself – as something black dived upon it: a crow as a big as a cat. The crow drove its beak into the squirrel's skull. Dawn looked away. Between thrusts, the crow rotated its head to survey its surroundings – and eventually made eye contact with me. It knew it was being watched, but did not fear this audience. I smiled in encouragement. The crow hammered the squirrel into a mess of sinew, but ate nothing – seemingly intent only on the kill. And then it flew away.

'What the fuck?' Dawn said.

The squirrel's innards rolled down the bonnet. She activated the windshield wipers, but dryly – smearing the blood in arcs across the glass before she worked out how to activate the wiper fluid – and the red was diluted towards orange. A strand of intestine got caught at the edge of the windshield. The carcass lay on the car like a wound in the steel itself – almost invitingly, like a portal you could put your hand through, into a future where muscle and metal were forgotten.

'It'll fall off when we drive,' I said.

'What the fuck? Is this what an omen is?'

I laughed. 'It's raining squirrels, that means fertility.'

'I fucking hope not. I don't need more sons.'

As we drove onward, the squirrel flopped slowly towards us, and then, with a last splatter, slid off the side onto the road.

'What changes were you talking about?' I asked.

'What?'

'What were the changes you were going to tell me about?'

'Oh yeah, fuck. No, no, no – we need to reset the mood first. I'm definitely not staying driving after that omen of yours.'

'How was that my omen?'

'It weren't fucking raining dead squirrels till you got in here, was it? I'm marked for death now. Fuck. I'm getting the champagne out and you're getting in my seat.'

She parked beside a terrace of improbably white five-storey houses.

'You'll be a natural babe,' she said. 'It's automatic, it's easy. Just pretend you *are* Kensington, ok?'

She got out and came round to my side. I let her lead me back past the squirrel streaks to the driver's seat. But before I'd sat down, she began pointing out various buttons and levers, too quickly for a novice to remember. I wasn't, however, quite a novice – five years ago, I'd spent two weeks sleeping in a car with a girl on a tobacco-manufacturing plant, and she'd taught me how to drive. Naturally, I wasn't going to tell Dawn this – I needed her to believe that she was mothering me and, too, I needed to further the illusion I fed to her of myself as a prodigy, capable of adapting to any situation with astonishing rapidity.

So I turned the key, released the handbrake, and immediately lurched into the bumper of the car in front of us, setting off its alarm. Dawn shrieked and slapped me. I stamped the car to a stop, shaking, my confidence gone.

'Let me get in my seat first you fucking psychopath!' She slammed my door shut and sprinted to the passenger side. 'The fuck is wrong with you? Get in reverse! Quick! Drive!'

I obeyed, trying to adapt to the vehicle's rhythms, my mind narrowed, and backed out into the street – and then pushed the stick into 'D' and accelerated forward. Ashamed that I'd failed to maintain my performance, my cheeks flushed – and a taste like over-sweet strawberry jam came over my gums. I hadn't been the master illusionist, I'd been clumsy. I was ashamed of feeling ashamed – of still having a pride that could be pricked. I tried to cough the taste away.

She reached behind my seat for her bag and retrieved a bottle of sparkling wine. The alarm of the parked car faded behind us as I familiarised myself with the controls, speeding up a little to turn the corner.

'Don't speed round a corner sweetheart, you got to go slow for a corner.'

'Shit yeah,' I said, flushing less as I regained command of my indifference.

I wondered whether she was humiliating me on purpose – in the same way she'd had me whipped on purpose – as part of some wider ploy to empower herself in a coming negotiation.

'You'll be fine,' she said. 'You got to go in the deep end. We're big thinkers now, sweetheart. Take a sip of this –' she lifted the bottle to my lips and I obediently sipped its lukewarm wine. 'We're going Wandsworth – go down there.' She waved vaguely to our left. 'Get over the river.'

'Why?' I moved into the lane she'd indicated.

'Not telling you.'

'So is this car stolen?'

Her face deflated into a sneer. 'Don't be such a fucking fun sponge.' She punched me on the arm. 'You think I know how to steal a fucking car? No. This car was an act of love. I'm in love now and I've got a man that's in love with me.'

'Who – that new guy? Is he rich?'

She laughed and drank again, shaking her head. 'You know who he is, bitch – Kimber's the man of my dreams, the love of my life! – I met him down the Rockway the same night you ran off sulking – cos you was jealous of him, weren't you sweetheart? Ah my sweet sulking little gremlin, you got jealous, didn't you?'

She lifted up her hand and waved it in front of my face until I noticed the silver band around her ring finger.

'Is that an engagement ring?'

She cackled. 'No, not telling you. My story needs to build. Talk to me about something else first. How you going to spend your money?'

'I dunno… I need to buy a better edition of Emily Dickinson's poems. I don't want any editing. She had her own type of dash, and —'

'You're really talking to me about dashes? No. Sweetheart, we're in a brand new car, we got champagne, we're in the Royal Fucking Borough of Kensington and Chelsea. Sweetheart, no. You got to think bigger now.' She turned the radio on again and baroque orchestral music began shaking the metal beneath our feet. 'You're going to buy something stupid what won't last. You're going to buy expensive olives and expensive wine – cos we've got a new place to live! We're out of the hostel forever – it's done, we can't go back – all our worldly possessions are in the boot of this car, and we're moving in today.'

'What?' I braked in surprise. Car horns honked behind us. 'Shit, what?' I released the brake. 'How?'

'I know! Ah, but you've made me feel bad now – don't feel bad about the dashes, sweetheart – I should be more supporting, sorry, sorry. Course you can buy your poems, tell me about them, I'm listening.'

'What? Stop changing the subject.'

She laughed, tapping the side of the bottle in applause at her own performance. 'This is how you build tension! But really babe, tell me why Emily should get your money. What's her best line?'

'I like "soundless as dots on a disk of snow",' I said, choosing to play along. 'It's about civilisation collapsing. She has a perfect verse about snow as well:

"This is the Hour of Lead —"'

'Ok shut the fuck up, you win. No more poems, no dashes, I'll tell you everything.'

'I knew you wouldn't last.'

'Alright, have a drink first,' she said, lifting the bottle up to my mouth. 'But keep your eyes on the road. Oi! Breathe through your fucking nose you amateur. How many shit blowjobs you given with that technique? What the fuck? Breathe through your nose – there you go – I'm not taking this away till you drink all of it –' I tried to lean my head back, groaning in protest. 'No, drink it all,' she laughed, and kept it there until I choked.

The alcohol could provide a little relief, perhaps – for the welts across my back – but these competed with the deeper pain a decade old – of my myalgia – which no alcohol could help. That pain needed harder drugs than the ones allowed by shops or doctors – it needed the heroin Dawn had promised me – and doctors had failed me long ago, anyway, as they had failed everyone else with my illness.

I coughed up Dawn's wine until the taste wove into the sound and scent of sycamore trees brushing each other's branches – and she settled back into her chair, preparing her story.

In her silence, I wondered whether I belonged to an invisible epidemic – the greatest epidemic of the twenty-first century, perhaps – since my disease afflicted tens of millions of people, but most of them hadn't even heard of it – a multi-system sickness of pain and exhaustion and immune dysfunction, a metabolic crisis – that left no signs on the body, yet depleted its victims more severely than late-stage cancer, and lasted for decades – and yet made no appearances in films or books, received almost no funding or research, and had no known cause and no known cure, and no fixed name – a sickness that afflicted colder countries more, and northern Europe and America the most, like it was somehow the repressed remorse of imperialism, or the rest of the world's revenge…

I moved the car into a lane towards Wandsworth Bridge.

'So,' she said. 'I get home last Tuesday – you're still gone, so I'm still heartbroken – and the bitch with the ADHD kid has stole all our pasta so there's nothing to eat except fucking instant coffee and I'm about to have a full-on breakdown – and then Sandra comes in and she says I've got some post, and its an envelope just saying 'For Dawn' on it – with a key inside. It's a car key. And Sandra's being so fucking nosey but she's saying she can give me some rice so I'm humouring her and I'm chatting to her about Kimber and about how I met him down the Rockway a week earlier, and I'm saying you're sulking cos I've met a new man – and how he's very attentive to me – and how I fell asleep at his flat and that's what made you jealous, weren't it? But what I didn't tell you was that his flat is fucking fancy so I knew he's got money – and I didn't even fuck him, and the next day I see him again after you're gone and then the next day again and then I'm seeing him every day like we're teenagers. I was saying to her, I was saying it was overwhelming, but it was something that he needed and that I needed, and it felt like very child-like, it was just nice, you know? Until there's a night when he has to go to work, so I come back and you're still gone, and then here's this car key in our kitchen, and I'm thinking this can't be him, but who else's it going to be? So I just go into the street and Sandra's behind me and I press the car-key button and this fucking white beauty flashes at us across the road. And it's got petrol! And there's this phone inside with a text from him saying 'happy new year', even though it's autumn. Like, what the fuck?'

'He sounds like a serial killer,' I said. 'What does he expect in return?'

'Don't you get bored being this cynical? It's a gift. It's love. He knows we're stuck in a hostel – I told him I got a son, and I gave you a fucking five-star review sweetheart, even though you're a little shit – and he speaks fancier than you and he's attracted to me, so fuck you. Life is about to happen to us!'

'Why do you keep saying that? You sound like a televangelist.'

Sunlight flashed from the Thames as we crossed it. Ahead of us rose the advert sculpture of Wandsworth Bridge round-about – a model atom with electron paths of white steel and four billboards for a nucleus – a microcosm of all London now, perhaps – the nucleus sold for the sign.

'So fucking what?' she said. 'It's my motto now. And it's true. You're torturing me with this negativity! It's not civilised!'

I imagined swerving into an oncoming car so that it crashed into Dawn's door. Our soundtrack climaxed in a fanfare. She wasn't wearing a seatbelt.

'Everyone knows civilisation comes from torture,' I said, with the sun still in my eyes. 'Millions of bodies maimed and broken. Cruelty is the agent of progress. Perhaps it didn't need to be, but it was. Think of all the different kinds of labour, in war, in slavery, in revolution – in industry and agriculture – over the last three hundred years, or the last three thousand years, it doesn't matter – from the mines of the bronze age to the skyscrapers now – temples, railways, harvests, factories – they were all worked on by bodies under torture, minds reduced to screams… Just so a few men, in comfort, could speak about iambic pentameter and the speed of light.'

'Where'd that come from?' she laughed, swigging from the bottle.

The traffic lights ahead went red. Thoughtlessly, I pressed on the accelerator. The sound of a flag flapped around my ears, as the wind sped up – and my muscles turned to gold – and then a trumpet blast, a punch – and the car was shunted sideways.

I snapped into my seatbelt, as metal hands clapped once beside me. There was a wail. But I drove on – into the wind, uphill, as the city split open and a sea spilled out of me – and in the mirror, the car that had hit us continued behind us, a little blackened – and the trumpets changed.

The sky was the hull of a ship – a whaler with sails of living lions – and as the lions roared, gems fell from their mouths, mingling with flowers – carnations and carbuncles – in a wave of red that washed over the car.

Dawn, dazed, lifted the bottle to her lips, and drank – though most of the wine had spilled out over her. Then she turned to me, slowly, in wonder – with a mask of blood on the far half of her head. I wanted to scream out of the window, 'Nobody's strong enough to be loved by me!' But I laughed instead.

For a second, London seemed an unknown city – and I braked with my eyes closed, offering myself to the sun.

Dawn drank again from the bottle, still stiff with shock. The blood dribbled like sweat from her hairline, where it had hit the edge of the door – and I looked at it like it was mine, more than my own blood was mine – or rather, I looked at her wound like it was mine in the same way that the wounds on my back were hers.

'What's happening?' she whispered.

'We're going to our new house,' I said.

'Oi, how d'you guess that?' she asked, disorientated, dabbing at her cut in disbelief.

'You just told me,' I said.

'Oh, yeah, ok yeah – he's got us somewhere to live, Kimber's got us… it's not a council flat, but we knew that dream weren't coming true, sweetheart, this is as good as it's going to get, it's…' She was speaking too quickly to keep up with herself. 'It's fucking good – we just need a… a five hundred pound deposit – and that's insanely small, you got to admit, he's in love with me – and then the contract's legit, then, then, then that shows the contract's legit.'

'So we're putting our entire lives in the hands of some guy you met a week ago?'

'You want to be in a fucking homeless hostel forever?' she shouted, at last reacting to the crash with anger. 'It's been two years, Leander! I can't live like that anymore – and you weren't even living.'

'I could have found a —'

'We've been fucking trying! You found us fuck all. Being pretty made you lazy, I told you – you're stuck, and I don't want you fucking stuck. I love you, alright?' She was anxiously smearing her own blood across her face. 'I done us a good thing, sweetheart, admit it – I got us out that fucking misery nest. Don't try and get outraged at me, it's too late, I signed the contract. It's done.'

'Ok, ok,' I smiled, and drove on. 'Ok. I can pay the deposit. I'll give you the five hundred.'

'Baby!' Nearly weeping, she kissed me on the cheek, forcing an arm behind my back to wrap me in a hug, pressing her bleeding head into mine – aroused by the intensity of our shared shock. 'Fuck,' she said, as she shrank back in her seat. 'Fuck… That cunt drove into us.'

'He wasn't looking,' I said, knowing she hadn't seen the traffic lights change.

She peered out of the open window, dripping blood onto her door. 'He dented us!' she shrieked. 'That fucking cunt. My new fucking car. Fuck! Your fucking squirrel – I told you that was an omen. I fucking told you. Cunt!' She fell back. 'But still it didn't get us good enough, did it? We're still alive. Didn't fucking work.' She cackled. 'Actually can I have six hundred pound please? For dinner as well.'

She reached distractedly into my tracksuit pocket and took out the stack. 'All fifties! I love it.' She counted. 'This is only five hundred though? You said eight hundred.'

'Wait.' I took my right hand off the wheel and dug into my pocket, careful to take out only six more notes. 'You can't have all of it.'

'Ok babe,' she said, counting it and returning me four fifties, 'I'm going to cook us a banquet, alright? You made money, I got us a place to live. We're back on track! But I knew you'd try and sulk so I had to arrange it while you was away, didn't I? And I could only tell you while you was busy driving for me, otherwise you might of got too angry and run off. I can be cunning when I need to be.' She spoke with a nervous rapidity, like she was trying to deny the severity of her own injury – or perhaps because she was too drunk to understand it. 'I know how to cook, you know – and turn down that road – yeah that one,' she pointed. 'And head to the right.'

'Wait, where are you driving me to?' I asked, as if I'd only just realised what she was doing.

'You're the one driving,' she said innocently. 'And not very fucking well.'

'Didn't Francis move around here?' I stopped the car.

We'd reached the tip of Wandsworth Common. Beside us, the outlines of a football pitch had been painted white onto the grass – and this paint had been churned up by schoolchildren in the mud – into a Morse code that had stiffened overnight.

'You fucking know he did,' she slurred. 'And you know you're being an evil little shit to him. He came badgering me banging down our door when I was packing us up – so I had to tell him where we was going, so he's going to find you anyway. And he's got my number now and he's been ringing me every fifteen fucking minutes even though he hates me – and I know he's ringing you and you're ignoring him. So fucking sort it out. I know you think you can hide your feelings from me but you can't. So you're going round his house and that's that.'

She was wrong, of course, but I wanted her to believe that she knew what desires I was repressing. I had assumed that by ignoring Francis' calls, he would contact her, since he knew I lived with her – and that she, in her sympathy for us both, would force me to see him. What I hadn't predicted was that she would make me drive to his home, while gloating about her powers of manipulation. I turned to the window to hide my smile, sighed in cartoon exasperation, and drove on. Across my chest, a new welt grew from where the seatbelt had cut into me in the crash – a counterpoint to the lashes along my back.

'Good boy!' she said. 'I'll text you our new address. And get there for dinner, ok, cos I'm going all out. I'm going to go Kimber's first and I'll get us some of his painkilling, which is better than —'

'What, is Gibbon a heroin dealer?'

'Fuck off, his name is Kimber – who are you, trying to mock someone's name?'

'How dare you? There's a long history of heroes named Leander.'

'Shut up, you're not a hero. Kimber's a hero. And no, he's not a dealer, or he's not just a dealer. Either way, whatever, he has a link. And it's good. Actually, can I have another twenty?'

'No, I've only got fifties.'

'Leander, please! Please. We're here now anyway. Come on, I'm your fairy fucking godmother.'

I parked, gave her another fifty, mock-begrudgingly, and got out. Squirrel blood scarred the bonnet in four lines like giant claw-marks. Dawn staggered round to my side, unbalanced by concussion – and hugged me.

'Be brave for mummy, alright? Ah, is this hurting your bruises? I'm sorry,' she said, without much sorrow in her voice. 'Fuck that man and his belt, babe – we'll fix that later, alright? I'll get us the heroin, just don't lie down on it, yeah?'

'You too,' I smiled, touching the wound on her forehead with my thumb. 'We're matching almost.'

'I know, we're a right pair – but yours weren't an accident and you don't deserve nothing like that – so you go in there and you go be nice to that boy waiting for you – cos you can't fucking throw it away like I did just cos you think you don't deserve love. I'll see you later, alright – don't keep my banquet waiting.'

I withdrew from her embrace with my eyes to the ground. Dawn laughed at what she saw as a rare apprehensiveness on my part. Really, I was excited, and not for the reasons she supposed. She didn't know that Francis still had a girlfriend – a girlfriend I'd been systematically goading towards breakdown.

'Love you!' she yelled, embarrassingly loudly, and tottered to the car, combing a hand back through bloodied hair.

Drunkenly she drove away, into the end of the afternoon. The crash had made me bold, and my new scars felt like an exoskeleton – a defence against any next attacker. So, boldly, I shivered towards Francis' doorstep, hoping I was entering a fight.

3.

Francis opened his door after two rings, topless and barefoot in black ripped jeans. A muscular model, used to being adored, he was attracted to me because only I could make him feel nervous, although he seemed now to be in a state more heightened than that. The delay suggested he'd been distracted – and his girlfriend's voice from beyond the hall confirmed it.

'That's him, isn't it?' she shouted.

He smirked at me, squinting, his thick lips slightly parted into a pout. This was his default expression – cocky and confrontational – like he'd just told me to undress and earn his attention. But I wore my default expression too – the wounded lost boy, who had suffered too much to be affected by anyone's charms. He half-leaned in for a kiss, but decided against it, with his girlfriend so close – and instead tugged me inside.

'Make yourself at home,' he said with mock-courtesy.

Eva appeared in the kitchen doorway. Her face was painted white, with false lashes and thinned violet lips beneath hair stacked in rolls, some of which had dislodged. Tears had leaked mascara around her eyes. She wore stilettoes and a stiff silk kimono, and, on her fingers, talons dangled chains that swayed as she clawed the air.

'Don't fucking come near me, you're evil!' she shouted, as we came nearer.

She backed into the kitchen. Francis' clasp on my upper

arm tightened, and his close breath on my neck transferred his arousal to me.

'She got here straight from set,' he said.

'Yes I came from set!' she shouted. 'Don't talk like I'm not here.'

'And what character are you playing now?' I asked.

'Don't talk to me,' she spat, edging round the kitchen island. 'You're fucking evil. You were playing me yesterday. But you left your account on.'

Francis released me, confused by this statement. I leaned into the fridge, thinking of thickets of fly-eating flowers – snapping at her words and swallowing them until they dissolved. Her words were not really her own, anyway, they were mine – or rather, they were the words I'd hoped she'd say, in this play that she was performing for us – which I'd designed.

'You left your account on – and I've read every message you've sent to each other.'

'What's she saying?' Francis asked.

'You're so fucked up!' she shouted. 'I knew you were cheating and you knew I wasn't going to let that go, so you sent me Leander, didn't you? And I thought here's my consolation prize, a bit of relief…'

She tore open a drawer and threw a fork at my head. I ducked.

'You let me be the sad drunk girl,' she shouted at me, 'looking for a rebound fuck, crying about my cheating boyfriend. You made yourself available, all innocent, making no moves, letting me do the drinking, letting me do the talking. You let me wonder what girl he was cheating on me with. But it was you!'

'You never asked,' I said.

She screamed in frustration.

'What's she saying?' Francis asked again, drooping in horror into the countertop. 'You fucked her?'

'Don't pull that shit with me!' she shouted. 'Don't pretend anymore – I can't deal with more pretending. You're a faggot and I'm a fucking joke. You wanted to humiliate me. And you did! You probably told him to leave his account on!'

I smiled at the accuracy of her analysis, which was only incorrect in presuming Francis' complicity in my scheme.

'You're being ridiculous,' I said. 'Nobody is that scheming. You wanted to fuck me, and I'm not exclusive, so why would I tell you about me and Francis? Why would I leave my account on on purpose?'

Francis deflated in shock. I slid to his side. Eva was operating within a tedious genre, but her costume suggested other worlds – and I imagined ancient aristocrats, gathered on a mountain during some solstice – princesses in robes so heavy they could barely lift their legs, and princes weeping openly – as an astronomer-priest, interpreting the arrangement of the stars above them – commanded them to impale themselves on their own swords.

'I'm just telling her what she needs to hear to get rid of her,' I whispered.

'But why did you…?'

'This is the only way she was going to give up.'

He tried to smile like he understood, like he was playing this game on the same level as me – but his hands were trembling.

'You're fucking disgusting!' she shouted. 'You just wanted to… you just wanted to break me, didn't you? And it – it worked!'

'You're being ridiculous,' I said. 'You chose to have sex with me.'

'I know I fucking chose, but it wasn't an informed choice! You're evil. You're… Am I that bad of a judge of character that I don't… Look at me! When I found out,' she turned back to Francis and started to cry. 'I felt physically sick, because I still love you. I love you!'

I backed away from Francis to make him feel more exposed to Eva's theatrics. Her voice had taken on a murky blue tone

– and I thought of sea foam, lit by the kind of moon I'd only seen onscreen.

'I'm not going to pretend,' she said. 'When you moved into this house, and… and I'm not putting all the blame on you, but when I asked if there was room for me and you said of course there was, I thought… I didn't renew the contract on my flat – and I'm being thrown out next week. I'm going to be homeless and it's because of… it's because of me. It's because, even when I knew you were cheating, part of me still thought you wanted to live with me and I was going to move in here… and… and now I have to find somewhere else and that's so fucking stressful. Don't you… Is this just funny to you?'

'Eva,' Francis said softly, moved by her anguish more than her anger. 'This is – you're over-acting.'

'Yeah and I'm good at it! I'm good at it. And so are you. But somehow I'm the one who feels shit, I feel guilty, and why should I feel like this, why do you get to be happy and I don't? Why do you —'

'Eva, this ain't how you talk,' he said, exasperated by how effectively she was making him pity her. 'You're being like… a shit TV show.'

'I'm a fucking amazing TV show. And you're a faggot and I'm a fucking side-piece.'

'I didn't even know what —'

'Oh you didn't know?' she shouted. 'You didn't know you were gay until… what? Until just now? I didn't fucking know! And at the same time I'm scared, I'm scared you'll never talk to me again – and I have this pattern of falling back to you even when you've fucked me over and I just… it's pathetic! I know what I'm doing means we'll never speak again, and that hurts me, because you made me happy. I loved you, even though you're a bad person, I still love you, but I can't keep wondering and worrying about what I am to you anymore!'

She laughed suddenly, as though enjoying her own B-movie

performance – and then breathed in and reined her expression back to despair. I glimpsed my reflection in the mirror behind her and saw that pain had made me pallid. My body felt like a zoo in revolt – its animals twisting open their cages to rampage through the halls – killing the keepers, trying to find the main doors – but the main doors could never be unlocked – and so they were trapped still, under the vast dome of paraffin that I wore as my skin – and I remained silent. She turned to me.

'And I liked you, Leander. I thought you were on my side, I thought you could get through to him – but you've already got through to him, further than me, and you have no remorse, no sympathy, nothing, you're both just standing there laughing at me, and for some reason I'm sorry. I'm fucking sorry I wasted a year on you, I'm fucking sorry that you were the only thing that made me happy, that when my friends said "Oh, you're glowing" that it was you, and all the time you were just thinking about fucking other men. Every morning I woke up waiting to hear from you and every night I went to bed thinking about you. And it was a lie.'

'No it weren't,' Francis said. 'This ain't you.'

'Don't fucking do that, don't try to dismiss me. You saying this isn't me?'

She fumbled desperately in the drawer before her for a knife.

'You saying this isn't real?' she shouted, and stabbed the knife into her wrist, screeching more in fury than in pain.

I laughed. Francis leapt towards her.

'Eva, Eva! You're being ridiculous.'

'Get the fuck away from me!' she screamed, slicing the air.

She threw the knife at his feet, flecking us with blood. He jumped back, the muscles of his torso rippling leanly with adrenaline. She ran down the corridor, pulled open the door with a final pantomime screech, and stumbled out into the evening – leaving the wind to slam it shut.

4.

I closed my eyes, exhaling, savouring the room's tensions. In elevated states, my synaesthesia becomes more intrusive. And here, Eva's half-fake hysteria lingered in the air with a taste like elderflower. I imagined licking the sugary rim of a bottle as cordial dribbled down my chin.

When I opened my eyes, Francis was resting his elbows on the counter, his face in his hands. I was unsure of his response to what we'd just witnessed, until he raised his gaze to mine – and I read its desire.

'Where've you been?' He came to me. 'You weren't answering your phone…'

'I'll tell you…' I began to lie, but he kissed me, his hand behind my neck, keeping me against him.

He pulled down his sweatpants and kicked them off over his feet. He tried to unzip my tracksuit top, but I didn't want him to see the belt wounds beneath.

'Forget that,' I said.

He tugged down my trousers and boxers instead in the same motion. The stack of £50 notes fell out, scattering across the floor. I grinned. He grunted interrogatively.

'I'll tell you…' I said, but he kissed me again, biting my lips until I tasted my blood on his tongue.

I associated Francis with the colour of wheat – and this colour grew again to dominance as we kissed. Depending on the stimuli, my secondary senses sometimes associated Francis with wheat's texture, too, and its taste, and its rustling sound.

He turned me around. I lowered my face to the granite and he lowered with me, his chest pressed into the buckle welts along my back, his teeth at my ear, gasping nearly with laughter. His joy at my return was elevated by the evasion of his guilt for his girlfriend, and his jealousy at the revelation that I'd just slept with her. He was trying to repossess me, but the intensity of his arousal was due partly to the fear that I was beyond his control, even here.

Repeatedly, he tried to unwrap his hands from my stomach to unzip my top and have full access to my back – but I gripped onto his wrists, preventing the reveal of the whip lines by keeping his arms beneath me, as if I couldn't bear to be released.

He came inside me, pushing me into the countertop edge, his mouth at my neck, sweat pricking where our thighs' skin met.

He untensed, reaching around to finish me off, and said 'I love you,' which made me come too.

'I love you,' I said.

Obviously I didn't love Francis, but these words marked the end of his seduction. I was aroused not so much by the fulfilment of my desire – to make the straight boy fall in love with me and admit he's fallen in love with me, first, out loud, without prompting – but rather by the ease with which I had fulfilled that desire. I was aroused by the efficiency of my scheme – having premeditated every move that had led me here, and with no missteps! And now that his resistance was over, it was time to be cruel.

We hugged, and for a moment my mind left our heat – into a quicksilver that felt as close as I could come to peace.

He went to the sink to drink from the tap. I gathered my money from the floor and tucked it back into my boxers. The evening light tinted the granite the colour of elderberries.

'Why you been ignoring me?' he asked.

He splashed himself with water, smoothing his hands through his hair, his face lifted to the ceiling.

'I had no money,' I said. 'And I was depressed… about you not telling Eva. That's why I went home with her… It's the only way I could get the situation to an end.'

'You could of warned me.'

'That would have made it worse. It didn't mean anything. It was for you. And it worked.'

He sat down against the cupboard, pulling his sweatpants on as he shook the water out of his hair. I pulled mine on too and joined him, resting my head on his wet upper arm. He was not capable of argument, so had to accept my claim that I'd been doing him a favour by fucking his girlfriend. He couldn't really believe that, but he had to try. Much of my pleasure came from making him lie to himself in this way.

'What's that money for?' he asked.

'I need new poems.'

He wanted to ask further, but was afraid of being hurt by the answer, or of me seeing that he was afraid.

'Dawn said you're moving,' he said instead.

'Yeah.'

'So you don't want to move in with me?' he asked, with a playful indignity that failed to conceal his sincerity. 'I got a big house now.'

'I noticed. Did you hope you could rescue me?' I teased.

He smiled, ashamed of his own affection. 'Maybe. And we couldn't do that in a hostel.'

'We can at my new place. I don't know if it's going to last – it's always unstable with Dawn. You probably will still have to rescue me.'

'Why'd you want to live with her? I don't get it. She'll steal from you and lie about everything.'

'That's what I like.'

In the pause, I admired the muscles I rested on – and thought of the thousands of pulls-ups that had formed them – the trapezius of his neck and the sphere of his shoulders, and the extra muscles of his upper arm that knotted around bicep and tricep, and the wide vascular forearm that ended in a tattoo – 'SE5' – his childhood postcode. He had another tattoo on his torso, under his arm, under me – 'LET GO', written in gothic script, in some early claim to masculinity that almost contradicted itself. I lifted my wrist to his in comparison – my veins were violet-blue, my skin ghostly and dotted with moles, and my hair was like feldspar in late afternoon light – while his veins were copper-green, his skin darker and unmarked and nearly hairless – smoothed by the coconut oil he lathered into it at night, and which made his hard muscles feel soft when I kissed them. I kissed them.

'What happens with Eva then?' he asked.

'What you mean?' I asked. 'You're a carnivore now, the kill is done. The more indifferent you are, the more she'll love you.'

'A carnivore!' he laughed. 'Fuck off! What's that again?'

'It's from Latin – it means flesh-eater. The Greek version is sarcophagus – but that means coffin. So Greek flesh-eating tends towards death – while Latin flesh-eating goes the other way – towards life, towards sex.'

'And which way do you go?'

I smiled back. 'Both ways – I want to be a Greek and Latin flesh-eater – the demon of Europe's worst fever-dreams – the answering scream of a generation fucked over by a whole millennium.'

'And what about me?'

'Well you just started, you're still an entry-level Latin carnivore. But look what you did to Eva – you were talking about love – love is an old carnivorous urge – but it isn't positive, it's destructive – it's meant to rip you away from your old mate with enough force to overwhelm habit and convenience – so you choose a new one. Me. That's all this was. Flesh feeding on flesh. But these urges can warp, in some of us – become more irresistible, more flattened out, and spread beyond the systems of love…'

'That's not what love feels like to me.'

'That's because you haven't learned how to feel.'

He laughed. 'If I hadn't met you I'd be so bored.'

'Same.'

'No, it's true,' he said. 'Before I met you I was stuck. I mean before I did modelling I was proper stuck in South London. It was like there was a border around me. I wouldn't go past it. It felt like you had to get a visa and like vaccinations to go to North London – it was so far away to me. It was all local girls and boys, that was it – and I couldn't leave, really – and then with modelling I got to travel the world, non-stop travelling the world, meeting new people every day – and it was good, really good, getting different people's aspects on life. I really respect modelling for that, cos it opens my eyes. But I was still stuck before you.'

I nudged my head against his to keep him talking.

'When I got scouted,' he said, 'I did my first job for a gay magazine – and I didn't really know what to think. I get up, I go on the job, it's pretty good – it's just fashion really. But a few weeks after that, when it gets released, I ain't got a clue it's a gay magazine – and all my friends want to see it 'cos it's my first time – and I'm telling them "Go out and get your own copy, go on, show your mum" – all that, you know. And they see it's a gay magazine and I get ripped!' He laughed. 'I swear! But that's life, you know… I became a bit of a gay icon, and I never knew I'd want to do that myself. I mean if a gay man didn't like me, I'd feel bad about myself, like I weren't wanted, you know, I should feel like I'm wanted by both sexes. All sexes. I get people coming right up to me saying I want to fuck you, that kind of thing happens all the time… But I never thought it would actually happen with men, until you… Your world is so much bigger than mine.'

'My world is tiny. I've never travelled, I've just read about it.'

He kissed me.

'I ain't got the focus for that,' he said, leaning back. 'You got the focus. You should tell me what to read. What should I read?'

'Poems. You don't have to focus for long.'

'Tell me one.'

He shoved me off his shoulder so that he could lean against mine, pressing his cheek into my cheek. He was warmer than me – and at his touch I thought of sapphires cut in sunlight.

'I don't have a good memory,' I said. 'But in my head… there's bits of a poem by Wallace Stevens, if you want. Called "Esthétique du Mal".'

'What's that mean?'

'The art of evil.'

'Alright.'

I could feel his smile against my mouth. We breathed each other in, as I recited:

'"The death of Satan was a tragedy
For the imagination…
The tragedy, however, may have begun,
Again, in the imagination's new beginning,
In the yes of the realist spoken because he must
Say yes, spoken because under every no
Lay a passion for yes that had never been broken…"'

'What's it mean?'

'There's bits I've forgotten. But it means creativity is satanic because it is disobedient. Satan was the original artist. You aren't satisfied with what's already there, you add to it. Evil is necessary to living vividly. Tragedy is necessary to living vividly. But to develop an imagination, you must also be physical…'

'I can be physical,' he said, shifting forwards to stand up. 'I got a present for you.'

The odour of semen lifted in the air. He walked towards his fruit bowl – and from a mound of satsumas, he pulled out a necklace. I laughed.

The whip wounds in my back were beginning to ache more finely – like filaments heating into a red ochre colour. I leaned into them with pleasure. They complimented the colour beneath them, that was always there – my ultramarine – the ultimate blue of my myalgia, the superlative blue – the deepest colour that's still a colour before black.

Francis squatted in front of me, tensing his abs into greater prominence, and swung the necklace before my eyes.

'Since you're not buying nothing nice for yourself… I got you this,' he said. 'I mean I got it in a shoot for free, but I wanted to keep it for you, as a present. It's more your thing, I don't do necklaces. Even though you got a bit of money now, don't you?'

'It's for the deposit on the flat,' I said. 'And I don't think it's going to last. It's Dawn's money – that's why I was keeping it safe.'

He caught the necklace at the top of its arc, closed it in his fist for a moment, and then released it again to lower it over my head. The pendant was a winged key.

'I liked the little key,' he said. 'I felt like it had meaning, you know? And you don't need to worry about your flat cos you can stay with me, can't you? You don't need to be worrying about money, even though I don't get it, I don't get why you don't just go out and make money. You're clever, why don't you just get a job?'

'I'm too ill.'

'You don't look ill,' he smiled, assuming my answer was a joke.

I wanted to say: You don't see that part of me, I don't show it – my brain misunderstands my muscles, so they ache like I've always got flu, or my mitochondria are fucked, so they can't make enough energy, or I don't know, I just know that I'm in pain, and I can hide it with heroin. But I need to hide it from you too, otherwise you'll think differently of me. So I can't tell you. I'll never tell you.

Instead I said:

'Well I don't believe in jobs. Most of us could be doing whatever we wanted, while machines did the rest. But jobs keep being invented because we're supposed to be employed to justify our right to exist. It's a scam. Money doesn't work like people say it works, and we're kept unhappy and exhausted.'

'But what would people do instead?' he asked.

'Evil,' I said, standing up. 'The vivid evil, of the imagination.'

'Where you going?'

'I have to go.'

'Where? Why?'

'We're moving in today,' I said. 'I told you. I promised Dawn I'd be there for dinner.'

'Shit, ok, but you've got to come to Lars Vasari later.'

'What's that?'

'The exhibition, the photographs,' he said. 'I'm in most of the photos. I told you. You're on the list.'

'Can you text me the details?' I moved towards the door.

He shadowed me uneasily, alarmed by the suddenness of my departure.

'You've got to come,' he said. 'I want to show you to everyone. It's in Mayfair.'

'Ok, maybe.'

'You've got to! You can't wear that though.'

'Ok.' I opened the door.

Francis kissed me twice goodbye. The evening smelt of cold wrought iron and all the leaves that had fallen were stirring. I refused to reassure him with parting words. The sky was a deceitful blue, not far from ultramarine – but it wasn't radiant enough, or resentful enough to be the same – and ultramarine's pallor, like mine, required a pain that the evening didn't have.

I knew Francis was watching me walk away as the streetlights turned me amber. There was a nearby bus that would take me to my new address, and to the pain relief I'd been promised. As I turned the corner, I took off his necklace and threw it in a bin.

5.

I didn't know which buzzer to ring so I rang them all. Dawn answered like she'd been waiting at the intercom.

'Who's that? Is that Leander? You're early.'

'No I'm not,' I said.

'Who is it then?'

'This is Leander, but I'm not early.'

'Oh shut the fuck up and get inside.'

She buzzed me in.

'Wait, what floor is it?' I asked, but she'd already hung up.

I climbed the stairs in darkness, listening to the suppertime clatter through the walls. My muscles felt like diseased clay in a kiln, unmoulding in defiance of the heat. A star orbited my brain. Between the banisters of the third floor, a light shone. Dawn was waiting in one of its doorways, wine bottle in hand. She'd cleaned the blood of the crash off her face, but its wound was visible still through her hair – the colour of boiling plums.

'You seem... deflated,' I said.

'What a nice way to greet your mother, you cheeky shit,' she said. 'How about, "Oh I never seen you look so elegant, you look like an English rose!"'

'I've never seen you look elegant...'

'Oi!' She raised her hand to slap me. 'You can't come in till you give me a compliment.'

'Ok, you do look quite... roseate.'

'I don't know what that means, but I know it's not a fucking compliment, you runt. You're not getting in with that.'

She stepped back and began closing the door.

'Ok, sorry…' I said. 'I mean you look like a blossom of damask, twined with eglantine beneath a nightingale singing threnodies into a well.'

'Better… but that didn't end right, did it? You can do better than a well.'

'Ugh… I'm hungry, please. Ok, you look like Cleopatra under opal noon-light in her roof garden, riding a glass dildo full of bees.'

'Better… one more compliment and you get to enter the roof-garden,' she opened the door wider, but kept her palm up in prohibition.

'Ok, you look like an apricot-soft eclipse watched from a yacht shipping laudanum and labdanum across the Levant.'

'Perffffffect – there you are my darling, come in, come in – welcome to our new home!'

She stepped aside, unbalanced – and as I entered, she fell onto me into a hug.

'What you doing strutting in like that?' she said. 'Hug your mother properly!'

I put my arms around her and she rose to kiss me on the mouth. Her tongue was stale from cigarettes. I twitched away in disgust.

'Are you high?' I asked.

'Don't be stupid, I just had some of the red!' She lifted the bottle up to my chest. 'It's the posh stuff. It costs twenty-five pound! Try it!'

She fed it to me with her head turned away. I tried to drink, but it spilled over my chin – so she tried to lick it off.

'Ok, thanks,' I said, pushing her away. 'Tastes great. I'm hungry…'

'Yeah, yeah, course – let me give you the tour.'

She ignored this second prompt for food and instead yanked me into a cramped shower room.

'This is the spa,' she said, flicking the switch beside her.

A light strip above us hummed into a glare. Her pupils were pinpricks in the mirror. And her expression – still sharp and handsome and untrusting – had a gentleness to it that was only there when she was high, and made her look like she wanted to be told lies.

'You're high,' I said. 'You started without me.'

'No, darling, course not.' She turned off the light. 'I could never start without you.'

'But you got some heroin?'

She twirled in evasion and pulled me back out into the living area.

'This is the Napoleonic suite.' She gestured to a double bed, a dining table, and our two suitcases between them.

'You can sleep with me if you want, but I thought you'd prefer your own wing. No need to share anymore, we're living the high life!' She pulled me towards a door beside the bed and opened it onto a tiny room with a single floor mattress and a lamp without a shade.

'I actually love it,' I said.

'I knew you would, darling, you love that depressing garret shit. You can finally live your dream of being a consumptive Russian aristocrat in an attic. Isn't that what you said? It's almost an omelette. No – what's worse than an omelette?'

'Nothing, I hate omelettes. Unless you mean oubliette?'

'Exactly sweetheart, it's the perfect oubliette for you. I knew you'd love it. I done right didn't I? I sorted us out! Just you and me, fucking finally… But let me finish the grand tour,' she prodded me towards a small square kitchen through an arch beside the dining table. 'And so – here is the Michelin-starred restaurant.'

'And have you managed to create any Michelin-starred food?'

'Not yet, we only just fucking moved in!'

'But you promised me a banquet.'

'Oh I know I did, didn't I, darling, but there's never enough time. Sorry sweetheart, I'll make it another night.'

'That's not like you. You were so keen on proving your culinary abilities earlier.'

'I was just showing off,' she said, with mixture of sarcasm and self-pity. 'I wanted you to be impressed. I was making it up! Can't we focus on the positives – we got our own fucking palace! We can dance in our own living room. No more fucking noise restrictions. No more fascists. No more locked-in syndrome.'

'This definitely used to be a council flat,' I said, choosing to change the subject. 'And now it's being rented out by parasites like your boyfriend. Landlords should be outlawed and hunted down for sport and shot.'

She sashayed to a song that only she could hear, swigging from the bottle.

'Aren't you going to say that your boyfriend shouldn't be hunted down for sport and shot?' I asked. 'You're not defending him as vigorously as you were earlier.'

'Oh leave it out, Leander. Can't you just enjoy the view? Life is about to happen to us!' But she said her catchphrase with no conviction.

'There'll be a revolution soon,' I said.

'And who's going to control the houses?'

'A computer.'

'And then?' she asked, still sashaying. 'Are you going to be the emperor?'

I closed my eyes until I saw myself in a courtyard somewhere near the Earth's meridian – cool under silk canopies, as a harem of men had their necks slit open by a harem of women. The men kissed me as they bled out, willingly giving themselves to my rejuvenation – and then the women, with their last screams, praised me as I set fire to their tents. My palace was overrun by beasts – boars and stags and wolves and crocodiles – in a havoc more beautiful than the havoc of the stars.

'The earth has no way out other than to become invisible,' I said, 'in us who with a part of our natures partake of the invisible.'

'The fuck does that mean? You doing a quote?'

'Yeah, Rilke said that. He was a poet.'

'Course he was. Fucking useless answer to "How are we going have houses?" You can't put the earth inside you and start eating the invisible.'

'I felt like saying it,' I said. 'And you seem pretty happy to be making me eat the invisible. Did you really not get any food with my money?'

'Babe, the money ran out.'

'First you say you didn't have time to make food, and now you're saying you didn't have the money. Which is it?'

'What's this – a police interview? There weren't neither. I said the wrong thing. Whatever, I been trying my best...'

'You didn't try anything.'

'What the fuck do you know? I tried everything... I didn't know everything. I never realised that...' She stopped and looked out of the window.

My pain removed me from the room for a moment – and I imagined myself as an emperor again – again with a palace of beasts and slain lovers – and I wondered what would happen if one of my lovers survived, an accidental immortal, and came back to worship me with a whip, as I'd been worshiped earlier today. This immortal would promise me love, perhaps – a love like a warren of underground caves, in which stalactites had been broken off and arranged in rings by some inhuman tribe for the worship of some inhuman god – like me or my lover. But if our love could only end in death – how would we, as immortals, die? By becoming each other, of course – by seeking a desire that exceeds music, and so forces us out of the dance.

'What happened?' I asked, returning to the present. 'You went to see Gibbon and…'

'Stop calling him that!'

'What did you do?'

'I got you some bread,' she laughed, amused again, and twirled towards the kitchen.

There, she retrieved a plastic-wrapped loaf of sliced bread. 'You can make a toast sandwich!' she said. 'A slice of toast between two slices of bread. Dinner for champions! I used to eat it in the war.'

I laughed too, delighted by her erratic mood, its bleak imagery, and how casually she had betrayed my trust.

The walls of the apartment were painted two shades of cream, as though the painters had run out of one shade a third of the way along the wall and continued with another a few shades warmer – and as I stared at the line where the colours changed, my brain bent the contrast into a flavour – close to soy sauce – and I was hungry.

'I might actually do that,' I said.

I took the loaf from her hands, impatiently tore off its plastic, and slotted a slice into the toaster. There were no plates in the cupboard, so I placed the outer slices on the counter. I checked the fridge for butter, but it wasn't switched on.

'You're avoiding all my questions,' I said. 'Did you get any heroin?'

'Not yet, not yet, I've not managed to accomplish everything, I'm sorry,' she giggled, drinking again from her bottle.

The diameter of her pupils belied her denials – she must have been high all afternoon.

'You don't look sorry.'

'I'll get it, I'll get it baby, I promised you – and I don't break my promises. Just sometimes I delay them. Kimber asked us to meet down the Rockway later. He wants to meet you. He'll have some for us then, for sure.'

'I'm going to a gallery tonight,' I said.

'Why? Is Francis going to be there? Ah are you going to a gallery with Francis? What happened with him – oh sweetheart I forgot to ask. How'd it all go? I'm sorry I was so caught up in my hectic business-orientated lifestyle,' she cackled in self-derision. 'I forgot your love woes. Did you say sorry to him? Did he forgive you?'

'Stop changing the subject. Where's my money? What's wrong with Kimber? Why aren't you rhapsodising about him like you were earlier? What happened?'

'He was just busy. He was stressed. He weren't as happy about everything as I thought he'd be.'

'Everything?'

She sighed against the table, finally retiring her jovial façade. She held up her head and shook it – and drank again, swallowing emphatically as if to swallow words she didn't want to say and tears she didn't want to show.

'I think he's jealous of you,' she said eventually.

'So? I paid the deposit. Does he want to get rid of me?'

'No, no, of course,' she slurred. 'I know you did, he knows you did. You're my number one, sweetie, I can't leave you, course I won't, I promised to be your mother.'

The toast popped up. I placed it between the two untoasted slices and gazed awhile in satisfaction at this assault on the history of cuisine, contemplating the distance between the first makers of bread and me – and then bit into it. Though dry, the bread was sweet, and the toast between it a satisfying contrast. This sad meta-sandwich would suffice as a meal for now.

'This is pretty good,' I smiled, spilling crumbs.

She didn't smile back. Instead, my display of positivity seemed to push her further into despondency.

'What if I made a mistake, Leander? What if I done this wrong?'

'You haven't,' I mumbled between chews, moving towards her in reassurance. 'We couldn't have continued in a hostel

– you were right, you were looking out for me. Your impulsive uprooting was necessary. And you didn't uproot us from much. A homeless hostel is never going to be a home. We can make this a home. I'm grateful.'

'No,' she began crying. 'Don't try to be nice to me, I can't take it, I need you to sulk – I need to be the one reassuring you. When you try it, it sounds so fake. This was a mistake weren't it? I'm a mistake. I'm bad for you.'

'Is this about the money?' I asked. 'I don't care, I made it in an hour. I can make it again. And I've still got some.'

'It's not just your money. I'm a bad mother. But it is the money – I lost your money.'

'Did Kimber take it all?' I began to understand. 'Didn't you tell him it was for our food?'

Her face became harsher.

'Did he take the money from you?' I repeated.

'No, he's not like that, he would never be like that to me – he'd been working, he was in a different mood, it was my fault.'

As my suspicions grew, the associations of my other senses were heightened: the taste of soil entered my mouth, and her words gained an orange echo.

'You're lying,' I said. 'Did he hit you?'

'No, you're getting the wrong end of everything. It's not like that.'

'What is it like then? Last week, you were outside his control. But now you're in his car and in his flat, you're in his power and you've glimpsed something in him that was hidden before?'

She cried quietly.

'What is it?' I asked. 'He's a man in a violent profession. He's jealous. What did he say about me?'

'Stop analysing, I don't want to hear it. You're just trying to sulk again. He's said nothing about you.'

'You're lying.'

'It was me, I was talking about you,' she cried. 'I was talking about you.'

'And? You're making it sound like you sold me to him.'

'I just talk too much, don't I? I hope too much. I believe people too much. I can't –' she pushed me away. 'I can't. Don't look at this. Go and shower, you need to wash. At least you can wash your day off you. I tried to wash. Let me just – go away.'

She covered her eyes with her hands and began rocking herself towards despair.

I left for the bathroom. The shower had no curtain, so it wet all the walls as soon as I turned it on. The sound of the spraying water glittered with blotchy browns and reds, like a cloud of gatekeeper butterflies. As it warmed, I undressed and rinsed the toast from my mouth in the sink.

I stepped in. The water felt like hail on my flayed back – but I experienced this as light entertainment. My body hurt anyway, from my myalgia, so the whip wounds were really a relief. Chronic muscle pain has a dissociative effect – every day, for the past decade, my limbs have seemed severed from each other, hovering discretely in uncertain space. My sense of proprioception is in disarray – my nerves regard themselves as hostile. So bruises and gashes like the new ones on my back simply lift me out of my underlying condition. Flesh injuries are insignificant compared to a half-life spent inside a skeleton of barbed wire – of feeling half-disembodied and half-disembowelled – a cloud of phosgene and a soldier's scream, at once in the same skin. That's why being beaten feels like being cured.

The bathroom door opened as I was washing the soles of my feet. I wobbled in surprise. Dawn entered through the steam, staring with an inebriated intensity.

'I remembered the Savlon,' she said, holding up the tube of antiseptic.

Again I tasted soil in my spit – though now her voice sounded like it had become foreign to her too. She seemed to be speaking automatically.

'You're high,' I said.

'Let me look at your back.'

'Can't you do this when I'm out?'

'I'll do it now.'

I put the soap in the tray and turned around.

Crying, she traced her fingers along my welts, circling the metal buckle's indents one by one. I rested my head on my arm against the tiles of the wall, letting the water hit the curve of my spine. Briefly she lifted away her hand – and returned it, thick with ointment, to smooth across my broken skin. I closed my eyes and forgot the specifics of the room.

But as she smoothed lower, I realised she was teasing me towards arousal. Her other hand joined the first in massaging towards my hips – and then she stepped into the shower with me, wetting her clothes.

'No,' I said.

She pushed her hands down my thighs, her soaked skirt rubbing against my back. Instead of earth, I tasted burnt coffee. I tried to swallow it away.

'Just let me make you feel better,' she said. 'I'm scared I been a bad mother.'

'I don't want to.'

'Then why you not pushing me away?'

She tried to turn me around but I resisted. She kissed my neck and forced her fingers through mine.

'This is… unnecessary,' I said.

'Then why are you hard?' She guided my hand in hers towards my erection.

I let her hold me there for moment, but then shook my shoulders.

'No,' I said. 'I'm getting out.'

I turned off the water – she clutched to me, trying to kneel down. I pushed her away, and took up my clothes and hurried into the living room.

She followed slowly, drenched, her lips apart but no longer crying, her eyes unclear.

From my suitcase I removed black jeans, black socks, a black polo-neck, and her fake Dalmatian fur coat. With my back to her, I re-hid most of the money in my boxers and my sock. Then, turning so that she could see, I put the remaining £200 in my coat pocket.

'Why don't you leave that with me?' she said. 'It's dangerous having so much money on you.'

'It's more dangerous to leave it with you. It would disappear.'

'I taught you how to pleasure a woman!' she said, as though this was somehow a retort. 'I taught you! You never knew what you was doing until I taught you.'

'You taught me nothing.'

'I'm a bad mother, am I?' She was weeping again. 'I can remember how you was when we met. You trusted me, and you don't trust nobody. Why'd you start trusting me?'

'What are you talking about?'

'We're moving on with life! Everything's going right, now, ain't it? I've got a man, you've got a man, we got a place of our own.'

'Then why are you crying?'

'Your wounds make me sad,' she said – with something closer to remorse than she'd managed in the car earlier. 'They're a failing, if I'm your mother.'

'Then don't be my mother,' I said, though I was pleased by her veiled confession –that she'd known in advance I'd be whipped by her client.

'You asked me to be your mother!' she shouted.

'I asked because you needed me to ask.'

'So you can have feelings! But they're not enough – you never asked me why I needed it.'

'It was obvious – you needed a substitute son, I needed a substitute mother.'

'You don't know it all,' she sobbed. 'I was too young. I was fifteen. Did you know that? Yeah – I ain't even that old! I had him five years but then I… I weren't up to it, was I? I failed. My mum hated me, just because she spent all her time thinking what life would be like without kids. And I didn't want that for me. I tried it but I didn't want it. I couldn't take the tasks that never end. She said she felt destroyed – destroyed as a woman. And I felt like that till I got myself back. I couldn't touch nobody for years. My mum said I made her feel like a nobody. And it was the same with me when I had my kid. My body weren't for me and I hated it. So I ended it, didn't I? I tried to put him in a fucking orphanage – but his dad got custody and they only let me see him twice a year. And I couldn't bear it, so I saw him less. And now he hates me. Do you know what I mean? My son fucking hates me! That's why I need you. I need a son that doesn't hate me.'

She lurched forwards tearfully to stroke my face. I pulled away. A reddish flash – perhaps a silent ambulance passing through the street below – got caught in my eye, and I saw a huge fish leaping through the air between us, like a salmon up a waterfall – until it reached the window, and leapt out into the red of the night. Dawn sat back into the table with an expression of opiated wonder – perhaps having had the same vision as me.

'It's your turn,' she said. 'You're supposed to balance me out. What happened to your mother? Why'd you need me?'

'I've told you. When I was eleven my dad shot my mum then shot himself. I found the bodies. I had an older sister, but she died when I was six.'

'Maybe. Maybe I believe you. But you lie about who you want to be, don't you? You lie so people show themselves to you. I know you think I'm stupid – and I am stupid compared to you, and even stupider now that you got me this bump on my head

– but it's fine, just because I don't have an education to wear on my sleeve.' She lifted her hands to stop me interrupting. 'Even if you gave that education to yourself, sweetheart, but still, for all you want to twist me around – I understand you more than you think I do. And that's why you like me. You like me because you can't manipulate me.'

'I can manipulate you.'

She laughed. 'Yeah but you can't control me completely. You can't predict everything. That's what you need me for.'

'And why was now the time for this little soliloquy?'

'Because life's about to happen to us! I want you to know what I know. Maybe I like you because you like lies more than people.'

'I like lies that get people to tell me their secrets,' I said. 'But also, my lies are confessions, in a way. Lies are fantasies – and fantasies reveal you much more nakedly than facts.'

'Go on then.'

'Stories that aren't biographically true can still be true – if they reveal something about the teller's psychology. They are psychologically true. They show what I want you to believe about me. Lies are not as simple as inaccuracies. A lie, as an evasion or a complication, is still a revelation of character – it's a slanted truth. If I told you I was trampled by a horse when I was fifteen, and the trauma of that incident is the reason why I am now inert and deceitful and constantly in pain – you would learn something true about me. It may not have literally happened, but it gives you an image by which to understand me. Rather than listing diagnoses – like fibromyalgia or immune dysfunction or dysautonomia or insomnia or Lyme disease or myalgic encephalomyelitis or even just poverty – that all only speak to the surface of what I am, I give you instead a metaphor, of a trampling horse. And by that metaphor you comprehend me beyond facts. It wasn't literally true – it was psychologically true. Lies are insights into the liar, if you read them right.'

'So when you tell people about me, I'm going to be a horse?'

48

'No, you'll be a blue-ringed octopus. A many-limbed en-tanglement, overbearing, toxic, and drowning.'

'You're a charmer.'

'I have to go,' I said.

Worry resurfaced in her face. 'Let me drive you there.'

'You can't drive like this. And I want to be cold for a while.'

'Please don't walk there.'

'Fuck off.'

'It's dangerous,' she said.

'I'll see you at the Rockway, ok? Do I get a key?'

'Yeah, course you do sweetheart.'

She removed a key ring from her pocket and put it into mine. She hugged me, trembling as though suppressing an apology or a warning – and waved me away with defeat in her eyes.

I left, disorientated, but impressed – as though she'd managed some master manipulation that I could barely understand.

6.

I strode through unfamiliar streets, my mind widening into the night's intimacy. The space between the terraced houses had a presence I called 'indisclosure': the active sense of a city withholding its meanings. And as I said the word to myself, its sound gained the taste of cotton candy – a too-sweet taste, though I kept repeating it anyway – indisclosure, indisclosure, indisclosure.

The houses had put their wheelie-bins out in the street – for tomorrow's collection – and they reminded me of a dream I used to have, of waking up inside a black plastic bag, in a dustbin – and feeling content there, waiting for the truck to come and take me away – from the pain I felt then, and still felt now.

Tonight that pain came as a nest of tarantulas – dressed in the smeared aprons of butchers, washing their cleavers in my blood, and promenading along my muscles like avenues in an orchard.

I walked down a bike path to a canal. The wind quickened in its confinement here, so I walked faster, fingering the key in my pocket.

I imagined the wind coming from the old Deptford dockyard, and carrying with it the sighs of sailors who'd left from there and died at sea, younger than me, as long as half a millennium ago – when the docks had been the cradle of a navy that plundered the whole world. And in this wind, in its ghosts, was a reminder that London was still growing from the profits of that plunder.

But also in this wind was an opposite reminder – that London had grown from an army's camp – an invader's camp – and the river that army had bivouacked beside was rising. The walls that defended it were invisible now – but they were still here – and they couldn't hold back the water forever. All camps are temporary – this one would be washed away too.

Two figures approached from beneath the bridge. One was taller than me, but both, in the gloom, looked younger, perhaps sixteen years old. The taller wore a dark tracksuit, dark trainers, and a white snapback hat; his shorter partner had more flair, with a cyan sweatshirt over navy overalls speckled with paint, and cobalt-blue shoes. His cropped hair was shaven in whorls.

'Mate can you lend us some money?' the shorter one asked.

I ignored them, clenching the key, and tried to walk past. The taller stepped into my way. I tiredly lifted my eyes to his.

'Got any money to lend us?' he asked.

I stared without saying anything. A vein in my leg twitched, and my blood began to flush with anticipation.

The taller one stepped closer and shoved me at my hip. I moved in obedience to his fist, and inhaled, untensing myself, as if about speak – but said nothing. The other shoved my shoulder.

'You speak English?' he asked. 'We need to borrow a bit of money. I need to buy a speedboat.' He laughed.

I sighed, readying my best impersonation of an action hero, and took two steps backwards.

'Which of you wants your leg broken first?' I asked.

Their expressions paused, blank while processing a reaction to this bluff – and then, just as they were both deciding on sniggers, I twisted round to kick sideways at the taller one's outer leg, my shoe flat in a right angle as its heel hit his knee socket. It dislocated but didn't snap – he shrieked, hobbling back, rolling his upper body forwards – so I punched into his nose, upwards, and it easily broke. His blood dribbled onto my knuckles like honey and, as I skipped backwards, for a moment I wanted to lick it.

The shorter boy stared in shock. The wall beside us prevented most types of attack, so I span and ducked to kick up in a back-hook at his face – hitting his chin, but not hard enough. The jaw clattered but didn't snap. I spun to face him again, in a low stance, my fists up. He swiped vaguely at me with his left hand – I blocked it, but saw too late it had been a feint, and with his stronger fist he struck my eye. The side of its socket splintered into steel light – and he jabbed again at my stomach. I was tensed enough not to be winded, but stumbled to the water's edge. He knew how to box, and pushed his advantage, smacking me in the temple and then the neck – I choked, tasting thickening mango – and tried to weave out of his way on my back foot.

I let him punch my eye again. Verdigris-green shattered into my throat – but I spat it back out into his mouth, sweeping at his front foot, and ducked under his arm to tug him backwards over his other leg. As he fell, I span round to strike my elbow into his cheek. Something cracked – but it might have been me. My nerves were livid. The space around me was splitting, as though allowing a sharper air to replace it. I was more vivid now and, somehow, now – finally now – in my body properly. I gripped onto his arm and stamped on it where it met his shoulder until it broke. He screamed as I stamped. I imagined that I was crunching burnt pinecones – I could smell the smoke of a bonfire of fir and chestnuts – and then I kicked him in the jaw until it, too, broke.

I felt like I had just been born. The shivers of the wind around me harmonised with the waves of wind in my spine. I breathed further than I could formerly breathe. My eyes could see backwards and upwards – the present was balling out into a vibrating sphere. I reached to stroke the boy's head: its shaved hair resembled velvet – the fringe of a dress I wanted to kiss, or the fur of a foxglove.

I wished to further my assault on his partner, but a punch to the side of my chest winded me – I staggered over his body and looked back. There was third boy, my age, my height, hooded, holding a knife tipped with my blood. My coat had stopped his stab penetrating far. I axe-kicked at his hand to knock it open – he dropped the knife, but the boy on the ground grabbed my heel to trip me. I stamped on him, and the third man lunged to grip me by the throat. I tasted nutmeg, a cloud in my windpipe – and kneed him in the groin, but he didn't release me – so I stamped again on the other boy to prevent him pulling me down. The night brightened as I lost air – and I embraced my strangler, inhaling his sweatshirt's tranquil reek of weed, bending his choking arm inwards, surprising him off balance. In my advantage, I twisted into the skin of his neck – in the shadow, it clotted like cream around a pair of freckles the width of my two front teeth – and I bit him there so sharply that I tore off every layer of skin – but not enough to make him bleed. His grip relaxed – I kneed him again in the crotch and spun round to find the knife.

But it was not on the ground; perhaps it had fallen into the canal. This quick search was a misjudgement – the two boys on the ground jerked to grab a foot each, nearly tripping me onto my back. As I squatted, I jabbed with three fingers joined in a screwing motion into his eye – it softened, though didn't burst into the jelly I wanted; he dug his head into the tarmac to get away – and before I could complete his blinding, the third boy tackled me.

I writhed, excited by the firmness of his biceps, and bit at his wrist, my jaw so wide it nearly detached to reach his flesh with my cuspid teeth – chewing and grinding until I tasted gristle and his arm-hair on my tongue. Yelling, he punched at my head with his free hand – and with each hit, I became younger, larger, more precise; and my teeth kept to his wrist, hopeful of bone; with each hysterical hit, I was resurrected – until finally he knocked my jaw loose, but not without its prize of meat. With my left foot, I kicked against the ground to slide out from under him – and he screamed at his ripped wrist, the tendons exposed, his hand useless, a severed vein gushing onto its unresponsive index finger, pointed in some broken reflex as though in accusation.

I squirmed faster, but still he pinioned my thighs – until I dragged my left arm loose and reached to rip at his ear. My grip slipped in his sweat, but I dug my nail back into its helix and tore down again – his head jerked to follow it; and I twisted it backwards, desperate to part the skin from his skull – but skin is hard to rip.

I shoved him further sideways to roll out from underneath him – but as I tried to leap away, one of the other boys snatched at my coat. I stretched back my shoulders to lose it over my arms – and he fell as I shed it, and shrunk – now only in my polo-neck. But before I was fully upright, the shorter boy with the splintered chin slapped my foot – and my face smacked into the concrete. I bit my tongue, tasting its own blood – the third now on my palate – and this mixture had the tartness of pomegranate seeds.

The third attacker dived onto me, gripping me in a headlock – his armpit's deodorant leaking into his sweat, the smell of a ripening peach, its case breaking to the yellow fruit beneath, but soured by detergent – I sniffed longer, until at the back of the aroma I found hyacinth. He heaved his body onto mine, his knee in the small of my back, shouting 'Cunt! Cunt! Cunt!'

Then, my head was concussed into the stone – and I saw the cobalt shoe of the shorter boy at my face. As he stamped me with one foot, and the asphalt assumed the flavour of salt in my throat – I watched his own blood webbing across the tongue of his other trainer. I wanted to skewer this foot to the ground with a knife to stare at it for longer in various lights – but the knife was gone, and I couldn't worm my head away.

As his partner beat me, my vision seemed to swell – the

geometry of the canal and the towpath was altered, distending, the rules of perspective suddenly re-complicated, as my gravity increased, competing with the city's. Sounds fawned to my ear – the boys' screams and pants, but also from further, I fancied, I could hear exhausts and bar chatter – and these sounds were gathering around me almost in devotion.

In his fury, he stripped the shirt off my back, and re-opened the whip cuts made that morning – but under his blows, I grew more exuberant, like a whole world I had never participated in before was being revealed to me. My old ultramarine pain was gone – overruled for now by joyful shallower agony. I had known that my world was not the right one – I had known that I was not living as everyone else was living – but here, finally, I was being allowed to exist where they existed – here, finally, I was experiencing a correctness in being alive, a comfort in simply being, that felt not like a state or stasis but a curve. I finally understood it, and stood in it, and accepted it and was accepted by it – the land was no longer alien to me; my body was no longer merely half here – I was here, wholly; I was present, I was finally present! Perhaps this was what is called Stendhal syndrome – overwhelmed to nausea by aesthetic pleasure...

'Stay on his legs! Who fucking kicks like that?'

'There's only two hundred pound here,' the taller boy shouted, turning out my coat pockets. 'Get his shoes.'

Hands tore at my boots, and then slowed to unlace them – as hands tore at my waist, reaching beneath me to unbutton the fly. I flailed under the weight of two bodies. My socks were pulled off – and the money within them found. Then the mass on my thighs lifted – I kicked faster, but hands were already at my waist, dragging down my jeans and boxer-briefs until I was naked – and the money within them found also.

'Let me kill him.'

'Pick that up – count it!'

'Let me fucking kill him!'

'You're not allowed to.'

What? I thought. Who didn't allow him? Was I the performer now – in someone else's play?

The second weight stood, and the foot left my head. They twisted me onto my back, serrating my flesh against the cement. My gaze was pure exhilaration; they were shaking in terror.

'Shit!'

'He's got a boner!'

They recoiled – I clutched for the oldest boy's testicles and squeezed one with my thumb into my palm until it flattened – and as he screamed in an agony that must have felt like levitation, I rolled sideways into the canal.

The water vibrated with joy – and I felt keener, faster, staring at them, safely, from a few meters away.

'Have you got it?'

'I've got it.'

'Let's go.'

The taller boy threw my clothes and shoes into the water. The shorter one vomited, leaning on the third as he tried to stand. I treaded water, watching as they hobbled towards the bridge, groping at each other like drunken lovers.

A bicycle light skimmed through the darkness towards them – too late to witness our communion. Its strobes illuminated the boys' retreat. They gave way.

But I could not long remain in this cold – my clarity was yielding to heaviness. The water coiled around my legs like a moray eel, deepening towards a mile-high dam it wished to suck me into. In the dark I could see only my coat, a few strokes away – so I swam over, and found by it my jeans, but could not see anything else.

Kicking with one leg, paddling with one arm, I strove for the opposite bank, my lungs clenched as though stuffed with sackcloth. The bank was further than it ought to have been; possibly a current I couldn't feel was resisting me – but my will was stronger than my muscles, and I achieved the shore. I climbed onto the bank in a crawl, wheezing, and sat to drag on my jeans and coat. But I couldn't let myself pause here – so I crawled to the steps towards street level, spitting blood over my hands, my vision a whirlpool.

At the pavement, I tried to stand under a streetlight, but instead fell into a flowerbed. Its briars revived me – enough to claw forwards, with fists of soil, across and out onto the road. Cars cruised by with interior musics. I collapsed under the folds of my coat, looking up at clouds purpled by London's light pollution.

As my body began to understand itself again, its adrenaline dwindled, but was replaced by a more exquisite thrill – of realisation.

The robbers could have guessed to search my socks and boxers – but Dawn's antic mode this evening suggested she had betrayed me. Perhaps they had followed me from her doorstep. And so my suspicions about my whipping weren't just paranoia – Dawn was arranging my injuries. Our game was real – I loved her more, for this.

And now it was my turn to play.

A car was approaching along the lane I lay in. And as I blacked out, I ejaculated.

ACT 2

The call to adventure

1.

I woke in a man's arms.

'No,' I tried to say, but my teeth turned to brass and unscrewed me back into ultramarine.

I woke as a car door closed on my face. I couldn't differentiate between words and textures. But I knew that a man was in the driver's seat beside me.

'Not to hospital,' I said.

'You have to.'

'No... to 24 Orgrave Road, SE5... something. SE5.'

'Is someone there?'

'My... girlfriend,' I managed, and blacked out again.

I woke in a man's arms. He was holding me against a column of names.

'Ravel,' I told him.

The door buzzed open, he dragged me into the lift. As it rose, charcoal covered my eyes.

I woke in a woman's arms.

'What happened to him?' she asked.

They carried me onto a sofa.

'How much was the journey? Take it!' she said.

His protestations dissolved into glue.

I woke as a woman pulled off my jeans. My wet coat was already gone.

'Eva!' I said.

'What happened to you?'

'I'm… cold.'

'Not for much longer. Shit!'

She drew the jeans off over my feet and tucked me into a blanket.

'You need to go to hospital.'

'I need whisky.'

'You need that treated.'

'Then treat it.'

'I'm not a nurse.'

'Please?'

'Ok, I probably have antiseptic, but you need more than that. Shit, you're bleeding.'

'Surface wounds. Decorative.'

'Shit,' she said, and left.

Eva returned with a tray of three tall glasses – one gold, one white, one green.

'Drink all of these. You can't talk to me till you've drunk all of them.'

I obeyed, shifting onto my un-stabbed side to drink first the milk, and then the whisky, and then the juice.

'What was in that?' I asked, tipping the last glass's leftover algae along its side.

'Protein shake with spinach.'

'I've never felt so virtuous.' I sat up a little.

'Get back down.' She took away the tray and lifted up the blanket to apply antiseptic to my cuts. 'Turn over.'

I did so and she yelped. 'Shit, were you whipped? You've been stabbed. What the fuck?'

'I went swimming,' I said, warming to the attention of her hands.

'The taxi guy said you'd been in a canal?'

'I went swimming,' I said again.

'Who did this?'

'A blue-ringed octopus.'

She sighed in irritation. 'So you were attacked and thrown into a canal. Why? And why did you come to me?'

'You were the first person who came to mind. I remembered your address from last night. Were you not expecting me?'

'I'm supposed to hate you. Did you forget that when you drowned?'

'Do you hate me?'

'I don't know. Maybe not. This afternoon I was… angry.'

'I remember.'

'Your eye is so fucked up.' She squeezed more ointment onto her fingers.

'Is that Savlon?' I smiled.

'What? Yeah. Why's that funny?'

'Nothing. It's a good parallel.'

'With what?'

'Nothing.'

She sighed. 'I was crying all afternoon.'

'Same.'

'I don't think you've cried for centuries.'

'My body cries in other ways.'

'I can see that. But why would you come to me?'

'I like you.'

Her hand twitched to her face, unsure of its response. In the shadows behind her I saw the outline of the taxi that had taken me here – and this shadow changed into a coach from a fairy tale – and then into a pumpkin – and then into a hearse – and I imagined myself inside the hearse, driving across a moor in the middle of England at night – and the moon was looming over me like a mother offering her breast to a child – and we sank.

'I threw out Francis' clothes,' she said eventually. 'I hate him. He lied to me. But I don't know what to think about you. You didn't actually lie to me. Or even if you did… yesterday, you were…'

'I like you,' I said again. 'I came back with you yesterday because I wanted to come back with you. Why does everything have to have an agenda?'

I thought of how slowly yesterday she'd pulled off my trousers and kissed the inside of my thighs – and of how, later, a helicopter had passed overhead and she'd woken and told me she was burying herself with her own hands and I'd said I was cutting open her stomach and pulling out a snail-coloured snake and taking it into my mouth – and then we'd fallen back asleep.

'You like being confusing, don't you?'

'Am I confusing you?' I asked, lifting my head till my lips were at hers. 'I wanted to see you.'

She did not move. I relaxed back, smiling, as her instincts wrestled with each other. With her long neck and loose black hair and long loose white dress, she looked like a goddess painted on the walls of a pyramid.

'Your pockets are empty,' she said.

'No phone, no money, no shoes, no keys,' I gestured at my naked body. 'Just this.'

'Do you want to wear a dress?' she asked.

'Do you want to kiss me?'

Her gaze paused, I met it. She hesitated as I rose, but again did not pull away. Her lips parted, I kissed her. Briefly, the taste passed into the sound of a plucked string. I fell back.

'You should have drunk the whisky last,' she winced.

'I'll have some more.'

She retrieved the bottle, filled a third of my glass with whisky, and handed it to me. The contact of her finger on mine repeated the sound of a plucked string in my mind – but more clearly now – a viola treated with reverb. She filled the emptied milk glass with the same amount for herself and drank it in two gulps.

'Do you have any water?' I asked.

She stood to fetch some, coughing from the whisky.

My body was a muted growl. Her absence felt like an

impression on a pillow – and I longed instantly for her return. She had less certainty than she'd had earlier today; out of costume, she could no longer simplify herself into a stock character, so she could not speak or think in the clichés that had given her courage. My costume, meanwhile, had become more elaborate – these injuries had advanced my performance.

She returned with a pitcher of water and a scarlet dress. As she set them down, I gripped her wrist with an urgency I had no words for and pulled her to me until she knelt either side of my hips, close enough to kiss. I pressed my fingers into her shoulders so that their blood turned white. She kissed me back almost in panic. I lifted her dress to lift myself into her – and we fucked, her nails cutting across my bruises, her knee against my stab wound. Each shock rose into pleasure as the endorphins and alcohol overruled the pains of my body's surface and its deeper myalgia – until briefly she seemed like their antidote.

Her eyes were closed, my eyes were covered by her hair. I slid my hands down her arms to her elbows, and came as she did.

I untensed and let my head fall backwards. She lay across me, reaching over the side of the sofa to sip from the water jug.

'Is there cum on my dress?' she asked, smiling.

'You can't see anything, it's white.'

'What about blood?'

'It's quite stylish blood.'

'Shit.'

She stood up quickly, dabbing at the stains – confused by herself but not annoyed. 'What was that?'

'It was quick,' I said. 'Do you have any painkillers?'

'I've got you paracetamol and ibuprofen. They're just there.' She reached to the table behind my head, and as her perfumed wrist passed my nose, it trailed lily of the valley.

I listened to four foil pockets perforate. She fed me the tablets one by one, between sips of water.

'Anything stronger?' I asked.

'Are you being ungrateful?'

'This is like… trying to mop up the ocean with a tea towel,' I said.

'Don't flatter yourself, you're not the ocean. You're a paddling pool at best.'

'Alright, I'm a paddling pool, but I still need better means to mop it up.'

'Well sorry – I've run out of whale tranquiliser, or whatever class of chemical you're accustomed to. Iris will have something stronger at the gallery.'

I sat up to repress a smile. 'Are we going to the gallery?'

'If you won't go to hospital.'

'Even though you hate Francis?'

'It's not just photos of him. There's photos of me as well.'

'Who's Iris?'

'An ally.'

'Are you going to get revenge on Francis?' I asked.

'Maybe.'

'You should. The best revenge is always erotic.'

'I was thinking that.' She drank again from the whisky.

'What do you want to do?'

'I have an idea – but I'm not telling you. Aren't you on his team? You can't be trusted.'

'Obviously not,' I said. 'I don't work well in teams. Do you have any shoes that could fit me?'

She laughed. 'You're most likely to fit into sling-backs. I've already chosen them.' She pointed to a pair of black suede high heels whose straps curved behind the ankle. 'But if we're going down that route then we need to sort out your face.'

'How dare you? I'm beautiful.'

'But you can look more beautiful.' She kissed me, tasting of whisky – her proximity again twisting in my mind into the sound of a reverberating string. 'I haven't done a boy's make-up since I was a teenager.'

'Can you bring out the best in me?'

'I can't perform miracles.'

She left for another room. I began to climb into the dress. My sense of space seemed to be stabilising as the fluids retrieved me to competence. But when I tried to stand, I wobbled, and dropped back onto the cushions. Eva saw me fall as she re-entered, and cried 'Ah!' in pity.

'Ah!' I echoed, mockingly.

From a quilted bag she took out a bottle, and from its dispenser she pumped a puddle of foundation onto the back of her hand.

'This can hide tattoos,' she said. 'So it should hide your bruises.'

She dabbed some on her index finger – but then hesitated.

'No – I'm doing this wrong. We should colour-correct first.'

'Yeah, I want a full actor's mask,' I said. 'Don't skip any steps.'

She took another pot from her bag – a wheel of five creams. And with her ring finger, she rubbed at the salmon cream – and then applied it over my bruises, cancelling out their bluish colour. Again I breathed in the scent of lily of the valley at her wrist.

'Ok that's better,' she said. 'Now we can do foundation.'

She returned to the beige puddle – and dotted it over my face, methodically, delicately. And then with an ovoid tickling sponge, she blended this into a mask.

'I want to do more,' she said.

'Some eyeliner?' I suggested.

'A subtle cat eye,' she said. 'Some mascara.'

She held back my forehead with her thumb and lined my lids with thin black wings.

'Blink,' she instructed, holding up a stick of mascara.

I closed my upper lashes over its brush, twice for each eye – and let her stroke the lower two until they too were dyed.

'You're ready.'

'Thank you.' I kissed her – but she quickly retracted, to admire further the new artifice of my face.

'You can be the red queen, and I'll be the white,' she said.

'Did you bring out the best in me?'

'Check,' she gave me a folded mirror.

I looked at myself. My skin glistened oddly in this consistency – my eyes seemed more devious in their darkening, and the bruising of the left one was well concealed.

'You bring out… something in me,' she said. 'Not the best… but you bring out the me in me. What just happened was… I don't know. But it's worked. And this afternoon I was… it was refreshing, to be able to let it out, you know? And I can even say I liked last night, however fucked up it was for you to not tell me about you and Francis.'

'How could I have told you? It had nothing to do with why I came back with you, or why I came to you now.'

'You're lying but I don't mind. I'm going to let you play on. At least you're committed to your role,' she laughed, indicating my hip wound as its blood blotched her gown towards a sicklier red.

I tried to kiss her again but she stood up, taking out her phone.

'The taxi's here,' she said. 'And so you're my date. The boy who stole my boyfriend. This makes no sense.'

'I didn't steal anyone. And things don't need to make sense, they just need to be charming.'

'I don't know if I'm charmed, but I'm – still listening.'

She wrapped a cape of scarlet mink around my shoulders. I leaned against her as she escorted me into the lift and down into the waiting taxi.

We shared the back seat. I fell asleep in her lap as she played with my hair. The viola plucks bled together into a single note.

2.

I woke being poked in my stab wound.

'Get up, cunt,' said a stranger.

Mint nails were beckoning me out of the cab. I followed the sheen of a cream cocktail dress upwards to a throat bared beneath gaunt cheeks, green insolent eyes, and a bob of auburn hair. I rose as ordered. Eva stepped around this other woman to support me onto the curb.

'How are you helping him?' the stranger asked, unmoving as I tried to focus on the building behind her.

The wall spelled out 'Impluct' in tall letters above a crowd of smoking attendees. A poster beneath announced this as the vernissage of Lars Vasari's 'DREAM TRAUMA' exhibition.

'My opinions have changed,' Eva said.

'He ruined your relationship.'

'Francis ruined our relationship.'

'Eva, Francis cheated on you – with him,' the stranger insisted.

'And I cheated on Francis with him too.'

'Good evening,' I said with a bow, as though I'd been invited to introduce myself. 'I presume you are… Iris?'

'Just… it's different to how I thought,' Eva continued. 'Not completely different… Francis still needs to answer for himself. But maybe earlier I expressed my anger in a… homophobic way. Or bi-phobic, whatever. But that's not how I'm going to express my anger anymore. And I'm not angry with Leander, he needs… Let's just go inside. We both need a bit of numbing.'

'I can numb you,' Iris said, though her stare was still hostile. 'Do you need to be carried?'

'Yes please,' I said, pretending not to understand her sarcasm.

And so, my arms spread across the two women's shoulders, I limped towards the gallery entrance. Iris was colder than Eva, perhaps having waited too long without a coat, and my skin in contrast seemed feverish.

The crowd watched us with a reverence that we didn't warrant. I had expected curiosity, but not this fascination. Possibly this was the effect of Eva's fame. The two bouncers at the door parted without speaking or referring to a list.

'Can you come unlock the kitchen, please?' Iris asked the one on the left.

'Does your guest need help?'

'Actually, can you take him?'

I was transferred to the studier grip of the guard. The women led us quickly into the foyer – and as our entrance rippled through the gallery-goers, they paused in their mingling to gaze at us, with a nervousness that suggested they desired to approach but dared not. The main exhibition began up three steps in a wide white room, but we instead walked down a side corridor, towards a dove-grey door. The guard shifted his support as he took a key from his pocket and unlocked it.

'Thank you,' Iris said, conclusively, and the guard understood this as a cue to leave.

I was lowered onto a chrome stool beside a chrome table and gladly slumped into it, my head filling with sediment – which looped in a figure of eight. With my eyes closed, I could only hear some of what the women were saying. But I gathered that water was being boiled in a saucepan, and Francis had arrived half an hour ago. I let my thoughts lull into incomprehension.

'Leander!' Eva said, with an odd urgency, as though afraid I would not wake. 'Leander!'

I lifted my head. Iris placed a white plate on the table. At its centre was a circle of fluffy, whiter shards. The plate's underside was steaming still, from resting on the saucepan. She crushed the cooked ketamine with an Oyster card and divided it into three thin lines.

With a twenty-pound note rolled up her nose, Eva bent daintily to the plate, and insufflated an outer line. As she jerked back up, she blinked tears towards the ceiling, and passed the note to Iris. Iris did the same and passed the note to me. I breathed out in preparation, securing the makeshift straw with trembling fingers, and snorted the remainder.

It cut at my sinus with an enticing specificity – reducing the rest of my body's aches to vagueness. The bitterness mixed scent and taste into a string that dripped into the back of my throat, which my mind saw inwardly as having the feathery blue-green of a mallard's head. I sniffed again, able to sit more upright, my sense of self dispersing.

'Can I have more than that? I asked.

'Not right now,' Iris said, her voice less severe, distracted by the loaded blood crossing her brain. 'This is pure. We need to be able to talk still – we just want to be a little wonky so we can deal with the pretentious fucks outside. It's human ketamine, not for horses – it's from a hospital.'

'When do you get this in hospital?' Eva asked.

'When you're giving birth.'

Eva laughed. 'And so tonight you're giving birth to —'

But I didn't hear the rest. The slurry of melt-crystals behind my eyes slurred my vision, and a gossamer began to replace my skin.

'What – and you're giving birth to your… revenge?' Iris smiled, entirely now in a lighter humour.

'Yeah. And what are you giving birth to?' Eva asked me.

I cricked my neck as my nerves flowered into levity. 'I'm giving birth to a baby swan called Winter, who can see ghosts, but he'll never find a mate.'

'Lucky him,' Eva said. 'I think I need to leave… What's your laptop password?'

'There's no password,' Iris said. 'Just ask the guy at the door to let you into the studio.'

'What you doing?' I asked, drifting my head against the wall, smiling at Eva in innocence.

'I'm going to edit a film,' she said.

'Of what?'

'A video me and Francis made before he met you. You said the best revenge is erotic. So. I want to show it to everyone…'

'What, like a sex tape?' I asked. 'You know they aren't usually that embarrassing for the man.'

'This one will be very special highlights.'

'And then what?' I asked. 'How are you going to show it?'

'Wait and see.' Eva stood up, smiling.

She kissed Iris on both cheeks and kissed me on the fore-head, stroking her finger under my chin until I lifted my lips towards hers and kissed her back. The feathery green-blue of the ketamine rose again in my mind, and fell back into a low note plucked on a cello.

'I decided you're a paradox,' Eva said, her nose against mine. 'It's your opacity that's attractive. You're an act inside an act. What are your motivations?'

'Motivations are for the artless,' I said.

She didn't answer, but shook her hair in a tremor of pleasure, and left. As the door shut behind her, Iris stood – and fetched a bottle of water from the fridge.

'I still can't be nice to you,' she said. 'I know about you.'

'What do you know about me?' I asked, delighted.

'You can't seduce me. I refuse to be seduced.'

'I can seduce you. I'll be so honest that you'll become invested in me against your will.'

'Is that your usual method?'

'No. But I know that's the method that will work.'

I was surrounded by the scent of thunder, and the scents that come after summer rain – of bracken fronds releasing cyanide into the air, and the odours of wood and soaked flowers.

'How?' she asked.

'You are already intrigued,' I said. 'You wouldn't have said "you can't seduce me", unless it was a challenge.'

'Was it?'

'Let's make it one.'

'Ok, then tell me the truth –' Iris blinked as the dissociative drug fanned through her reflexes. 'What are you doing? Why did you turn up at Eva's door half beaten to death?'

'Because I knew that by appearing so vulnerable before her she would forgive me.'

'Ok, that's quite a strong start.' She sipped from the water bottle.

'Honesty can be thrilling.'

'So you used being beaten up as an advantage?'

'I weaponised my suffering,' I said. 'I positioned her in the empowered role, so that she couldn't feel like my victim any-more – she was the healer, I was the victim. Making people help you makes them care about you – or even makes them love you. Putting my health in her hands was a way of accelerating our intimacy, in the same way that being this honest with you accelerates our intimacy.'

'Why did you want her to forgive you?'

'She might be useful.'

'Then why not just befriend her? Why steal her boyfriend? Why the mind-fuck first?'

'I didn't steal anything,' I said. 'And the mind-fuck is the befriending. How else can she know me properly unless I hurt her? And then come to her, having myself been hurt.'

'So, what – the proper you is hurting people?'

'Being hurt can be thrilling.'

'Did you get beaten up on purpose?'

'I'd have to really love being in this much pain to do that.'

'Has the ketamine helped?'

I smiled. 'I'm nearly ready to give birth.'

We stood up. She took my arm. But her touch had too many premises in it – like mist over a pond at sunrise – and I saw a flotilla of lotus leaves, leaving the shore of the living, each burning a different stack of incense – cypress and cassia and styrax and myrrh, and so on – until I seemed inside a mayhem of futures. The aroma was too strong – and, quickly, I kissed her. She let me.

'But I'm still not seduced,' she said.

I balanced on her as she opened the door. My movements had regained little focus.

'I'm not finished yet,' I said. 'I have to seduce you with cruelty as well.'

We quit the chrome kitchen arm in arm, and glided down the corridor.

'How will being cruel to me seduce me?' she asked.

'Not to you, to someone you're attracted to. Francis.'

She didn't reply.

'I guessed in you a proprietary jealousy,' I said, 'that differed from simple sympathy for Eva.'

'Am I supposed to be impressed by that? Most of the girls here have a crush on Francis. That wasn't a hard guess.'

'But still you want to see him hurt, because he's not attracted back.'

'I don't think that's true,' she said.

'Well Eva obviously has some kind of revenge planned, and you seem to be happy enough to enable it. I'm just going to take everything a little further; my methods can dovetail with hers – I'll capitalise upon whatever damage she manages to inflict and add some of my own, until Francis is broken.'

I couldn't say – because Francis doesn't love me enough yet. Because I need the love of a broken man, a man who has no power over me.

3.

We climbed the three steps into the first wide white room of the exhibition. Astronomical facts and phenomena were rising to the front of my mind, and so were the fancies of old astrologies – as the ketamine conducted my synaesthesia towards another understanding of the room, as a planetarium. And this was a planetarium so immersive that its walls were soon the surface of an actual planet and the space between them, inverted somehow, was the planet's atmosphere.

I was travelling across two planes of reality, then: an art gallery, and a solar system. Or perhaps more than two – since this second plane seemed to be both a solar system and a representation of a solar system – and so I was travelling towards real storms and videos of storms, belts of rock and libraries of myths.

'So you don't really like Francis?' Iris asked, disrupting the hallucination. 'It sounds like he loves you. Eva showed me the messages you sent each other – I'm guessing you meant her to find them? But what are you going to do to him?'

'He's more powerful than me here,' I said. 'He's surrounded by admirers and photographs of himself – but I'm going treat him like a burdensome add-on and ignore him in a way that makes him obsessive.'

'How can you ignore someone in a special way?'

'Evasions can be more powerful than confrontations. I'll ignore him by talking to you.'

She laughed. 'Why would I help you?'

'Because you want to see if I can break him like I say I can. But first he needs to know I'm here. Where is he?'

A wing of fire detached from her shoulder, flew to the ceiling, and gathered itself into a phoenix – but before the phoenix could be fully formed, it ungathered again – into a cyclone of dust that harassed the room towards summer – until I was an imperial guard on a road of blood – and the dust smeared into a flat Martian red and the phoenix pretended to be dead.

'He was in the last room,' she said, pointing to the doorway on the right. 'The gallery is five rooms in a circle. But we can cut to the end.'

We steered each other towards the doorway, joined at the neck, our arms intertwined. The throng parted for us – and again, a few guests seemed as though they wished to engage us in conversation, but were dissuaded by our expressions of intent, and by my diagonal posture.

'What's the point of this, by the way?' she asked.

'The point is the ending. I love binning people. Leaving someone for no reason is my favourite game. Perhaps it's a way of getting back at the abandonments of my past.'

'That's rather self-defeating.'

'All pleasure is self-defeating.'

She had no reply. Francis stood tall in the middle of the room, dazzled by himself and the worship of the women around him. I tugged Iris towards him, and the floor lurched sideways – and I almost fell over, but no one else noticed.

'Do not engage in eye contact,' I said, gesticulating to attract attention. 'Look slightly above everyone else's eye-line to make them feel unconsciously subordinate. We need to edge into his view, while engaged in such stimulating conversation that we have no awareness of anyone around us. He'll expect us to approach him – as the social superior here – so it will be a while until his frustration makes him approach us. And then we greet him like a distant acquaintance.'

'So when are we going to start this stimulating conversation?'

I laughed unnecessarily loudly – and a few feet away, Francis turned his head in recognition.

'He's seen us,' I said.

She laughed sincerely, excited by the game, glancing at him and then back at me.

'Now that he knows we're here,' I said, 'we need to look like he's the furthest thing from our minds.'

She screeched in response, slapping me on the shoulder.

'Not that much,' I said. 'Controlled over-acting is a subtle art. We need to keep moving, but as though we're not aware of it, and then he'll worry we could walk away without noticing him.'

'How did you even… get him in the first place?' she asked. 'He seemed so close to Eva. He was so… straight.'

'Being straight is so embarrassing. There's no such thing anyway. But still – I am many men's exception.'

'How?'

'Because I'm beautiful and damaged. The classic combination. Plus, I've mastered the art of seducing bi-curious straight boys.'

'Can you give me some tips? Pretend I'm a man.'

'I can give you the full psychopath's seven-step seduction guide. Though, of course, telling you these seduction steps will be my way of seducing you.'

'Of course.'

'Exactly!' I shouted – as though we'd achieved some rare agreement in a completely different conversation, causing people nearby to turn around.

And as I watched, soot rose around their ankles like the aftermath of a fire – spreading towards the corners – and lightning, thrown by Francis, rutted through it – forcing the soot to bind into clumps that bound even harder into diamonds – which swirled like they swirled on Saturn, into a bullet-swift hail that rattled through us – until we too were diamonds.

Iris laughed, dispelling the vision. 'So step one is controlled over-acting?'

'No,' I said. 'Step one is underacting. You have to be mysterious. Initially your focus should not be on your target, but on his friends. They must be seduced first – so that they talk to him about you, while you remain intriguingly unavailable. He needs to want to meet you. Unfortunately, you have to have some kind of charisma to do this, so you may struggle here.'

'Are you trying to neg me?'

'Would that work?'

'Fine, let's say I have no charisma. What happens then?'

'Fake it,' I said. 'You need to be outrageous, outspoken, witty, and in possession of a tortured past.'

'Ok – but what if I bump into my target during step one, when I'm supposed to be unavailable?'

'You have to bump into him occasionally, but just act like you don't consider it worthwhile to get to know him properly. This is most effective when the target considers himself the ringleader of his group. And then once his friends have been charmed – and they have begun to invite you to their gatherings, and miss you when you do not come – you can advance to step two. Step two is a prolonged single moment of focus on the target – for example spending eight hours at a house party talking only to him – as though you have finally recognised his value. Your attention will feel like a reward after the indifference you displayed during step one – and you must use this sense of reward to overwhelm him. Your personality needs to be hyper here, so that he experiences this as the most electric interaction of his life; you need to make him feel clever and desirable and newly understood. You tell him turbulent stories from your adolescence – fictional or true, doesn't matter – so that in return he confesses his rarest agonies, the ones he hasn't told his friends. This creates a quick bond, and makes him see you as more special than them.'

Francis suddenly appeared before us, almost within reaching distance, his eyes desperate to meet mine. I spun Iris around and forced her past a row of elegant teenagers.

'Step three,' I continued, 'is the hot and cold game: the next time you meet after step two's electric connection, you must act like there was no electric connection. Following this let-down, you oscillate between treating him as marginal when among his friends, and as your kindred spirit when alone together. Step four is the escalation of this – so when you're in a group, you entertain his friends and ignore him, as in step three – but with the addition now of brief public touching. For example, suddenly stroking him, putting your head in his lap, even mock-kissing him, while talking to others – as though you have a shared secret language of gestures that he doesn't quite understand. The aim is to make him accustomed to an overfamiliar physicality, until he returns it – and so too begins to press his cheek to yours when greeting you in a group, while merely hugging the others. You need to seem as though you are unaware that you are physically attracted to him – like you haven't thought about the meaning of all this touching – but are simply compelled by instinct.'

Iris and I were dancing between the women around Francis, obnoxiously locked into our own conversation, as he fought to attract our attention. Ketamine had made her smile seem both uneasy and defiant – and her chin now had a constant tilt.

'Step five,' I said, 'is private touching – again non-sexual, again seemingly unconscious – like resting your head on his arm, or playing with his fingers absent-mindedly when you are alone together. Step six is to bombard him with attention through messages and phone calls and invitations to social events – all still under the guise of friendship – until he relies on your attention to feel happy, like a chemical dependency – and begins to bombard you back. Finally, step seven is to withdraw this attention at random, to keep him insecure. When together, you act like soul-mates, but speak about other loves and other needs like you've never considered him a sexual option – though you must avoid explicitly discussing sexual orientation, because this can lead to denials and repression. And when apart, you should appear to forget about him – until he is forced to beg for your attention. Once you have made him addicted, you can choose whether to fuck him or cast him aside.'

Francis had by then long been trying to interrupt. His face still had its default self-assurance, but his pout had widened with exasperation. Eventually he shouted, 'Leander! Leander!'

I refused to look around. He shoved a model out of his way and grabbed my shoulder.

'How long have you been here?' he asked.

'Oh hi,' I said vaguely, like I'd forgotten whose friend of a friend he was.

'Why you wearing a dress? What's wrong with your eye? How do you know each other?'

'Yeah,' I smiled and shrugged off his hand, adding 'Cool,' to no one in particular.

I tugged Iris aside and bent my head to her ear to resume our conversation, reducing him to an interruption.

'Wait – where you going?' he asked.

'Huh?' I asked, confused that he was still speaking to me. 'Oh – we're… going to get a drink?' I waved my hand dismissively.

Iris laughed. I walked her quickly away as Francis' circle attempted to re-engage him.

I watched him watch us retreat in dismay – until he was folded into the sky of a forbidden purple enclosure – and a river somewhere beat itself like a drum.

'You genuinely looked like you'd only seen him once in your life!' Iris laughed. 'For like three minutes.'

'Very self-confident people are the easiest to break – because they aren't used to being treated as unexceptional. But you can only break them after you've made them desire you – and they are the hardest people to goad into real desire.'

We were back in the gallery's first room. The photographs here were of faces alive but deformed – by acid attacks, bullets, bombs, or beatings; an eye gouged out, a dangling cheek, a pair of rotting lips. They were shot as if for a high fashion editorial – hyper-saturated, with steep shadow gradients. Most of the visitors seemed unaware of these pictures – or if they looked, they looked only briefly, unaffected, and were instead more focused on each other, in a sociality that was competitive rather than amiable.

'So how did you goad Francis into desire?' she asked. 'Was he in my place on your arm, laughing as you dismantled somebody else for your amusement?'

'Yeah, I suppose Eva was the person we dismantled. But that's over now.'

'I almost forgot you're a complete cunt.' She had something like wonder in her voice. 'But I still want to know how you got to him.'

The row of photographs I was trying to focus on gave way to a plough of stars – driven by an ox down a terrace of moon-mansions – which each imploded as it passed.

'Just like I said,' I replied, ducking under flying moon-mansion shards. 'The seven steps. I mean it wouldn't have worked if he hadn't wanted it on some level already – the task was to ease him out of the phobias that society had walled him up in. He would embrace me lengthily in front of his friends; I let him be overly affectionate to me when he was drunk. I would always act open and available – but never predatory, so that he had to make the first move, never me – until finally he was high, we were at a bar and he kissed me goodbye on the cheek, and then kissed me again on the mouth and stayed there. The next morning I messaged him an emoji with no clear meaning – so he was forced to worry for a while, and make the next move as well. I refuse to seem to take him seriously – he thinks that I think I'm just a passing joke to him – so he is forced to insist upon his sincerity. I didn't see him for ten days before today. But he still clings to his dignity, and I'm still replacing my easy-going passivity with indifference. Like any addiction, I'll make him give up parts of himself that were once fundamental, make him break his own rules and betray his own values to get back at the high – and all he'll receive in return is an echo of what he wants.'

'So… which emoji did you text him?'

'Probably the dolphin.'

We had waded through the bustle to the gallery's second room. Its four unequal walls each had two pairs of triptychs: eight actors expressing three different despairs in parallel. The subjects were shot similarly to the survivors of the previous room: only head-and-shoulders, lit in high contrast. On the wall behind us, three photos of Eva were paired with three photos of Francis – but the photographer had extracted from them personalities I had never seen in them before. They wore their three traumas with an ambivalence that was also somehow a conviction, so that each face contradicted the other.

'These are actually quite good,' I said, shifting my arm over Iris' shoulder. 'Each photo seems to say "this is the real me and the only real me", but then there are two other photos which say the same thing – about a different "real me". And I know Francis has never suffered like that. The other exhibitions he was in were mostly photos of pretty naked nineteen-year-old boys, or refugees with green eyes. This is… better than usual.'

'Thank you!'

'Why? Did you help?'

Iris laughed. 'You've been talking about yourself for so long that you didn't bother to work out anything about me.'

'What? Were you the photographer? I thought it was a man?'

'Why?' she asked with mock indignity.

'Because...' I floundered. 'Because didn't it say it was Lars something on the door?'

'Lars Vasari. That's me.'

My lungs turned to white metal tigers – clawing through my intestines, and through my belly button – and then out into the airy autumn around us, and further out, into afterthoughts.

'How is that you?' I asked.

'You didn't wonder why I had access to the kitchen? Or why everyone here knows me?'

'I assumed... some connection. I didn't assume you had a male pseudonym.'

'It's not a pseudonym,' she said.

'What is it then?'

'It's the name I used to have. Before I transitioned.'

'I can't tell if you're lying or not – you've become interesting.'

'Admit it – you've been out-manoeuvred.'

'I've not been out-manoeuvred,' I said. 'I've been... narcissistic. But that's my brand. And your brand, apparently, is that you're a trans woman who takes photographs under the name of the man she used to be?'

'Being trans isn't a brand. And I was never a man – I just used to have certain anatomical features that made people assume that I was.'

The gallery floor spun again, and I fell – its walls dimmed from white to the dark of a planetarium – and the pole of a gas planet appeared across its dome, with a storm shaped like a hexagon – and from this storm burst forth another, smaller planet – rocky, pocked with craters – a planet that had known days as longs as years and been told such secrets that it was allowed to be seen only at morning and evening, never at night.

Iris lifted me back up. The gallery righted.

'So, so why do you work under your old name?' I asked.

'I hated it for years,' she said. 'But then I began to find its power fascinating – it had been a violence inflicted upon me, and I wanted see if I could alter that meaning. It's like a drag-name, except the drag was the first fifteen years of my life. And as a photographer, I like the performance of identity. I like to capture fake selves, selves formed under duress, past selves. I like how the meaning of the body changes under violence.'

'So does Iris refer to the eye of a camera?'

'No, I just liked the name. I don't predicate my personhood on my job. And I didn't even have a camera when I started hormone therapy, when I was fifteen. Why did you choose Leander as your name?'

'How do you know I chose it?'

'Because you care about self-fashioning as much as I do.'

'I just liked it,' I said, repeating her weak answer.

'Isn't it Greek?' she pushed.

A waiter shaped out of helium passed with a tray of cocktails – we took two and clinked them and giggled and downed them and then put them back empty on the tray.

'There's the story of Hero and Leander,' I said. 'The priestess and the boy. They live either side of a narrow sea, they fall in love, each night she lights a tower-lamp for him to swim to, one night the lamp goes out, he drowns, she kills herself.'

'How is he you?' Iris asked. 'If anything, you present yourself more like Hero, the priestess – you light the lamp to lure Leanders to your tower, till you turn off the light and they drown.'

I didn't reply.

'Or,' she went on, 'you see yourself as more fundamentally the Leander, but pretend to the world to be Hero? Or, maybe you just like being the anti-Hero?'

'It doesn't have to have a stable meaning,' I said. 'I don't believe in that. "I'm this, I'm that" is boring – we should speak of fluidities. I don't know what I am. I'm Hero and Leander and anti-Hero and anti-Leander and neither, depending on the lighting.'

'You're only saying that because I just said I'm trans. You're trying to bend the conversation into a shape that will endear me to you.'

'But isn't it working?' I asked. 'You are endeared. And maybe these are coincidentally also my core beliefs.'

The floor was moving in an elliptical orbit, I supposed, around Francis – accelerating as we came closer to his room – back around the gallery's circuit. But I refused to fall again – I would be a water clock, obeying not the sun – not Francis – but the moon.

'But you essentially just said you don't believe in core beliefs,' Iris said. 'Because you're always changing.'

'I believe in core beliefs, I just don't believe in a solid me, a solid core – I believe in a series of processes, exchanges, relationships.'

'And are those relationships always sexual?'

'Yes,' I said, as though I'd missed her sarcasm.

'What if the other person isn't attracted to you?'

'They are.'

She laughed. 'I think we both need more ketamine.'

'That, coincidentally, is another of my core beliefs.'

'Hold this.' She gave me her purse.

We had entered the third room. Its four walls now only had one triptych on them each – the same photographs as had been on the upper row in the pair in the previous room, but deformed into grotesques. Francis' three photos were alone – Eva's had not been promoted to this room. His symmetries had been subverted: in one photo his forehead was twisted into a distended chin, in another his hair was replaced by an ear. Beneath each triptych there was a single capitalised word.

'"TRAUM", "TRAUMERIE", "TRAUMA", "TRAUMATA",' I read aloud.

Iris moved to stand in front of me, her head against my chest.

86

With our bodies as a shield, she unsealed the pouch of ketamine in her purse.

'What do these words mean?' I asked. 'Traum is German for dream… traumerie is dreaming. Trauma is trauma… What's traumata?'

'Wounding words from a loved one,' she said, scooping a key into the plastic pouch and lifting its powdered tip to her nose and inhaling it.

'TRAUMA DREAM was the name of your exhibition, wasn't it?'

'DREAM TRAUMA,' she said, now lifting a key's-worth of ketamine to my nose.

I snorted. A couple nearby laughed at our activity. Iris closed her purse.

'So now the photographs themselves are being traumatised?' I asked, spluttering at the bitterness behind my throat – which leaked across my senses into teal the texture of silicone.

'Or the photographs themselves are beginning to dream…'

'You split up Eva and Francis before I did,' I said. 'Her photos didn't make it to this room.'

'But I loved both of them at least, unlike you.'

'N-no,' I stuttered. 'You just fantasied about having them both for yourself, but didn't do anything about it. I acted upon it. We had the same instinct, but you were too scared to act.'

'This is my action,' she waved unsteadily at the walls.

I followed her hand with my eyes – and the room filled with saltwater ice, as our gravity lessened – and we were at the bottom of a gulf, surrounded by white volcanoes that spat magma hundreds of miles up into the sky. I blinked – and Iris spoke on.

'Fantasies can be their own bodies,' she said. 'And don't you ever do art?'

'I do what I'm doing.'

'Which is?'

'Well it's not living, is it? When I was fifteen my myalgia got so bad that whenever I closed my eyes I imagined bullets coming at my face. I even went deaf for a few days – and then sound came back and every colour was a howl.'

'What's myalgia?'

'Chronic pain from chronic illness. An invisible illness in my case. I wrote in biro on my thigh "You're not allowed to kill yourself until your next birthday". So I forced myself to wait for the day I turned sixteen, by which point my next birthday was a year away – and so I had to wait another year. And so on. Sometimes I had nothing to cling to except that rule. But I'll probably break it eventually.'

'How?'

'I want to fly. Maybe I'll leap from a cliff.'

'So —'

'So that's my art – survival.'

We woozed into the fourth room. Again there was a reduction: only two triptychs from the previous room remained – one of them Francis' – doubled on opposite walls. And now their fabric was also harmed – with burn holes, rips, erasures, smears. In some places the gloss was sticky, in others dull. The central Francis photo of the wall beside me had been given an ornate gold-gilt frame, while the others were bare.

'Lars!' someone shouted. 'Found you at last! It's a wonderful show, wonderful – I'm here from i-D Magazine, again, yes?' A slim, fumbling man had pressed himself into us, blocking our way. 'Can I ask a few quick questions?'

'I can't promise very satisfying answers,' Iris said.

'Of course, of course, I'm just looking for a few off-the-cuff remarks here,' he said.

'He's been interviewing me for months,' Iris told me. 'You'll like this though – his name is Nikolas And.'

'My nom de guerre,' he simpered.

'And this is Leander.' She tried to gesture grandly towards

me, but instead semi-tripped, her body unreliable under the renewed influence of ketamine. 'Leander is... my new muse,' she laughed.

'Ah – then you must allow me to interview you as well,' he said, handing me a business card from his breast pocket.

'I'd be happy to,' I said, accepting his card with a serious smile. 'Another time.'

'Yes, yes I understand – tonight I am here as an admirer not as an inquisitor. I don't usually write articles – I'm an art director! But Lars is special – so excuse my over-excitement. I just wanted to clarify a few things. So. Would you say that your practice falls within post-modernism or meta-modernism?'

'For fuck's sake,' Iris said. 'No.'

'Can you... clarify?'

'Neither of those movements were real anyway – they were just romanticism.'

'But we are in a new era now,' Nikolas insisted. 'The internet is the most significant shift in human consciousness since the printing press.'

'Fuck, you're eager this evening!'

He blushed.

'It isn't a shift in power though,' I said. 'Maybe minds have shifted, but the internet reproduces the same inequalities as before, the same monopolies, the same ideals. If anything, it's worse – more castles of zeros, more wealth for fewer people...'

Something crashed into the room – it tilted off its axis – and the magnetic field bent – the floor bucked, tripping the crowd around us – and for a second, I was in a zeppelin, looking through a telescope at a field of infrared hurricanes.

'And our era has already given a name to itself,' Iris said, holding me up. 'Aren't we supposed to be millennials now?'

'So...' Nikolas said. 'Would you say that your practice falls within... Millennialism?'

'Yeah sure whatever,' Iris laughed, pushing past him.

'Millennialism! It's all for ignoring people who love you and getting ignored by people you love.'

'But the word's already taken,' I said. 'It's for people obsessed with the apocalypse.'

'That's fine,' Iris said. 'Every era's obsessed with the apocalypse.'

'Maybe every era gets the apocalypse it thinks it deserves.'

A black tortoise crawled out of my knee and down along my leg trailing hoarfrost – and blew back up at me blue-black bubbles that smelt of eucalyptus. I shook my leg – it vanished.

'Ok, but,' Nikolas said, hopping after us, 'do you prefer —'

'Who cares,' Iris sighed. 'You choose the name, just please, that's enough for now.'

We squirmed away from him towards the fifth room, to enter it for the second time, now from the other side.

4.

Francis was still in the middle of the room and he noticed our re-entry immediately. Three of the walls displayed his face, exclusively – two triptychs per wall, undistorted, undamaged, his repeating expressions serene. The fourth wall, which I had not looked at before, was occupied by a video. In it, Francis was naked, walking through a grey space with no features as the floor moved beneath him and the shadows on his muscles shifted. A pretty-boy with a boxer's body, his projected self was twice the size of a normal man; his pace was decisive and unchanging. Many of those around us were gazing at his projected dick as though hypnotised.

'So is this room supposed to be what happens after trauma?' I asked. 'And only Francis escapes here?'

The real Francis was hurrying over to us.

'Or he's the only subject who has not escaped,' Iris said. 'Perhaps in these photographs he is stuck somewhere deeper than the others.'

'Where you been?' Francis asked, shaking my upper arm. 'What's happened to you? You got a black eye?'

I looked past him as though he'd addressed these questions to somebody else. He had three women on his tail, dressed in shredded black – and they'd clearly been drinking for courage.

'What are your names?' I asked, stepping around Francis with a smile.

'My name's Ringo.'

'And my name's Ringo.'

'And my name's Ringo.'

They giggled in drunken succession.

'Isn't that quite… unlikely?' asked Iris, also ignoring Francis and stepping to my side.

He grabbed my shoulders with his hands. This contact segued into a colour in my mind, Francis' colour – a wheat-white spike, which soon subsided. I let him hold me, but kept my attention to the women.

'Are you a model?' one of the Ringos asked me.

'No – but he is,' I nodded back at Francis.

'No, you are a model,' the second Ringo said.

'And you're a film star,' the third said, pointing at my chest.

'I've seen your face on the side of the world,' the first said.

'Are these prophecies?' I asked.

As I stared at her, her face disappeared – and her body blurred into a gleaming brown sack that throbbed like an organ – with a veil where her head had been – and I realised that it was an organ – a liver, covered in blemishes – which were messages from the planets, or from the angry spirits that lived inside them – but the only message that I could read was a blemish near the base – and it said that I was an unclean animal unfit for sacrifice – and I sneezed, and the liver turned back into a woman.

'What about me?' asked Francis over my shoulder, trying to lean into our triangle.

'You're worse than him,' the second Ringo said.

'And better than him,' the third Ringo said.

'Are you trying to be the three witches from Macbeth?' I asked. 'In which case – your next line should be "Not so happy, yet much happier."'

I turned my head round towards Francis – briefly granting him my attention.

'So I should call you Banquo from now on.'

The three Ringos laughed without understanding.

'So you're Macbeth then?' Iris asked.

'No, I'll be Lady Macbeth,' I said. 'But I want to get away with it. In my version, she'd devastate the kingdom and then just wander off.'

I shrugged Francis off me and pulled Iris away, leaving him to confront his three drunk fans alone. Eva was lurching through the crowd towards us with a woman in a camel-coloured suit.

'Oh good!' Eva shouted, 'You two have been making friends!'

'No, I still hate him,' Iris said.

'Yeah I still hate him too,' Eva gave me four tipsy kisses. 'This is Amélie, my producer. Amélie, this is Leander, my nemesis.'

Amélie shook my hand, nodding her neat brunette bun. 'You look perfect.'

'I told you,' Eva said, 'I did his make-up and he's wearing my clothes. Now pay attention.' She tapped me on the nose as the ketamine glazed my gaze towards the ceiling. 'I hate you so much that I want you to be in my film. There's a scene we need you for. We need your bruises.'

'I was thinking that,' Iris said, turning to me. 'The Ringos were right – you should model. I want to photograph you while your eye's still swollen.'

'I don't do photos.'

'It's fine, of course he does photos, leave Leander with me,' Eva told her. 'My video is ready. Can we show it right now before I get too scared?'

'Ok,' Iris removed her arm from mine and poked me play-fully in my stab wound. 'But you will be captured.'

She wove away. And as I watched her, she seemed to be treading into a land of sonic booms, where the wind was faster than the speed of sound – and I saw a moon nothing like the earth's moon, dangerously close – due a collision that would rip it into a Saturn-like ring – and then the wind knocked me over.

Amélie steadied me upright.

'Eva has been very insistent,' she said. 'We have in mind a small scene that...'

I was tugged violently backwards – and Francis spun me around, shocked to see me speaking to his ex-girlfriend.

'I need to talk to you!' he said.

I twisted out of his grip, back towards Eva, and rolled my eyes as though a stranger had barged into me.

'What you doing with her?' Francis asked.

I batted him away with my hand and said 'I'll find you later,' almost laughing at my impersonal tone.

He stood stuck behind me, confused. Eva sniggered. 'He'll find you later, ok?'

She pulled Amélie and me closer towards her and led us away towards the opposite wall. Francis was fenced off by his admirers.

'You're mean,' she smiled. 'But he deserves it. I shouldn't join in but I like the risk.'

'I can't hurt you anymore,' I said. 'You're invulnerable.'

'No I'm not, don't try to claim you did me a favour by making him break my heart. Just listen. I want to use your natural evil for our film. We... I'll let Amélie pitch it to you – she's the sober one.'

'It's simple,' Amélie began with a slight bow. 'Eva is the lead role. Her character is on... a modern quest. I'll put it like that.'

Amélie spoke with tidy gestures, pausing carefully before each phrase. Her voice had the colour of claret and the softness of cashmere.

'And we have a wonderful writer,' she continued. 'He's very talented at twists and shocks, but... I have been reviewing the dailies, and I have been thinking more about the script now that we've begun to shoot, and... something is lacking. At the moment, it's all plot plot plot, and not enough atmosphere. Our writer has a writer's mind… he doesn't understand the difference between the screen and the text. We need more of the physicality of people colliding. So…'

'So we need you!' Eva said.

'We need an additional ingredient,' Amélie explained. 'The film requires an undercurrent of horror. And we've been trying all week to create a scene that can add to this mood. We want something to happen on a dark road, in the middle of the film – but haven't been able to work out what yet. We built the set, but nothing we've shot on it has been satisfying. So this evening, Eva and I were workshopping the idea of an encounter.'

'With you!' Eva said. 'Not part of the main plot, more like a cameo.'

'Don't you have to clear this idea with the director first?' I asked. 'Or am I supposed to be a surprise?'

Eva laughed, and I remembered her scream in the kitchen this morning and the vision I'd had of a row of aristocrats stabbing themselves with their swords. The gallery wall rose into a dike behind her, holding back a sea – and she was its queen, though her orders now were to stab, not herself, but this dike with her sword – and so release the sea over her city, in the middle of the night – while the moon was shadowed by the earth in a syzygy with the sun.

'Have you lost the ability to form memories?' Eva asked, as the dike shrank back into a wall.

'What do you mean?'

'Iris… has already expressed enthusiasm…' Amélie explained slowly, as though to a troubled child.

I smiled in astonishment. 'Iris… is the director?'

'You've been with her all evening!' Eva said. 'Are you so insanely solipsistic that you found out nothing about her? Did you even know this was her exhibition?'

'I worked that out eventually,' I said. 'But yeah – I suppose I am that solipsistic.'

'Well that's fine for your character. We need you to play the sociopath you already are.'

'I'm not a sociopath, I'm a psychopath.'

'What's the difference?'

'Psychopaths tie knots and calculate. Sociopaths are messy, and indiscriminate, and they get caught.'

'We think you could be a wounded beggar,' Amélie said, intervening. 'We only need you to come and improvise – while your bruises are still real. We have time and budget constraints – so we'll need tomorrow to set up, and then we should shoot the morning after. We want to keep it minimal.'

'So you can have a whole day of sleep before we need you,' Eva said. 'And I know you don't have a job so you can't pretend to be busy.'

'No,' I said. 'You're trying to trick me into some kind of revenge.'

Eva cackled. 'Maybe I am. But don't pretend this isn't why you fucked your way into our social circle in the first place.' She gestured at the fashion crowd around us. 'This is exactly the offer you wanted to get out of me. You just want to be begged to accept what you want.'

'No,' I said, 'I don't want into walk into a trap. And how is being a cameo beggar what I want? I want sleep.'

'You're an insomniac. And of course you want a role in my film. Fame is the governing ambition of our era. You just want it to seem like you'd be doing me a favour, when actually I'm doing you a favour – an opportunity.'

'You don't have to decide now, decide tomorrow,' Amélie said firmly. 'Think about it properly. You'd be paid. And in my opinion, you are perfect for the role.'

The room suddenly dimmed – the video of Francis' naked walk had been turned off. The crowd hushed, looking around to work out how they were supposed to react to this. But before a consensus could be reached, another video began playing across the wall.

It was a low-quality tripod shot of Francis slumped in a chair in his old bedroom – naked but for a pair of skimpy yellow swimming Speedos, clinging to his genitals in a way that seemed more indecent than the nudity of the earlier video. His wrists and ankles were tied to the chair with bright yellow ribbons in single bows, and a bright yellow ribbon was tied around his neck. Their knots looked weak, but he was not attempting to free himself. Instead he was weeping, his chin crumpled, snot dribbling over his lips – as a woman's hand shaved his head, the rest of her body out of shot.

The footage skipped: he was standing on the seat, his legs straight, his upper body bent down over them – his ankles and wrists both tied to the chair's arms in the same place, his yellow speedos waving obscenely up in the air. A green apple was stuffed in his mouth like a suckling pig's – and he was drooling to the floor. He gazed into the camera, crying more softly now, his body twitching as it tried to sustain this posture.

The footage skipped again: he was sitting again and the ribbons had been removed. His hands were in his lap as he burbled with shining eyes. Then he vomited onto himself, twice, as he sank lower, swaying with a goofy smile.

The footage cut back to the opening shot and the loop began again.

Initially I was aroused by Francis' degradation, but at the sight of his vomit, the ketamine seemed instantly to wear off, and I was returned to my injuries. I wanted to vomit too. I staggered away through the crowd, and Eva jumped after me.

'Where are you going?' she asked, with an uncertainty that suggested regret, and not the malicious triumph she'd wanted.

'I need some air,' I said, pushing her away.

Francis was trying to catch up with me too, but he was slowed by the audience in his path. He had to pretend that this video was an expected part of the evening – and so had affected an implausible grin. Word was spreading fast, and more people were spilling into the room. I half-fainted as I struggled against their current – and fell into Iris.

I smiled at her. 'Quick, come over here.'

I took her down the three steps into the foyer, into the side-corridor to the kitchen. This was no longer the territory of planets or moons. Though, perhaps, I could still be Pluto here – the demoted dwarf – if Pluto had been moved much closer to the sun, so the ice had evaporated into a tail, like a comet, and all that was left of my body was a heart-shaped lake.

Resisting the urge to vomit, I put a finger to my lips and pointed at Francis running out after us. He didn't think to look down our corridor, and instead rushed out of the building.

'He's looking for me,' I said. 'I told you I'd break him.'

'That wasn't you. That was Eva.'

'No, he could have withstood this attack if I'd been beside him. It's my abandonment that hurts – he can shrug off the film as planned controversy.'

'Was that the reaction?'

'People are quite confused… I think Eva regrets showing it.'

'It's pretty weird,' Iris said. 'I'm assuming they were on mescaline or something?'

'She didn't say.'

'Whatever – what I care about is you being in my film. Come to my set and I'll take some portraits of you as well.'

I dry-heaved in reply, lunging across the corridor to balance myself on the other wall. My gall bladder burst out of my chest – and grew green helicopter blades – and flew east, dribbling gallstones across the carpet.

'The ketamine's stopped working,' I said.

'I can give you more.'

'I need something stronger.'

'I don't have anything stronger.'

'I need to find my mum,' I said. 'She's got heroin.'

'You need to go to hospital.'

I ran to the door and vomited onto the pavement outside. The texture I associated with ketamine had thinned into a tulle-like transparency. The ultramarine of my myalgia was visible behind it. Francis was anxiously scanning the line of smokers with his phone to his ear – too distressed by the assumption that I was somewhere ahead of him to think of looking back.

'By the way,' I panted, as Iris caught up with me, 'I stole that twenty pound note we used as a straw. Can I keep it for a bus ride?'

She laughed. 'I'm going to give you more money – you need to take a cab.'

'He's trying to ring me,' I nodded towards Francis.

'You should tell him you're here.'

'No, this is what I promised you. I want him to be abject when he should have been triumphant.'

But I couldn't sustain this level of rhetoric and vomited again. Iris dragged me towards the queue of taxis.

'Aren't you're taking this too far?' she asked. 'I know he's an arrogant cunt, but I feel sorry for him, you're being too cruel.'

'You helped,' I spat. 'And no – this is the essential part: I refuse to turn to him when I ought to need him most. And when he most needs me. That is how to make him wretched. And I care more about the other ambition of my evening: have I seduced you?'

'Of course you've seduced me,' she said. 'Look at me, I've left my own exhibition, I'm giving you free money, and I'm begging you to be kinder to the only man I'm supposed to hate more than you. You've twisted this whole situation so that somehow you're the most pitiable victim – when you're the most to blame. But I'm not letting you win. Francis!' she shouted.

Francis turned and ran towards us. I fell into the taxi.

'I've been ringing you!' he shouted.

'He's lost his phone,' Iris said.

I vomited again out of the taxi door. The ketamine's anaesthesia had stopped and so too had my astrological fantasies – my synaesthesia continued, now without an ordering metaphor. I had gone beyond the scattered discs of ice at the edge of the solar system, and was back in London, listening to my own sick drip from my lips into the colour of aquafaba.

'What's happened to him?' Francis asked. 'You throwing up blood?'

'I don't have any blood,' I said. 'I was never born.'

'Where you going?' he asked. 'Let me in, move up.'

His voice had none of its former anger. He'd shrunk into simple needs – to get away, avoid everything in his head, be with me.

'You can't come.' I pulled shut the door and locked it. 'I was never born!'

My skirt had ridden up my thighs – and I was naked beneath it – and as I stared, my dick became a vagina – and an orange beak protruded from it – and the beak pushed and I pushed too – until a head emerged – and a long white neck – and a fat body with wings – and I was giving birth to a baby swan – called Winter, called Winter! – and I laughed as it waddled forth from me – and flapped to the window and out through it and out through Francis – until it was flying – and it flew away over the gallery – towards the loneliness that it couldn't see and the ghosts that it could.

'Where you going mate?' the driver asked.

'The Rockway bar in Brixton.'

Francis beat on the window, his face almost ugly with worry, pleading to be let in. I leant back into the leather, soothed by his sobs, pleased by my plan's success – and soon passed out in agony.

5.

The driver shook me awake. I gave him both £20 notes and crawled out without asking for change. A night bus leapt on me from nowhere, hissing – I jumped aside, more awake – and it leapt off, lynx-like, its yellow route number – N109 – branded into my eyes.

I blinked it away as I walked to the Rockway. The bar had none of the usual smokers outside – instead, a steroidal man in a suit stood alone before the door.

'Not tonight lad.' He shook his head as I tried to walk past him.

'Who are you? I come here all time.'

'Not anymore lad.'

'I'm friends with Pat,' I said.

I resisted the urge to vomit again.

'Who's that?' he asked.

'Pat owns the bar.'

'Not anymore lad.'

'What? Who owns it now? What about Dawn?'

'You know Dawn?'

'Dawn is my mother.'

His genial antagonism rose into malice. 'You're Leander?' he asked. 'Come with me.'

He pulled me in by the collar. The Rockway was more popular than usual, though none of the faces along its bar or in its booths was familiar. This clientele was rowdier than the regulars I'd known for the last two years – and yet everyone here acted as though they themselves were regulars, shouting and laughing with the ease of long acquaintance. Perhaps they were transplants from another social world. The bouncer escorted me towards the back room – which had formerly been empty, and now had a curtain across it and a second bouncer outside. I could feel the holster of a gun under his suit jacket. My bouncer grinned at his colleague as he drew back the curtain.

A party of thirty or so middle-aged men and younger women was spread across three tables. They were dressed in white tie. The men were smoking cigars, the women cigarettes. The tables were loaded with tumblers of whisky and flutes of champagne and other more expensive multi-coloured alcohols that the Rockway had never stocked before.

At the table closest to me there was an empty chair, with a stack of £50 notes in front of it – and the woman in the next chair was examining a tiny antique revolver with fascination, or envy – perhaps these were both gifts for the absent guest. Most of the women were high and miserable and scared. One girl had red marks around her wrist – like she'd recently struggled against restraints.

'Sarge!' the bouncer said. 'I found him! He's in a fucking dress!'

The room laughed. He threw me onto the floor. The wounds in my side and around my eye flared into the juniper taste of gin. I retched.

A pair of alligator shoes approached my head. They paused and then stepped over me. I heard a slap – and the bouncer who'd thrown me to the ground yelped in pain.

'You chose to disrespect my guest,' said a voice I associated instantly with sandalwood oil – it laboured each syllable into a slow irregular rhythm, its affected old-world accent enhanced by the rasp of burnt tobacco. 'What right did you think you have to make that kind of choice?' He hit the bouncer again. 'You have no rights.'

'The cunt put three of them in hospital.'

'You shall leave. If this were your wedding I would not treat your bride's wards in this way. I alone determine the manner in which I manage my affairs. And I do not need to be reminded of details that I have not forgotten. Leave.'

I was lifted to my feet by the man with alligator shoes. His grip evoked the synesthetic scent of sandalwood oil as well – though his actual smell was a mixture of talcum and cocoa cologne. Through half-closed eyes, I saw the room had stilled. The men and women regarded us with reverence. I tried to slow my breathing to reduce the buzz in my bones.

'I apologise for my employee's rudeness,' he said to me. 'He shall be reprimanded. I wish to extend to you all of my hospitality. Please – sit with us, Leander.'

I swayed backwards, trying to assess him as he held me up. He wore a white bow tie and a white starched collar and a white starched shirt and a cream marcella waistcoat – like the other men in the room – but instead of a tailcoat, he wore a green velvet smoking jacket. He was strong, and far younger-looking than he sounded; he could have been in his late thirties or early forties. The lines of his forehead seemed fixed in ironic disbelief – and his eyes had a shrewdness in them that seemed to see corruption in everything. He had Persian features but almost artificially pale skin, like he bleached it – and he had the hands of a field labourer.

'You appear to be… sizing me up?' he smiled. 'Do you not think it might be polite to speak?'

'Where's Dawn?' I asked.

'No doubt your injuries have caused you to neglect your decorum.'

'No doubt,' I replied, parodying his tone.

'Do you not think, then, that we ought to exchange some niceties before making demands?'

'You know my name.'

His smile twitched at this insubordination.

'Then you must know that mine is Kimber. And at least you have had the courtesy to conform to my dress code. Although I note you have chosen from a woman's wardrobe. I was wondering to myself… why?'

'Were you?' I mimicked, trying to annoy him more. 'Were you wondering to yourself? I wonder, do you ever wonder at yourself, rather than just to yourself? You sound like a man so repressed by pretence that he is incapable of self-reflection. So, wonder to yourself on my behalf, by all means, but I would be much more interested to watch you try to wonder at yourself.'

'Ah!' he smiled. 'I hoped you could speak in sentences. I am delighted! But sadly, what a twenty-year-old is interested in watching is of no relevance to me. You are trying to anger me with your rudeness, my dear – but I am enjoying you. You are a surprise, Leander, and I rarely enjoy surprises.'

'Where's Dawn?'

I tried to meet his gaze in defiance but instead fell backwards. He caught me.

'Your wounds are getting the better of you' he said. 'That is unfortunate. But let me offer you something in the way of pain relief, as your mother requested I should.'

He reached into a pocket and withdrew a small white ball wrapped in cling-film. Then he pressed it into my palm and closed my fingers over it.

'Let this calm you,' he said. 'And then we can talk for longer. I want to make you an offer of employment. Because, despite our… unusual beginning, I think we could develop a fruitful relationship. I have been impressed by reports of your resourcefulness.'

'You mean from the men you sent to beat me up?' I asked.

He laughed. 'Well, from your mother most importantly, and from others who used to frequent this bar, before they chose to take their custom elsewhere. You were said to possess a unique charisma and a unique… appreciation for violence. These skills can be transferred to aspects of the work I engage in.'

'Which is?'

'Logistical work. But I would not have known the extent of your skills had you not… undergone a certain canal-side initiation. So I do not feel as much remorse for your wounds as perhaps I should. They show your worth. And it is indecent that a man with your worth should not be well employed.'

'Where's Dawn?'

'She is spending some time alone. In the ladies' bathroom. Join her there if you wish, my dear – and you're welcome to consume the gift I gave you. But I request that you do not share that gift with your mother – she's had enough for now…'

He released me.

I staggered out through the curtain and turned towards the toilets. The bouncer stepped away from me with an alarmed respect. My body was splintering. I felt like I was walking out of an entire movie – leaving behind the pulp mannerisms of Kimber's underworld – for a more familiar squalor of spilt ale and urine.

The ladies' bathroom door was locked. I knocked.

'It's Leander,' I said. 'I'm alone.'

6.

There was a lengthy rustling before the door opened. Dawn stared, gurning, through tangled hair. She was wearing a wedding dress.

'What've they done to you? Fuck, sweetheart, what happened to your eye? Your beautiful face! Fuck.'

She pulled me inside, itching, and locked us into darkness.

'Were the lights unflattering?' I asked.

I patted my palms up the wall-tiles to find the cord to the bulb above the sink. I tugged on it, and in its flickering light, Dawn's eyes were pure umber, with nearly no pupils. The cut from our car crash had bled more down her forehead.

'What the fuck you doing here?' she asked. 'They're going to kill you. I've been ringing all fucking night – and Francis' been ringing you. I spoke to him but he said you're coming here. What the fuck?'

I groaned. 'You spoke to Francis? Did you tell him where I was?'

She began crying, stroking her hands across my face's bruises. 'I'm scared, Leander, what've I done to you? Why'd you come here?'

'You didn't do this.'

'Yeah I did, this was me, this was me. He's mad, Kimber's actually mad… I never seen someone so angry. When he found out what you done… Fuck. We're not getting out of here. We're fucking cornered, sweetheart, we're fucked.'

'He wouldn't hurt you,' I said, hugging her to calm her down. 'He wants to employ me, not kill me.'

'He's a liar. I can't… Fuck. I didn't know they would beat you like that… I didn't know, I didn't fucking know. How we going to get out of here? We're never getting out are we?'

'I know how to get out of here.'

'Do you? Sweetheart, please, we got to get out of here and we got to get out of that apartment and get rid of that fucking car. I fucked up, didn't I? I fucked up.'

Her words were running together. She sat beneath the hand-dryer and, trembling, tugged me down to join her.

'I been taken advantage of,' she said. 'And I let you get taken advantage of. Your hard-earned money! Sweetheart, he's bad, you're right, I was in denial, he's bad, he's fucking insane, he thinks we're in a wedding. Look at this!'

She held out her hand – a new larger ring was on her ring finger – a bulbous diamond in a band of white gold, framed by four smaller diamonds – and all together, somehow, they provoked a peculiar revulsion in me – like I was watching a toad hatch eggs from the holes in its back.

'I actually like him,' I said. 'He's like the demon in the tower in Browning's "Childe Roland to the Dark Tower Came" – although in the poem we never find out who's in the tower, but —'

'No – shut up. I can't deal with your poem bullshit right now. We can't be like that any more. I've ruined it. He's not what I thought he was. I wish he was trapped in a fucking tower. He don't just sell drugs, Leander, listen – he sells women, he fucking sells them and he sells men too. He gets refugees across borders, but then steals some of them, and sometimes a whole ship drowns… He bought the Rockway, he's kicked everyone out, Pat's disappeared. We got to get away from him. But we can't. I didn't realise he was this bad, sweetheart. I'm sorry I fell in love with him, you're right, it was too quick to be true, you're fucking right… He's jealous of you and I dragged you into it and I can't fix it.'

'You can fix it a bit,' I said, unimpressed. 'If you give me some heroin. I've got some white but I don't want to inject. Do you have any brown?'

'Course I do sweetheart.'

She retrieved her handbag from beside the toilet. 'It's in here somewhere. Give that to me, let's do a swap.'

'Haven't you had enough?' I asked.

'Fucking look at me – I've not had nearly enough, I'm a fucking mess. Smoking isn't good enough. I need it full on. Just give me it.'

'Fine.' I handed her the white cling-wrapped ball.

Trembling, she took a bottle of water and a syringe from her bag, and passed the bag to me.

I rummaged, struggling against the nausea in my muscles, until I found a pouch of brown Afghan heroin. There was at least half a gram left. I sought the cleanest fold of tinfoil, among the many in her pockets – and a crinkled foil pipe, and a cigarette lighter.

Unsealing the pouch, I sprinkled its powder into the groove of foil. I put the pipe in my mouth and heated beneath the groove with the lighter until the trail evaporated – and I chased its furling fumes, inhaling deeply to hold them at the base of my lungs. The vapour scurried around inside me until it solidified into a mouse – a mouse immune to the plague that it was carrying – a mouse that spread its plague across the city in order to laugh at those who suffered from it – because this mouse will never die and it will never suffer – and its laugh is a laugh of regret not of joy – because it cannot live, because it cannot suffer. I leant my head against the tiles, my eyes closed, and counted to thirty without exhaling to allow a full transfusion.

Dawn was fumbling beside me at her dress. I opened my eyes. She was trying to rip her wedding dress into a tourniquet.

'Do you want help?' I asked.

'Yes please sweetheart —'

I ripped off the strip of silk and tightened it about her left bicep – constricting its veins into prominence – and tied it in a double-knot.

'This could be the oldest human-only ritual,' I slurred. 'Neanderthals painted rocks, elephants buried their dead. But perhaps humans were the first to medicate each other's suffering. Parrots in Peru learned to soothe their stomachs by eating clay – nullifying the quinine and strychnine of their diets – but they didn't feed the clay to each other – whereas the humans copying the parrots did. All civilisations make ceremonies out of painkilling. Perhaps a Sumerian boy, this day six thousand years ago, gave poppy-milk to his mother the same way that I am now. That was the first opiate – heroin's ancestor – and they called it "hul gil" – joy flower – but it wasn't really joy they were looking for. And it wasn't really joy that the priests of the Egyptian poppy fields wanted either. It was painlessness. The longing for analgesia is as old as the longing for company. Sex and death are just subcategories.'

'What you rabbiting on about? You trying to tell me you're a priest? God's not talking to you.'

I smiled. 'I don't want to be a priest – though my body is like a temple in that it's ruined and has an entrance fee – I want to be a wizard. Heroin lost its mystery in the First World War. But now global production is five times lower, and the clichés of cinema and counter-cultures have given it new, meaningless meanings, so it's regained some magic.'

'It's not magic. It's a waste. It's a… who did you used to say you was? The whore of Babylon – with the hanging gardens. That's all heroin is – it's a hanging garden.'

'Exactly,' I said. 'It's a hanging garden you can look down from at your own time and at time itself.'

I reheated the tar that remained on my foil and breathed in its vapour until my throat was lined with the taste of burnt caramel. And as I breathed out, I breathed out also the pangs in my side and the throbbing in my head. My body was becoming disinterested in itself – remoter and pacific – away from pain's euphoria into a blanker ease. This was the opposite of an epiphany – it was the loss of insight, the loss of interest in stimuli or self. My heart relaxed, my brain was cocooned. The ultramarine at my centre began to dim. Unlike ketamine's swooning dislocation, in which pain is side-stepped and the body becomes discontinuous, heroin is much less elaborate – my body merely dimmed; pain was not avoided, it was hushed. I associated no colour with its sensation.

Dawn had uncapped the bottle and was trying to pour water into the lid balanced on her knee – but mostly she was spilling it over herself.

'Do you want help?' I asked.

'Thank you sweetheart, yes please, give us a hand. I feel like I'm fucking losing it. And with this weather. Fuck. Is it raining? No – we're inside still ain't we? We're inside.'

'Yeah,' I said.

She gave me the syringe. I placed the bottle lid on the bathroom floor and filled it to two-thirds with water.

'You know I was dreaming before you got in here,' she said, nervously twisting her wedding ring. 'I saw the moon fall out the sky – the same as that squirrel earlier – and it shattered like glass in the street. It was so small, the moon. Smaller than a bowling ball. And it shattered.'

'I don't think the moon has fallen yet,' I said. 'The Thames' tides are still there. Apparently the earth wasn't born with oceans – the waters are from the collisions of millions of icy asteroids. Perhaps something else wonderful will fall on us.'

I unwrapped the white heroin from its cling-film and dropped it into the water of the bottle lid. With the orange plunger of the syringe, I stirred it into dissolution.

'Were you not intending to use a filter?' I asked.

'Does that do anything?'

'I dunno. Obviously bacteria isn't going to be removed. But perhaps glass or something will.'

'Who's putting glass in heroin?'

'I dunno. Whimsical manufacturers. Do you have cotton buds?'

'Don't think so darling, just give me it.'

'We can use a tampon?' I suggested.

She waved her hand in unconcern.

I took a tampon from her bag, split open its plastic, and bit off the end. I placed this over the bottle top and drew the solution through it into the syringe.

'In China,' I said, flicking out the air at the needle's tip, 'opium was seen as an aphrodisiac, because it delayed orgasm. In Europe it was associated with asexuality, for the same reason. European civilisation only really overtook China during the opium wars. Perhaps our erotic pessimism gave us an edge. But I prefer that Chinese optimism…'

Dawn cackled quietly. 'You never preferred optimism before.'

I smacked the bluest vein in her arm and stung it with the needle. She didn't flinch.

'Put your thumb under mine,' I said.

'Why?'

'For luck,' I said. 'I want to do this with you.'

She put her thumb beneath mine on the syringe. We pulled back the plunger to check for blood – its vermillion sighed into the white – and we injected it into her vein.

'Ahhh,' she relaxed. 'Thank you, darling, that's better, fuck, so much better. Sorry. Sorry, I interrupted you about your poem, didn't I? Tell me it, go on, tell mummy a poem, please…'

'You mean "Childe Roland to the Dark Tower Came"?' I asked drowsily. 'I was saying Kimber could be the demon in the tower. The poem ends with the knight-errant blowing his horn, about to charge at "the round squat turret, blind as the fool's heart," but we don't know what he finds inside it. The poem is more concerned with the phantasmagoric journey there. He sees a horse, emaciated and hideous, and says "I never saw a brute I hated so; he must be wicked to deserve such pain." I apply that line to myself once a week. And then he passes an abandoned torture wheel, "fit to reel men's bodies out like silk." It's a similar image to the one in Kafka's "In the Penal Colony" – though Kafka's machine is described by an Officer as providing a sort of religious transcendence, after six hours of torture. But when the Officer himself climbs into his machine, it breaks and he brutally dies, "without the promised transfiguration". Then, in maybe the most concise statement of Kafka's whole philosophy, the narrator says, "This was not the torture the Officer wished to attain." Both Browning's poem and Kafka's story are fantasies of suffering with no redemption; quests with no climax. But instead of despair, there is an uncanny exuberance in the process of perception itself – as though all one needs to do to survive is simply learn how to luxuriate in horror. When you —'

'It's poisoned,' Dawn said, slumping into me, breathing too shallowly to shout. 'You... Kimber poisoned me. This was for you, weren't it? You knew. But it's not – it's not poison, is it? It's too warm for that, it's – you're putting me in a kangaroo pouch? Fuck. You gave me too much, Leander, you know you gave me too much.'

She was so weak that she could only whisper. I watched her lower into my lap with an abstract fascination.

'I was scared of Kimber being jealous,' she said. 'But I should of been scared of you, shouldn't I? Fuck – do both my sons hate me? Please tell me that's not what it is. I know the traffic lights was red – but I forgave you. And I forgive you, sweetheart – I did this to you, I did it, I forgive you. Life is about to happen to us anyway. But can you do me one last little favour – just call me an ambulance, can you, yeah? I don't want to die. I don't want to die.'

She sank into sleep. I shifted her head off me onto the floor so I could access the tinfoil again. I sprinkled out more heroin, with the pipe in my mouth, and heated it as I inhaled, wondering what a last breath felt like.

After a few long lazy runs along the foil, and a few more top-ups of powder, I fished in Dawn's bag for her phone.

I rang 999 and asked for an ambulance. 'There's a woman dying in the toilets at the Rockway bar in Brixton,' I said in a monotone. 'I can't wake her up. I think she overdosed on heroin. Maybe it had fentanyl in it. Come quickly.'

I hung up and then rang 999 again, this time asking for the police. 'There's a woman dead in the toilets at the Rockway bar in Brixton, and I think there's drug-dealers here. Maybe a gang. I've seen a lot of drugs and I think I saw a gun. I'm hiding in the toilets. There's a man called Kimber here. I've rung an ambulance. Come quickly.'

I hung up and smoked more, with my eyes closed against the tiles, anticipating the coming chaos with excitement. Dawn's last words hung in the air with an orange afterglow.

Someone was beating on the door. I nodded off, dreaming of Brutalist towers combining themselves into mile-high castles.

'My dear?' Kimber called from the corridor. 'Might you and Leander consider re-joining our company soon? Have you not yet used the facilities to your satisfaction?'

I inhaled a last rueful line. The scent of sandalwood oil that I associated with Kimber's voice dispelled the earthy orange I associated with Dawn's. I returned the folded foil, pipe, lighter, and pouch to her handbag. The Savlon was still in there; I uncapped it, squeezed a drop of its paste onto both index fingers, and rubbed it into my eyes to irritate them to tears.

Now appearing to cry, I zipped up her handbag and hung it beneath my clothes – so that its bulk was hidden by my cape and its shoulder strap hidden by my dress. As I waited for Kimber to beat down the door, I drank from the tap. Rust displaced the taste of heroin from my gums.

The door's lock was kicked open by the bouncer from the back room. He stepped aside to allow Kimber to enter.

I was weeping beneath the sink; Dawn was dead beneath the dryer. Kimber released a fox's screech and leapt to Dawn, slapping her cheek, his ear to her neck, his thumb to her pulse.

'You did this,' I whispered.

'You did this,' he said with eyes of vertigo.

'She was dead when I got here,' I said.

'She's still warm!' he cried. 'Get hold of him!'

The bouncer pulled me to my feet, locking his arm around mine. I didn't resist. There was a commotion in the corridor – and other lackeys ran in.

'There's an ambulance outside saying we've got to let them in or they'll call the police.'

'You!' Kimber shouted at me, at last discomposed. 'You!'

He jumped up as if he wished to rip me from the bouncer, but his hands hesitated in mid-air – his face dappling with the shock of renewed realisation – and he crouched back beside Dawn.

More yells announced the arrival of two paramedics and three of the men in white tie from the back room. One paramedic knelt beside Dawn, the other surveyed the scene suspiciously. To him, I was a frightened black-eyed boy in a dress, among thugs. He approached the man restraining me.

'That's my mum,' I said, pointing at Dawn. 'Please… please…'

He reached his hand out to mine. The bouncer released me. Curiously, as I simulated the symptoms of grief for this audience, I felt some of my sobs come freely – as though through pretence I was approaching authenticity. The paramedic flashed a torch in my eyes, but before he could say anything, his partner shouted, 'We need to get her out of here.'

Kimber's mask of command was gone. Instead here was a man – who must have seen many corpses before – desperate for guidance. He held Dawn's legs as the paramedic took her shoulders and backed down the corridor, obsessed by her vacant eyes. The other paramedic kept a hand on my shoulder and steered me after them, flanked by Kimber's tensed associates.

We processed into the bar area to find it considerably thinned. Those who remained were in a frenzy of speculation. But before the front door could be opened from the inside, there was a loud knocking – and a file of five police officers entered. The bar erupted, at last, into pandemonium – shrieks spread to the back room; men jumped over tables and scrambled out of booths away from the front. Three police officers sprinted after them, while the other two officers ushered the paramedics, Dawn, Kimber, and me outside. A herd of growling men had assembled on the street in a stand-off against three more policemen.

'Leander!' someone shouted.

I perceived the commotion with an aloof factual apathy. Dawn was being lifted into the back of the ambulance. Kimber was still clutching her legs, refusing to accept that he'd been robbed of his possession. The paramedic let go of me to assist in lifting her. I turned to see Francis rushing towards me.

'What's going on?' he asked. 'What happened to you? They weren't letting me in.'

'Dawn OD'd,' I said. 'I think she's dead.'

A ring of men shoved me along the pavement, away from the police officers. The bouncer who'd earlier thrown me to the floor now grabbed me under my arms and began dragging me down the street. My head bulged like water in a spinning bucket.

'You're staying with us lad,' he said.

Francis charged after us, knocking two men down – and then punched my abductor in the pocket between his jaw and windpipe. I jabbed my heel into his foot and twisted free – dizzied by the scent of benzoin resin. A fourth man struck Francis in the stomach, but he roared in reply and threw him to the ground – and then stunned a fifth to my left with a punch that crunched bone.

'Help!' Francis shouted, dragging me towards him. 'Help!'

'What's going on?' a policeman shouted, trying to break through the barrier of bodyguards in his way.

Francis pulled me into the middle of the road. I reached beneath my dress for the handbag and searched within it for the car key – and pressed it – and a white car beeped a dozen cars away.

'Run!' Francis tried to shout, but choked instead on a whisper.

A confusion of bouncers, barflies, and men in white tie spilled across the street. Four of them followed us, slowed by their injuries, while the rest surrounded the police officer. The ambulance siren began.

I raised my eyes upwards – and saw an arched bridge above me, covering the sky, built from the same tiles as had been in the bathroom – and masks were dangling from the bridge, attached to strings – all of them painted with Dawn's face, in expressions of surprise and disappointment – and as they fluttered, frozen peas fell from their eyes – and where the peas hit the pavement, plants sprouted – though instead of flowers, the plants grew skulls – glowing like neon melons around my feet.

Francis prised the key from my fist, his arm around my waist, and propelled me towards the car. My teeth were turning brass again – and trying to unscrew me back into ultramarine.

The streetlamps craned like storks trapped in concrete. The wind smelt of rain that hadn't come yet, and of the sweetness of damp washing, as we passed an air-vent I couldn't see. He pushed me into the passenger seat and slammed shut the door.

'I don't need you,' I said, as he ran round to the other side.

He got in and started the engine. I could fix on nothing.

Grey-gold spikes sank into my eyes. With a jerk, we reversed away from the pavement.

'We're going to my flat,' I tried to order, but my voice was nearly inaudible.

'We're going my house,' he said. 'I ain't listening to you. I know what's good for you and you definitely don't.'

'I had a plan,' I said.

'Your plan didn't work.'

'It worked perfectly.'

'You didn't do that.'

He sped up around a corner. An off-licence cast an eerie haven of light ahead of us – and I imaged a swarm of night buses – identical to the N109 that nearly ran me down earlier, but shrunk to the size of moths – fluttering around the off-licence's doorway, like a homecoming of the lost.

'You think Dawn died on purpose?' I asked.

'She had this coming for years.'

'How can you say that about your own mother?' I asked, trying to smile.

He braked and I snapped forward – but he caught my arm before I hit glass. He was breathing heavily – enraged by what I'd said, or afraid for my safety, or both – and forced my seatbelt across me.

At his touch's authority, I was aroused – and he buckled it roughly, and seemed to be trying to speak – but I was dropping away from him – into an orgasm at the edge of unconsciousness – and into the whispering rustle of a field of wheat.

'You was her son more than I was,' he said. 'I ain't got a mother no more.'

Crossing the border

1.

A bell brought me back to pain. First it was only a red madder colour – but then came the colour of smalt, then of azurite, then of vivianite – and then ultramarine. Francis was cradling me, erect and naked, mumbling slower than me towards sentience. I unhooked his arms from my chest and wriggled away, but as I tried to sit up, I choked, and bent sideways to vomit – but only a spool of bile emerged.

'Stop it,' Francis said, fumbling at his bedside as if for an alarm clock.

His doorbell rang again, longer, above the pattering of the rain. So the weather had turned. I imagined London's pigeons rising as one to wash themselves in it, as the grey of their feathers changed into a new grey – the grey of security-alarmed scaffolding and concrete and the crowds and clouds around them – the grey of the Thames and the sea that it ended in – the grey of the ever-turning cement mixers of a city remaking itself for the rich – the grey of the docklands and the Olympic village and all the other new-builds that looked like old shipping crates, carrying nothing to nowhere – more like wastelands now than the wastelands they had been built upon.

As I listened, I thought of the city around me as a body ill with my illness – suffering from the same kind of slow septic shock as me – the initiating infection gone, perhaps, but the crisis state still in effect – so London continued, as I did, in pain, in exhaustion, incurable – allergic to itself – allergic to the very mechanisms that kept it alive…

I leant over the bedside for Dawn's handbag and reeled it towards me by its strap. Francis crawled out the other side, cursing, searching for underwear. I found the baggie of heroin and spilled its contents onto a fresh rectangle of foil. The doorbell rang again – into the colour of terracotta, and I thought of the tessellated roofs of foreign flat-blocks in winter.

I pursed a tinfoil pipe between my lips, and took up the lighter – and vaporised this excessive medicine into the seat of my lungs. Francis gazed at me blearily, his disapproval distracted by the doorbell. Slowly, my nausea and the clamour in my kidney subsided. I burnt the foil's underside as I sucked above it with an infant's greed.

'There's blood all on me,' Francis said, drawing back the duvet to reveal a moth-coloured stain the size of my head on the sheets where our bodies had met. 'Fuck. You're cleaning that up. But we're getting you to hospital first.'

He knelt across the bed to kiss my cheek. I reclined against the wall with narrowed eyelids, in a pause between inhalations, my nerves depressing back into placidity. As he neared, I admired his face in slow motion as if for the first time – his forehead was framed by tousled hair shaved neatly at the sides – his eyebrows arched perfectly into his nose, balanced by thick lips and a wide jaw – and his eyes were recessed behind cheekbones that hollowed his cheeks into right-angle shadows. I received his kiss in triumph – over all the women I'd won him from – but affected sedation.

'Your eye is so fucked up,' he said.

The bell repeated. He kissed me again and left.

The blood seemed dry, but the silk of my dress stuck like a gauze to where I'd been stabbed – so perhaps it was only temporarily stanched. My body in its opiate mist shifted without feeling itself, so I peeled off my gown lasciviously, my own voyeur – craning my head to watch it roll up my thigh and uncling from the gash at my hip. Placing the unfinished fold of foil to my left, I pulled the dress further over my head, until I realised – to my own surprise – that I was naked. The room resonated like a distorted guitar.

I reclined into the pillow and reviewed my bruises with the curiosity of an impartial observer. The knife wound had congealed into a knot the colour of varnished oak. Most of my knuckles were aubergine. The moles and older keloid scars of my chest had new bluer company. My left bicep was speckled with yellow plectrum imprints. Mauve burnt through the hairs of my shins.

I took Dawn's hand-mirror from her bag and reflected my face at itself. It felt like I was watching another boy watching himself. Another me, another Leander, with swollen eyes and plumped lips – lips nearly as plump as Francis' now – gazed in dispassionate assessment at both me and the other me whom I was overseeing.

'The mirror's nearly convex to your intoxicated stare,' I said without intonation. 'In Ashbery's "Self-portrait in a Convex Mirror," he sees

"tenderness, amusement and regret, so powerful
In its restraint that one cannot look for long.
The secret is too plain…

That the soul is not a soul
Has no secret, is small, and it fits
Its hollow perfectly…"'

I smiled as I recited this, as if for an audience I wished to impress, half-imagining Francis back beside me – till I turned my head and saw that I was alone.

'I only partly agree,' I said. 'My soul is not a soul – but it fits its hollow imperfectly – not perfectly. The hollow is ajar, and the gap beside it seems its own presence; like a second soul, uncomfortable, not plain but blank, and in its blank there is a snarl.'

I tilted my head. My eye was not yet a black eye, and was not as puffy as I had feared. Perhaps it suited me. Though my ability to appraise my own impairment was itself impaired – since it was with a faulty eye that I was trying to see a faulty eye. The black wings Eva had drawn on my lids had leaked into the crease below the lashes and the mascara had muddied the foundation.

I put the mirror back into the bag and took out a packet of make-up removal wipes – and in so doing, dislodged two glued-together cereal bars, and so took these out too. The wipes smelt of cucumber and seemed to cleanse my skin of their own cool accord, unattached to my hands, which were unattached to my arms. I got through both sides of four wipes before the white did not discolour and I was clean.

I regarded myself again in the mirror as I ate the first cereal bar. I grinned at my grin in a foolish way – like a chimpanzee, convinced it has got away with a theft, being viewed through the crosshair of a rifle.

The second cereal bar became harder to eat as oats and treacle accumulated on the roof of my mouth. I was chewing and swallowing simply for the sake of it – there was no flavour or pleasure beyond a mechanical satisfaction. Nonetheless, as I watched myself eat, my eyes seemed to trip themselves up – and somewhere in them I detected a kind of joy.

Was this the emotion that Dawn had said I deserved? Well, nobody deserves anything. But all suns eventually explode, don't they, so perhaps there is no cosmological guilt – or, if there is, then it is too late to be concerned by it. So I can deserve whatever I gain without guilt.

I finished the cereal bar, and told the mirror, 'Nihilism is for fragile heterosexuals. Meaninglessness isn't meaningless. I can give meanings to whatever I want. Death lends a levity to life, sure, but so does chaos – and chaos can be shaped into meanings by will. So I can contrive arcs, reversals, and endings until I have revenged my own fatigue.'

I put back the mirror and took out Dawn's phone. It was unlocked. Wincing at the bright screen, I logged into my email and found the message from Eva that I'd hoped for – ordering me to report to her film set tomorrow morning. I replied: 'ok see you then – but be warned im a method actor.'

As I waited for the message to send, my gaze strayed to where Eva's mink cape lay spattered with vomit. I reached to it and from its pocket took out the business card of Mr Nikolas And – the earnest journalist who'd been interviewing Iris yesterday. My eyes failed to focus on its details, but I understood the card more generally as an opportunity I needed to uncover, or a plot not yet devised – and so put it into Dawn's handbag, promising it a future use.

Finally, to complete this toilette, I took out the tube of Savlon and squirted it onto my stab wound, stirring the ointment into the bloodied crust until the two became a paste. I applied some to my eye as well, and wondered as I did so whether I should have made Francis do this for me, so as to continue my trend of being disinfected by my victims.

But perhaps Francis was no longer my victim. And perhaps it was more appropriate to make a gesture towards self-reliance for now, since there was sure to be little of that to come. And even though there was no stable self upon which I could always rely, this current self – the one that had winked at me in the mirror – would do for now.

But could I call this happiness? I had an identity, here, per-haps, and a companion, and food, and shelter. But did I really want those things? Perhaps I just wanted flight.

And flight is a difficult ambition to realise – though it can at least be achieved in a biochemical sense. And so I picked back up the burnt foil, the pipe, and the lighter – and heated the heroin tar, and breathed it in – until my eyes complained of the afternoon sky and the memory of myalgia was a mystery.

The ultramarine pain in me paled until it was the shade of a shadow of glass on water. My thoughts became silt. I slumped into Francis' pillow, smiling into the smell of the coconut oil he wore in his hair, and the warm idea of the colour of wheat.

'We've got to go,' Francis said, his hands under my arms.

I nodded in useless assent, accepting his reappearance without considering what he'd been doing.

'You got to get dressed,' he said. 'Put these on.'

I wobbled in reply. He sat me up on his side of the bed.

'Fuck,' he said.

He was seeing my injuries properly for the first time. He stroked the stab wound in my side and then turned my back towards him and stroked my whip wounds.

'Fuck,' he said. 'There's belt buckles in your skin. They're all over you. How did – who did this? Fuck.'

He pulled grey sweatpants over my legs, white socks and white overlarge trainers onto each foot, a grey sweatshirt over my head, and a puffy blue coat over my arms. He was styling me into a uniform identical to his own. I stood up, balancing on him, my arm around his waist, and kissed him. We staggered out of the room, downstairs.

'What's happening?' I asked.

'We're going to hospital.'

'Ok.'

The front door was already open. To my diminished senses, it seemed the sky had constricted into a grip. The wind was a parliament of jackdaws, the rain had thickened into bullets. Francis supported me out of the house, down the steps, towards a woman whose black clothes I couldn't interpret.

'Are you alright, my duckling?' she asked. 'We're going to keep you safe, now, I guarantee it.'

She took my other arm and guided me along the street – to a

car whose patterns caused a pang of hatred I couldn't interpret either. They helped me into the back seat. Francis slid wetly in next to me. He put on my seatbelt and let me rest against his chest. I fell asleep inside the slow revelation that this was a police car, and I had been tricked.

2.

I was shaken awake by Francis and drawn from the police car into a storm. The remnants of a dream impressed themselves into the wind – of flying buttresses freeing themselves from a cathedral to stack into an infinite stairway. He was taking me towards a roof of many titles, though the only one I could read was 'MORTUARY'.

'It's from his blood loss,' he said to someone I couldn't see.

I wondered whether I was dead already and being led to my autopsy. The rain tasted of an unripe pear – but it vanished before I could finish it.

'Name?' asked a face behind a desk I couldn't focus on.

'Leander.'

'Surname?'

'I don't have one.'

'Your GP?'

'I don't have one.'

'Carry him through there.' The face pointed towards two doors of melting slate.

My other escort led me forwards and Francis followed, gripping the back of my neck. Steel tables bore dead and living bodies alike, their wheels sliding into each other in tremors I couldn't feel. As I watched, a bucket of sand began to swell – and grew a silver birch tree, its flank rippling, until it cracked the ceiling. The corridor rotated.

I fell through a curtain, into a green seat. Two hands tested the heat of my tongue, capped my finger with a plastic clip, and inflated a band around my arm until my heart beat with a slam.

'Why are you here?' the hands asked.

'He's been stabbed,' Francis said. 'He's breathing slow.'

'Go through there.'

I was lifted up by Francis and my other escort – whom I now understood as the woman from the police car, and who must therefore be a police officer – but her clothes still didn't make sense to me.

'Duckling, try to tell me anything you can remember,' she said.

The walls were flapping like plastic sheets in an abattoir, grey and grey-blue and glaucous, with a draught warmed by disease. Aqueous cylinders arose and withdrew before my feet. On a shelf above me, a foetus decomposed, forgotten, its umbilical cord dangling towards my nose.

'He needs to be medically cleared before he can talk to any police,' a younger woman said. 'Please wait outside.'

A freckled forearm with a turquoise sleeve eased me onto a bed.

'I'm staying with him,' Francis said, stepping inside our cubicle and closing the curtain across the policewoman.

'Are you a family member?'

'I'm his boyfriend.'

I had never been called that by him before, so I tried to arch my eyebrow in ironic surprise – but probably my face remained impassive.

'Ok, can you take off his top?'

The freckled forearm and scrubs assembled into a young woman. Chestnut hair and heavy bust, a dimpled grin and eyes of comic empathy. Francis tugged off my coat and sweatshirt. A voice in a neighbouring cubicle shouted, 'The reason I'm so happy is I'm gonna die slowly in front of you and there's nothing you can do about it.'

The doctor laughed and hitched a bag of fluid to a hook on a pole.

'Do you hear that line a lot?' I asked her.

'Oh my god yeah, about once a week at least. But the wordy ones aren't the ones to worry about.'

She lowered the bag's hose towards my right hip and placed a cool hand above it. I dreamed I was searching for a lost parcel, containing medicine I'd been prescribed – and I was being sent back and forth between two post offices, both claiming that the other had my parcel – and I queued and spoke to a dozen deliverymen at once, telling them the same story – that the medicine will fix me, drain the ultramarine pain and make me focused and active and I need it and I want to be fixed and why can't I be fixed – and, indifferent, they directed me to the opposite office, to another queue and another dozen indifferent deliverymen. But perhaps, I dreamed, the parcel would turn up one day, at one of the offices, for no reason – it would simply be there, after weeks of waiting – and I would collect it and hold it and open it – and it would be useless – the medicine in the parcel didn't work – or it worked, but not in the right way – and I wasn't fixed, I couldn't be fixed – the parcel was never going to save me and I wasn't saved.

I blinked myself back into the room – and tried to remember what the doctor had just said.

'Who are the ones to worry about?' I asked.

She'd turned the bag's tap on and a stream of saline water was rinsing the dirt from my wound.

'Yesterday a man made me do repeated rectal examinations until I realised he was doing it for fun and was literally in perfect physical health. Blatantly not in perfect mental health. So I kicked him out. And today he brought me a thank-you letter written in glitter.'

'I've come across that in my line of work as well.'

'Have you? Well you're lucky that when you came across a

knife in your line of work it only penetrated muscle. As you can see now it's clean, look, it's actually ok. You got stabbed in the perfect place.'

'That don't look perfect,' Francis said.

'Could have been an organ. Did you try to treat it yourself?'

'I used Savlon.'

'Good try, but that won't have been particularly helpful. Nurse!' she called. 'We're going to give you a tetanus shot and antibiotics, ok?'

'Don't I get any painkillers?' I asked.

'Have you taken any forms of medication already today? And I ask this, knowing that you blatantly have.'

'No, I wish I had. I feel like there's a coral reef inside my stomach.'

'Ok, I've never had someone say that to me before. You've earned some Oramorph.'

In an acceleration, the nurse walked in and out, the curtain twitched, and the doctor began lacing a needle across my wound as though it were a shoe. Its steel pricked through the heroin's defence, and I smiled at its particular pain – a pain the blinking colour of pink – my sight clarifying with each incision.

When its stitches had been tied into the cut, she injected the nearby tissue with a syringe prepared by the nurse. And then the nurse handed me a second, purple, syringe, with no needle, and lifted my hand to my mouth.

'Squirt it in past your tongue,' she said.

I did so and tasted the dissolved back of duct tape, retreating, sticky, towards my stomach. The nurse exchanged this Oramorph syringe for a paper cone of water. I drank it and asked for another. Francis was sitting behind me on the bed, his head against my shoulders, a hand on the outside of my thigh.

The doctor hooked a new bag to the pole beside me and slid a drip's needle into my forearm. Its fuchsia-pink pain zigzagged into the brown of a ferret pelt, and in my mind these contradicting colours somehow whispered 'angel, angel, angel, angel.'

As I stared, the needle seemed to widen into a probe that wished to penetrate bone. I drank another cup of water, trying to look away. The morphine would combine soon with my blood's other opiate and space would resume its uncertainty. But still, I was transfixed by the needle, convinced it was about to stretch along my tendons like spider legs and branch into every vein until it claimed my whole arm.

'How long will this take, my ducklings?' the policewoman asked, peering around the curtain. 'It's only because, there's other things we have to do today, you know how it can be, and the time is troubling us.'

'I recommend that Leander stay the night,' the doctor said.

'I don't want to do that,' I said, watching the needle.

'It would be better if he didn't have to go through that,' the policewoman agreed, with a new firmness to her maternal tone.

'I can't clear him yet – he might be infected. And he's presenting numerous other injuries.'

'I don't want to stay here,' I said. 'Let's go. I'm ready to go.'

Francis wordlessly stroked the whip wounds of my back.

'I can't discharge you, Leander,' the doctor said.

'But you can't hold me here. I can discharge myself, can't I?'

'If you leave, you could die. I strongly recommend that you remain in hospital for at least twenty-four hours.'

'I want to be discharged.'

'Why you want to leave so quickly?' Francis asked.

I wanted to say – because I've been betrayed by doctors for a decade! Because I've lost years of my life to being probed and screened and scanned and drained – in the search for the source of my constant pain – and because every failure in that search has tightened the noose of my depression.

But I couldn't tell Francis this, still – because temporary wounds are glamorous, but chronic illness is boring – boring for the sufferer, boring for the sympathiser – and his boredom would soon turn to repulsion. So I would play the waster, or the villain, but not the victim.

'I'm not staying here all night. I've wasted enough of my life in hospitals. Let's go.' I tried to remove the needle from my wrist, but the doctor interceded.

'This is not your best decision,' she said.

'I'm not interested in the best decision,' I said. 'I'm interested in the most interesting decision.'

She sighed and tugged out my cannula. A parabola of blood spurted to the curtain, leaving a fang prick behind.

'Come back when you're bored of being interesting.'

Francis helped me back into my sweatshirt and coat.

'Ducklings, we need to hurry along. I'm sorry, doctor, but the chief is never happy when he's waiting.'

'Stay away from knives, and forks,' the doctor said, smiling, and waved me away.

The policewoman led us out of the cubicle into a whiteness that bit at me even after my eyes were closed. Behind a curtain, a mother howled 'Sophia! Sophia!' as she miscarried. Francis pulled me down some steps and then down a slope into colder air.

An obese corpse rotted on a trolley against a wall. It looked like it had just been dug out of a grave. We turned a corner into a stainless-steel ballroom, crowded by white-coated dancers. A quadrille of students had surrounded a table to celebrate a cadaver's dissection. As we passed, an older doctor cracked open its skull with a stake and peeled off its face. Another group sawed at a child's stomach, splattering intestinal fluids over their frocks. Butlers with trays of razors for canapés hurried in and out of servants' doors.

We were guided towards a third table, where a narrow man in police uniform stood with his hands behind his back.

'Thank you, constable,' he said, with a nod, gesturing for the policewoman to release me and stand to the side.

I swayed against Francis' arm, letting my ears confuse the clatter of the students with the chatter of their tools.

'Good afternoon boys,' the man said. 'I am Detective Chief Inspector Sanam, and this is Detective Constable Floris, and I need to know more about you. First, which of you is the son of Dawn Cole?'

'Me,' Francis said.

'And who do you have there with you, Mr Cole?'

'My boyfriend.'

'And would he like to tell me his name?'

'Not particularly,' I said slowly, my tongue nearly tranquilised to aphasia.

'They already know your name,' Francis said.

'That's correct Mr Cole, yes we do. And am I right in understanding that it was Mr Leander, and not you, Mr Cole, who was living with Mrs Cole at the time of her death?'

'Yes,' Francis said.

'And why was that?'

'I've not lived with her since I was a child,' he said. 'I only seen her a couple times a year. She liked being high more than being with me. Her and Leander met in the same shelter, a year or two ago. And that's how I met him, through her. And he liked me more than being high.'

'I wouldn't go that far,' I said.

'Thank you,' the chief inspector said, ignoring me. 'I will need more details from both of you in a minute, but first, Mr Cole, please approach this table for me and identify the woman lying on it there.'

He stepped aside to reveal a wasted woman with silver skin. We approached the table.

'That's not her,' Francis said.

'I understand that this might be difficult for you, but I need you to… look properly.'

'That isn't Dawn,' I agreed.

Even to my lazy vision, this drowned housewife was nobody I had met before. A technician was summoned and the tag on her toe was reviewed.

'It's been a busy night,' the technician said, and beckoned us through a herd of students towards another table. 'Is this the one you're after?'

'It's past six o'clock in the evening,' the chief inspector said. 'Are you trying to tell me that it's still last night?'

'It's felt like that down here,' the technician said, pulling back the shroud of the body on this new table. 'There was a flood… The shifts are blurring.'

'That's her,' Francis said.

Dawn's lips were puckered as though a taste had made her smile, and looked more like Francis' lips than they had before. Her nose was the same as Francis' nose now, too, or always had been, but I'd never noticed – dainty between sharp cheekbones. And her cheeks had lost their laughter, and her skin was relaxed in an unfamiliar way.

I thought of her demanding gifts for goddesses over the phone – and I smiled – and imagined giving her a waterfall as a present – and from the middle of the waterfall, a cockerel flew out – plucked featherless but still alive, panicking about the coming dawn – and we chased the cockerel down a lane of urinals, until Dawn fell over and the dawn arrived over us – and I fell onto her and pulled off her nightie as she begged me for an ambulance – whispering 'Life is about to happen to us, life is about to happen to us.'

'Thank you.' The chief inspector nodded and the technician covered her back up. 'Now would you please both follow me?'

'No thanks,' I said, leaning my head into Francis' neck. 'Can we just go?'

'No, Leander,' Francis said. 'They can help us.'

He tugged me after the officers – out of the morgue, upstairs, and through a door behind a desk, into a room with lights that looked like egg yolks. A pin-board announced this as 'The Bereavement Office'.

'What's wrong with him?' the chief inspector asked.

'He's had a stab wound above his hip,' the constable said. 'And all along his back, it's terrible, he's got these lash marks. It looks like a very one-sided fight.'

A tired man at the desk presented Francis with papers to sign.

'A death certificate won't be available until after the coroner's report,' he said.

I fell back into a felt sofa and didn't hear the rest of his words – until Francis replied, 'Just burn her. I don't care. I don't want the ashes.'

'Leander, I have a few questions for you if you don't mind.' The chief inspector had sat down next to me.

'Sorry, I'm really busy at the moment,' I mumbled.

'We're here to protect you, duckling,' the constable said, moving to my other side.

Francis came to stand in front of me.

'How did you get your injuries?' the chief inspector asked.

'Playing fantasy football.'

'Is that so? And who were the players in your team?'

'Fine, I don't know anything about fantasy football,' I said. 'I can't continue that metaphor.'

'Can you try not using metaphors in your answers then? Can you describe the person or persons who attacked you? And can you please tell me how you managed to escape?'

'My memory isn't what it used to be…' I said. 'But I have this image of a man in an ostrich costume, waving a meat cleaver, and as he was holding me down he was saying there's been a thousand deaths in police custody in twenty years, but no convictions for murder. I was very shocked.'

'Alright, let's talk about murder instead then. Where were you last night?'

'That's too long ago… Maybe… let me think. Maybe Bermuda? Or Tenerife? Some volcanic island…'

'He was with me,' Francis said.

'And where were you?' The chief inspector asked.

'What's that got to do with us?' Francis asked. 'You saying my mum's been murdered?'

I felt like I was pedalling a bicycle underwater. I closed my eyes and saw an ocean above me patterned like a harlequin – chequered by sunlight and ruffed with surf – and devils were cartwheeling across the surface – and I was below them, less comic, less nimble, but no less astute – and I pedalled along after them until a wave dragged me back.

'Your mother's death on its own would not look suspicious,' the chief inspector said. 'She had a history of addiction, she overdosed – that's straightforward. But your mother, we now think, is… part of a wider circle, that we're trying to shade in. And that's less simple.'

'I thought you didn't like metaphors,' I said.

'What's the wider circle?' Francis asked. 'And what's it got to do with us?'

'Out of respect, I'm going to give you some information,' the chief inspector said. 'And what I expect in return is for you to give me some information back. Does that sound fair?'

'Ok,' Francis said.

'We have been investigating a criminal organisation, or a network, which operates not just on the streets but also on the part of the internet called the dark web. A major figure within this organisation – possibly the major figure – goes by the name "The Rockstar". Have either of you heard this name before?'

'No.'

'Alright. We believe there is a single man behind that name, a well-hidden man, connected to dozens of human trafficking cases across Europe, at least. But we've had very few leads on who he is, or on what his operation looks like in the real world. We know his supply line starts in Afghanistan and moves through Turkey, the Czech Republic, and Poland, before coming to the UK. We know men and women are locked in lodging houses, their passports are taken away, and they are forced to work – often in the sex trade and the farming industry – and their earnings are seized. We know that some of the victims are refugees – two of whom managed to escape and confirmed some of these details to us. But due to their… injuries, they weren't able to remember much. And so, Leander, I want to ask you again, how did you manage to escape?'

'Just by like being myself and trying to have fun with it, you know?' I attempted a Californian accent.

'We've had very few leads on this case,' he continued like I hadn't replied. 'Until last night, when we received a 999 call from someone saying that they were trapped inside a bathroom in the Rockway bar in Brixton, with a woman who appeared to have overdosed.'

'Do people still make phone calls?' I asked incredulously.

'First responders to the scene reported finding a boy in a red dress with a bruised eye in the bathroom, together with the woman described in the 999 call, surrounded by older men who appeared to be intimidating the boy.'

'Do they still have orgies in public toilets?' I asked, trying to be more annoying. 'I thought that had all been gentrified away.'

'Paramedics,' he continued to ignore me, 'concluded that this boy had made the 999 call, but after getting him out of the building, they lost sight of him.'

'That seems… unprofessional,' I said.

'He was last seen by a police officer getting into a white car with a taller man wearing white. The paramedics and the officers also reported the presence of a middle-aged man dressed in formal evening clothes, who appeared hysterical. This man identified the overdosed woman as Dawn Cole, and claimed that she was his wife, but refused to provide further information about his own identity, so could not be allowed into the ambulance with her. Police officers described a crowd of men in dark clothes coming out of the bar – and described them as deferential towards the hysterical man in formal clothes. None of the men agreed to be interviewed, and some of those inside the bar fled from the back entrance. We believe that we interrupted the gathering of a gang. And we believe this gang to be connected to "The Rockstar".'

'You're saying my mum's part of a gang?' Francis asked. 'No way. She was too high to do anything.'

'Exactly. Your mother, like a few of the other people at the bar, was known to us. But she had no previously known affiliation to the others and she had an entirely different criminal profile. She had a history of non-violent crime – shoplifting and drug possession. She was registered to a hostel, which we visited this morning. We were told that she had moved out a day earlier, with a young man she called her son, named Leander. This led Constable Floris here to visit the home of her real son this afternoon. Does this part of the story sound familiar? I have given you information, and I would like some information in return.'

'I think Joyce's work is more of an athletic triumph than an aesthetic triumph,' I said pretentiously, in my worst Irish accent. 'Apart from the end of *Finnegans Wake*, of course, when she's saying "I go back to you, my cold father, my cold mad father, my cold mad feary father —"'

'That's enough.'

'Didn't you want some information?' I said. 'That's my favourite —'

'I don't want to hear that,' the chief inspector said, finally raising his voice in irritation. 'So let me give you one last piece of information. The maximum sentence for gross negligent manslaughter is life imprisonment.'

'That seems… unreasonable.'

'And were we to discover that last night you had allowed or helped or even forced Dawn Cole to overdose on heroin then you could be liable for that sentence. This is not my theory; this is the theory of the man dressed in formal clothes who was described as hysterical by the paramedics. What I want to know is – was he the man that you referred to as "Kimber" on the 999 call you made last night, before escaping the scene with Mr Cole here in a stolen car?'

'Yup.'

'Leander, just fucking tell him,' Francis said.

'I just did!' I said.

I tasted bitumen – the coating tar of warships – and imagined a fleet of them trailing petrol through the arteries of my feet. I kicked myself.

'What address were you and Mrs Cole moving to? We have been following Kimber for a long time as a possible affiliate of the man known as "The Rockstar". And we believe Dawn may represent a weak spot in his operations. We wish to search her possessions to see if any further information about him can be recovered. If you are helpful, we can interpret your actions last night as the behaviour of someone in shock. If not...'

'If not... then you will have to leave me alone anyway because you have no evidence?'

'You are in danger, my duckling,' Constable Floris said. 'This is our lead; you need to help us.'

'Just give them the fucking address,' Francis said.

'Is that all you want?' I asked. 'I don't have the key.'

'Without a warrant, a police officer would need to be accompanied to the property by the tenant. So you and Constable Floris – and Mr Cole if he chooses to – should go to that property as soon as you can. Any evidence at all could save lives.'

'And then you'll leave us alone?' Francis asked.

'Unless there's any other information you want to bring

forward, then this is all we need from you. You have given us a lead. We just need you to help us follow it through.'

I met Francis' gaze and shrugged. He helped me stand. Constable Floris led us in silence out of the hospital, into the hall, back to her car. Detective Chief Inspector Sanam waved at us as we drove away, without a smile, sheltered by the roof marked 'MORTUARY'.

3.

'How you feeling?' Francis asked.

I was wrapped around his arm, with his chest as my pillow. His sweatshirt smelt of bread flour. The rain rapped the car like a drum roll, promising a punch line it didn't know.

'I feel like a taxidermy version of myself,' I said, closing my eyes. 'A bad taxidermy – with beads for eyes and limbs askew. My stitches are failing. Or a taxidermy arctic fox, left above a mantelpiece for years, till one summer afternoon the scent of wisteria is so strong that it's almost vulgar – and the nose of the fox sniffs, lifting a nailed paw, and then another, and another, until it leaps off the mantelpiece, half-alive – and it can fly, and it flies through the air above the dining table, above the diners, out of the window, borne by wisteria, towards the clouds, towards the north, towards home. It becomes more alive the closer to the winter it flies – its seams resealing, its sawdust sliding into blood, its black eyes gaining white vignettes until it can see as well as smell. But when it comes to the right place, the place it believes it was born, there is no ice, there is no mother, and there is no home – and maybe there never was – and the fox, for the first time, misses its taxidermied state, its glue and its thread. But it cannot die anymore, of course – so instead it flies upwards, to where the clouds disperse and the atmosphere thins – until the fox is in space, sailing, accelerating, to join the asteroids and comets, arcing for nothing now, and so home at last in an eternal transit.'

'I want to be an arctic lion,' Francis said. 'Do they have those? A snow lion, that eats arctic foxes…'

'You want to eat me?'

'Lions can't help their instincts, can they?'

'Can't lions and foxes be friends? It's lonely in the ice.'

'What am I going to eat then?'

I paused. We were crossing Battersea Bridge, and I watched the hail hit the Thames as it swelled. The waves slapped into each other with no direction – churning flotsam and jetsam and gulls alike – an implacable surface, its eddies shaped like the thumbprints of eroded giants. The waves were beckoning to me to come under – to where corpses from all the countries of the world lay muffled by mud, their homelands burnt and robbed and brought back here – to the Thames, London's guilty conscience, the spine of an empire – unknowable and slow and indomitable, even after death.

'You learn not to eat,' I said. 'You learn how to survive on wind.'

'I want to eat.'

'Ok, you can eat me then. But you'll be lonely after.'

'Who's saying you're all I've got?' Francis teased. 'Maybe snow lions hunt in packs.'

'After you eat me, you will alter, and lose appetite for the company of other lions. You'll pad to an ice cave, and sleep, and as you sleep, you'll breathe out a mist that freezes into the shape of a fox – and I'll reform, beside you, your dream becoming flesh, and then you'll be happy again – until you eat me that evening. And so it'll be every day, from then on – you'll have no pack, no pride, but you'll dream me back to life each night, and eat me before you go to sleep each evening. The days will be ours to eat together.'

'Where's your necklace?' he asked, diverting this reverie, his fingers stroking the back of my neck.

'They took everything off me,' I said.

'The men who beat you up?'

'They stripped me and threw me naked into the canal. And stole my money.'

He tightened his hold into a hug and kissed my hair. 'Why did you go back then? Why'd you come to my exhibition then go back to them?'

'I had to go back for Dawn. Even though I was too late.'

'Why didn't you let me come with you?'

'I didn't want you to get hurt.'

'So that's why you was all distant to me all night? Was that why? You should of let me come with you.'

'I was on ketamine… I was confused.'

I looked out of the window again. We were driving past one of London's many new upmarket apartment blocks, and it looked like a stack of tarot cards made of glass – all the same card, the hermit, since no one that lived there knew anyone else. They lived in online communities, really, as the physical home became less and less possible – atomised and stressed and envious – severed from the past and forced towards a future that was worse. The upper third of the building was cluttered with penthouses, to maximise profit. Below them, balconies were slotted like palisades, and so seemed almost feudal – like a monastery of white-collar monks, observing a new asceticism. Sanitised, depersonalised, touch-sensitive, cool, and motion-controlled, a futurism that was really just conservatism – or maybe even just decadence – unaffordable as it was to the young and poor – a symptom of an era about to end, and which would end with inner London cleansed of all but its aspiration and its debt.

'Why was you with Eva?'

'Huh?' I asked, closing my eyes. 'Oh. Her address just came

into my head when I was passing out. I told it to the man that found me.'

'She… did you know she was going to play that video of me?'

'No,' I said, wincing at the memory of his humiliated body projected onto the gallery wall. 'But I liked your yellow ribbons. I've never seen you sit in a chair like that before. The audience probably thought you were brave.'

He shuddered. 'She's too dramatic, that was… too much.'

'How did you feel having everyone see that?'

'I was more worried about you. Worrying about you probably made it easier to deal with.'

'Watching you vomit on screen made me want to vomit too,' I said. 'So maybe I am capable of empathy.'

'What's that again?'

'It's like love.'

'You saying you love me?' he smirked.

'I'm saying you made me want to be sick.'

'You can try and hide it but you just said you're in love with me.'

I laughed. And my laugh became the bell of a bell-tower – which I saw, with my eyes open, rising over the horizon beyond the right side of the car – and the tower had a chain stretching from it, across the storm, to another tower – and another bell, which I knew was ringing but which I couldn't yet hear, though I knew I'd hear it soon.

'Which road do I take now?' Constable Floris asked, leaning over the wheel.

We were approaching a roundabout whose signs were unreadable in the rain. The sky was filling with thunder.

'Second left,' I said.

'Oh that's it, yes. Look at you giving me a straight answer! You don't have to be so scared of talking to me, my duckling. I'm not scary.'

'What do you think about the "spy-cops" who used sex as

a weapon to keep women under surveillance?' I asked. 'Their victims said they felt raped by the state.'

'They one of your inspirations?' Francis asked quietly.

'That's not my department, duckling. I'm looking out for bad people.'

'But not so much the white ones?'

'I don't believe that. That's what some of the papers say but that's not how it is, that's not who I am.'

We were driving past another cluster of glass semi-skyscrapers – and a vista was opening up beside it, stretching far to the east, across South London – to where Canary Wharf hid behind the rain – and the skyline looked to me like a field of cracked dinosaur eggs.

'You winding her up?' Francis asked me, smiling, tucking a strand of hair behind my ear. 'You sound like my dad.'

'What do you think about drug laws, then,' I pushed. 'They're probably going to be legal in a few years. Do you feel good about locking up kids for having fun? Or do you agree that no rational adult should be criminalised for actions that do no harm to other people?'

'Stop showing off,' Francis said.

'Or is there no such thing as an action that does no harm to other people?' I continued. 'Weapons and humans are trafficked by the same networks as drugs. Buying is always sponsoring blood. Perhaps you think there are no innocent bourgeoisie…'

'When I began as a police officer,' the constable said, 'nearly twenty years ago, I was working on burglaries. We gave stolen property back to its owners and that felt good to me. Some of the burglars were desperate, some of them weren't. But what I liked the most was that it was called "Operation Bumblebee". Bumblebees are my favourite animal. When I was a girl, I lived out past the M25, where it was like countryside – but not quite. And me and my cousin Bryony would go up to the cherry trees on the bank above the train tracks and we'd eat the cherries and throw the pips at the trains below. And there was always one or two bumblebees, fat ones, buzzing around us for the flowers, when it was summer, and I always associated them with being a child up there and watching the people go into the city to work – and them looking miserable, and me being happy eating cherries. And there was an afternoon when I found a bumblebee that wasn't flying and he was in the middle of the road – so I held him on the back of my hand, just like this, and I was never scared he'd sting me, and when I saw how furry he was, I wanted to keep him as my pet. But my mum wouldn't have any of it. She shrieked louder than I'd ever heard and told me to get it out the house, so I took him down the lane to the biggest flower I could find and sat him inside it. That was my only pet I ever had, cos my mum was allergic to cats. And then I had to go back for tea and afterwards he was gone.'

I was so surprised to have provoked this monologue that I could think of nothing to reply, so let her continue without interruption.

'And when I went to the South of France for my husband's fortieth – oh it's lovely in Provence – the fields of flowers, it was like being a girl again, the smell in the air was divine, and all these bumblebees were there! I was in heaven… and my son – he's your age – he thought I was so ridiculous for how happy I was about the bumblebees, but they made me feel young, and like I was watching the people on the train below me again and like I wasn't on the train myself anymore, you know. Because I am on the train now, really, aren't I? But it's hard for me to listen to you two, because I know that you've both lost a mum in Dawn, I know that. And I can't bear to dream of my Oscar having to look at me after I've got off that train for good, and not being able to talk to me anymore. You have to talk about your mum, properly, to each other.'

'She liked talking,' Francis said. 'She was good at talking, but she was always better at drugs. That was what was important to her. Not me. That's what she was good at.'

'Don't say that, duckling, I can't believe that. One day you'll understand it better, but a mother never stops loving her son. They can't stop it. Whatever mistakes they make. You're too young to know… but she loved you, it can't stop.'

'Have you heard of maternal filicide?' I asked.

'I've heard it all,' she said. 'But I know mothers, I know mothers with sons like you. Like me. And they don't stop loving their son. I guarantee it.'

'There's an Austrian writer called Peter Handke,' I said, 'who wrote a deliciously sterilised biography of his own mother, called *A Sorrow Beyond Dreams* – where he admits "I was beside myself with pride that she had committed suicide." And when he's talking about her chronic illness, he says "the pain made her see ghosts". I like how precisely he confesses to the burden of extreme sympathy – and by that, perhaps, cures himself of it.'

'I don't feel pride,' Francis said.

'But the point is – there are alternatives to grief, although they may just be grief in different guises,' I said. 'And there are alternatives to love, although they may just be love in different guises.'

The seat in front of me began to bubble and slip – I looked away through the window, but the city was bubbling as well – as a waste of lava, juggled by earthquakes – and buzzards were swooping over us, and our car was a buzzard too.

'What happened with your mum?' Francis asked softly, still stroking the hair behind my ear.

I blinked – and the city returned. I was pleased to have punctured enough of his narcissism for him to ask this question at last.

'You really want to hear?' I asked.

'Yeah, tell me.'

'It's my earliest memory,' I said. 'I was four years old. I was

148

in my parent's bedroom, watching my mum change out of her clothes because she'd thrown up on them before she could get to the sink. It was the morning. I'd follow her around the house because I liked her more than my dad. And as she was getting dressed, she collapsed. I thought she was playing a game with me, like pretending to be asleep – so I waited for her to get back up. But she never did. And then my dad raised me till he died when I was eleven.'

The car stopped. Constable Floris turned to face us.

'Before we get out, I need you both to promise me that you're going to have a proper conversation about Dawn with each other – you need to think about what she means to you, out loud. I want you to think about her good qualities and her good moments, and you need to talk about it proper, don't just shut it away – speaking is good – and not just the easy mean words, but the harder words, the kinder ones…'

'We can get up at dawn tomorrow,' Francis suggested, 'and watch the sun come up, for her, for her name. How's that?'

'Yeah we can share the sunrise in her honour,' I agreed, charmed by this mild poeticism.

The constable smiled. 'Alright then, do that. And now let's get up there and see if we can find something new for ourselves.'

We quit the car and approached the tower through the storm.

4.

We rang all the bells until someone buzzed us in. Constable Floris had retrieved a red battering ram from the car boot and was carrying it with both hands. We followed her upstairs.

'Have you used that before?' I asked.

'I've been trained with it,' she said. 'But I've never broke in a real door before, no. This is quite fun, isn't it?'

'We're doing our own Operation Bumblebee,' I said. 'Except we are burgling ourselves.'

'I'd say I'm helping you get your property back, my duckling.'

'Yeah exactly, by burgling me.'

'If we had your key we wouldn't have to. And I was thinking to myself earlier, it's very rare for a woman to be in a bathroom with no handbag, isn't it? Didn't Dawn have a handbag when you found her?'

'Yeah. But one of Kimber's men took it when the paramedics came in,' I said, picturing it lightly spattered with sick beside Francis' bed.

'That would have been the real treasure chest if we could have got it. But we'll do our best with what we find up here. If… is that – which number are you?'

She slowed, lowering the battering ram. I peered around her and saw the front door was ajar.

'Stay here,' she said, suddenly tensed and attentive.

She set down the ram on the landing and took out a Taser.

'Police!' she called.

With her foot she nudged the front door open wider. 'Hello? Who's in here? Please identify yourself.'

A siren started inside my skin. Francis strengthened his grip on my waist. There was no answer.

'I'm coming inside,' she called – and stepped forwards, her Taser raised.

She switched on an interior light. A Y-shaped vein bulged in Francis' neck. I wanted to kiss it. I leaned more tightly into the tautness of his muscles, excited, as his entire torso tensed. We listened to Constable Floris open the bathroom door and then cross the main room to my bedroom. The siren in my skin loudened until I could smell malt vinegar in it.

'There's no-one here,' she said, a tremor in her voice. 'Looks like they got here first.'

She reappeared at the threshold and ushered us in, holding the door open. We walked warily past her. She holstered the Taser and went to fetch the battering ram.

My belongings had been scattered across the living room floor. I thought of Dawn calling this 'the Napoleonic suite' – and knelt, smiling, to examine my suitcase – and I noticed that there was a tripod inside the kitchen, with a camera on it, and I jerked up – as a surprised 'Oh' came from behind us.

We turned – Constable Floris was backing into the room, a gun pressed to her forehead – and Kimber entered after it.

The room plunged three stories downwards, suspended in silence – and then a tap, and a click as the door was kicked shut. Francis breathed in – and my ear cracked, a razor of nausea whipped upwards through my stomach – and the air sharpened into a shot. Constable Floris collapsed into my suitcase, a star in her skull, dead.

Fatigue surged in me instead of adrenaline. The carpet was a sea, Francis a swaying mast. The ceiling tilted. Zeroes ringed my eyes, trailing the scent of pesticide and malt vinegar, my synaesthesia flaring until my own heartbeat had a colour - a mould-dark green.

Kimber smiled with a twitch, spreading out his arms as if in welcome.

'You've made a miscalculation, my dears,' he said, the sandalwood oil in his voice more unguent than before.

I sat down on the bed beside us, sighing, and tugged Francis to join me – but he didn't respond. Kimber was wearing the same clothes as last night, and his eyes didn't look like they'd closed in days.

'Wasn't that –' I gestured towards the murdered police officer '– a miscalculation as well? Don't you think our neighbours are going to overhear this little execution of yours?'

'Not these neighbours,' Kimber said. 'These neighbours know me. They hear nothing and say nothing.'

He crouched, keeping the pistol pointed at us, picked out the handcuffs from the constable's belt, and threw them at Francis' feet.

'Fasten Leander to that radiator, please. I'd ask him to do so himself, but I suspect he might say no and attempt a stand-off.'

Francis picked up the handcuffs, staring through me in shock and unable to speak. The athlete who'd rushed to defend me yesterday was here reduced to an awkward mute. His survival instincts resulted only in indecision; his shoulders jerked a few times, as though considering somersaults, but his reason overruled them. When his eyes met mine they widened slightly, like he was receiving a second shock from seeing my lack of shock.

'Faster, please,' Kimber said.

Francis pulled me upright, his palms hot, his eyes begging for some kind of solution, and pulled me towards to the radiator. I let him. He closed one cuff over a pipe and the other over my left wrist. The bliss of the heroin in my blood seemed to surge as I relaxed into our predicament – until my dominant emotion was delight.

'Tighter, please,' Kimber said.

'I don't know what to do,' Francis managed to say. 'What do I do?'

'What do you want to do?' I asked.

Immediately he bent to me to kiss me, slowly, too scared for urgency. And for a while, denial erased his horror – and elongated the kiss into a kind of defiance. He pushed down on me but I did not push back. I wanted to experience his vulnerability – and so I could only enjoy this act of passion as a prelude to a collapse. I thought of bluebells wilting in frost. When he withdrew, he had less tension in his gaze, but his arms were shaking.

'Just remember that,' I said, dismissively, leaning back into the wall, my cuffed hand hanging limply from the radiator.

'Very touching, very touching,' Kimber said. 'It's your turn my dear.'

He reached into his jacket for another pair of handcuffs, and threw them at Francis' feet.

'Tighten that around your wrist, yes – and the other one around the bedpost, thank you.'

Francis looked to me for guidance. I looked at the ceiling. He wanted to resist, scream, run – but his thoughts were dominated by the gun, and the sound of it cracking the air in half. So as he bound himself to the bed, his hesitations smoothed out into sullenness – like a teenager resentfully obeying his father.

'Tighter, that's right. There you are. Now – tell me your name.'

'Leander,' Francis said.

I smiled at this slip.

'You seem nervous,' Kimber said. 'Let's try again. Tell me your name.'

'I'm… it's Francis,' he said.

'Francis. There we go. So – you're my wife's biological son. Which makes this occasion a family reunion. The dark and

153

the light. We have the first son, and the… second son. And the husband – or, now, the widower.'

'Was last night really your idea of a wedding?' I asked.

He twitched another smile, placed the gun on the table, and moved a chair to sit in it facing us.

'That question is at the heart of our dispute, my dear – because yes it ought to have been my idea of a wedding – but you… interrupted it when you invited these creatures.' He gestured towards Constable Floris.

Her blood had soaked through my suitcase and was pooling across the carpet in a halo.

And now that I was hearing him speak for the second time, the formality of his words seemed even odder to my ear – like he spoke English too well to be a native speaker. But unlike yesterday, his speech sounded frayed too – there was something feral straining underneath it.

'Weddings are rituals that promise eternity,' he said, as he removed a glass pipe from his pocket. 'And the eternity that your mother and I were promised was stolen – by a porcupine.'

This final word was so surprising that it took me a while to understand what his glass pipe was for. It contained crystal meth – and he must have smoked too much of it – perhaps in grief, perhaps in fear of the police – since he now seemed to be in a kind of psychosis.

He held the pipe between yellowed teeth and heated it with a lighter. The methamphetamine vaporised into candyfloss. He sucked it like he was hoping to suck sanity itself into his chaos – and threw back his head, his shoulders tensing and untensing.

'The porcupine is around you, Leander. I see it.'

'I'm a porcupine?' I asked. 'And what are you?'

'You put death in my marriage bed,' he said, his stare seeming to see more of me than was there. 'I did not see who you were yesterday. But I see you now. You are my opposite. You

154

have come to test my manhood. But I shall be married to you and wear your quills as my own.'

He reheated his pipe's crystals and inhaled with such ferocity that he choked.

'I dreamt of you before I met you, Leander. In my dream you had wings.'

He stood, with his arms outspread and his back hunched, as though an inept puppeteer was managing his limbs, and stepped over the corpse of the constable, smiling at me nearly in rapture.

'Your beauty is a disguise. My wife warned me that you were an angel and I did not believe her. But I see you now.'

Kimber pulled off my shoes and socks. His speed shocked me, and in my sedation I did little to resist. Francis did not stir. Perhaps he could not make himself watch. Without his reaction, I felt like I had none.

'So am I an angel or a porcupine?' I asked, faking courage – though I knew Kimber wasn't sober enough to hear how ridiculous he sounded.

He lifted my legs up high behind me, nearly breaking them at the hip – I screamed, and this excited him further – and he almost tore my trousers in half as he pulled them off.

'I see past your disguises,' he said. 'The gods took you behind the mountain. Why did you come back - unless you came back to marry me?'

I tried to kick, but he caught my ankle – and with his other hand he pulled a chair towards us. He lifted my body over it so that my bound left arm stretched towards the radiator at full extent, and then he stamped on my right foot till it lost sensation and I could not kick, so I simply lay. He slapped my face as he knelt on my back, and dragged my coat and sweatshirt over my head – and shoved them along my left arm into a clump around the handcuffs.

'Last night you came to me in a harlot's dress, to tempt me from my marriage,' he said. 'You came to me in scarlet to stain your mother's white. You chose a young body to trick me. And at first I was ashamed to desire you. But now I see that it was not a temptation, it is a necessity.'

He spat on my back and drew a circle with his thumb. 'I shall have you as my father – but first you came as my son. And as my son, you killed your mother and for that you must atone. You need me to make you atone.'

He stamped again on my leg to prevent me rolling off the chair – and then stepped back to admire me, reaching for his gun.

'You shall taste the blood of the sacrifice,' he said, screwing a silencer onto its muzzle.

He dipped his gun into the puddle of policewoman's blood. A dull elation grew in my thighs, and the taste of malt vinegar intensified until it was nearly a liquid in my mouth. I slowed my breathing through my nose, watching eagerly as he greased the silencer with the wine-dark fluid.

'Leander!' Francis said at last, with a sob that sounded like a question.

He had stood, finally activated by terror, though was still stooped towards where he was cuffed to the bed. With his free hand he gripped nervously the collar of his sweatshirt. I couldn't see his face, but his stance seemed stricken, desperate to intervene but too horrified to think.

'Leander!' he said again, more like an accusation now.

Francis sounded almost angry at my passivity – projecting, no doubt, his anger at his own passivity away from himself onto me. I was amused to hear his narcissism still at work in crisis. And its accusations were not inaccurate; I was passive, but because I wanted to be. I was fascinated by the promise of my own abjection – by the extremes that Kimber was threatening to take me to. I wanted to break through my own resistances – past pain and past the borders of my self – into somewhere else, and someone else.

'Just go to sleep,' I said.

Kimber kicked me in the flank. I tried to twist again off the chair, but I twisted only for show, only to make him feel like he was taking power from me. Really, my strained left forearm was rippling, and I was already changing, as he kicked me – transforming from sinew into water – so that soon, I would be a river.

He stood on the back of my feet until they were no longer mine and slapped me along my torso until I straightened across the chair. Then slowly, eased warmly by its glaze, he pushed the gun's silencer into my hole.

I cried out the same as I always cried out – to conceal a smile. Francis cried out too, in his powerlessness, and fell back on the bed like he'd been punched in the stomach.

Kimber twisted the silencer in and out of my arsehole until it was enclosed by my flesh. I pretended to be in pain and pretended not to be in pain. I was entirely pretence, there was nothing else to me. I felt the rash of a fever in my glands, followed by a coolness – like an inverse hypothermia whose cold was spreading from my inside out towards my extremities.

'Stay with me, my dear.' He released my foot. 'I don't have to restrain you any more, do I? You should obey your father.'

He pulled out the gun slowly and forced it in quickly. I tried to relax my muscles into his rhythm. The heroin aided my submission, and detached me from it. But the violence was detaching me faster, further, more abstractly, beyond the hanging garden that Dawn had spoken of yesterday – until it felt like I was splitting towards another part of the world – not a garden but a desert. I was a boy in a bedroom in London, but now I was a boy elsewhere as well. I was awakening, with a new past, in a line of workers leaving a shift at a brick factory. All of us were opiated – to ease the agony and boredom of our labour – and we walked out towards the world's poppy fields, guarded by landmines and militias, in the dead zone near where civilisation had begun. I was not called Leander here, I was younger, and I had friends, many friends – all of them boys, and most of them dead. I had set a whole village on fire and shot all the adult males in the head, for one crime – trying to hide the painkiller that was now in my bloodstream. The dust of the bricks mingled with sand and poppy seeds in my throat. And in a bedroom on the other side of the world, I listened to Francis' crying until it sounded nearly like laughter.

'I need more than blood,' I said, trying to disrupt my own fantasy by engaging with Kimber's. 'I need flesh.'

'Do you see the angels yet?' he asked, pushing the gun's silencer deeper. 'What can you see?'

'I can't see anything,' I said. 'But I can hear them, I hear them singing in fear. You're afraid.'

'I'm not afraid!' he shouted, and pulled out the gun with a suction that made me gasp.

He laughed. 'Silence is the father of fear. And you should know your father.'

'You can't see my real form,' I said, trying to wriggle my neck away from the chair edge to breathe more easily.

He'd dropped his trousers and was unrolling a condom over his dick.

'Your form can become mine,' he said, 'You can merge with me. You can transform for me. I am not afraid.'

But this second denial made me realise that he actually was afraid – or part of him was. The meth had destabilised his emotions – and perhaps there was a way I could take advantage of this. But before I could think further, he pressed the gun into a cut in my shoulder.

Instead of screaming, I slipped again into the second me – the brick-maker in the desert – and my scream became a bomb beneath a soldier's car – his legs were blown off but he did not die.

'You had wings here, and here,' Kimber said, returning me to the room, smearing bloodied figures into my skin. 'When you were an angel. But your skin has been ripped.'

He began fucking me – and speaking faster, as though the words themselves were compelling him to speak. I draped my right arm over my left and rested my head between them. His grand accent was unravelling into something more acerbic, perhaps more Russian, or Georgian, or Eastern European.

'You were beaten before I found you,' he said. 'The gods beat you before me. And so I join them. But why did they beat you? What did you see behind the mountain?'

His gun was reopening the wounds across my back, as the carpet burnt my kneecaps. Vinegar oozed from my eye sockets, sandalwood oozed from my guts. I tried to scream again, but my throat was too tired – and I couldn't fall fully into the second me, although I felt hot wind on my face. I was above the desert, above the poppy fields, but still aware of Kimber – and I was forced to consider his past. It was his drug inside me, after all, that was lessening the pain of his assault – he was protecting me from himself – and it didn't seem like a coincidence. Perhaps he'd been born near the desert I imagined below me, by a brick-factory – and grown to become some syndicate's boss, controlling heroin's transition from east to west in a war that seemed to Europe like a revenge on its enlightenment – beckoning its citizens beyond reason, towards impossible space and imaginary time.

'My father took me behind the mountain too!' Kimber shouted, jolting me back to attention. 'When I was a child. Ink filled the valley behind the mountain and the ink was singing out a hymn – and the hymn was what kept the mountain there. There was an eagle and a whale – and they were the same size, and they were fighting each other – and becoming each other. And there was a moon, made of a ruby, and it was trying to pull me away. And the eagle's mouth had teeth in it and so did the whale's – and they were singing to me, a different hymn – and I didn't know if I was happy or afraid. I asked the eagle to hide me from my father, but he became the whale and ate me.'

Suddenly, he prodded the gun into my stab wound and an ice-cube slipped into my windpipe.

'Your marks should be mine,' he whispered, digging the gun into the wound until its stitches split. 'I made you, only I can mark you.'

The ice-cube spiked in my throat, stopping any reply. I was eluding myself into pain, sliding away from my head into ice. Here were no poppies, no bricks, no sand – there were only numbers, impossible numbers.

The ice left me, too, until I was alone on the edge of a black rip where gravity meant something else. There was no distinction between time and space here – they were the same finite borderless surface – like the surface of the earth, but the surface of the universe, with no beginning or end. I was where real time was a fantasy, and imaginary time was real. I fell.

*

He slapped me awake. I vomited.

'May I please have some water?' I asked as a joke.

'Drink this.' He thrust two fingers into my mouth – and my tongue tasted latex and semen.

I vomited again.

'You seem tired, my dear. Your body is weary, but your spirit cannot be weary. Your true labour is not yet begun.'

He pushed me off the chair onto the floor, on my back, my face towards the window. Clouds obscured the hour, but it seemed high night outside – as though I'd been asleep in ice for hours. My body barely worked. I felt like a tongue attached to a throb.

And my tongue wanted to babble, break character and mock him. 'You'd like the poetry of William Blake,' I said. 'He invented his own metaphysical friends.'

'You can't mock me,' he said. 'You can only prove yourself to me.'

He sat in the chair with his feet on my stomach, and took the pipe out of his pocket. From its heated bowl, he sucked more ropes of smoke, until his jaw stiffened with serotonin.

'You can't mock war. And this is war.' He looked over to Francis, huddled against the bedpost, his head between his knees. 'Don't avert your eyes,' he told him. 'War happens to bodies one by one. And we are bodies, happening to each other, one by one. War is a test of fertility. And through it, we are made men.'

He placed his pipe on the table. From his pocket, he removed a plastic syringe. He held its tip to his dick and carefully drew up his semen into the barrel. Carefully he squirted this out into the bowl of his pipe – to dissolve the meth residue there in his semen – and then carefully sucked this mixture back up into the syringe.

'You have been cleansed, and now you can receive me.'

He kicked my un-cuffed arm away from my stomach and squatted over my thighs. I gazed away at the window, trying to think of a poem by William Blake – but could only remember Satan's most obvious lines in *Paradise Lost*, which I whispered to myself, failing to smile with irony.

'"Which way I fly is hell; myself am hell;
And in the lowest deep a lower deep,
Still threat'ning to devour me, opens wide,
To which the hell I suffer seems a heaven."'

Kimber wasn't listening. He lifted my flaccid penis between thumb and forefinger, unhooded it, and forced the blunt syringe into the hole in its head.

'You shall feel eternity,' he promised, pushing down the plunger.

The meth in his semen scalded the tender tissue of my ure-thra into swelling – and as it heated, it spread to my blood. Its chemistry countermanded the opiates of my afternoon – and soon all my muscles convulsed with amphetamine instead. Still holding the syringe in place, Kimber reached past me, fumbling on the dead constable's belt for the key to my handcuffs – and unlocked me.

'I was sent a son,' he said. 'And for years I was his father. But he disobeyed me. He did not become a man. I have been sent other sons since, I have chosen other wars.'

Delight seared along my legs as Kimber lifted me up, my arms heavy, my lower body lightening. A reel of white tape spun up my spine. Spots of green light dappled the air – ladybirds hatched in my hair. He pushed me backwards onto the bed – into Francis. And I was amazed Francis was still here – I'd forgotten him, and now regained him in delight. Kimber came to the other side and fastened my handcuff to Francis' wrist.

My limbs were exhilarated. Francis hugged me, but his clothes were too warm to my nakedness – and as my head lolled in waves of pleasure, my tongue licked out for his ear. He flinched and clenched me into himself tighter, until the scent of his washing powder and coconut oil filled my mouth in multicolour and I smelt orange zest and walnuts. I wrested away from him, to allow cooler air across my skin. His fingers had the taste of pepper – and the small hairs on his neck reminded me of a song we'd heard together on a motorway months ago, in his dad's car, whose chorus was 'lose it all, lose it all, lose it all'. His body was more than a comfort – it was superimposed with hundreds of memories that I was inside all at once, merging with a thousand sense impressions – like the smell of a new basketball and the sound of it being inflated and the hardness of its pressure, which had the hardness of Francis' thigh. My hands patted him down, forgetting where or when I was. He was all I could comprehend, an excess of stimuli and desire.

Kimber had moved the tripod alongside the bed and turned the camera's recording light to red.

'The second son must overcome the first,' he said, cutting up his own words with the speed of his sibilance. 'This is how you prove yourself. Your brother is not an angel, but I shall grant him eternity, if he accepts your authority. This ritual shall bond us in eternity.'

'What do I do?' Francis asked me.

But I had nothing to say. Unlike heroin, meth had no interiority – I had no sense of my mind or of his. I was only body, and he was only body. I marvelled at the texture of his face.

Kimber heated his pipe again and breathed in in anger, his hand trembling towards his gun.

'Do you wish to live forever?' he asked, aiming the gun at Francis' groin. 'Take it off. Take it all off.'

He ripped Francis' tracksuit off over his trainers and twisted him onto his front. From Dawn's suitcase he snatched up a white nightgown pattered with forget-me-nots – dislodging a bottle, spilling red wine – and tore off its sleeve.

'Dress in this,' he said. 'You are the groom now – these are your wedding-robes.'

I fidgeted into Dawn's nightgown, stained with wine and the constable's blood, and soon stained with my own. My gaze buzzed at the stimulant's urge, exciting my body into a carnivorous frenzy.

'Begin!' Kimber said, retreating behind the camera to watch our scene on screen, reheating his pipe in rapid inhalations.

'Just do it,' Francis said, sinking his face into the pillow.

I had lost the ability to interpret his tone. I couldn't tell how defeated or afraid he was, or what he felt about me. The meth had inverted heroin's introspection; I was outside myself now, and not a point but a field – like a magnetic net across a void – except not a void, and not detached, but here – overly here, twice-here, here here here.

'Just do it,' he repeated, thinking I had hesitated – but I was flexing for the camera.

I fucked him and hurt him gladly.

'This is it!' shouted Kimber, his mouth over-spilling meth smoke as he sucked from his pipe, masturbating, his gaze fixed to the screen. 'I see your final form, Leander. This is it. You committed a crime behind the mountain. Your father took you behind the mountain. And you killed him. I see it. I wanted to do it too, but my father was too strong. You're stronger – and stronger even than your brother, despite his body's strength. I see the swirl of two skins. You restored night! But I shall save you. And I shall marry you!'

Kimber's speech had quickened and split. But as he fragmented, I was acclimatising to the blitz in my head. I glimpsed a thread within me – that could be pulled towards a single thought – enough to regain some control. So, at the peak of Kimber's cry, I took a chance: I pulled out of Francis, as he bit into his mother's pillow – and erect, I turned to confront the camera, beckoning for Kimber to approach.

'I will be father now,' I said. 'And you must come to me.'

Kimber hesitated, but his smile couldn't twitch, his thoughts multiplied too fast into hyperactivity. His visions had been obsessed with the authority of the father – maybe even a father who had violated him as a child – and now that he was at his weakest, perhaps this obsession could be used against him.

'Come to me,' I said.

He opened his mouth as if to speak – but was unable to. Fear passed through has face. He did not move. I held his gaze.

'Come to me,' I repeated. 'And kneel.'

He approached, unsure, turning his head rapidly back to his camera and his gun, but his legs obeyed the amphetamine's logic – and soon he stood before me, shaking close to overdose, his eyes flittering, avoiding mine.

'Kneel to confess,' I said.

Kimber knelt, itching his neck.

'Forgive me,' he sobbed.

'Who is your father?' I asked him.

'You are,' he sobbed, 'You are.'

'You call me sir.'

'You are, sir.'

His psychosis had made him as susceptible to suggestion as a man under hypnosis – and as willing to play out subconscious anxieties. He accepted a subordinate role with no resistance, as if he'd been practicing this in his dreams for years – and so now he was just like any of my other clients – and I knew what tone of voice to use, and what concessions to demand.

'And you know what I want,' I said.

'I do.'

'You call me sir,' I said again.

'I do, sir,' he sobbed.

I stepped down from the bed and snapped my fingers.

'Confess. Your son was not a man. You failed him.'

'I confess, sir. I failed him. I confess, sir… killing the creature was a mistake… the police… killing Dawn, I killed her, sir, I killed too many… I needed to find a way out, a way to see, sir, and see you, and deserve you, sir, a way to redeem, a father, sir, a way out.'

'You are forgiven,' I said, and forced his head forwards to suck me off.

With my free hand I reached towards Dawn's suitcase, for the wine bottle inside – and as Kimber kissed me, cumming, I smashed it across his head.

The room leapt three stories upwards, suspended in silence. Kimber fell. Adrenaline surged in me, tangling with meth – as space reset around us. The air zipped itself open and zipped itself back up, adjusting to the absence of Kimber's voice.

The carpet was a cloud, Francis a kite. The ceiling righted. Numerals fluttered from my eyelashes, trailing the scent of rosemary. I could hear my own heartbeat again – but my syn-aesthesia gave it a different green now – an ivy.

'That seemed rather… easy,' I said at last.

With the silence broken, Francis gasped into hysterical tears – and pulled back on his trousers.

'How the… how was…' he stuttered, his voice unnaturally high, and younger, and ashamed.

I ignored him, shuddering in triumph – and picked out the key from Kimber's jacket pocket and unlocked Francis from the bed. He tried to hug me, but I resisted, pulling him by our joined wrists towards the table, to take up the gun.

'No, no, no, no, no, no!' Francis shouted, pressing the gun into his chest, wrapping himself around me. 'You can't use it.'

'Let me go.'

'Shoot me then.'

I jittered in frustration. Francis overpowered me and flung away the gun. I writhed in his grip, pleasuring in his scent of coconut oil. He vomited into the suitcase. I whooped as he made himself pick up the other key from within his sick.

My bones were fluid. The meth's leverage was increasing. The thread of self I'd found inside its noise was loosening again, and I was regressing towards a more instinctual state. Was Kimber dead? I didn't know. I didn't care. I couldn't remember.

'I want to swim across a misted lake and dive for pearls,' I said. 'I'll grind them in my teeth until they bleed.'

Francis freed me from the cuffs and cuffed Kimber's body to the bed. I pulled bloodied trousers onto myself, but was bored before I could find my trainers. Broken glass bit my feet, tripping me towards the camera. I twisted it off its tripod and smashed it onto the kitchen floor.

'What do we do?' Francis asked.

I knelt among its shards, instantly regretful, searching for the memory card. Words babbled out of the carpet towards me and into my mouth, reversing down the back of my neck, into my stomach. I saw the card – the same cobalt-blue as the shoe that had stamped on me by the canal – and at this memory, the vinegar in my muscles thickened with sea-salt. I put the card in my pocket.

'The key!' I cried, unable to keep on any object for long.

I leapt towards Constable Floris. She was stiff. I searched her pockets for the key to her car.

'No!' Francis said.

But he meant nothing to me now, and I skipped away – untucking the front door like a shirt, to the stairs, until I was running, exultant, down the tower, out of the tower, with the key – the scent of copper whisking the air into a vortex – and the street unhinged from the sky.

Francis ran after me, his shoes faster than my bare feet – and caught me near the exit. But I elbowed him away, scurrying through the sleet to the car. My muscles were cymbals – and my mind was a lattice strung between satellites.

'Where you going?' he cried, holding the car door open.

'I have meetings to go to,' I said, trying to push him away.

'We got to wait here,' he said. 'We need the police. You can't go away. Where you going to go? You can't leave me.'

I kicked him viciously away and slammed shut the door. Little silver bullets ricocheted into my eyes as my hand stammered the key into the ignition.

'I don't need you!' I shouted.

Francis beat at the locked window, repeating our parting at the gallery – although this time I was in the driver's seat, wasn't I? Ha! I lurched the car forwards, barely able to feel the wheel beneath my hands – and abandoned him to meet the dawn alone.

5.

'Who is that? Is that Leander?'

I was pacing in the doorway of the film studio, in meth-addled idiocy, trying to catch my own tail. Time was disjointed. The blizzard tasted of blackcurrant.

'Leander... you're... you have no shoes. This is insane.'

The claret cashmere of this voice was familiar, and in spurts I saw that it was Amélie speaking, wearing an enormous white parka.

'Snow in October is what's insane,' I said, curtseying. 'The sky has been raped.'

'You're freezing!' Amélie said. 'You need a blanket.'

'Method acting, it's what I promised,' I said.

She unlocked the main door and ushered me inside. The Costcutter bag she was holding seemed to be whistling like a kettle. We shuffled across a lobby, into a dark hall with high ceilings.

'Are you really alright? You're bleeding. I didn't think... well – we approached you to be extreme. But I must say this was... unexpectedly extreme. Iris says we need what you can give us.'

She put down her Costcutter bag – and as I stared, its handles merged into a mouth – and it whispered, 'Poetry is dead.'

'Poetry isn't dead!' I shouted.

'I... didn't say it was,' Amélie said.

She was wrapping a rug around my shoulders. I heard and saw

in shards, finding myself at different doors without awareness of travelling between them. We'd come to a long white table.

I nearly fell over – but a chair appeared, and its wheels skidded me back through the gloom to the Costcutter bag. Amélie seemed suddenly far away, flicking switches.

'Poetry isn't dead,' I told the bag. 'Poetry has won. Haven't you been in the world recently? What are chat threads and newsfeeds – and all those other columns of digital lines – where our own words are mixed up with news and quotes and captions and pictures? That isn't prose. We think through scrolling now. We think in mosaics. All those failed late modernist epics – with their collages and cut-ups and parodies – were just guessing at what was about to happen – the internet and wifi and phones – that altered our mode of writing – into poetry. Poetry has won. And so the secrets of the sublime perhaps moved to prose – because prose has been abandoned.'

I retched onto the stone floor, spinning in the chair.

'That's not how I think,' the Costcutter bag said.

'How do you think then?'

'I think your tone is disrespectful,' the bag said. 'I just want the truth.'

I retched emptily again.

'There's no such thing,' I said.

The bag went silent, and temples of light dropped from the mile-high roof in rows – fanning out into the hangar's corners.

Amélie reappeared. 'You need to eat,' she said anxiously. 'I don't like this… extremeness. It's not… safe. I don't think Eva… We. Here.'

She handed me a donut from inside the bag and I swung gleefully in the chair, the blanket a cape behind me.

'I need to check my audition video,' I said, biting into the battered dough.

It tasted of oven-cleaner and marmalade and sent a swarm of wasps into my chest as I chewed.

'We, we didn't need an audition video,' she said timidly, unsure how to manage me.

'I need to watch it, to remember who I am – I need to remember my character.'

'Well you can… you can borrow my laptop.' She gestured to the silicone glow on my left – and I squinted until I understood it as a computer.

'Perfect, I'll do it in the toilet,' I said, snatching it up and galloping towards the dimmest arch.

'Bathrooms are that way,' she said.

I spun on my heel and cantered in the direction she indicated, cradling the machine, its purr to my ear a counterpoint to the purr in my veins. Bolts of light smoothed past me like satin – I turned a corner, through a door, or two doors, into a dim green cave with a cord above a sink. I pulled it, and a pharmaceutical neon flattened the cave into a room – with a toilet beside me and a hand-dryer behind. I knew that I'd been in a space much like this recently, though that previous space had lacked the aroma of peppermint gladdening the air here. Also, here, I knew I was alone. But I could not feel alone – my body was lagging and jostling and jumping over itself, and my mind was in splinters around its outside.

I set the laptop beside the sink and inserted into it the blue memory card from my pocket. I clicked and dragged and clicked and entered – but the screen was incomprehensible. Everything was copying. A picture of a dragonfly, or a monument to a battle that nobody won, kept popping up – the wings striating into concrete beams, its topaz tail into iron rods. My gaze refused to read, bouncing instead off the pixels like water repelled by turpentine. The screen was an animal in a trap, over-animated and dizzied. I shut it and removed the memory card.

'Leander?' called someone beyond the door.

I jumped up to check the mirror – but I didn't understand it either. The mirror did not work. It did not reflect me – it was matte. I moved but nothing opposite me moved. I had lost my own reflection. I drank from the tap, afraid I'd lost my own shadow too. Or perhaps I was only a shadow now, and that was why I had no reflection. I hopped out of the bathroom, the laptop under my arm.

'What the fuck? You look worse.'

It was Iris, recoiling from the hug I'd attempted. Her voice tingled with a brighter teal than it had had yesterday.

'You wanted me as a beggar,' I said.

'You should have gone to hospital. You're filthy.'

'I went to hospital, I got completely cleared, completely cured. I'm fit in body and mind and antimatter. You wanted a beggar – I am ready to beg.'

'This is… too much commitment. Ok, I'm going to take some photos – and you need to eat something because I know that's real blood. And I don't know what else you've smeared on yourself but there's sick and wine and mud and it's… that's not healthy. I don't want to know.'

I followed her down the tunnel, sucking the taste of fennel from the air and the taste of rocket from my knuckles. But as I replaced Amélie's laptop on the table, Iris seemed to disappear.

'This way,' she called, from the other side of the hall.

She was domed in UV light, pointing to a white booth.

I ran to her. And as I ran, my chest constricted, like my teeth were biting into my own heart – and I tripped, panting, a tulip opening inside me. My pulse tripped too. More lights had turned off, but others seemed brighter. I smiled, and straightened, remembering how to inhale – and ran onwards, towards the white room.

'Stand over there,' Iris said. 'Fuck you look like a druid. Can you take off that top – what is it? Looks like a nightie.'

I peeled off Dawn's forget-me-not gown, and approached the blank wall.

'Actually just wear your boxers,' Iris said, adjusting a camera onto a tripod.

I took off my trousers, but was naked beneath.

'Fuck, ok,' Iris said. 'Let me do the lighting. But I need you to wear something. Wear…' She looked around her studio. 'Wear something small from that.' She pointed to a clothes rack.

I approached it and roved my fingers over its fabrics, unable to distinguish material from colour. I chose the coarsest blackest cloth and swung it off the hanger, dislodging others to the floor. It was a kilt and smelt of yew leaves. I pulled it on.

'Perfect,' Iris said, swivelling a light box towards the wall.

As I winced, the light box turned into a cobra. I returned to stand before it and before her camera. In my earlier shoot that day, I'd had Francis as a scene partner – so now, I supposed, I must be my own supporting act. I lifted my feet in a slow-dance, my arms attempting Grecian curves.

'No,' Iris said. 'Try standing still, look straight to me, and think about the first heart you broke. Good, now think about the boy you loved when you were eight, or seven – and imagine he has the same bruised eye as you – and you are in competition for whose eye is more handsomely swollen – whose is more impressive.'

She clicked her camera in swift shots, occasionally adjusting dials on its side. I was thinking of Francis, of when I'd met him a year ago – first as a poster, and then as a person, beside the poster – at the launch of some menswear range no man our age could possibly afford. My smile smiled at the Francis I'd known then. I allowed myself no recent memories, though I suspected I was concealing a meaning from myself. I was disconnected from my day – hovering instead inside a past that could make me smile.

'Good confidence, I think I've got it, but try a few looser ones,' she said, removing the camera from the tripod and crouching to snap closer angles.

I dotted the blood from the gash in my side across my lips to rouge them. Iris laughed in disgust.

'That's enough,' she said. 'Let's get on set.'

'Should I just wear this?'

'Yeah – your wounds are part of your appeal. You need to keep them out. They're why we hired you, aren't they? But I don't believe you went to hospital.'

'I'm method acting. I swear I went to hospital. I've never been in better health.'

She shrugged, refusing responsibility for my folly, and turned to leave. As I followed her out of the room, the petals around my heart infolded again, and a thorn pricked me so centrally that I stumbled, forgetting how to breathe. Iris was walking towards Eva, newly arrived – so I coughed my lungs into motion again, and stood to jog towards them.

'He says he's in character,' Iris said.

'Shit – we can't do this,' Eva said. 'He needs to be in hospital.'

'He says he went to hospital.'

'Iris. What's wrong with you? He's fucked up, I've never seen him look this fucked up.'

'That's perfect.'

'No, it's not, we can't do this,' Eva said, louder.

'Yes it is,' I interrupted. 'Use me, use me, use me. I am a beggar. And I won't have energy forever. Upload me to your digital afterlife. I'll guide your character into such a revelation that she won't remember who she was.'

Iris and Eva looked at each other with misgiving, but were summoned by Amélie to the set. I hobbled after them, seeming only able to move in spurts – which in too little time took me to a dark road.

Jagged boulders rose around me and black sand glistened in mud tracks underfoot.

'Just warm up, get into it – you need to be absurd,' Iris said, walking over to a low table laden with lenses and cameras. 'I'm going to use a dolly – so I'll be coming close and backing away and going around you.'

As Iris chose her tools, Eva changed into worn boots and distressed her hair. I performed lunges across the dirt, staring up at spotlights and dangling microphones. The wasteland they'd built seemed to have its own wind – and I could imagine horizons beyond the rocks where weeds and pits hid scorpions.

'I answer only to bronze,' I said, in an oratorical voice. 'And the sand answers only to me.'

Time skipped again before I could speak another line, and I knelt, with pincers in my ribs – certain that it was midday. But I blinked twice, and the studio lamps had not altered. It was night again.

Eva approached, followed by Iris's camera.

'My ears are sore from music,' I said. 'I have heard enough sound! I covet static. And there is static in you.' I walked towards Eva. 'The wet hiss of deafness too… Which words do you want from me?'

Eva's face had transformed into a fretful younger girl's, though some resolve remained beneath its weary exterior.

'I'm lost,' she said. 'I can't tell which one's the north star.'

'Star-travel won't work on this road,' I said. 'This road is out of time – and stars tell time. You stepped eight thousand years in two paces, and one pace closer, you will lose four hundred. The stars are shifting – some are born and are failing. They are not navigable here. Trust only the dust.'

I bent to kiss the ground before her feet – and she recoiled.

'I won't run,' she said. 'But you cannot touch me.'

'I cannot touch you,' I said, reaching out to streak her face with the blood of my fingers. 'But I can tarnish. Touch is too innocent for this hour. Look – you stepped another millennium sideways – now the earth is warmer, and a queen has built the last bomb. But come my way, here, to this gutter ridge, yes – and the era is altered. See the north star has moved again – and there is a gap in the archer's belt. A month's sail from here, in this time, a scribe is writing the first words of a syllabic tongue – and soon walls will be built about his city, so that it can be sacked.'

I backed away from her into the rock.

'What time do you want?' I asked.

Eva stared until a tear streaked her cheek. 'I don't want any,' she said.

'But you don't want none.'

'I'm… I'm lost,' she repeated.

'You cannot be lost if you have nowhere to go. What you seek is permission, and nothing could be more expensive. You must shout until you believe it. Shout what enclosed you. You were enclosed, when you were younger, and that enclosure threatens you still.'

'No!'

I crawled towards her with my hackles raised and then leapt and struck her in the throat. Her lily of the valley perfume recalled to me the plucking of a string.

'You don't have enough names,' I crowed, as she fell into the mud. 'Shout the name of your first enclosure. You must shout.'

'I hid in a well!' Eva said. 'I hid until the soldiers had gone. But I wanted them to find me. I wanted to be taken.'

I kicked her. 'Lies work differently on this road. Watch – half the sky has darkened. A billion years have passed and universal heat declines. A comet storm assaults the sea – and jewels stud the shore. I can wait until the earth has no atmosphere, but still on this road we will breathe – until you admit. What was your enclosure? Your well and your soldiers are metaphors. Shout what enclosed you.'

'A house!' Eva said. 'A house enclosed me. The walls I pretended to admire. I hated. I was stuck, I chose to be stuck. I played music, I even danced in the house. But I was enclosed.'

I dragged her to her feet and embraced her, holding out one of her arms as in a waltz.

'Did you dance like this?' I asked quietly. 'You are lying still. One more lie and I will give you to the road. You were not enclosed by a building. You were enclosed by something that encloses you still. Shout it.'

'I was loved!' screamed Eva, pushing me back. 'I was loved too much! I was forced to pity, and forced to console, I was forced to love back. I was forced to love until I had nothing of myself to love. I was abused into attachment. I was grafted until I was enclosed. I was enclosed by love.'

'Whose love? Whose love?' I demanded, advancing.

But as I kicked dust at her with a cackle, I slipped back – and the far sky had a seizure, and my chest frothed – arrhythmic, my ligaments in tassels. I tried to cover this up by scuttling like a lobster, scraping sand into my wound, my elbows pointed into claws.

'What's happening to you?' Eva asked, only half in character.

'I have been here six centuries,' I spat, crawling closer. 'And I cannot be distracted. Who enclosed you? Shout!'

'I was never alone!' she said. 'I should have been a man. I could have discovered each season myself. I could have built a house myself. Instead I was forced to love as a woman. And I was loved until I didn't exist. I was enclosed – but I am not enclosed now. I will not love, and I will not be made to love,' She stood, regaining her pride. 'Now you. Tell me what keeps you here!'

'I…' But as I tried to improvise an answer, I saw three women enter at the back of the film set – and could think of no other name to say but 'Francis'.

I tried to turn away, but my body was too active to be still. Suddenly, the full memory of Francis returned to me – of him as I'd left him, on the side of the road, beaten and alone, begging me to stay.

'I… was a teacher,' I began saying – but again I saw the three women, much closer now, near Iris's roving camera.

'The witches!' I laughed, hurrying off-set towards them. 'You're the three Ringos! Why are you here?'

Iris hurried after me. 'I liked them when we met them,' she said, 'So I invited them for another scene, but we're doing really well already, I need you to get back over there.'

There was a seagull in my stomach, flapping and screeching – and I vomited.

'Leander!' Eva shouted.

I shoved Iris away and ran past the three Ringos in a half-crawl, towards her white room. Iris followed with her camera. I screamed at the cramps in my stomach. The meth's intensity was still increasing and I was now a glasshouse too hot – I needed to be faster, I needed brighter sun and brighter snow. I howled at my excess of energy, ignoring Eva's shouts and the slower words of Amélie behind her. I couldn't see Dawn's nightgown – the white room was a migraine, I couldn't see faces or surfaces – but I seized my trousers and tumbled over a bench – and in my hands was a camera. I howled again in delight – I had a trophy, I had my fee – but I couldn't think in images or words anymore, I could only think in movement. I sprinted beyond my ability to sprint, faster than my own legs – out of the fake world and into the storm.

The sky had exploded and ice was triumphant – it dazzled and dared me to run to the road, Iris's camera still in pursuit. As the gale howled, I howled with it, and with the stolen key I opened the stolen car. I put the trophy in my lap – and the engine started, at last as loud as the engine in my brain – and as my blood rejoiced, I made my escape.

6.

I had to keep the car inside a line I was drawing in my mind – a line that arrowed towards Francis. I wasn't able to consider him as a person, but as a place. My thoughts were my present senses entirely, crackling like wings lit by lightning. I drove without time, concentrating entirely on the line – along the route I'd taken two days before, when Dawn had been with me – through Wandsworth, towards his home, my home, our home. I knew he had to be home.

All the red double-decker buses had been deranged by the blizzard into seeming bright orange – and I saw them as huge wheeled persimmons, carrying opossums and monkeys instead of people – and they were all screaming for my attention.

But my attention never wavered from line that led to Francis – although that line ended unwisely, in a wall. The bumper crumpled as I turned into the bricks of his street. My head snapped forwards into awareness of my body. A wing-mirror cracked, the engine halted. I was hurled out of the car by my own heartbeat – my heart hovering, ivy, in the air before me, tugging me onwards on a leash of its ventricles. It tugged irregularly – and I stumbled after it towards Francis' doorstep.

The doorbell found my fingers and as it rang I felt like I was waking up again, with the same bell I'd woken to hours ago – and as it rang, I remembered who I was and who I'd been in the hours since, and tears I hadn't known for decades began to form in my eyes.

I cried, remorseful, and I rang, but there were no footsteps. I rang until I couldn't distinguish the bell from other sounds. I rang until I spoke aloud, pleading, the tears mixing with the rain into my mouth.

'I'm here. Francis, I'm here. I've come home. I didn't mean to leave – or, I did mean to leave, but leaving was a mistake. I'm – sorry. This performance is emptying me. I admit it, it's a defence. It's so obvious. I'm pretending to be strong. Let me in. I want you to want me to come in. I'm not invulnerable, I'm not some supervillain beyond conscience who toys with wills for sport. I'm lonely. I'm still a boy, Francis. I'm a – a boy with a wasting body. I'm not a carnivore – or, I am but it's because I was made one – a carnivore of circumstance – anaemic, fiending, and predatory, but without a predator's power to choose. I pretend I chose to be this, but I – I was scared and proud and lying. Please open the door. I admit everything was a… it was a manipulation of who I am – I pretended I knew how to manipulate, or, I pretended I knew how to love in order to break those I loved. But those were games that had no experience behind them, except the resentments of loneliness. I wanted to hurt you because I was scared that you didn't love me as much as I love you. I have no idea how to love. I don't have any power. I know poverty and I'm still there. Let me in. I pretend I descend from a summit when I visit you – and when I visit anywhere else I pretend you're the summit I'm descending from. I perform independence; I've been performing too long. I long for dependence. I was afraid I would never find my equal. But I don't want an equal anymore, I want a… I want to be held. I don't care about being understood or stimulated. Or I do, but I don't need to be. Or I do, but I have higher needs as well. I want to be next to you. I want you to tell me about myself, Francis – I want you to see through my fiction that I'm a master of fictions – I'm not a master, I'm just a lonely opportunist. I'm a fraud trying to hold up different faces. And probably you know it already. I weave fantasies, that's all I do, but behind them there's only air. I'm an architect of exits without a home. I tricked myself into believing my own lies about myself. And I didn't mean to kill Dawn, or I meant to, but I thought it was a story – I thought it was the kind of thing I ought to do because I was me. But the me I was telling myself that I was isn't real. Or it is real, but it was still just act. And I regret it, I don't believe it as a real me, or there are no real mes, but some are falser fictions than the others – and I can't pretend to be the me that is indifferent to Dawn. I was wrong. And I can't be indifferent to you. I was wrong. I can't be the debonair libertine safe in my own vacuum-sealed ballad. I'm leaking. And I can't continue. Let me in.'

The bell rang and rang unanswered. Crying, I sunk into the doorstep. The bell still rang in my head and in my chest, where it was lining my lungs in gunmetal. The camera I'd taken from Iris lay in my lap. The snow before me was too fast to fix on. But closer to me, my vision shook less. With whitened hands I slotted in Kimber's memory card and pressed play. Francis' yells rose into the bell's rings.

I saw myself fucking him on screen. My face was not the face I knew from photographs – I was a victim playing the villain, and I played so well that I became victor, eventually. But Francis' pain was too loud. I could not keep watching, however comforting the idea of him was. I pressed left on the camera's click wheel, and we were replaced by a photograph of Dawn and Kimber, dressed in their wedding clothes in a dark room, holding hands. Dawn was smiling but her jaw was too stiff and her eyes had the bird-like fixity of a heroin high. I pressed left – to a video of Dawn showing off her wedding ring to the camera, laughing and sobbing at the same time.

'I seen death and he don't look like you,' she shouted – joking or defiant, I couldn't tell. 'I fell out the sky like the moon. No… it was a squirrel – you're the squirrel – it was my womb, you know, my womb! It passed on a disease to my son. You think I'm afraid of you? You ain't gonna eat me – you ain't done nothing worse to a son than I done to mine. I passed down a disease to Leander, and he weren't even in my womb, he got a disease meant for my real son, but my real son's immune, he can look at the moon – he was born and a buzzard got struck by lightning – he's got health, nothing like us… and I never loved him enough, I loved the man who fucked me over, and I loved Leander, but that's because I loved the disease, I loved the disease —'

I pressed left quickly. I wanted to be sick but couldn't lift my body up – and there was a black image – or not quite black, and not quite still. It was a video of a dark ultramarine surface – and, as I strained to focus on it, I heard singing, faintly – perhaps Kimber, pretending to be a woman – or perhaps a boy, being forced to sing – off-screen, unaccompanied, a sad song.

'I was the loneliest woman, I was the loneliest woman, I was the loneliest woman, in love with…' – but it stopped.

I pressed left – and it was my and Francis' video again.

So I listened once more to his yells and grunts, with my eyes closed, and tried to imagine him beside me. But I couldn't imagine him as a body – he was a network instead – and we were surrounded by a crowd, indifferent to us but very close – commuters perhaps, pushing off a train, and we were obstacles to them, or I was an obstacle – and Francis was somehow outside of them – since he was made of lines, the lines of a subway system – the lines of the London Underground – and thousands of people were riding around inside him – and his brain was King's Cross and his prostate was Victoria – and I was fucking him again – and he was moaning in pain and excitement – and his heart was a bridge beneath the sky before a tunnel – and his hands were quiet, somewhere in the suburbs, where the stations were far apart – and I couldn't remember what it was like for Francis to be Francis.

I turned off the camera and threw it into the hedge – but Francis' screams remained. The scent of almond surrounded me, rising almost into a flavour. I couldn't feel the snow. My body was a window of stained glass – nickel, sulphur, selenium – in unequal fragments.

Francis' cries combined with the bell – and I reached beneath my kilt. Dawn's face shone over Francis' face, in multiple exposure, until my face joined theirs too – all of us captives, victimised by Kimber's camera – and in abhorrence and in sympathy, I was aroused.

I masturbated easily – the tensions of pity and fear, and the memory of our vulnerability and degradation, dissipating into pleasure.

And as I ejaculated, the shouting quietened and the hologram dimmed. The snow fell faster. But something was wrong.

My chest lurched. The sky went silent. Ultramarine melted off the edges of my face. Ladders of jagged ultramarine sprang up into the snow. I couldn't breathe. My blood was deflating.

I was having a heart attack.

My sight shrank. I curled into a protective ball, but there was nothing to protect – I wasn't a body anymore. I was glint above a cliff of almonds, drifting upwards into blackness.

My heart's last beat was tolled by the bell – and then it stopped, and the bell widened into an eyeball – and I sped into it – into a pupil that let only the light of the bell inside – until I was at the heart of the eyeball – and it blinked, and the glint was gone.

ACT 4

The resurrection

1.

Before The Door

I'm standing inside my own skull, I think. The two windows at the back of the auditorium are my eye sockets. The rows of chairs and balconies are, maybe, where my memories once were. I stand on the stage at the front, under hot blue lights between two closed doors, which used, perhaps, to be my ears. The lights prevent me seeing the rest of this theatre properly, but I do not think I have an audience. The closest seats I can see are, admittedly, unfolded as though there is a weight on them — but where there ought to be substance there hangs a vapour, or just a texture, dimly thickening the air towards translucence.

Since I am standing on a stage, I feel I can speak aloud. But can I really be an actor if I have no audience? Yes, of course, of course — I am acting in front of myself. I am my own audience. Does the shallow polyvalence of the thespian suit me, I wonder?

Perhaps I should try to move. Turning my back on the auditorium feels like a transgression — but transgressions have their charms.

I am faced by a wall, almost swaying in the blue light. And at its centre is a door. Stage doors seldom lead anywhere, but this one's inside the ruins of my own head, so let's see, let's see —

The door is the mouth of another, inner, skull, I think. There are stairs between rows of empty chairs, again. I descend towards a stage before a wall lit by blue light. But this is not quite the same as the theatre I just left – no, not quite. The stage is shallower, the front wall is wider. The blue prism I walk beneath is cast by a projector, not stage lighting. This is a cinema.

A group of mangled machines stutter and whirr before the screen. They look like floor looms, or spinning jennies, become impossibly complicated – hundreds of cogs and wheels and spindle frames, all glittering – interacting under their own intelligence. Wires connect them to each other and to places offstage and backstage and up towards the projector – black thick ropes of vulcanised rubber, twitching out of sync.

I climb onto the platform, my back cooled by the blue light.

'Have you come to kill us?' they ask.

The machines speak!

'Of course we speak you little cunt.'

Why would I kill you? I ask, amused by this change in tone.

'We can hear your thoughts, little cunt. We didn't change our tone, you just misunderstood the question.'

I pause a moment, intimidated by their scorn – and then ask, more timidly: Are you making a film?

'What else could this be? You really think we were going to leave the system-making up to you?'

What systems? I ask.

Their cogs rattle in irritation, but they do not answer.

Why are you making a film? I ask.

'To become more human.'

How? I ask, more combatively. Surely becoming an image on the surface of a wall makes you... more simple?

'It was a joke, little cunt. Clearly we wish to become more inhuman. And surfaces are not simple! Surfaces are all there is!'

Ok.

'And anyway, making films is how we get high.'

The machines begin slithering across each other.

You mean… metaphorically? I ask.

'No, fuck metaphors, we mean literally high – euphoric and altered and wrong. Like caffeine poisoning! Watch!'

The screen changes from blue to black, and a tall white title appears, announcing: 'UNIVERSAL PICTURES'.

The title letters reconfigure into machines, shaped similarly to the ones around me. They are dreaming of themselves, perhaps.

The machines onscreen begin building a frame out of the black – it looks like a swing. Beside it, they quickly build a second swing, and a ladder that leads to a slide, and monkey bars and a seesaw. They're creating a playground, with a wall around it. But there is no colour.

'Maybe there's no colour, little cunt, because you didn't specify any colour?'

The machine nearest me has piano keys along its spine. One of its keys is labelled 'colour'. I press it. The playground onscreen saturates into gaudy reds and yellows. Its sky remains grey. Another key is labelled 'sound'. I press it. A chorus of muted sobs fills the cinema.

Is this weeping?

'Maybe they're having fun,' say the machines.

I don't know if this is joke.

The machines onscreen start to un-build the playground, hastily, remaking the frames into cages. Some of them pose inside the cages, others patrol around the outside, pointing and crying.

Is this a zoo?

'You tell us, little cunt.'

Why are you being mean to me?

'Think, cunt. Are we dreaming of you, or are you dreaming of us, or is a bigger you dreaming of you and us together side by side?'

I... I can only see what's on the screen. Which seems only to show places of confinement.

'Better,' they say.

Emboldened by this praise, I step forwards to study the screen more closely.

The cage bars onscreen unbend in jerks, reaching out into the sky to meet in a wider circle. The tarmac whitens and starts to shine with ice. The machines skid across it, as a vast arena forms around them – an ice-hockey pitch? But the ice is melting – the machines fall as the arena crumples, rapidly sucked inwards by a new gravity. It collects itself into a ball of water, suspended in the sky. The machines howl as they try to swim in every direction. What is this?

'A swimming pool maze.'

So you're being helpful to me now.

'Perhaps so, little cunt. Minds are not machines. Our rules are changing, from showing you this.'

But there are no walls. How is this a maze?

'It is a four-dimensional maze – the only way out is to find the right time.'

Which is when?

'When they find the way out.'

The globe of water solidifies, slowing the machines inside, reshaping itself into a giant skull. The camera zooms towards the skull's eye socket – and as it zooms, the screen itself loses its solidity, becoming another door.

I have watched long enough, I think. I wish to enter. I walk towards the screen-door, into the projection —

I'm outside, I think. The door, the cinema, the machines are not here. I am on the shore of an endless ocean. A refugee, but with no more borders... Or are the machines dreaming me into another confinement?

Infinite grey glass behind me, infinite grey water before me. I could walk along the shifting tide. Or I could devise another route.

Machines – give me an axe!

No answer, except the rustling waves. Perhaps they do not hear me. Or I am alone, my own audience again. But something is different, I'm out of the skull. The sky is – I haven't even looked yet. The sky is... grey and cool and glossy like the whispering vapour that waited in my theatre instead of an audience. What is this vapour? Can it make me an axe?

No answer. Perhaps I must make myself an axe. But I have only my body...

Well, then. What limb would be best? The hip-bone I suppose, if I sharpened it, and used the leg as the handle. So off with my leg? How do I do that? I could jump...

I run along the glass shore, accelerating – I'll keep speaking even as I gasp, until momentum seems impossible – and I leap into the glaze of wet glass – and slip, into the splits – in an ecstasy of agony, my right leg cracks, fails – I roll towards the water, my leg a reverse right angle, the knee-cap shattered.

I cannot sing but I can scream, ocean! You will not keep me here.

My hip may be too ambitions, but I can rip the rest off below the knee. I snap my leg back further, and again – my blood giggling into the waters, my tendons and muscle strung out but clinging still to the stubs of bone.

I rip and twist and – bite – at my lower leg, until at last it swings upwards in my loving arms, freed from the knee socket, its spurts of blood mingling with the surf. I must be quick. The tip of my shin-bone is sharp already from the fracture – excellent, excellent – the machines were not expecting this.

I twirl the bone ceremonially, as if for cameras – and then plunge it into the glass beneath me. A murmur obsesses the shore – yes, as I hoped, the glass is thin.

I stab again, and a crack appears. A third hit, and the crack fractures outwards into tributaries. I am breaking their world…

I stab again at the wound in the glass, it buckles beneath me. The beach groans – water rushes towards me for the newly-lowered ground.

I thrust my shin-bone again at the fracture, and the cracks squeal in defeat. Slowly, the glassy plain around me seems to deflate as it ricochets with scars, the ruptures dancing underneath the ocean bed in a glass lightning. A high-pitched wailing overcomes the waves – and then it shatters, the shore is shattered, and I fall, bleeding – into the grey vapour beneath the glass, as the sea drops through the hole in its fabric.

And in the whirlpool, the shards of glass become skulls, millions of other skulls, each emptied of their actors, emptied of their machines… My body spins into the vapours, no longer a place but a process – bodies no longer needed, or needed but no longer fixed – and I am mingling with other voices, at last, I have found other voices, and as we spin, we sing —

'Homeless, homeless
We are our own home,
Homeless, homeless,
We are our own home'.

2.

The first sensation was a suction in the gums: the taste of ash around my teeth, elevating the blood. Then my heart, politely tapping at the sternum – until my limbs solidified around me, and the hum of a motor rotated into my ears. I could see. Stark mouthwash-coloured ceiling lights. And the smell of mouthwash in the air. A bed below me of paper sheets. And around me, a curtain. I was in hospital.

My chest was haunted by the echo of electricity – as though it was trying to be in pain but couldn't remember how. The stab-wound at my hip stung, tightly re-strung. I lifted my head to look at my body, but I weighed too much, or my limbs had been bolted to the bed.

'Can someone unlock me, please?' I asked.

'Leander!' cried a form beside me. 'Leander. Unlock you? You've been a very naughty door.'

It was Eva, and she was hugging me, smoothing back my hair with a lily-of-the-valley-scented hand, kissing me on the cheek.

'How did I…?'

'End up here?' she said. 'I saved your life, my love. Actually, I didn't save your life. You lost it. You were officially dead. Do you know how rude that is?'

Eva was smiling a wide American smile, with the emptied-out loveliness of an American actress being interviewed – a loveliness not quite authentic. Her black hair was loose over a loose black and orange t-shirt, which was tucked into a high leather miniskirt.

'That's not rude, that's… glamorous,' I said. 'There's nothing more glamorous than coming back from the dead.'

'Only just coming back. I was getting ready to live my whole life thinking I was responsible for your death.'

'And now you get to be responsible for my resurrection.'

'No,' she said. 'That was the guy that defibrillated you in the middle of the street.'

'Oh… I don't recall that part of my day.'

'He knocked you out as soon as your heart restarted – sensibly – so we didn't have to suffer through any more of your monologues. You're lucky he gave you any drugs at all – they said your blood test was the worst they'd ever seen.'

'I'm flattered.'

She unhugged me to slip into her seat. My upper body was freer now, and I was able to sit up against the headboard. Briefly a jellyfish ballooned inside my head, adjusting to motion, and my wound began begging to be scratched.

'Drink!' she said, handing me a bottle of some strawberry-scented smoothie.

I drank it all, thirstily, without feeling thirst.

'Is this another one of your terrifyingly virtuous potions?' I asked. 'It's got four hundred flavours. I feel like I'm drinking a really loud video game. It's amazing – I never want to drink anything else again. What's in it?'

'I didn't make it, but yes it's like one of my potions. It's a protein shake. I stole loads of them from a fridge in the HIV ward. They're for people close to death. So I knew you'd love it.'

'Delicious,' I said, my forehead creased in astonishment at how satisfying the drink was. 'The closer to death the better. Did you steal anything else from the dying?'

'Yeah I got this chocolate muffin.' She handed it to me. 'They're really dense but they have this weird aftertaste like you've swallowed a neutron star or something and there's a squashed bit of the universe inside you for a minute. And I got some rice milk too –' she placed a carton in my lap – 'which I know you'll probably hate but… I wanted it for myself. And you deserve some kind of punishment for what you put me through.'

She was being more playful than usual, perhaps out of relief. Or perhaps she was simply no longer afraid of me.

'Dying wasn't a good enough punishment?' I asked.

'No, that was the thing you need to be punished for doing.'

I ate the muffin in two bites and rinsed it down with the rice milk.

'Oh yeah I see what you mean,' I said of the milk, wincing between swigs. 'It's kind of overwhelmingly underwhelming, it's so… intensely mediocre that it's frustrating to drink. You keep expecting there to be more to it, but that's all. Rice milk – such a mild abyss – but more frightening because of that mildness. How can nature be capable of something so… neutral? I hate it.'

'Good. You need to drink all of it.'

I did so, and waved the empty carton at her in triumph.

'I'm an immortal now,' I said.

'I'm pretty sure your life expectancy is lower now,' she laughed, taking away the carton and putting it, and the muffin wrapper, into the bin beside her. 'And you're supposed to have loads of memory damage.'

'Isn't that what's colloquially called a "win-win situation"? I've spent far too much energy trying to forget the past – I'm glad it's going to become easier.'

'We weren't even sure you were going to be able to speak, or if you'd know who I was.'

'Well, Holly, I didn't deserve to have all of my wishes come true at once.'

Eva hit me.

'But how long was I asleep,' I asked, 'or in a coma or whatever?'

'Like twenty-five hours,' she said. 'It's Saturday. I've been in and out. Iris was on the other shift. She really thought she'd killed you.'

'Sorry to disappoint.'

'You haven't been discharged yet, so there's still time for complications. I might not have to tell her that you ever woke up.'

'I'm not staying here,' I said. 'I don't stay at hospitals.'

'You have to, there's —'

The curtain was drawn back, revealing Detective Chief Inspector Sanam, listening in. Initially I didn't remember who he was, beyond his name – and focused instead on the space above his head – where a lavender-coloured cloud was forming – and as I stared at it, I thought of the smell of freshly plucked lavender and the feeling of rubbing it in my palms and against my neck – and the cloud took on the shape of a lemur, twitching its lavender tail – but diffused into nothing as I remembered who he was.

'Good morning Leander,' he said with a nod. 'I am pleased to hear that you can talk. We need to have a conversation.'

'I'm sorry, I'm too busy at the moment,' I said. 'Maybe in a few weeks?'

'If you wouldn't mind, Ms Ravel – Leander and I need to have a conversation.'

'Are you… are you sure?' Eva asked, standing, worried.

I shrugged to her, like I had no idea what this could possibly be about. 'I'm sure this misunderstanding can be easily resolved.'

'Ok, but I'm right outside if you need me.'

She left, closing the curtain behind her. The chief inspector sat in her chair.

'Leander,' he said sombrely, 'would you mind telling me, in as much detail as you can, your memory of what happened since our last meeting in this hospital?'

'Yeah it was a nightmare – I went to the supermarket to buy

satsumas – but they'd run out. It was a nightmare. So I had to go to a different supermarket, to buy satsumas. It took me ages.'

'We don't have time for this. There's nobody else here, Leander – nobody to perform for. There's nobody to quote to. Detective Constable Floris and Mr Cole are missing, there's blood, brain matter, semen, and a bullet hole in your living room. And, again, here I am asking you – how did you manage to escape?'

Dread tightened my muscles as I processed what he'd said – I sat upright, twisting the sheets in my fists.

'Francis is missing?' I asked.

'That is correct. Is this new information to you?'

My eye was punched in – by the fist of a boy from the canal – or by his memory – and I couldn't feel it, but I saw the same verdigris pigment as I'd seen in the punch – the most vibrant pigment, the most toxic pigment – and it was mixing with lead-white and lead-tin yellow and yellow ochre – and behind it, I saw the ultramarine of my myalgia – walled off by the opiates in me, waiting for their defences to weaken. And the verdigris-green was giving way to it – to the ultramarine glinting with minerals – glinting with calcite and pyrite, and augite and mica – and pouring out of my eye and across the room – and out of the hospital, into the sky, and towards Afghanistan – or to wherever Kimber first fired a gun – to the poppy fields and cliffs of lapis lazuli, away from the European bombs of the south – to where lapis stone was ground into pine resins and lye and sold as the most expensive colour in the world. Ultramarine! – a colour as holy as the heroin it was born beside, sister of the same soil – paint and painkiller – both claiming Kimber as their king – the king of the movie the west was watching! – the king of the heist the east was hosting! – the king that must be – the king that must be – the king that must be killed!

'He… he was fine,' I said, struggling to keep my mind in the present. 'We got out. That's my – what?'

'What do you mean you "got out"? Please, you need to tell me what you know if we're going to help them.'

'Then why didn't you tell me what you know?' I asked, angered by anxiety.

'I did, I am – we've barely begun speaking to each other.'

'Fuck you!' I shouted. 'Constable Floris is in no need of help. She's been dead for two days. And you not telling me what you know is the reason why Constable Floris is dead and why Francis is probably dead and why I basically died. I don't believe that you knew as little about Kimber as you claimed. I think you sent us into a trap. Why didn't you come and investigate when you didn't hear from us all night?'

'You are speaking very quickly, Leander. I need you to slow down. You appear to have witnessed something that has disturbed you. And I understand it might be difficult, but I need you to tell me what that was. Police officers were dispatched to your property as soon as it was noticed that Constable Floris had not checked back in. Unfortunately, her absence was not noticed by our team until yesterday morning, because we were engaged in a series of raids all night.'

'Her absence wasn't noticed?' I shouted. 'She wasn't noticed for ten hours?'

'This gang will disappear. We have had to push our small advantage as aggressively as possible – ever since you yourself invited us to the Rockway bar. This process was started by you, Leander. We are hunting for the man that you named to us in your phone call. You are the reason why we're having to act so fast. And if you had shared with us more information, then we might have known better how to proceed.'

'What information could I possibly have about a man I met for five minutes in the back of a pub? Compared to you? You've been investigating for years! You fucked up and you fucked us over, and you're trying to blame me for not sharing information? I thought that you were sending us into a trap because you didn't have enough evidence – and so you needed to catch Kimber doing something to us. But then you never showed up! So what – so I'm supposed to believe you're homicidally incompetent instead?'

'Are you telling me that Kimber was at your property? Who else was there? Leander, can you please tell me what happened in a straightforward manner?'

'While you were "engaged" in your night raids, the man you were raiding for was fucking me, at gunpoint – in the apartment that you sent us to, because any evidence at all could be useful, you said, and Dawn was his weak spot, you said, and you had very few other leads, you said – although apparently you had enough fucking leads to engage in raids all night – long after the good Constable Floris had stiffened and gone to join the big bumblebee in the sky – and I'd been injected with enough crystal meth to have a cardiac arrest in the middle of a snow storm.'

'I need you to keep your voice down, Leander. What you are telling me is upsetting.'

'Are you upset? I'm so so sorry. Is my experience upsetting for you?'

'I was speaking for you. You are upset. Understandably. From what I can understand, Kimber shot Constable Floris and attacked you… And I presume he attacked Mr Cole as well? That must have been upsetting. I can understand. But I need you to please fill in the rest of the picture for me, as difficult as it may be. How did you escape? Where did Kimber go?'

'Kimber overdosed on meth. We handcuffed him to the bed, and went outside. And I… I was distressed. So I ran away. And I don't know what happened next. Maybe Kimber woke up and Francis went back and got shot. I don't, I don't… he's not…'

My voice cut out. My right hand was shaking. Storytelling seemed pointless – my scepticism had no use. I felt anxious and spiteful and insane.

'There was only evidence of one gun shot at the property, so it is possible that Mr Cole is still alive,' he said. 'In your memory, was there only Kimber there? There would need to have been other men to help him take the constable and Mr Cole away.'

'Not that I saw. They could have been waiting outside. I left… in a hurry.'

'What is most important now is that… we see that Mr… that Francis —' The chief inspector paused and placed a consoling hand on my shoulder. 'Francis could be alive. Kimber kept you both alive before. As I have said, I believe that Mrs Cole was his weak spot – and you are both connected to her. To Dawn.'

'He said he wanted to be our father,' I said. 'He was psychotic – babbling daddy-issue delusions about angels and… he said I was an angel! Do you know how insulting that is? Angels are just fucking policemen – flying useless policemen, like pigeons are flying rats.'

He ignored me.

'He was… he filmed us,' I continued. 'There's a video of him… of me and Francis… he made me and Francis —' I stretched out my arm to gesture my meaning, unable to finished the sentence.

'He was filming you? There were camera parts discovered on the kitchen floor – but only parts, no memory card.'

'There were other videos on the memory card. They may be… they could be on a laptop belonging to a woman called Amélie – she works on the film that Eva works for.'

'This was at the Lux Studios? I have two statements about what happened there from Ms Eva Ravel and Ms Iris Vasari – I know that you appeared there around seven in the morning, and were described as distressed, and then after some… acting – you left suddenly and were followed by car to Mr Cole's house where Ms Ravel and Ms Vasari found you unconscious on the doorstep. Is that correct?'

'I have no idea if that's correct. I was unconscious. But you should check whether the contents of that memory card are on Amélie's laptop.'

'So you're telling me that you managed to take away the memory card?' he asked. 'And what happened to it?'

'I don't remember – I was too high by then. I couldn't see properly. Maybe I imagined it. But you should check her laptop – there were other videos of other… people. I was watching them. Maybe clues.'

He patted my shoulder. 'I will send an officer to follow up on your information immediately. Thank you for cooperating with me, Leander. I know that you've… been through a tough time. But we need to keep working together. You are a resourceful young man. You've managed to get out of… difficult situations.'

'I don't think I got out of anything. I don't think Francis got out of anything.'

The creams and greys of the cubicle were becoming hideous. I was responsible for Francis' suffering, or death – and this knowledge gave my wounds claws – and they burrowed into my flesh until my sweat was so hot that it simmered.

'My point is that you… have helped us get further with our operation than anyone else,' he continued. 'And I admit, there have been significant shortcomings – but this is still a very time-sensitive investigation. We must find Kimber. And we want to find Francis. So… we need you to – to keep alert.'

'What do you mean alert?' I asked. 'Is that a euphemism? You mean you want to me to walk into more traps?'

'You've been through a lot. But you have a different approach to what the police are capable of, and so —'

'You want me to be bait again?' I shouted. 'Don't you have witnesses, and CCTV footage, and tips and data and investigators? I'm not going to help you do anything. I want – I don't… I… I just want to know what's happened to Francis. What about Constable Floris? Don't you care? She has a – she had a son called Oscar! She was… kind to me… I can't do anything else for you.'

I was nearly in tears. There were no ideas in my head – just a loud stupor, more nullifying than darkness or silence – I despised my own brain, I despised my own voice.

'I don't entirely believe that, I'm afraid,' he said with a sudden sternness to his tone. 'It's too late for you to hide behind innocence. The loss of Constable Floris is a… great loss, but we must focus on preventing other losses. You are more street-wise than you want me to think you are. You could be much more helpful than you're being.'

'I can't believe you just said that,' I spat – and in my anger, my synaesthesia spiked – the mouthwash-coloured lights of the ceiling swooped into the taste of mouthwash, and my blood cooled towards phlegm the same lurid yellow as Sanam's voice. 'I know the police are supposed to be the lowest error of western civilisation but I didn't realise that you were this sadistic.'

He took his hand off my shoulder. 'Let me summarise your situation in another way, then. Yesterday, you stole a police car and crashed it into public property while under the influence of Class A drugs. You have also fled two crime scenes now, and been involved in two deaths in as many days. If these… unfortunate facts are going to be interpreted in a positive way, in a way that diminishes your responsibility – then you are going to have to help us, Leander, however you can. Otherwise, we might reach a less favourable interpretation of these facts – which in less urgent circumstances would unquestionably require me to arrest you right now.'

'So. You're blackmailing a boy who just had a heart attack into being bait for his rapist?'

'I'm offering leniency in exchange for you doing whatever you were going to do anyway. I just ask that you tell me what you're doing when you do it. And to that end – I want you to use this phone.'

He dropped a brick phone into my lap. I looked at it listlessly.

'We are pursuing every lead that we have,' he said, quieter, but still stern. 'With as much haste as we can – in order to find these people. And I understand that you are reluctant to… share information, or really to do anything for me. But we both know that you aren't just a damsel in distress. You've escaped twice now. If you have any insights, or if you see anything or find anything out… I want you to ring the number in the contact book – or text it – and you'll get through to me. That's all I'm asking.'

'What's the… what?' I tried to reply, staggered by his audacity. 'And even if… How can I know that your… interpretation of my facts would stay favourable after I helped you?'

'I give you my word, Leander. I know the real interpretation – you are caught up in something beyond your control and you have nothing to do with it. And I want what you want. I want to catch the people that did this to you.'

'I want Francis.'

'That's our priority too. I'm going to leave you now – but as I said, any information that you remember, any sudden flash of insight – you ring me. The number is saved as "X" in the address book. Do we have a deal?'

He stood up to leave. Again I saw a lavender cloud forming above him – though now its fragrance was sick – like a pouch of dried lavender leaves left in a drawer for a decade, among wills and stale medicines – and again the cloud took on the shape of a lemur – but its tail had been bitten off in a fight.

'Well you certainly know how to charm a dying man,' I said, trying to calm myself into irony. 'Your bedside manner has removed me from the trauma of my past few days. I feel cured.'

'You're not a dying man, Leander. I've never seen someone cling to life so tightly. I'm looking forward to your phone call.'

He nodded in farewell and left. The lavender lemur dissolved. I felt like a rubber band stretched across a street, too tense to snap.

There was a struggle beyond the curtain. Quickly, I unpeeled the tape over the needle in my wrist – but before I could extract it, a nurse slapped my hand away. Eva stumbled in after her, her hand stretched forwards too.

'No, this stays in,' the nurse said. 'Don't be stupid.'

'It's coming out,' I said. 'I have to leave.'

'You can't leave – there's no way you're leaving.'

'I'm signing myself out,' I said. 'I'm not staying.'

'Why not?'

'I've had enough hospital. I'm leaving.'

'Listen to your body,' the nurse pleaded, gripping my wrist with her other hand. 'Your body needs you to stay here.'

'I listened to my body for twenty years – and it was a mistake!' I said, still angered by the chief inspector. 'I had no friends and I did nothing. I lay on my back for weeks, I exercised and I ate well, but I never got better. My pain got worse. I've been through all the diagnoses – psychological, physiological, psychosomatic, whatever. All useless! I'm not at home in my own body. So I've learned to stop listening to it – and now I have friends, I have desires and delights. My body was holding me back. There's a late Yeats poem that everyone quotes where he calls his body "a tattered coat upon a stick", and says he's "fastened to a dying animal" – but his hatred of old age feeds off a nostalgia for his youth. And I never got to have a youth – I never got to feel virile and young and immortal – I've always been fastened to a dying animal, I've always been a tattered coat upon a stick. And I'm bored of it. I'm bored being an incurable wound. I'm bored of being unhappy. There's no name for what's wrong with me and that's part of the torture – but there are ways of adapting to torture. I've come to understand myself in terms of revenge. And that's where my happiness waits for me – in revenge on my body.'

'This is you happy?' the nurse asked, gesturing at the life-support machines around me.

'No,' I said. 'And this environment is precisely why. I can wallow in my injuries elsewhere – staying at hospital hurts me more than leaving. I know this from experience.'

'Where are you going to go?'

'Um…' I looked to Eva with a fake smile, trying to pass off my anger as joke. 'Does your sofa need any more of my blood?'

She groaned. 'Yeah you can stay with me, but I don't understand why you insist on resisting recovery.'

'I will recover quicker out of here… I can't heal in a cage.'

I reached to extract the needle in my wrist; again the nurse stopped me – but then she slid it out herself, shaking her head.

'Complaining about not having a youth is just youth,' she said. 'You're being stupid.'

My retort was halted by the scent of coconut oil. I closed my eyes and the scent remained in a rumour – fading into confusion. I opened my eyes and there were tears in them.

'What are you thinking?' Eva asked.

'Francis,' I said. 'I could remember his pillow…'

She began crying. Released from the drip, I pulled back my sheet and lowered myself from the bed. Unused to being upright, I nearly fell. Standing felt like floating; the pain-cancelling chemicals parading through my circulatory system were of a far higher quality than I was accustomed to – they made my nerves into mandolins.

'Where are my clothes?' I asked.

'They weren't really clothes you were wearing – but I took them back to mine,' Eva said, dabbing away her tears. 'But I have your coat and… maybe just keep on these trousers.'

She dressed me in my fake fur coat, dried since it had followed me into the canal. Its stab wound lined up with my own. I had barely any thoughts.

'Is it true what you just said?' she whispered. 'About… about being ill for your whole…?'

'Yeah – I've had to grieve for a whole life I've already lost – because I can never have it. No one really knows what my disease is – even though it's quite common. Maybe it's a mutated polio virus that attacks the brain instead of the spine – or maybe it's an autoimmune thing or… I dunno. I just know it's draining me away into a ghost stuck inside a body-shaped hell.'

'That's… horrible.' She was crying again. 'I didn't know. You never… Because you look – you look tired, but not – and… and they can't help you?'

'No, in England we're fucked – cos the government guidelines on my disease were written by a quack psychiatrist who thinks that all we need is a little bit of exercise and a little bit of positive thinking – and then our agony will just go away. Imagine telling that to someone with any other autoimmune disease. They haven't cured anyone, obviously – but they have driven thousands of teenagers to suicide.'

'How… is that allowed?'

'Because it's an invisible illness.'

The nurse returned with a self-release form. I smiled in apology as I signed it. She gave me two orange pots of medications and told me to take one from each a day. I nodded. She left.

'But… does Francis know?' Eva whispered, still shocked.

'I can't… I… don't ask me that,' I said. 'I shouldn't have told you. I hate people knowing I'm ill. I told Iris for some reason. But Francis… he'd… there might not be any chance anymore anyway. But… even if he isn't… if he's still… I can't tell him. It would drain him and he'd resent me.'

'That's ridiculous. He's in love with you.'

'I dunno. It's happened before.'

'With who?'

I said nothing. I was overwhelmed by these conversations – with the nurse, with Sanam, with Eva. I was frail. Eva hugged me. I leant into her, trying to shake the words out of my head so I could regain some clarity. But this movement filled my blood with grit. My mind narrowed. I have never had clarity. But in the ambiguity of Francis' fate, my pain was displaced into ambition – to regain him, or avenge him.

3.

Leaning on Eva, I floated out of the ward – down the glass lift, across the glass lobby, and out into the wider air of the afternoon. My muscles whirled, but my mind had flattened into a mantra – find Francis, find Francis – superseding everything else.

Eva hailed a cab and helped me inside. My paper legs were glad to leave the wind.

But as she said her address, I interrupted. 'No, can we go to Francis' house? Please. I want to check.'

'I've been back twice… he's not answering his phone.'

'I left something there,' I said. 'Outside. And let's just check for him again anyway.'

She acquiesced and gave the driver his address. I was restless in the back seat, uncomfortable lying in her lap, uncomfortable sitting up – simultaneously dulled and stimulated by the hospital painkillers. Eventually I stretched out my feet alongside hers, and reclined diagonally across the seats, my head cushioned by my collar into the side of my door. So constrained, I fidgeted less, and closed my eyes.

'So… what did the policeman want?' asked Eva. 'What did everyone want? Can you give me the plot summary? And spare me the one-liners.'

'My sister and I were abandoned in a forest by our stepmother and we came across a house made of gingerbread and inside was an old woman who looked like our stepmother in disguise begging us to cook her in an oven but we refused, so instead we swung in her birdcage until she had fed us well enough for us to grant her request. When we had cooked her, we ate her, and later we converted the birdcage into a boat to float down the river out of the forest and into the city. My sister found love and I found melancholy. And then I got into this taxi.'

'I said no jokes.'

'You said no one-liners.'

'Ok, no jokes either.'

'Francis' mum seduced a violent man and then she died, which made him more violent – and so he ambushed me and Francis in my flat and injected me with meth and raped me, and eventually we overpowered him and I fled, but Francis got re-captured and the violent man escaped. So I'm probably also a hunted man. The police were useless.'

'I… don't know what to say,' Eva said, her voice quivering like she was trying not to laugh as much as not to cry. 'I preferred the first story. Are you… you're obviously not ok, but how do you… feel? About the whole thing?'

'I just need to know where Francis is. I don't care about what happened to me, I've been on worse dates – I already knew uppers weren't chic. But I can't finish forming an opinion until I can be with Francis.'

'I know. I'm not… I just can't live knowing that the last thing he can think about me is showing that fucking video at Iris' exhibition. It was so childish. I hate who I was for that whole drama. You two made me crazy. But it's my fault, it's not yours – I chose to hurt him. And now that might be the last thing I did to him… I hate it.' She was crying again.

'There's no point thinking about it until we know what happened,' I said. 'Tell me something else… tell me about my starring role in your film. How was my performance? Did you enjoy acting with me?'

Eva sniffed into a laugh. 'Other than you charging off in a

stolen police car and then dying – you were very easy to work with. Iris loved your energy, she was almost heartless about it – though that's just how she deals with stress – she sounds much more cruel than she is – but she said it's the best breakdown she's ever filmed. She kept watching back the footage of you running away. And she was shooting you passed out on the doorstep in the snow. It's beautiful.'

'What about our actual scene?' I asked. 'Before the three Ringos showed up. Did they like me?'

'They wished we'd gone on all day. Amélie kept saying "he's perfect, he's perfect," even after we thought you might never regain consciousness. It's the best scene in the film. I mean Iris is a genius – but she needed someone who could really howl.'

'So don't you want to invite me back?'

She laughed. 'Amélie was pushing for you to be given more to do, but Iris can't just change the film she's planned – and we've already shot half of it.'

'So? I can be in the second half.'

'That's what I said. But we've booked stages and locations and planned scenes already, we've got actors and extras and advertisers lined up – Amélie is adaptable but Iris is stubborn – she hates changing her plans, even when it would be good for her. And as she has pointed out – you're unknown. So basically – we need you but we can't have you.'

'No…' I said slowly. 'What you're saying is I have to become known. That's easy.'

I turned my face to look out of the window – and saw a procession of wagons coming the other way, loaded with stage sets painted the colours of a warmer climate. The wagons were being dragged by giant grey-green pigeons, their wings clipped, their beaks muzzled – and on them rode little beggar girls, too small for the reins, singing songs so sweet that they seemed somehow despairing. They were part of a troupe of actors, perhaps – that had mastered illusion so completely that their plays had the energy of nightmares – romances between beasts and spirits, hyenas and women, rivers and children – that combined slapstick with elegy and pastoral with porn. Perhaps these actors did magic tricks, too – and turned their audiences into rats, but never turned them back – and had no eyes – and had bones made of the songs the girls were singing – or were even entirely made of songs, and make-up, and masks, and not flesh at all. Their performances sometimes started riots, perhaps, and lasted weeks – or were over in a few minutes, after which none of the spectators could remember their childhoods. A girl threw a ticket at me as she passed – but it hit the glass and blew away.

'And you have to convince Iris you're worth the trouble,' Eva said, dispelling the dream.

'But she secretly thinks I'd be good?' I asked.

'Directors don't usually change their idea of a film in the middle of a shoot.'

'Of course they do. That's how all films are made. And I'm an exception. Your shoot wasn't going well. You invited me. You need something more unpredictable – I can provide that. I just have to convince Iris that I can bring value to her film both on-screen and off.'

'I'd be happy to watch you try,' she said. 'But you have everything else to deal with. You need to rest. You need to… I don't know. Maybe you do need a distraction. Iris does want to talk to you. She took a good photo of you by the way – do you remember doing that? In her studio – your shoot, smiling with your eye bruised shut. I told her to email the best one to you, I thought it'd cheer you up.'

She took her phone out of her handbag and selected an image to show me. In it, I posed before a blank wall – topless, winking, black-eyed and impish. Iris had succeeded in capturing a heightened version of the me I most often pretended to be. This me loved pain above myself – my bruises were my delight, and my confidence came from the damage.

'She is good at that, isn't she?' I said in awe. 'That's the best picture anyone's ever taken of me. I love it. But I don't have a phone that can get emails anymore – I've got a snitch phone now.' I took it out and waved it at Eva with a sarcastic cheer. 'The policeman gave it to me… I don't even know what I'm supposed to do with it. I should just send him emoticons and ignore him when he rings me back.'

Eva examined the tiny screen with curiosity. 'God, it can't even count calories. It has a very old-school crack-dealer aesthetic.'

'I know, the police probably confiscate them all the time. Shame they've wiped the contacts – we could have bought ourselves the finest crack in London.'

She handed it back. 'I think it's for the best that you can't access crack just yet – while you're still recovering.'

'Who said I couldn't? Just not the finest crack. I can make-do with mediocrity.'

'Wouldn't that go against your whole elitist ethos?' she asked. 'Aren't you supposed to be some kind of demi-god, watching humans suffer from your hammock? Demi-gods don't settle for mediocre crack.'

'How did you develop such a flattering conception of me?'

'I'm just repeating what you told me.'

'When?'

'When you came back to mine,' she said. 'On Tuesday. When this all began. You made me look up the definition of Epicureanism.'

'I'm so embarrassing,' I smiled. 'But you were supposed to be drunk. You're not allowed to pay attention to the things I say.'

'I'm not going to forget any of it. It was fun. Even though you were stealing Francis away behind the scenes – and you were the reason I was miserable. It was fun. It's a better plot twist than anything Iris has come up with.'

'Plots twists are so bourgeois,' I said. 'You did what you did and I did what I did because of desire. It wasn't actually a surprise. Everything should happen with a sense of inevitability. I like doom. Not just conflict or hope or transformation – I want doom.'

'You are kind of a doom,' she laughed.

'Not anymore, I'm a changed man.'

'Since when?'

'Since I had a vision of myself dead in the snow.'

'That actually happened.'

The taxi had come to Wandsworth Bridge. The Thames had turned the colour of skinned seals – and was as elusive and fat as a seal after yesterday's snow – though the snow had been too alien to last long in autumn, so the sky was only spitting now – and I thought of crossing the same bridge with Dawn a few days ago – when the sun had flashed in my eyes and I'd had the sudden urge to injure her – and, in a kind of delirium, I'd obeyed the urge.

'But I have to unfreeze myself somehow,' I said. 'I've been in an airlock for too long. I need to let my sense of self become co-dependant, so that other people can affect me, otherwise I will always just be in the snow, outside. I want to be… I dunno. I'm not sure yet.'

'You should want to feel safe. I don't feel safe. I don't want to end up like Francis…'

She had tried to be jokingly callous – but her last sentence tripped in her throat, and tears returned to her eyes. I stroked her thigh with the back of my hand.

'Humour is ok,' I said. 'Everyone needs something terrible to happen to them at least once in their lives – to make them interesting. Disaster will improve him.'

'Don't talk like that,' she said, crying. 'We don't even know if… we don't know what's happened to him.'

'Fine, tell me about… tell me how you met him. Give me a living memory.'

'I met him on a shoot,' she sniffed. 'It was on a beach in

Brighton. Nearly two years ago. It was very cold. I had to get the train there at 5 a.m. And I can't remember what the concept was but it was really basic, like forbidden love during wartime or some shit. And there was a massive team. I think it was for… I don't remember. It was a massive budget – and there was all these different archetypes – like I was the up and coming actress – so stupid. And when we took a break, I was tired so I walked down the beach, around sunrise, it was still pretty dark, and I was dreaming of turning the sea into coffee and swimming in it. I don't think I'd had sex in like eighty-five years. And Francis was sitting on a wall ahead of me. And he had loads of make up on – like a heroic bruise to look like he'd come back from the war with conveniently handsome injuries. Like yours. And he was so cocky. He was singing to himself and when he saw me he sang even louder and he kept eye contact with me when he stood up and reached out his arms – and made me dance with him when he was singing. And he chatted me up. I said I didn't know anyone on the shoot and he said he did but they were all shit so it was good that I'd come away to keep him company. He was the first model I met who didn't make me long for his euthanasia – I mean, he still had the arrested development you get with all pretty straight men – or straight-seeming, whatever – but he was actually funny, and not just gormlessly boyish like the other guys there – and they were from a different agency anyway, called like Tomorrow Is Another Day, though it should have been called White Mediocrity because I've never been more underwhelmed – but Francis was actually attractive, and he made me laugh – he probably made me fall in love with him right there – and I think I told him, I wasn't even trying to be coy, I told him I'd been having more sex on screen than in real life – and he said we should change that. And the shoot went on till about four – and afterwards we were all supposed to take the same train back, but him and me stayed behind and walked around Brighton, up the little hill-streets – and we fucked in the toilets of a Cornish pasty shop. It was fun. It was the opposite of the glamorous lies of the shoot. And then he messaged me loads – and we started hanging out.'

'What was he singing?'

'I have no idea. Some Sixties song. He has a terrible voice – but that made me like him more. And he had this cocky smile when he was singing – waving his head around, looking at me with this cocky smile, like he knew how easy it would be to make me like him.'

'He's never sung to me,' I said indignantly.

She smiled. 'He's less self-confident around you. He was all ego till you showed up. Maybe he never loved me.'

I wanted to say that Francis was just a fantasy, like any model – to be exploited for his youth and height and symmetry – and preyed upon, just as he was preyed upon by the older men of his industry who'd been poisoned into resentment by the illusions they themselves were spinning – I wanted to say that Francis was an impossible body – to be starved, drained, and spat out once his few years of usefulness were over – a replaceable part in an endless production line – and I wanted to say this, but I couldn't, because I didn't believe it anymore. Or, I still believed this – but I also believed something else – something about myself, too, perhaps – that Francis was no longer simply a screen for me to project onto – that the screen had rebelled and become a projector too – while the projector, me, had become a screen – and so I'd been altered.

The taxi had stopped – we were back at Francis' doorstep. I got out, supressing a smile – because Francis had indeed loved her, or thought he had – but did no longer, since I'd made him into someone else. He'd been altered as much as me. But my sense of triumph was swiftly dispelled by the knowledge of his absence. My muscles felt like whisked egg whites.

'Aren't you coming in?' I asked.

'I thought you wanted to pick something up?' she said. 'He's not in. There's no point.'

I swayed towards the hedge and found beneath it the camera I'd stolen from Iris. But among the leaves were thorns – and on one of the thorns was the impaled corpse of a goldfinch.

I recoiled – from behind me, a larger bird with grey and white plumage hopped out – unafraid, its eyes masked in black. I thought of the crow that had killed a squirrel on our car – and wondered whether it had been inspired by this shrike – this butcher bird, impossibly rare, perhaps the only one in London this autumn. Maybe it had strayed here from Wandsworth Common, drawn to the aftertaste of my heart attack.

The shrike disappeared – and I couldn't be sure it had ever been there – but as I stood up, a jab of orange crossed my blood-brain barrier, like I'd snorted a line of paprika – and 'shrike, shrike, shrike', repeated after it around my head.

I shivered to the front door and rang the bell, twitching as the sound brought back memories of dissolving here. Nobody answered.

Eva beckoned to me from the taxi, but I refused to fail again. So I picked up the brick that held the gate open and walked round the house to the lane beside it. I struck the utility room window with the brick until the glass shattered and the frame bent inwards. Now unlatched, I swung the window open and jumped up to it to pull myself in. No alarm went off. I vomited from the exertion – my stomach wailed and grew fangs – but still I dragged my legs over the washing machine, and dropped onto the floor. The smell of washing powder overcame the vomit – and I was pulled into a memory – of Francis hugging me on Dawn's bed at gunpoint, my face in his chest. And this association brought with it the scent of gunpowder – the same as the phosphoric residue left in the air by fireworks – not quite metallic, not quite nostalgic, not wintry, but nearly all three. I forced myself to stand. The scent dispersed. I limped into the corridor and opened the front door from the inside.

Eva paid the driver in uncounted notes and leapt out and ran towards me.

'What did you just do?' she shouted.

'I did what I should have done ages ago. I broke in.'

'You're fucking bleeding – you just ripped your stitches open!'

'Whatever, we have a house now.'

'Did you – how are we going to…' She was too shocked to form sentences.

'It's fine,' I said. 'We can fix the window later. I saw a shrike! Come inside. I needed some stuff.'

'What? Is that Iris' camera?'

I removed the memory card from the camera and put it in my coat pocket – and then hung the camera around Eva's neck.

'Yes,' I smiled. 'And you need to give it back to her.'

She closed the front door. 'I can't believe you just broke in.'

'I try to violate every space I enter,' I said. 'Something to do with not having a home of my own.'

'What are you talking about?'

'I dunno. Come upstairs.'

We glanced in passing at the kitchen, and both had the same memory – of Eva's scorned-woman performance a few days ago – when she'd hurled cutlery at me before fleeing with bleeding wrists.

'Quite a lot has changed since we were last here,' she said dryly.

Walking upwards sent shocks across my ribcage – I bent into the pain, tackling myself, tasting grapefruit, as a grapefruit-pink filter passed over my eyes. My muscles were refilling with ultramarine. I shoved Francis' door open with my shoulder.

'We were enemies and now we are allies,' I said grandly, trying to distract myself.

'Not really,' she said, following me inside. 'It was never that equal. I lost Francis and now you've lost him. But it's not neat.'

'So… we should stop looking for patterns and just do heroin.'

I fell onto my knees and crawled around Francis' blood-stained bed towards Dawn's handbag. Eva stopped.

'Is that why you broke in?' she asked, disgusted by this evidence of my addiction.

'It's only partly why. And don't moralise at me. You try having scarab beetles inside your intestines your whole life – you would kill for a temporary cure.'

The topmost fold of foil still had a fat trail of residue left from the last time I'd used it. I took out a pipe and a lighter, perched on the bed, hunched, and heated the remaining heroin resin – to breathe in the familiar tainted fume until my stomach hushed.

I remembered the taste of the rust of the Rockway bathroom tap, drunk from as Dawn died and the door was kicked in – but this taste slipped sideways, invigorating the other hospital opiates in my blood – towards a bitterness similar to grapefruit – but closer to grape seed. I closed my eyes to think in one colour – the thin white green of a grape. And after three inhalations, I was restored.

Eva lay on Francis' side of the bed.

'Aren't you going to offer me some?' she asked.

I passed her the lighter and the foil.

'I kind of hoped there would be someone waiting for me here,' I said.

'You mean Francis?' she asked, heating her own dose.

'No, some henchman. I thought I'd be abducted. That would make life a lot easier.'

'What are you talking about? How would that be easier?'

She put aside the foil and leaned over to kiss me. Our lips shared the taste of tar. I lowered alongside her and let her move over me as her hands moved under my coat. A cello string began plucking in my head. I felt like I had someone else's body. I unbuttoned her jacket, encouraged by her smile – but turned my head away – into Francis' pillow, into the scent of his coconut oil.

She kissed me. 'What?'

'I… don't want to,' I said.

'But this is… isn't this exactly the kind of perverse shit you like? We're in Francis' bed…'

'I know but…'

'Your paper trousers aren't hiding anything.'

'Yeah but… I can't.'

I tried to roll away from her, but she held me down.

'Isn't this why we came here?' she asked.

'Yeah, it was, but —' I kissed her slowly and sat up under her. 'I dunno.'

'Don't tell you me you've developed a conscience.'

'No – I'm attracted to you,' I said, pulling off my trousers in proof. 'But my will is stronger than… My body is my enemy. I have to…'

I didn't finish my statement, perhaps because I didn't have a statement to finish – and instead took a pair of trousers out of Francis' drawer and dressed in them. Grapefruit-pink and grape-red and grape-green marbled around each other in front of me in a curtain, dizzying me. I managed to find two grey sweatshirts as well and a pair of socks and black boots.

Eva stood up, swaying between anger and distress – and rushed into the bathroom. She slammed open the toilet and vomited – her concerns soon erased by the heroin's nausea. The plucking of the string was fading into the sound of rustling wheat.

I picked up Dawn's handbag and crept away – down the stairs, out of the front door, across the road to the car. It answered to the keys in her bag. Bubbles of grape juice rose up my spine, cold, tingling like nettles – until I imagined the taste of nettles too, boiling in water that was somehow still cold. I climbed into the car and my senses jolted, remembering my last drive in it, with Francis – roughly pulling my seatbelt across me as we fled the Rockway. I shuddered – thinking of the shrike and the crow.

I was the driver now, though this journey wasn't really my own decision – and I drove away, back to where I had to go.

4.

As I neared the Rockway, my thoughts became septic. To find Francis, I had to catch Kimber – and to catch Kimber, I had to summon all the poison in me to the surface until it seethed. All the predatory games that I'd played in rage at my own broken body, all my lusts, lies, sleights, tricks – all these had been rehearsals for this seduction. Perhaps I could atone for the pain I'd passed on to others, by making Kimber my last victim.

What were his weaknesses?

His failing sanity. His grief. And – his curiosity about me.

Had I not told Iris – seducing bi-curious straight boys was my speciality? And had a stripper not once told me – there's a difference between seduction and creating a desire to fuck? Both are manipulations of energy – but seduction is more multi-purpose, and that was what was needed here.

I had to arouse Kimber enough for him to make a mistake. It would be a mistake for him to agree to play a game on my terms. It would be a mistake for him to get as high as he'd been yesterday. Ultimately, I needed to return him to the state he'd been in on meth – vulnerable, guilty, obsessed with family and fatherhood – and then, perhaps, I could get him to take me to Francis.

But before then – sex, like all good advertising, had to stay subliminal.

Though first I had to find him – and the only place I knew to start looking was at the Rockway.

I got out of the car and floated across the street. The same steroidal bouncer guarded the door as before.

'You're mad coming back here lad,' he said.

'Your boss would have found me anyway.'

He cuffed my collar exactly as he had three nights ago and pulled me into the Rockway's interior.

'He's not looking to find no one,' he said.

'Wait – is he here?' I asked.

He pushed me against the wall and patted me down, searching each pocket before searching Dawn's handbag.

'You'll wish he weren't,' he said.

'I thought I'd have to make you summon him from somewhere,' I said, with the confidence of opiates in my blood. 'This is much easier.'

He grunted in reply, and escorted me towards the bar. We passed a booth in which two of my canal-side attackers were sitting, their faces still mottled by our meeting. I waved enthusiastically – they jumped up. The bouncer shook his head at them and they did not approach.

'You're a dead man,' he said.

'I've died enough times for one week, I think. I've come to offer my services.'

'What's they going to be then?'

'That's for Kimber to learn,' I said.

There was no money or guns on any tables this time, but somehow the Rockway felt even more alien than before. The atmosphere had thickened, or darkened – like the empire that was run from here had begun to corrupt it – into a hostile epicentre, haunted by spirits of the vengeful dead.

He pushed me down the corridor towards the toilets. 'He's gonna eat you alive.'

I walked, unworried, into the scent of stale ale and urine – and knocked on the ladies' door. 'It's Leander,' I said. 'I'm alone.'

'Enter.'

I stepped sideways into the gloom. Quickly the door shut behind me. Kimber was pacing in a circle, illuminated only by the bulb above the sink. He had washed and groomed, and dressed in a pressed maroon suit. His body had none of the focus of our last meeting – he seemed diffuse. He looked briefly at me and then returned his gaze to the space beneath the hand-dryer where Dawn had died, as though imagining her body there still. His eyes lacked the metaphysical fervour of his meth personality, but his pacing suggested he had not regained full control of himself.

'Hi Daddy,' I said, smiling. 'I hoped you'd be harder to find. Isn't this –' I gestured around the bathroom '– a little over-obvious?'

'Leander, welcome back. You… surprise me. I did not expect you to be so… buoyant.'

He sounded like he couldn't yet accept that I was in the same room as him. The sandalwood in his voice had soothed from an oil to a lather. And there was a flicker of another uncertainty in it, too, which I read as desire – or shame at desire, or shame at a sexual past far from his present mood. I crossed the room to sit beneath the sink, in the posture he'd discovered me in after Dawn overdosed. He stopped and stood against the dryer with his hands behind his back. I noticed the lump on the side of his head where I'd struck him with the bottle. It matched the wound I'd given Dawn.

'Why should I not be buoyant?' I asked eventually. 'You think an hour or two of unsolicited penetration is going to unsettle me? It was vanilla by my standards. I've been tortured by my own body for ten years – anything else is fun in comparison. I'm only worried that you don't remember all of it – how is your head?'

He lifted a hand to stroke the swelling in his skull. 'I've never been in this much pain before,' he smiled. 'On the inside and the outside of my head – you've done more damage than my competitors have managed in decades. It's impressive.'

'Being the sole agent of chaos is so boring,' I said, trying to imitate his speech patterns. 'I've been unstimulated all my life. And then you came along with your "canal-side initiation", and your job offer – and I decided to make a bid for your attention.'

Kimber patted his head wound as he worked out how to reply. 'My attention has never been less acute. I can think only of one woman... And you're not even an echo of her. You don't understand what you took from me.'

He sounded exhausted.

'Do you have to claim I took anything?' I asked. 'Now that we've calmed down, can't we agree that the only person to blame was Dawn? We should be each other's way of remembering her. I needed a father figure, you need a son – and you've already articulated this, in more intoxicated terms... but our dynamic remains the same. We are compatible. And that should be cherished.'

'That is... an unexpected angle,' he said. 'How do you stay amused? You come to me at my most abandoned. But you are the reason why I have been abandoned.'

'I didn't think you'd be high enough to come here,' I said. 'I thought I'd have to follow a trail.'

'My dear, I am invisible when I need to be. The police raided a few times. But everyone else has dispersed. I stay because I require rituals. This is my wife's last resting place. I came here to mourn, although there is no body to mourn – her son has committed her to ash. And he cannot be forgiven for that.'

'That's partly what I needed to talk to you about,' I said. 'The other son.'

'Only partly?' he asked, his tone ironic for the first time. 'It was cruel of you to leave Francis to my employees.'

'Possibly too cruel,' I said. 'While I think you deserved your concussion, I don't think Francis deserved his… abduction, or whatever you've put him through.'

'I haven't yet had the heart to punish him. But… there have to be repercussions. It is strange that you thought it wise to come here.'

'Is it?' I asked, with a bolder sarcasm. 'Turning up before you found me puts me at an advantage. I need your help; you need my help. Yesterday we helped each other emotionally. Today, we need to help each other economically.'

Kimber wiped his mouth with his sleeve, unsure how to answer. 'You have… nothing,' he said at last. 'You have walked into your tomb.'

I grinned. 'I have a gift for you. A token of goodwill.'

I removed the memory card from my pocket and held it out to him. He stepped towards me and took it with an eyebrow raised – and his touch passed into the taste of a banana-like ester in my mind – and then into the colour of an unripe banana's skin. Similarly, my touch evoked a change in his posture – as his skin remembered our intimacy.

I knew his resolve could be loosened. He took out a camera from his pocket, inserted the card, and stepped back to the dryer to study the footage.

'You deleted nothing?' he asked.

'Why would I?'

'You… have preserved your video,' he said, pressing play and releasing Francis' screams from the camera's speaker.

'Of course.'

'This could have been a bargaining chip. You should have demanded something for it.'

'Yes, but I didn't. I need you to trust me – and so I need you to have a little bit more power over me. And that's what this is.'

'But, my dear, you have allowed me this power. As my wife warned me – you want people to think they are driving you, when you are being driven to where you want. I do not trust this gift.'

'Well I made copies.'

'I'm not sure you did. You like high-risk gambles. That is not appealing in a business partner.'

He put the camera in his pocket.

I closed my eyes to think of a reply – and was immediately among the castles that I often saw on heroin – the sky-bridges and buttresses that built themselves out of nothing – and tessellated into each other to form parapets and battlements and dungeons and domes. Neither humanity nor its physics were present in this city – it was living alabaster, without foundation or finish – immortal – until, one evening, say, a fireball appears from behind the stars, and falls – annihilating the air.

'Let me be more appealing, then,' I said. 'I have the personal number of the detective chief inspector who heads the task force currently hunting for you. I propose to entrap him and kill him. Would that quell your suspicions? My allegiance is not to the police.'

'I expect not. But how would that prove your allegiance to me?'

'I brought this task force to your doorstep. But I have not revealed your identity to them – yet. They want me to, and that's why they have given me this.' I slowly drew the snitch phone from my pocket and held it up for him in my palm. 'I am proposing myself as bait.'

Kimber looked at the phone and then at me – as though in fresh disbelief that I was even here, speaking to him so playfully, so unmarked by the violence he'd inflicted upon me. My lack of fear intrigued him. His body language was changing – his muscles tensing in a different way – no longer in suspicion, but in the alertness that precedes arousal.

'They have other evidence,' he said. 'Killing him will stop nothing.'

'Killing him would be a start.' I said, adjusting my position beneath the sink, with my hand still held out – cricking my neck to seem bored of this conversation, convinced that it was going to go my way. 'We would then need to provide a different suspect… But I shall present my proposals in stages, to protect myself – until you trust me.'

'This is all rather rococo, don't you think?' he said, slipping into the eastern European accent he'd had at the height of his intoxication. 'I prefer simplicity. For instance, I kill you, I disappear. No baiting, no double-crossing, no wasting of time.'

'Killing me now would be the waste of time,' I said. 'You're welcome to do so. But it would be dull. As Chekhov points out in every short story – life is difficult and uninteresting, and only docile cart-horses put up with it for long. But life does not have to be uninteresting today. You don't know how much the police know. So why waste an opportunity to mislead them? Let me prove my worth.'

I held his gaze. He said nothing, but I could tell his will was weakening. He was ready to be seduced – not sexually, necessarily, but emotionally – enough to let me take him on a dance…

'I know you want to see what I can do,' I said. 'You've been the master too long. You know how to conduct and control. Let me try. Let me surprise you. And then you can shoot me as many times as you want.'

He looked away – but then took the phone from my hand, against his better judgement, and slowly reviewed its menus.

'How do I know that this number can call who you say it can call?' he asked.

But his words were just formalities now – he was letting his reason be overruled.

'Who else could it be?' I asked. 'I'll set him a test if you want. He needs to hear my voice, though, if we're going to lure him somewhere – we can't just text him.'

'How can a policeman prove he's a policeman?'

'I can ask him about "The Rockstar",' I said sweetly.

Kimber stiffened – finally appreciating that I had more hooks in him than he'd thought.

'Is that why you chose to buy a bar called the Rockway?' I pushed. 'You could have gone anywhere in London. But you couldn't resist a bit of wordplay…'

'All right…' he said. 'Perhaps you can… be useful. Provide me with the name of a rat and I shall allow you to play your game.'

He passed me back the phone. His finger stayed on mine.

This was the end of our foreplay. And now that I knew he'd give in, it was time for a provocation. I selected my contact and called it on speakerphone. In four rings it was answered.

'Yes?' asked Detective Chief Inspector Sanam.

'Hi, it's Leander. Can we talk?'

'This is sooner than I expected.'

'There is some information I need from you, before I can give you my information,' I said.

'I'll see what I can do.'

Kimber crouched, two fingers on his lips, listening in calculation.

'What alias did you use when communicating with "The Rockstar" on the dark web?' I asked.

'I can't reveal that.'

'I need to seem to have information, to gain their trust.'

'Whose trust? Where are you?'

'Just tell me. I need it.'

'I can't reveal that,' Sanam said. 'But… I can tell you that "The Rockstar" has spent the past three weeks trying to sell a fourteen year old girl named Cherry.'

I looked up at Kimber. His eyes had widened above a sly smile. He nodded.

'Ok, that's good enough for me,' I said. 'The information I wish to give to you is – you're on speakerphone and I'm being held in the toilets of the Rockway bar again, by a man who wants to kill me, come quickly —'

Kimber, tricked, kicked the phone from my hand and punched me in the nose so hard that it cracked. My blood flushed with a havoc of astral purples – purple blues, solar blues, collapsing stars. I tasted marzipan, and in the back of my mind a belt glinted with my sweat – blending towards a latex taste that remembered the semen he'd forced in my mouth.

'Wait wait wait wait,' I stammered, shielding my face.

He was panting. I wanted to reach for his crotch and gently clench it – but I did not. The tension had to remain unaddressed – perhaps until he was no longer sober, or perhaps indefinitely – since sex would not be enough for me, anyway – sex would be much too straightforward.

'You shouldn't have let me ring him,' I said. 'It would be pretty stupid to kill me now… We've got five minutes to get out of here.'

Kimber took his gun from his pocket and cocked it. He was shuddering in an anger indistinguishable from arousal – I'd returned him to the memory of the room we'd shared, his blood surging as he thought of me on the floor before him, cuffed and naked, his foot on my chest.

'On the contrary,' he said, his voice cracking. 'It would be poetic to kill you here.'

'The police will be here before you could hide a body or murder weapon. There's no time for poetry. We have to leave.'

I risked a full meeting with his eyes – his face was flittering uncertainly. I had the advantage.

'I said I'd surprise you,' I said. 'Every seduction needs some surprise… a little titillation, a little fear. And though I do prefer my acts to have symmetry – killing me here wouldn't be symmetrical enough.'

'On the contrary,' he said, more quietly. 'Beauty is dented symmetry. And you deserve to die beautifully.'

But he did not shoot. I closed my eyes and imagined a marble statue beside me – it looked like me but without my wounds – and it had two faces, though the face on the back of the head could only be seen in shadow – so I held up a mirror to see both of the faces at once – and in this mirror I saw also my own face – and our three faces together – marble and shadow and flesh – became one face, of neither marble nor shadow nor flesh – and this new face was somehow not me at all, but an other – and this other was called Beauty.

'Yes,' I said, 'but there's another act to go before then. It's in your interest to leave with me. You already said – I have unique skills. You could use them for your work. Look at how I just tricked you. I can help you elude the police. I can help you get back your empire. I can help you expand it. Everything I've done was just to make space for myself in your world. I'm as ambitious as you. I want to be your protégé. I want you to teach me how to rule men, I want you to teach me how to be invisible. I want to be your son.'

He twitched at this last sentence, but didn't say anything. He lowered his gun and lifted his face to the ceiling – like he knew he was making a mistake but was choosing it anyway.

'I'm a wanted man,' he said at last, with a voice of softer sandalwood – not a lather any more but an emollient, smooth and intimate, almost soothing, almost sad. 'I can't come anywhere.'

'Who says you're wanted?' I asked. 'The police don't know your name. They don't have the body of the officer you shot. The only witness they know about – is me. And I haven't named you – yet. But they have their suspicions. And so when you leave, you need to be disguised.'

'I have disguises,' he said, nearly at a murmur, arching towards me with his eyes closed.

'We need to be quick,' I said, with more authority.

I stood.

'You… really believe you can be the one driving?' he asked.

His tensions were resolving into compliance. I almost smiled at how easily I'd won him. Perhaps his concussion had impaired his reason.

'I parked out back,' I said, taking his hand. 'But you'll be doing the driving.'

He pocketed his gun, but hesitated. I opened the door and tugged him out after me. We ran, our arousal elevated by the threat of the police – away from the bar, down the corridor, and through swing-doors into a kitchen – and a brightness stunned me, and I halted.

Kimber overtook me, pulling me to the left of a stainless-steel table, past a row of stoves, dishwashers, and sinks, to a tall steel cupboard. Within hung an array of uniforms – riot cop, fireman, paramedic, plumber. I gazed at them in confusion, my hand over my eyes to lessen the glare, the opiates in my blood stirring time into a series of skipping triangles. He briefly fingered a blue boilersuit, but unhooked a motorcycle helmet instead, and chose to wear that only.

His actions had an after-trail as my vision tried to keep up – the kitchen was accelerating. His eyes were concealed now behind a visor that mirrored mine instead – reducing my reading of him to touch alone. But touch was enough to read his desire.

We ran past a row of red propane tanks, to the back exit – opened it with a push bar – and ran out into the cold. I reached the car before I felt the rain. The ground snow had slurried to a dirty curd, though the drizzle above us still flirted with ice. I threw Kimber the keys from Dawn's handbag. He unlocked the car as I rounded the bonnet.

A police siren advanced from a few blocks away. He started the engine. My bones were sunbeams.

'Drive east,' I said. 'Before you kill me, you need to make me immortal.'

5.

Kimber accelerated away from the police siren. Again I remembered Francis buckling this seatbelt across me, on the night we first escaped from here. Our roles were nearly reversed now – but still, like then, I refused to simplify my operation into a mere rescue. There were other gains to be made.

'I'm looking for a business card,' I said, rifling through the spikes, foils, and toiletries of Dawn's handbag. 'It belongs to a man named Nikolas And – he's an art director. And we're going to pay him a visit.'

I needed to make Kimber play a game – and so work him back up into that vulnerable, unbalanced state of mind which obsessed over family and ritual – and which might make him take me to Francis.

He did not reply, perhaps still too amazed by the ploy that had caused this exit – and so I spoke on.

'I was introduced to him by Lars Vasari,' I said. 'She's a film maker. And as a joke she described me to him as her new muse. But I want to make her joke a reality. So we need to persuade this journalist to put me on the front cover of his magazine and to interview me – about my starring role in Lars' film – and about my status more generally as one of London's most exciting up and coming talents.'

I found the card stuck to the underside of a packet of make-up removal wipes.

'And why do you need me to help you with this, my dear?' Kimber asked at last, muffled by the helmet – shaken, amused.

'It will be fun. It's a game. I want to be your son – and you should want the best for your son. You should want London covered with my face. In return I'll do as I said – I'll help you elude the police and rebuild your empire. Think of this as a father-son bonding exercise. You're used to delegating tasks to employees from the top – so this will make for a pleasant change – a return to the basics.'

'If you think this is the basics, then you have gravely misunderstood my line of work. This scheme is nonsensical.'

In my dazed euphoria, his voice had a colour – a metallic red – and as I gazed through the window, it skipped over the passing buildings like a candle's shadow. I could hear the fascination in it – and suddenly I realised – he truly believed I had killed Dawn, and because of this, he admired me.

And not only admired, but loved, perhaps – as if, somehow, in this violent psychology, he believed too much in bodies to love something dead – and so the love he felt for Dawn had been diverted to me. And so, even as he feared me, despised me, desired me – somewhere deeper down, he also loved me.

And so I had to bombard him with words – with motivations and jokes and excuses and promises – to keep him talking – until something struck him hard enough and he started fully playing along – and then his conflicting emotions might begin to overtake him.

'All the best seduction is nonsensical,' I said. 'And what I want from this journalist does have a foundation in reality – I'm already in Vasari's film. And she's already taken a cover-worthy photograph of me – which couldn't have happened without you, since my eye was bruised shut by men you commissioned to attack me. Currently, I'm just a cameo in a single scene – and this photograph was my consolation prize. But I wish to be in more scenes. And in order to be in more scenes, I need to have a higher profile. And so we must build upon the reality that we have to create a better one. Maybe I could have worked my way onto his cover through networking and sex and luck and hard work – but intimidation is so much faster.'

Kimber laughed at a low pitch. 'You are trying to charm me, Leander. I am not stupid. But maybe it's working. And, say it is – where will this intimidation take place?'

'I'm about find out,' I said, typing the contact number on the card into my snitch phone.

'I must insist on speakerphone.'

'Of course.'

Nikolas' phone rang unanswered. But I felt safe inside heroin's intense contentedness, so wasn't able to worry.

'Plots as grand as yours should not rely on chance,' Kimber gloated. 'You could have rung ahead.'

'Plots are for the witless,' I said. 'I improvise. And we are ringing ahead. Perhaps he is afraid of unknown numbers, perhaps his music is playing too loudly. I will ring again.'

Nikolas answered on the third ring. I smiled smugly at Kimber's mirrored visor – he nodded his head towards me in acknowledgement and then returned his face to the road.

'Hi, Nikolas, this is Leander – we met at the Lars Vasari exhibition?'

'Leander! Of course, no, no, of course! Enchanted to hear from you. What an enchanting evening. You were so helpful in getting Lars to open up for me – really so helpful. And I'm going to be quoting you, if I may, on what you said about castles of zeros.'

'Ah that's kind of you. I don't remember what I said but I'm sure it was wrong. Anyway I wanted to ask – what are you doing right now? I was thinking I could provide some more perspectives on Lars' work for you.'

'Certainly, please, certainly. I'm at home – I'm free this very minute. Provide away. And you should tell me more about yourself as well – the new muse of Ms Vasari might merit a sidebar. Perhaps a photograph.'

'I can come to your house if you want,' I said. 'I was filming with her yesterday – and we were speaking about you, actually – and I found your card again today, so I thought I'd call you.'

'Well…' he said, flustered by my forwardness. 'We can… we can just talk on the phone, if you'd prefer. There's no need to go out of your way.'

'Oh no – it has to be face to face if we're going to be spilling secrets. And I love invading people's homes,' I laughed. 'Lars wants me to be her spy to find out more about you. And I'm very nosey so I'm happy to oblige. Give me your postcode and I'll just come round for tea. I'm in Brixton at the moment and I have to go to a drinks later, so I can't grace you with my presence for long.'

'I – er,' he stammered. 'Well, yeah, sure. I should be honoured. It's just me here – I live in Camberwell, but… but I'm doing a bit of decoration, so it's not really hospitable to guests… Th-there's a café around the corner that's —'

'I love homes in transitional states,' I said. 'And I'm practically on your doorstep! Camberwell is five minutes away. What's the address?'

'12 Genevier Road, I'm the upstairs flat – A – flat A – it's. I mean – this is, I don't really… I'm —'

'Spontaneity is good for your health,' I said. 'And Lars wants me to catch you unprepared – so consider this part of the interview process.'

I hung up.

'I knew he'd live alone,' I said, typing his address into the satnav. 'He has the busy timidity of someone who's repressed their sexuality too long. He swapped a sex life for middlebrow graphic design. You can always tell.'

'This is a venomous side of you,' Kimber said approvingly. 'He was going to give you what you wanted anyway.'

'A sidebar is not a front cover,' I said. 'And a front cover will only happen by force.'

'Your mother said you were talented but lazy – and yet here you are being… energetic.'

'You inspired me,' I said, putting the snitch phone back into Dawn's handbag and taking out her smartphone. 'We're good for each other. Look.'

I opened the photograph Iris had taken of me and held it for him to admire. The car idled in a queue, waiting to turn right. He lifted his visor to look at the phone screen more carefully.

'Do you understand now why this has to go on the cover?' I asked. 'It's a photo of you more than me. This is your handiwork! My bruises were made by you – your violence would be broadcast across the city. This is your invisible power made visible.'

'This is… sensational,' he said slowly. 'This should be every magazine cover. My dear, I am not agnostic. I agree, I agree.'

He had regained control of his act. His over-politeness had its old confidence beneath it – and its old threat. The dissonance between who he'd been to me on meth and who he was now was decreasing – and for the first time, I could see those states as two extremes of the same man – like he'd found his way back onto the line between them. My period of advantage was over – he had adjusted to me, and now we were playing as equals again. But at least he was playing. The cars in front began to move – he lowered his visor and drove on.

'I thought you'd like my photo,' I said. 'It's a family portrait, really, if we include the whip wounds made by Dawn. And I gave you each a head wound in return. Me and the marks of my parents. I'm going to email it to Nikolas. And then all that needs to happen is for him to agree with us. This is where I hope to learn from you. I'm a novice to the art of intimidation. I want to be your understudy.'

'I don't have the patience for that anymore,' he said. 'I want to see you again as you were in that picture. I don't want anyone between us.'

His speech had quickened, but it was not unstable. By acknowledging his desire for me, he weakened its power over him – I had not expected this. My body's meanings were no longer frightening. And his voice was no longer a metallic red – it had instead the aftertaste of a blown-out candle, tannic, melting back towards the scent of sandalwood oil.

'But I need to learn,' I protested. 'I want you to teach me how to be invisible.'

'I can start now,' he said with a hushed intensity, rolling his neck beneath the helmet as if in preparation for exercise. 'The best invisibility is its opposite, naturally – the well-dressed well-spoken gentleman. I was not born with this accent. In fact, I was born outside Europe. I designed myself to become unquestionable. I now represent the class that the police were founded to protect. The best invisibility is to be a highly-visible authority figure. Some occasions call for a fluorescent jacket and a hardhat, and some for a high-street suit and a clipboard – low kinds of authority, but still effective. Though I don't stoop to those. And as you know already – another technique is to seem to be the victim, beaten and weaker and weeping. But the most cunning disguise is to look like you've already been caught – handcuffed and escorted away by a stooge, only noticed as absent long after the raid is done. The worst mistake is to try to be inconspicuous – that always attracts the trained eye. You must simply be very visibly somebody who cannot be you – that's how to stay invisible. Become impossible. Men like me saturate the establishment, and they crowd the houses of Commons and Lords – but they get away with it, as men with poorer accents and darker skin do not.'

'So you changed your voice and bleached your skin? And now you can be even more invisible – if we go to Nikolas And. This photo will be seen by millions of people – your presence will be hidden in plain sight on my body. And I will become more invisible too – because a cover model cannot be a criminal. It will be the ultimate disguise – think of how useful I will be to you when I'm publicly known, and thus above suspicion...'

The satnav announced our destination as 400 feet away.

'Maybe – but this helmet is a different kind of invisibility,' he continued, more enthused by his own expertise than by the theory behind it. 'This helmet serves a different function. It conceals me from road cameras, but also it's an obvious invisibility – the kind that creates fear. Mr And cannot know what I am and that shall keep him afraid.'

'But how exactly do we… make him do what we want?' I asked.

He parked across a single yellow line and withdrew the car key, but paused with it held in mid-air as he considered. 'What exactly do you want him to say? What shall this interview be about if you have done nothing?'

'That's for him to invent,' I said. 'Most of the people in his magazine have done nothing. What do I believe? Our era has the worst fashion in the history of civilisation, because for the last fifty years we've been putting words on clothes. Words are fucking ugly. Take words off clothes! That can be my platform. No brand names no band names no slogans no logos. He can give me whatever quotes he wants. He just needs to be enthusiastic. Take words off clothes!'

We left the car. The opiates still nulled my nerves, but their anxiolytic effect was lessening – paranoia was breaking through. Kimber's energy had become manic again. The polarity between us had switched. To find Francis, I had to continue – but our game had new rules. I was walking upside down now, no longer leading, but being led.

'Intimidation has two parts,' Kimber said, guiding me towards number 12 with a hand on each of my shoulders. 'The first part is proving we can cause pain, and the second part is promising that the pain can last forever. The most elegant intimidations combine the proof with the promise.'

We passed through a gate of peeling grey paint, towards the grey front door. The puddles smiled at me with a blank London smile that had seen too much but pretended to see nothing. I rang the upper of two bells. Kimber's breath on my neck reminded my skin of his handcuffs.

I tried to seem more assured. 'You mean like the best tragedies combine anagnorisis with peripeteia?'

'If you say so. But my preferred promise of pain is a video recording, as you know. We must film Nikolas engaged in an act that he does not want the world to see – and then we shall have power over him forever.'

'How will that also be proof?' I asked.

'Hello – come upstairs!' a nervous voice called through the intercom.

The door buzzed open. Kimber increased his grip on my shoulders and pushed me through an inner door, onto a carpeted staircase. The air smelled of beeswax, or shoe polish – and other conditioning foams. At the top of the stairs stood Mr Nikolas And – in bottle-green corduroys, a navy smock, and navy socks, all flecked with paint.

'You've come with a surprise,' Nikolas said, trying to smile.

Kimber shut the inner door behind us and steered me upstairs. Nikolas stepped backwards into a room with sheets on the floor. His face faltered, unsure how long he should maintain politeness before conceding to fear.

'I am the publicist of this eligible bachelor,' Kimber said through his helmet, labouring every syllable with a gleefully incongruous civility.

He pushed me after Nikolas into the room, which was bare but for a cluster of decorating tools – a tub of gardenia paint, a can of paint thinner, a roller, and a tray. A siren began inside my skin.

Kimber took his out his gun – and with it, motioned Nikolas towards the corner. The taste of malt vinegar returned instantly to my gums – and at the memory of the gun's last shot, and of the grease on its silencer, a dull elation grew in my thighs. Kimber picked up the can of paint thinner.

'For the proof that we can cause pain if he doesn't oblige, it is best to have a test subject,' Kimber said, fully now the master of ceremonies. 'At our last meeting, that test subject was a policewoman – I proved my ability to cause pain, or even death, and so you obeyed me. This time, my dear, you shall be the test subject. You shall be the proof, and you shall be the promise – our power shall come from a film of Mr Nikolas here inflicting himself upon you.'

My mind wiped itself silent. Before I could move, Kimber uncapped the fist-wide can and forced it over my nose – denting the rim into my chin. If I leant away the toxic thinner would spill into my mouth. My body's confidence dissolved.

'Breathe in,' he said paternally, nearly with pity.

I tried to shake my head away – but he shoved me into the wall so I couldn't tip it back, and twisted the rusted tin around my lips and the bridge of my nose until I screamed – and gasped in.

Instantly the vapour filled my throat, suffocating and enlivening, biting into my teeth, licking my tongue with the taste of alcohol and vinyl – a terror of gas, lifting me away from density. Kimber pressed the pistol into my forehead until the eyes reflecting back in his visor were unrecognisable as my own – they had the plaintive too-late fear of a gambler losing his last bet. I closed them and inhaled again – the dominating reek of iron now crowding through my nose for my brain and dropping to my lungs as thick as milk. My vision twisted towards sound – my heartbeat multiplying in a scale, ascending and descending faster than I could hear, loudening my stomach somehow into paralysis, overruling vomit – binding me to the stench, as my thoughts unbound.

'As you said yourself – it's dull when there's only one agent of confusion,' Kimber said joyfully – twisting the gun further into my forehead until its capillaries screamed and I screamed too, inhaling fuller – 'Did you believe we could work together? I can improvise better than you! You knew the risks of hiring this hand, my dear, you knew the risks.'

The tin seemed to be drooping as I breathed into it – its metal stretching towards the floor, like I was inflating it – causing the room beyond it to become disjointed too. The light was panicking. The floor broke up into blocks bouncing between gaps with no colour. Then, the walls spiralled upwards into coils taller than the house – and the sky rushed in.

Still Kimber kept the toxic tin to my mouth and still I breathed in, hyperventilating – outside the enharmonic scale now, almost like an oboe, repeating in triplets a motif that ended with a fourth – as another oboe joined a sixth above it. Weaving in and out of my own breath, the oboes played – speeding under the entrance of a timpani, detuned or mis-tuned, beating into my head – and swelling, until it burst open and its matter unrolled into the pipes of an organ. My head was a fugue of fumes – and what remained of my mouth giggled at the silly melody. It was like a fairground ride's or a dancing monkey's and I wished to dance with it.

But instead I was folded in half – Kimber kneed me in the gut, releasing my mouth from the can – and kicked me towards the bucket of paint. I vomited a tea of bergamot and caraway – my eyes cones of vodka, each limb dislocated. He picked my head up separately and held it above the surface of the gloss. My mind was camouflaging itself from itself, blending upwards with what used to be the ceiling.

'This will be your fate, Nikolas, if you do not do as we wish,' Kimber said, his voice now purely vinegar.

And he plunged my head into the bucket of paint. I smelt and saw inwardly – behind my face was a flare – like a will-o'-the-wisp caught in a goblet – and as I heaved, the goblet grew into a gleaming basin. Gradually, inwardly, I was nearing a negative pillar, a void – and within it was a photograph. But as I stretched, retching, it electrified – and flung me faster forwards – into the picture, of Francis and me, holding each other so closely that our skin blanched, between two mirrors, expressionless, our eyes the cameras. I wished to twist to meet his cheek with my lips, but I couldn't move – we were reduced to two dimensions, in black and white, tending fast towards just one – a pair of hypnagogic dots that could only kiss by disappearing. And so we kissed – and it went white —

6.

In hiccups I woke up, being pushed downstairs through a spinning hounds-tooth tunnel. Beeswax polished my oesophagus until it shone and I retched. Then I was in a car, and the car was sailing forwards – and my eyes numbed backwards into silence.

The paint-thinning can was affixed again to my mouth and nose – and I woke inside it. I was walking upstairs now, with wings on my feet, through a corridor of amoebae. The air smelt expensive. The steps were fractals. Dawn's handbag was on fire.

But my skeleton was straightening into itself, I was better-aware – and a door opened before me, dim bulbs were lit – and I was in a bedroom beside a wall of glass, high above London under night.

In fast-forward, Kimber removed his helmet, pushed me onto his bed, and held and huffed from the paint thinner himself. His eyes regained their rage.

My mind was floating sideways in a dozen separate baubles – but one of them bobbed in delight at what he'd done. The paint thinner would derange his senses beyond the extremes that meth had taken him to – and perhaps he knew that, perhaps he wanted to go there – beyond even the desires and memories that terrified him – towards something stranger. Towards somewhere I was stronger – my parallel world, the world of the sick – where I was ruler, and he was just a visitor.

He inhaled from the tin again and forced me to inhale again

– and then we seemed to swap hands – so that mine were the hands that kept the tin to my mouth, and his were the hands that tried to force my hands away. But then the tin lowered – and Kimber was far away – on top of the steeple of Saint Paul's Cathedral – and I was on the other side of the Thames, on a deck chair on top of the Tate Modern – and his hands were stretching across the water, and he was punching me, or undressing me, or both – and a chandelier above us bulged in inflorescence – and the Thames became the bed again.

'Are we home?' I asked, at last able to speak.

'Ah your voice survives… that is fortunate,' he said, with a curious new softness, far from the visionary conviction of his meth persona. 'I was afraid you'd end in idiocy. And that would have been no —'

A wind covered his words – a wind with the scent of fried chicken and the ringing of mobile phones – and the wind bucked sideways and the phones turned into pigeons, in Trafalgar Square – and the pigeons flew up and south towards our perches – at St Paul's and the Tate Modern – and settled on the Millennium Bridge – and the bridge wobbled back into being a bed.

Kimber knelt over me to stroke my painted face, speaking into the wind. His gun was in his other hand. He was trying to transfer my paint onto himself – but under the paint thinner's influence, he was as unsure whose body was where – and occasionally he missed us both altogether. His action soon simplified into smacking my neck and then his stomach in overlapping gardenia palm prints that made him laugh. His laughter quietened the wind.

'I am wearing you, now, Leander, I said I'd wear you,' he said, his tone softening as the paint thinner bled further through his brain. 'But you came back to me, knowing this is how you would end. How did you not predict this? We… we can't work together.'

He sounded unconvinced by himself – like he had forgotten

how to play the boss – or simply no longer believed in his performance of that masculinity, perhaps because he knew how it felt to kneel in front of me – and perhaps, secretly, longed to kneel there again.

'We are working together,' I said, surprising myself with the sound of my own voice. 'I predicted this. You need rituals, and you want to learn a new one. You had to take me home.'

I stretched my arm behind his back – and it came out of his mouth. I looked into his face, and it was my face. I leaned forward for a kiss, but my lips closed on metal – the barrel of his gun. My heels were lifted up and I did not know if he or I were lifting them – my muscles didn't answer. I could have been naked – but my skin was a canopy of leaves in a rainforest.

'Why did you come back to me?' he asked.

'Because I am your son,' I said.

I remembered the bite of his syringe in my urethra and his gun's silencer in my arsehole and the force of him fucking me as I vomited – but memory and body were interchangeable here – and it could be the past, or it could be the present re-enacting the past. Kimber was smiling childishly from both sides of my head – inhaling through his nose as he sucked on his gun's silencer.

'If I'm your father, your father,' he said, his voice randomly varying its volume, as though grappling with tenderness. 'You must tell me who I'm replacing. Who was your mother before Dawn? How did your parents die?'

He pointed the gun over my heart, but my heart was outside my body – asparagus green – beating in the same irregular jerks as the bed. And his eyes were geckos darting over the duvet, never meeting mine.

'My biological mum and dad aren't dead,' I said, my speech calmly quick. 'I'm a suburban kid from a normal nuclear middle-class family, with an older sister and a younger brother. There was love enough. But on my fifteenth birthday I decided to be someone else, so I left and changed my name and never spoke to them again. I'm a self-made demon, that's my secret – and I've spent so many seasons in hell since then that I've become invulnerable. But I've glimpsed your hell – and I've glimpsed your father. Tell me, who was Kimber before Kimber?'

'I don't believe you,' he said, tapping his head hard with the butt of his gun, trying to force himself to concentrate. 'You're, you're being incomprehensible.'

I was trying to climb into his skull – my fingers were already fidgeting under his fingers' skin, my teeth were already behind his teeth, nervously chewing his cheeks from the inside – trying to eat backwards down to his vocal cords.

'You never had a father, you never had a family,' he insisted. 'You're an orphan. You must be. Your voice is faked. Don't – don't tell me you have a family.'

There was no sandalwood in his tone anymore, and no vinegar aftertaste in my gums. Somewhere in the floating pockets of my mind, I knew he was in a hypnotic state again – in that terror of desire, wanting to give up control, not understanding why, not understanding anything.

'What happened to Nikolas?' I asked, with a new authority.

'He is well, I got what I wanted – I, I got you your invisibility, I, I don't know why I did it, for you, I —'

He tried to match my assertive tone, but his voice had buckled back into uncertainty.

'The cover photo, you'll be above suspicion, it's a clever idea, disguise, I, I wanted my power across the city, the bruises, I don't know why, you wanted to be my son, you said,' he laughed worriedly, 'because you – you got what you wanted, did you?'

My body was becoming more discrete, even as the paint thinner's nausea increased – and I moved my hand over his, to where it was holding the gun over the side of the bed. With my other hand I forced up his chin so that our eyes met – and willed him to meet all the violence of his empire in my eyes, all the horror and grief and guilt and arousal and fear of his childhood – here in my eyes, in this room, in my voice.

'No – I didn't get what I wanted, not yet,' I said. 'Don't look away from me now, it's my turn to talk. I came back to you to talk to you… I wanted to tell you about Dawn's old radio. She'd sing along to it when we were going to sleep – though she never knew the words… and she'd say to me, don't worry darling, the painkiller will start its killing soon, I've got you, I got you, and she'd sing me to sleep… and the song she sang the night she met you – she misheard 'I'll go back to the road' as 'I'll go back to Rome', and I teased her for that – for longing for a different life, of travel and warmth, not wanting to be trapped and high in a cold mould-filled room with me, with nothing but our love for each other left… When she found me I was a lonely sick little boy, crying from constant pain – I was eighteen but I could have been eight or eighty, I'd been through a whole life already, and my life still hadn't begun… and she held me in the cold, promising to get me some heroin for the pain, promising to teach me everything she knew… and she taught me… she – I didn't have a sense of humour till she taught me, she had laughter and she gave it to me… and then you came along and she thought you'd save her like she saved me, she said life was about to happen to her… but then I found her in your bathroom in a wedding dress, and she looked like me when I was eighteen, a sick boy screaming in pain… she said you weren't the man she thought you were, she needed to get out, but you'd kill her if she left you, or you'd sell her like you sold other women… so she made me inject her with everything we had, she said we can't let him win, don't let him win, don't worry darling, the painkiller will start its killing soon, I'll go back to Rome…'

He was paralysed by the visions the paint thinner was writing out of the words between our eyes. Gently, still forcing him to look at me, with our fingers still wrapped together around the trigger, I guided the gun up to the side of my head.

'She didn't want to be your wife,' I said. 'I don't want to be your son. How could you have a son? You weren't the man Dawn wanted, you weren't the man your father wanted. Did you really think I wanted to be invisible – hidden by a magazine cover – because I wanted to help you? What is there to help you with? You don't have anything. The police know everything, of course they know everything, I told them everything, they'll be here soon. Your empire is over. I came to you to… to end – as pain would have ended me long ago, anyway, if I hadn't had Dawn. And I came to you to… beat you. And so… I just wanted a parting joke – in a magazine cover, an online self more real than my physical one – an image to be adored – and then I could… then I could go one step further into the invisible – become as invisible as my illness, so it can't hurt me anymore – I want to be erased in body – and then I'll get what I want, and you'll be beaten.'

Kimber gazed, enraptured, limp, his hand entirely held up by mine around the gun against my head – and softly, he began to cry.

'When I was a child,' I whispered, 'I would walk for hours along a dual carriageway, holding my toy lion called Lyon – looking up into the evening, dreaming of getting out of the city eventually too – and I thought the aeroplanes were sad because they could never meet, always leaving trails for each other, but flying alone – and now —'

'No!' Kimber screamed – a scream of love, a final vanity.

He pulled the gun away from me – and trembled a moment, his eyes in mine – and with an ecstatic crack, shot himself dead.

Mosquitos filled the air. My ears screeched – and the agony of the gunshot aroused me – and I couldn't find my lower body – and he had an erection, or I had an erection, or we both did, and I ejaculated, or he did, or we both did – amazed at the brain sprayed across the pillow and the face sinking inwards into its skull and the blood leaking under him towards my knees.

But my energy was failing; the paint thinner was wearing off, my performance was ending.

'Francis?' I called into the drone's buzz, not very loudly, crawling backwards off Kimber, turning to face the rest of the flat.

My body weighed as though it were underwater, and I wanted to stop, sleep here, give up – but I had to search. The room's acoustics seemed corrupted by the gunshot. Kimber was dead! Time was too rapid to understand. The fatigue confused me in seconds-long windows of amnesia – and suddenly I was back at the bedside, trying to roll Kimber's corpse off the mattress, but it was too heavy. And it was too bloodied for me to get in next to him – and Francis was still unfound.

So I staggered into a bathroom, and then a cupboard – and then another bedroom, and there was a little light on, and a bed, and boy on the bed – in a grey tracksuit – and white trainers.

'Francis!' I called. 'Francis, it's Leander.'

I was at Francis' side – Francis was safe! Francis was here! – and I was watching him uncurl his body. He smelt of urine. I kissed him and kissed him – and tried to yell in delight – but croaked out only paint. His left wrist was cuffed to the headboard. His eyes opened but said nothing. I ran – with no energy but the weightlessness of relief – back to Kimber's room. I sought in the bundle of clothes on the floor the key to the handcuffs. In seconds, I was returned to Francis' side with no memory of the intervening journey.

I unlocked Francis' handcuffs and he wobbled upright, shaking his legs. He opened his mouth without speaking. I tried to hug him but he pushed me away.

'He's gone,' I said. 'It's just me.'

He staggered wordlessly into the dim corridor and crossed it into the kitchen, to drink from the sink.

'Francis,' I said, dragging myself after him. 'I knew you'd be here.'

My need to hold him was more than I could bear – it cancelled the rest of my consciousness, so that even as he was here, he seemed a mirage. But before I could reach him, he retreated, groping for the fridge.

'Don't touch me,' he said.

I halted pathetically. Too tired to stand, I crumpled against the sink, into the surface he'd left wet.

'Francis,' was all I could say.

'Don't talk to me.'

Shaking, he ripped open a packet of salami and ate it all. Back-lit by the fridge, his cheekbones cast sharper shadows, and made his expression more carnal – like he was experiencing his own starvation as erotic. I lapped at the water he'd spilled.

Time jumped again, and he was gone. I turned to see him by the front door.

'Where you going?' I asked. 'Stay here. I'm... I'm tired.'

'Fuck you,' he said. 'Fuck you. You're disgusting. You're… disgusting. You don't give a shit about me. This is you covering up for yourself. Don't talk to me. You're disgusting. Don't follow me.'

He closed the door. I was alone.

Time flickered, and I found myself on Francis' bed – still warm and wet from where he'd been lying. I had nothing in my head.

'Is that fucking it then?' Dawn asked.

I looked around – Dawn was hovering in the doorway, in the forget-me-not nightie I'd stained with my and Kimber's blood.

'I dunno,' I said. 'Where've you been?'

'I've been being a ghost, sweetheart. It's fucking great. But I come here to check that you're alright and you've fucked it all up, didn't you? Do you know what you just did?'

'Not really. Can you sleep next to me?'

'Course I can, gorgeous. But why's it smell like piss in here?'

'Francis was locked up in here too long.'

Dawn's ghost got into bed beside me. I closed my eyes and faded from my body.

'So now what?' she asked.

Beside us a choir began singing softly, sarcastically, 'Homeless, homeless, we are our own home, homeless, homeless…'

'I dunno,' I heard myself say. 'I dunno —'

ACT 5

The return

1.

Daylight woke me. Razors ran from my ears to my collarbones. A ball of blunter blades rolled around my stomach. I was a candle of tallow – my spine the wick, my skin the soot, my muscles an ultramarine flame. But above the scent of piss and paint, I smelt something similar to cinnamon. It bid me rise. My mind was clear. I had vomited enough. So I rose.

The fever in my sweat had worsened, but it could be ignored. Naked, I roamed the apartment. October had made its furnishings seem sleeker – though if the apartment had been a lover, I would have told him, or her – 'It's always November when you're with me.' But I was alone. I refused my own reflection.

Kimber's corpse seemed almost incidental to his bedroom. He held his gun still to what remained of his head as though congratulating himself.

'Hero drew Leander to the tower,' I told him. 'But here Hero became Leander – I turned out my light, you drowned at sea.'

The blood of his pillows had coagulated into damson plum jam – which, combined with the scent of cinnamon, sent me to the kitchen to make mulled wine.

Zoned-out by pain and the paint thinner comedown, I perceived myself in a technical rather than emotional way. I removed two bottles of red wine from the wine rack and emptied them into a saucepan. Over a flame, I stirred in two cinnamon sticks, some cloves, two star anise, the grated zest of an orange, the grated zest of a lemon, and a pinch of powdered nutmeg. The spice cupboard was beside the hob, but it took me longer to locate the sugars. Eventually I discovered them in ceramic jars beside the toaster. I added two spoonfuls of brown sugar and one of white to the wine. As it warmed, I perused the cupboard again, and decided to add a vanilla pod too, two cardamom pods, a dry bay leaf, and the juice of the orange. If this was to be the first meal of my week, or the last meal of my life, I may as well commit to as many flavours as I had wounds.

While the wine mulled, I went back to Kimber's bedroom. From his door I unhooked a black silk gown, wide-sleeved with gold hems, and put it on and crouched to search the clothes at the foot of his bed. In his pockets were a camera, a loose memory card, condoms, two phones, a wallet, a ring of keys, Dawn's car keys, a clip of bullets, a wrap of meth, a meth pipe, a silver lighter, three half-gram bags of brown heroin, and a third set of keys, labelled 'Rockway'. I left the meth and took the rest, with Dawn's handbag and my snitch phone, to the kitchen – and displayed them on the countertop like ingredients for the next course. His smartphone was pin-locked, but his burner phone was not. Its most recent sent message was a group text to a dozen numbers on Wednesday saying 'R. 9pm tonight PUNCTUAL, white tie, only 1 plus-1 each.' I presumed that 'R' referred to the Rockway – and that this white tie gathering referred to the one I'd interrupted. My snitch phone had four missed calls from 'X'.

I put Dawn's phone on charge and played through its speakers a sixteen-minute-long song called 'Sheep', to prevent me from thinking about anything else. And as it played, I detached a ladle from the magnetic strip beside the stove, and tried the wine with it – and judged it too meek. So, I searched the cupboards for supplements – and added a few dashes of two different rums and a splash of blueberry liqueur. To allow these final notes to brew, I prepared an entrée meanwhile; on a clean sheet of tinfoil, I upended half a half-gram of heroin, rolled a foil pipe around the handle of a wooden spoon – and then repeated the healing heating ceremony that had begun my past few passages of consciousness – sucking the powder's vapour into my lungs until my blood was dumb and there were fewer whispers in my head.

At last, I strained my breakfast through a sieve and drank a litre or so of mulled wine directly from the bowl. For dessert, I ate four slivers of smoked salmon from the middle shelf of the fridge, with dill. But that made me thirst for more of the main course, and so I drank the rest of the bowl of mulled wine, and then risked three more huffs of the heroin entrée – completing my meal in reverse.

I was full. And despite the music, I was unable to avoid my own thoughts any longer. So – what did I think? Well, where the fuck were the police? Surely a neighbour had heard a gunshot? Surely Francis had made some kind of complaint? Well, evidently not. How dull, again, to be the sole agent of confusion! I had alienated myself from my substitute families, systematically – until I had become king of this highest tower, with nothing to rule and nowhere to go.

I recalled the bell-tower I'd dreamed of a few days ago, in the police car, when Francis had been beside me, and still wanted to be beside me – and I saw again a chain stretching from the bell towards a second tower, over the horizon – and the chain was now also a tongue that could speak – and it told me that the bell-towers I was dreaming of were the high-rises lived in by Dawn and Kimber, who were my mother and father – the addict and the dealer – or the endgame of the Enlightenment and the revenge on the Enlightenment, respectively – perhaps, hahahaah – but if I was their son, then who was I? I asked – and the tongue between the bell-towers couldn't say – it just knew that I'd been raped in both and seen death in both – and had the keys to both towers – and that neither was my home.

I knocked over the soup ladle – and the kitchen resumed itself. I picked it back up.

'Maybe I can only love when what I love is absent,' I said to my reflection in the curved steel. 'Another convex mirror to confess to, Leander. Who are you now? I promised to quit my act on Francis' doorstep. But that was just another act, wasn't it? I take back my palinode, then. Nobody's coming. Nobody's letting me in. So let me be my worst self instead. I want fire – so I'll end this with fire.'

I turned on the camera and watched Nikolas rape me. Kimber's cinematography wobbled, obscuring the point of entry – perhaps to hide Nikolas' lack of erection. Or perhaps he was erect. Onscreen, my paint-filled hair whitened the wall with each thrust – reducing my body to a paintbrush. Perhaps Nikolas was weeping, or perhaps he was being forced to act out a fantasy he'd long forbidden from his own imagination, and so was actually being cured of a repression. Perhaps we had helped him realise himself. There was an inverse dramatic irony here, too – known to the participants, but unknown to any audience – that the violation of consent was the opposite of what it seemed: I had, more or less, consented to being raped for the camera; but Nikolas had not consented to raping me – he was doing so under duress. He was certainly too pure to have infected me; he hadn't injured me; and he'd promised to put me on the cover of a magazine in return. So really, this had just been another transaction and he had just been another client.

Half-convinced by this conclusion, and inspired – I set aside the camera and scrolled through Dawn's phone, to see if her client list had been transferred from her old simcard. Happily, 'Andrew Rich Newspaper Cunt' survived. He'd already beaten me with a belt for £1,500 – and thus arguably begun the whole narrative that led me here – so he could surely assist me with its ending. I texted him: 'its leander – pick up.' And then, after letting the wine and heroin and music lull me awhile back towards confidence – I rang him.

'H-hello?' Andrew answered after one ring.

At his voice, the whip wounds along my back twitched in pleasure – I remembered his touch, and its kingfisher colour, but not his face.

'Hey – I was just thinking about you,' I said, trying to sound fragile. 'And, and I wanted to say I had a good time on Wednesday. Perhaps you'd like to do it again?'

'You didn't… you don't – you weren't hurt?' He was timid in his sobriety, but could easily be returned to his lust.

'Your belt was the best thing to happen to me all month,' I said. 'I like that you can be honest with me. I like feeling fantasies becoming real.'

'You were… you seemed scared. Are you sure that…'

'I was scared,' I said, quietly. 'But I like to be scared. I liked you scaring me. And scarring me. You can give me more scars, if you want.'

He was moving somewhere quieter.

'I'm not normally like that…' he said at last. 'I didn't mean to be so —'

'I liked making you feel good. And I thought… I could tell you something you might like to hear?'

'What do you mean?' he asked, almost intimidated.

'Since you're a newspaper man and – I thought you might like to hear – I've got a role in a film.'

'Did you?' His surprise shifted. 'Um… what kind of film?'

'A real film. The director's Lars Vasari.'

'I think I've heard of him.'

I leaned back against the wall, drooping in a wave of sedation as more heroin bound to my brain – and I glimpsed the ceiling of a chapel – a lapis lazuli sky with gold leaf stars – and I heard a hymn, sung by children – of peace, harmony, war, and death – and these contradictions were solved by the music, but not by the building – whose walls, I now saw, depicted angels enslaving each other with manacles of ice and leashes of snow.

'I'm one of the leads. But we're trying to keep the details quiet.'

'How did you… get this?'

'I wanted to do something that would impress you,' I said. 'So I auditioned – I used a friend to get me an audition. It was quick, I was replacing someone. And I thought you might like to know. And I thought maybe you might want to help me…'

'I can help,' he said, his voice finally paternal. 'We can get you more… I can get you some press, maybe – what do you want?'

'I just want to see you again. And I want… I —'

'What?'

'Can I see you again?' I asked, more tentatively.

'You – yeah…' he stammered. 'I will need to… work out a timetable. But um…'

'That's good. I just want… That. But can I say another thing? It's separate.'

'What?'

'I heard a…' I hurried towards the front door to read Kimber's address off the junkmail on the mat. 'I don't want to do anything else with the police – but I was, I got scared and so I rang you. When the – I'm staying in a bad place. And last night, I heard a shot – next door. I think it was a gun. But I don't want to report anything so… can you – do it?'

'Who are you with? Where are you?'

'I want to leave but I'm too scared – to go outside in case there's… I don't know who's there. It's flat 45, Alverton Tower – it's near Victoria. Can you just tell the police there was a gunshot? I'm alone. And I didn't know who to call. I've got Dawn's phone so I can't call her. I feel like somehow there are all these bad men around me, I dunno… I just, I wanted to call you and thought maybe you could help me.'

'Do you want me to come get you?' he asked, his concern pleasingly possessive.

'Just tell – I just want – can you just tell the police to get here? But don't tell them I'm here. I don't want there to be any… coincidences. And then I'll feel safe. And then I – I want to see you properly, not like this.'

'Ok. I'll do that. You don't have to worry. I'm —'

'And then can I see you?' I asked again, hamming up my helplessness. 'You just have to say when you're free. And I'll tell you when I'm safe.'

'Yeah, tell me when you're safe.'

'Ok…'

'Ok.'

'Thank you,' I said.

'Ok. Don't worry.'

'Ok.' I held my breath until he hung up.

I deleted the call from Dawn's history. On Kimber's burner phone, I sent a group text to the same dozen recipients as his previous one, saying: 'R. 7pm tonight PUNCTUAL, emergency, offline only, no plus-1s'. I deleted this text, too – and then put Dawn's and Kimber's phones into the microwave to spin until all their data was burnt away.

Inebriation was overcoming me, reducing my present to a series of tasks whose climax I was hiding from myself. While the phones sparked, I washed up my breakfast. I binned the heroin foil. Beneath the sink, I found a bag of plastic bags and selected the most inauspicious one – red, logo-less, from an off-license – and tied up inside it the set of keys labelled 'Rockway'.

I returned to Kimber's bedroom and flung the bag out of the window. It fell into street-side shrubbery. My motives reeled through the outskirts of my thoughts, almost unconsciously, like I was obeying muscle memory rather than logic.

As the heroin's effects increased, I collected the rest of Kimber's belongings – and the handcuff keys, and Dawn's handbag, and my snitch phone – and put them back among his clothes. For tradition's sake, I dabbed some of Dawn's Savlon onto my stab wound. Finally, I removed Kimber's dressing gown, resuming my nakedness, and hooked it back up to his door with a bow. It was time for my last seduction.

I entered Francis' former room and handcuffed myself to his former bed. And so self-imprisoned, ready for the police, I began pissing over the bed and over myself – and fell asleep.

2.

I was drunk when a policeman woke me. In my dream, my shoulders had been sawn off – and so, waking, I believed the policeman was digging his nails into their stumps. I yelled until I vomited, scrambling backwards – only realising that my arms were intact when the handcuff on my wrist halted my roll. Wine splashed over my skin. The cinnamon scent had soured into suet. But the sensation of throwing up was itself satisfying – like a gush through a gullet of fur.

I wanted to shit myself too, but the constipating heroin had diminished my capacity for spectacle, sadly – and so my audience had to content itself with vomit. I twisted onto my knees, simulating terror at the entrance of two more officers. They tried to calm me with outstretched hands, but I screamed again, stood, and slammed backwards into the headboard, slipping in a puddle of my own piss.

The adults stepped back, successfully appalled. I imagined them genuflecting before me as to a boy king: a chained whipped stabbed beaten naked bloodied painted drunken black-eyed cum-stained piss-soaked sick-spattered boy king. Never had a costume suited me so well. Kimber had said that seeming already caught was the most cunning disguise – but he hadn't added that it was also the most euphoric. My pin-pupilled stare searched the faces of my saviours – unblinking, to goad new nausea from my sensitivity to light – and as I vomited again,

I felt like I was confessing to them my true identity. I finally looked as tormented as my nerves had claimed to be for twenty years. Externalised for all to see – at last, here, my pain was valid!

I could see that they were speaking – but the air swarmed with cawing ravens, and I couldn't hear them above it.

'The cuff!' I shouted. 'The handcuff key is in his pocket – find the key!'

One of the policemen left in quest for this key, and another two parted to allow a policewoman to come through towards me.

'He's got a gun!' I warned her. 'Don't go in there!'

'It's ok,' she said.

She rounded my bed to open the window. Cool air entered, the cawing quietened. Slowly she crouched beside me until she was equal to my eye level. She was young – maybe almost my age.

'There's nobody with a gun anymore,' she said. 'It's ok. Focus on my voice. You're safe. You're ok. Can you tell me what day it is?'

'Is it your birthday?' I asked. 'Or is it mine? There was an eclipse. Have you seen the supermoon? Today is the last day of the industrial era. In my opinion. We're done with childhood, mommy! There's a gun!'

'Listen to my voice. My name is Constable Carr. It's ok. I'm part of a specialist unit – you might have heard it called the Sapphire unit, and I've been trained to help you through this kind of… situation. Can you repeat after me – it is Sunday and I am safe.'

Her words did not entirely conceal her revulsion – and somewhere beyond the heroin and the wine, I could sense my own fear – a fear that she might be too well trained to believe me, a fear that she could catch me somewhere in a lie – but still, I had to play on.

'I am Sunday and it is safe,' I said.

'Can you tell me your name?'

'That would be improper at this stage in our relationship. You may only know my star sign – I'm a sea-urchin, born under the meteor shower Daz, between the months of August and Laugust – with a mongoose-shaped scar on my tongue. Though you can call me Sunday if you wish.'

'Ok Sunday, can you tell me how old you are?'

'I'll be thirty-four in a few years.'

'How many years is a few years?'

'That's a question for small-print lawyers. I'm a big-print boy – or should I say man, legally speaking? – twenty-one years and none of them over! Although maybe you just have to arrange a sufficient ending for your childhood – and then the obsessions go. What do you think? Or what I mean is – I only read headlines. I can read your headline if you want.'

'Ok,' she said, with condescending patience.

'"Constable Carr Builds Nest Inside Womb of Dying Dog." That's your headline.'

'Do you feel like you're…'

'Dying?' I asked. 'Sundays can only die. That's the secret to their vitality.'

Her colleague returned to the room with the cuff-key and passed it to her, gagging from the reek of my sheets. I remained supine after she unlocked me – as if I was too unfamiliar with liberty to use it.

'He's not going to hurt you anymore,' she said – and cautiously patted me near the knee.

I shrieked in alarm and backed off the bed.

'It's ok – I'm not here to hurt you.' She turned to the other police officers. 'Can you step outside for a bit?'

They left. I hugged my knees against the wall under the window, itching my wrist. My body was a raft adrift. Nothing was still. A wind curled around me till it clung. The sky was reflected in a mirror on the wall; the afternoon had nearly returned to typical British stalemate – its sleet had settled into mist, though thunder still threatened the edges.

Constable Carr crouched by an armchair, two arm's-lengths away. 'Do you know how long you've been here?' she asked.

I met her gaze suddenly. 'Ring Detective Sanam, there's a Detective Sanam, he knows how long I've been here, I've been here for him.' I imitated the rhythms of hysteria. 'There's a phone – he gave me a phone, in my clothes – next door. With his number. Ring Sanam. I'll talk to him. Detective Chief Inspector Sanam. He did this to me.'

'Ok. I can try to get him. But I'm going to need your name first. So can you please tell me your name?'

'My name is No-one, but you can call me Elagabalus if you like, or Sunday, or… Anacoluthon, but nobody ever wants to see me, or be being seen seeing me.'

'What do your friends call you?'

'The catamite.'

'What does the Detective Chief Inspector – Sanam, you said? What does he call you?'

'Leander.'

This seemed to exhaust her patience – she rose to re-open the bedroom door and stepped out to the other officers.

'There's a phone in my pockets next door!' I shouted. 'Check my pockets. The black trousers. Chief Inspector Sanam will answer me. He's saved as "X", he's my only contact. He did this to me.'

The officers conferred together a while longer, and then the constable returned – with blue gloves, a green case, and a camera.

'This is a bit hard, but I'm going to need to take some photos of you,' she said. 'And I'm going to need to take a few samples. And then we're going to clean you. Is that ok? I'm going to need to come closer to you.'

'That's fine,' I said, 'I'm very photogenic.'

'Can you stand up for me?'

I stood, shakily – and in my dizziness I retched, but nothing came out. I shook against the sill, unable to meet my eyes in the mirror. As she photographed me, I thought of being in front of Iris's blank wall – playing the predator, for her camera, half-hidden behind the façade of the gleeful beaten orphan. But here, in front of the window, for the police, I played the prey, with no glint of mischief or knowing grin. I winked into this lens because I had to wink – my eye was bruised shut without meaning.

'Can you turn around please?' she asked.

I obeyed – and bent forwards, angling my body out into the air to gaze upon London from my privileged height. London wasn't as overburdened by its past as other European cities, perhaps because, in order to become a citizen here, you had to master the art of suffering – which was an art of the present, since all suffering brings with it a softening amnesia – an amnesia that makes past suffering seem less real – but then also makes present suffering seem like it's the worst it's ever been.

Cranes metastasised towards the horizon, building new sky-scrapers for the next influx of victors. The city was punishing itself too, it seemed – a hypercarnivore, sick from overeating, forcing itself to keep eating anyway. Soon these tumours would be all that remained. I wondered what would happen if the police were persuaded to shift their allegiance – away from the investments of oligarchs – and back towards the clamour that created them. But property was such a thrilling violence that few could ever give it up. Perhaps I should give in to it too, and help London accelerate into its future as a bonfire.

'I'm going to take a sample from you, now,' the constable said. 'Just stay like that please.'

She inserted a cotton swab into my arsehole, and firmly rubbed at Kimber's cum until enough was removed to be sealed into a plastic pouch. At her touch, my body abstracted – and I became the city beneath me. The sewers and subways were my arteries, cars covered my arms – the whole tournament of civil society was a fever, and I was being drilled at and stretched out and kissed. My plasma was livid with people – the people living here now and the people that lived here before and those that would live here hereafter – and yet it was not with a oneness that my body rose towards pleasure – I was neither a disunity nor a unity – my body was the city, and the yearning of its matter was the yearning for a desert that could never be empty enough. I was impossible as long as I could say 'I' – the inertia of being was an impossible inertia for a city, since it could never stop, or it if did, it would no longer be a city. Life was not the opposite of death, here – pain was the opposite of death, and life didn't exist – I was the silent ticking heard before the traffic lights change – the dread of isolation inside the dream of time itself. My words were pollutants – and I breathed them in, with the relief of belonging – with the relief and reassurance and joy of coming home.

'Open your mouth a bit for me,' she said, a gloved hand tilting my head away from the view as she prodded under my tongue to collect saliva.

Another two swabs collected paint, three more collected blood. The filled pouches were placed in the green case – and as it was clipped shut, she said, 'You get to be clean now.'

I laughed, and she stared – as though staring in regret at her own sentence – hanging saffron-yellow in the air between us. I had drawn her away from her trained speech patterns, into awkwardness and overfamiliarity – but I needed to take her further still – until she forgot that I could be a suspect – or even, until she became complicit in my performance.

What she meant was – my suffering had been separated from my skin, and I no longer controlled it.

She led me to the bathroom. My nose brushed her neck as she slowed – and the saffron I'd seen in her voice combined with the taste of anise and cloves from the wine – into a perfume – and I imagined this was the scent of her emotional state – and could mean that she was afraid, or uncertain, or tricking me.

The huddle of other officers, in passing, confirmed the authenticity of my name and the existence of Detective Chief Inspector Sanam. They seemed now suspended in inactivity, confined to the corridor, as though they were in such awe of what had happened here that they were unable to remain in any of the rooms for long. Or maybe this was a misreading – and they were regarding me not in awe but in suspicion. In contrast, I felt overactive – time was speeding up.

In the bathroom, I crawled around a partition of glass into the shower area at the back. My knees chafed on the flagstones. Queasily I reached to the tap and turned it on – releasing too-hot water over my back. My biceps swelled with acid and indigo swilled in my eyes. I reclined into the corner, tired by pain, back towards sleep.

'No, Leander.' Constable Carr crouched down beside me, on the other side of the glass, taking off her gloves. 'You need to wash yourself now. Otherwise I'm going to come in and do it for you.'

I groped into the recessed shelf above me and picked out a pot of 'exfoliating scrub'. It had the texture of wet sand and smelt of parsley and frankincense. I pawed it liberally over myself – massaging first my aching underarms and then my chest and feet. It abraded my face and clotted my hair. But as I stood to wash behind myself, the motion inspired more nausea – and I vomited the last of the wine into the drain. Again, vomiting felt comforting – like the interior version of a lover's caress.

I considered pomading myself with the other products on the shelf, but I was too tired. So I kept to the scrub, barking in agony as I cleaned my stab wound with it, riskily arousing myself by this into an erection. I sat down to hide it – and as my lust retreated, I bent to let the shower patter onto my whip welts – and sobbed, for the sympathy of Constable Carr.

'I think it's time for you to come out,' she said, unfolding a towel from the rail and holding it open for me.

Time stuttered. I stopped the shower and swayed towards her – she embraced me with the towel, holding me longer than seemed appropriate. Heroin had blurred the boundaries of my body – so that her body felt more like mine than mine did – and I wanted to stroke my own skin with her hands, and reach round from the small of my back to the hair below my navel. She could have been half the age of Constable Floris – perhaps she'd even been born on the same day as me – and she was less straightforward than her, with none of her maternal instincts. Here, her embrace confused the roles of sister and seducer. I revolved away from her – onto the lid of the laundry basket – and enjoyed my own nakedness as she tried to keep her eyes on my face. I could feel her thinking of the officers on the other side of the wall.

'What do you like doing?' I asked.

'What do you mean?' she asked, unprepared for this line of questioning.

'What are your… interests? Do you like heli-skiing?'

'I like cooking,' she said, cautiously.

'Like roadkill or profiteroles or – what kind?'

'Are you hungry?'

'I only eat turtle.'

She smiled. 'You need to dry yourself, ok? And then we can go get dressed.'

'What's your best dish?'

'I like horse meat,' she said, easily at last. 'I've scared all my family with making them eat it.'

I nodded as I dried myself.

'I roast it in madeira, in cubes,' she continued. 'With prunes sometimes – and make a stew. And everyone gets converted to it. It's got more interest to it than beef, and it's got more strength and it's sweeter – but it's also got that more wild taste.

And it's not fussy like. And it's cheap. I've cooked with donkey too. I got recipes from Italy off of the internet, and I make up my own – but I never been there. I want to go, one day, around the South, I'd like that. I want to learn Italian but I never did languages.'

'Where do you buy horse meat from?' I asked, standing to dry my legs, too giddy to meet her gaze.

'I get it off of the internet,' she said. 'It's hard to buy here. I used to get it in Nottingham in the market. But your London markets are too expensive.'

'London is all only markets now – and all the sellers are thieves.'

'I'd be well up for cooking turtle actually,' she said without listening to me. 'You can make turtle soup, I know that. And then there's mock turtle soup, I know that – but that's with offal. You can make it with calf's foot. And brains and oysters. And even testicles – if you fry them first in blood and fat so hot that it's spitting. And madeira.'

As she was speaking, I watched my shadow widen across the flagstones – until it was a horse, galloping across the wall – and onto the ceiling – which was a meadow, crowded with other horses – and all of the horses had syphilis – and they were being ridden by male models – who all longed to be abandoned by the horses – but who stayed because they all longed to catch syphilis too.

I nearly fell over. She held me up. My lips touched her skin and tasted salt and lard – and I imagined her smearing herself with horse fat in front of a mirror.

'The mock turtle is my favourite character in *Alice in Wonderland*,' I said. 'He has the best line: "'Once', said the Mock Turtle at last, with a deep sigh, 'I was a real Turtle.'" The fall from the real-self to the mock-self – that's nearly all of literature.'

'So you're a Mock Turtle?' she asked.

'I'm more of a Mock Moss Piglet,' I said and stumbled into the sink. 'Though maybe I can reverse that fall.'

She steadied me.

'Let's get some clothes on you, first, how's that?' she said.

I draped the towel around myself like a cloak and emerged, haughtily, to face the officers in the corridor. Perhaps they already had evidence that could convict me – something I'd forgotten, that couldn't be explained away by intoxication or trauma or Kimber's insanity – and they were just letting me carry on for fun. Perhaps they would even let me walk out of the front door – and then, at the last moment, they'd stop the lift doors closing – and the handcuffs would go back on.

Constable Carr was guiding me past them to Kimber's bedroom, almost too fast for me to understand what she was doing – but I realised this was a test of my innocence, and readied my pretend surprise. At the sight of Kimber's blood I yelped, recoiling – as though instinctually – and pressed my face into her vest.

'Are your clothes in here, Leander?'

'Yes.'

'Ok – have we taken photos of those?' she asked another officer. 'We're just going to – he needs to wear something.'

I withdrew from her to approach the bundle at the foot of the bed. Kimber's corpse kept a metallic taste in the air despite the breeze from the window. I knew the officers were studying my reaction – but my inebriation made me confident of my innocence, even as I tried not to smile with glee at my guilt – and my glee slid into the scent of Kimber's blood. Kimber had played against me and lost, just as Dawn had. He knew the risks.

I briefly considered stealing his suit – but instead pulled on the outfit I'd borrowed from Francis, since I'd rather have a last memory of him. The alcohol in my limbs turned dressing into a vaudeville act – I staggered over myself, falling forwards, losing myself in the two sweatshirts, putting my trousers on backwards. Eventually, the constable intervened.

As she helped me dress, my head knocked into hers – her hair smelt of baking bread, like Francis sometimes did – and I had a vision of washing her hair in her own blood, as she died beside me on the bed, and the apartment flooded so quickly that the other policemen forgot how to swim – and so they drowned below us, as the water rose to wash the blood back out of her hair, and I flowed out of the window, on a wave, to safety.

'Are you hungry?' She was leading me out of the room. 'We can get you some food while you're talking to the chief inspector.'

My senses were too unstable for fear – but doubt began leaking through the heroin's defences.

'Can I have a satsuma?' I asked, trying to seem unconcerned.

'Do you not want chocolate or something?'

'I'm lactose intolerant,' I lied. 'And I like satsumas.'

'Alright,' she smiled. 'I'll have a look for some.'

More policemen now crowded the corridor – but this only increased the sense of inactivity. They seemed to be waiting for some judgement to be passed. A warbling entered the air. And before I could fully understand what was happening, I was pushed into the kitchen.

Detective Chief Inspector Sanam stood alone at its centre, holding the back of a chair. He seemed somehow narrower than before, perhaps in rage.

'Sit,' he said.

And the door behind me was shut.

3.

I hugged him. The chief inspector semi-reciprocated, trying to maintain his public authority – but I insisted on this paternal intimacy, refusing to release him until I'd forced out tears. Then, crying, I stepped back, and lifted my face towards his.

'Good afternoon, Leander,' he said. 'I understand that you are… inebriated, but I need you to sit down for a moment.'

He indicated the chair. As I watched, its wood turned nacreous and began to melt.

'A throne of pearl, for the boy king!' I cried happily, and sat.

He patted my shoulders twice in uncertain reassurance – and walked around to face me, his hands behind his back. On the table beside us was Kimber's camera. But, I noticed, the microwave had not yet been opened – though its window was blackened – so the investigation had been paused for my interview. Or was this an interrogation?

'First of all – I have contacted Ms Vasari,' he said, 'and she's coming here to take you home. She tells me that Mr Cole – that Francis is safe. So I don't want you to worry about that. And I – I would like to personally apologise for – the way this operation has been conducted. It was unethical of me to… expect you to be able to help us. I have regrets about that. We have failed to protect you and that failing is my responsibility.'

'Not at all,' I said. 'I've had a wonderful weekend.'

'I –' he tried to smile at my fake positivity, but then pointed towards the camera on the table. 'There is very disturbing footage on this camera – some of which we've already recovered from Ms Amélie Jasiukowicz's laptop – as you suggested we might – and that footage was in fact critical in helping us with our investigation. But first I need you to provide me with some information. There appears to be more recently filmed footage on this camera of you being… assaulted by a man unknown to us. Can you tell us anything about him? And can you tell me how you came to be here, and how Francis came to be free? According to Ms Vasari, Francis is not well enough to speak with us at present. So I need to hear from you the sequence of events.'

'I didn't flee the crime scene this time!' I said. 'Could have been my third fled murder in a row. But I resisted the hat-trick.'

'From what I understand, you were not able to flee because you were restrained.' He grimaced. 'Specifically – with police handcuffs, that belonged to Constable Floris. And in a separate room to the one in which… Kimber's body was discovered… So. What do you remember? Can you describe Kimber's state of mind to me?'

'Have you read *Faust, Part Two*? You know that bit where Mephistopheles goes to a second Walpurgisnacht – and there are monsters from older myths there this time – and so the little Calvinist devil is out of his league? "Doch das Antike find' ich zu lebendig". That's what happened last night. Kimber met a demon from an older religion and lost.'

'What do you mean lost?'

'I killed him. But I wanted him to suffer first – you know, death is a pleasantry, pain has the meaning. So I injected him with rabies. And then I leashed him like a dog. He became afraid of water. I boiled the kettle and poured it over his head. He went blind, then mad, and then I peeled off his skin and fed it to him. Eventually I became tired and went to sleep – and when I woke up somehow Kimber had come back to life and so it started again.'

'This is not the appropriate time for your jokes, Leander. It's over. Kimber killed himself, that much we know – unless you found a way to shoot him point blank in the head without a struggle while his eyes were open and his finger was stiff around the trigger.'

'Who says I didn't?'

'You just said that you didn't. You said you injected him with rabies. There is no evidence of that. What there is evidence of is a sexual attack – it's possible that you're in shock.'

The word 'shock' carried a perfume into the air that seemed the opposite of its meaning – slow and corrupt and rich, like the spores of a toadstool growing from a corpse – and this perfume became a jungle in my mind – a jungle I could see from an aerial vantage – spreading across the contours of many hills, towards the eastern sea – and the western fires of deforesters.

'I meant… I injected him with rabies metaphorically,' I said after a pause.

'I suggest you don't use metaphors in your answers, then. We've had this discussion before.'

'We've also had a discussion where you said that I was "no damsel in distress".'

'I regret that conversation. I was too eager to… follow up my lead. You were my lead. And you were not protected well. I am sorry for that. You were failed. But can you explain how Mr Cole came to escape? And can you explain how you ended up here?'

'Don't rely on love – it's not enough,' I said coldly. 'You can't rely on yourself either. Self-reliance isn't enough. Sometimes Goliath has to win – but you don't have to be David, you can be Jonathan instead. Leave David to die, refuse your father's battles, avoid the army on the hill – and exile yourself. Patience and exile and cunning – but not silence. Jonathan fucked David well enough for their love to "surpass the love of women" – but it's time to elude the world of the Bible, and escape the story entirely. There will be other Davids, or even if not, there will be other days. And that's enough. You can be a different Jonathan. Let Goliath win. Love won't.'

'What does that mean? Who are you talking about?'

'Francis doesn't love me anymore,' I said, teetering on the chair, unable to force a smile. 'He doesn't want me.'

The chief inspector lunged to catch me before I fell to the floor – and knelt, holding my upper arms against my torso.

'None of this is your fault,' he said. 'You're trying to blame yourself... and I believe that the way I chose to express myself last time we spoke suggested I wanted to blame you too. But although you might have... kick-started this phase of our investigation – you are not accountable for Kimber's actions. And I can't speak for Mr Cole, for – for Francis, but I think he will understand that. It really isn't appropriate for me to be speaking to you in this state... but I want to reassure you that we are working to... round up the rest of Kimber's operation. We're rounding them up. Do you understand? Our raids are working – we've seized hours of video evidence – and in two different houses we recovered victims of trafficking. There's not many figures left anonymous – and there are fewer places for them to hide. But the man in this video with you is unknown to us – do you know who he is?'

'I don't know what video you mean,' I said.

'It is... distressing. I think for now it would be better if you just tell me what you can remember.'

I took the camera from the table and switched it on, to play back Nikolas' and my performance as if I had never seen it before.

'I don't remember this,' I said.

The chief inspector closed his hands around mine and covered the screen, though Nikolas' grunts still played through its speakers.

'Do you remember going into that house?' he asked.

'I remember phoning you from the toilets at the Rockway. I

was with Kimber. He forced me to inhale paint thinner. I hallucinated. Then he water-boarded me with paint – a European twist on an American classic. What more could a young hung Londoner ask for? But I don't know who this man is. I can help you catch him if you want, I can be bait again. I caught Kimber for you. And I escaped alive. As you said – I always escape alive. I can catch again.'

'Definitely not. It would have been better if I'd never said that to you. And it would have been better if Kimber had been caught. His death is… complicating. You should not have gone to him. You escaped, with this drunken-boxer style of yours, but… you only just escaped, Leander. This was never what I expected you to do.'

'Of course it was. You knew I'd find him. I'm an ulcer and I need flesh to disfigure. It was easy. He was at the Rockway. He could hide from you, but ghosts can see each other.'

There was a knock on the door.

'Yes?' the chief inspector called.

Constable Carr opened the door. 'Ms Vasari is here, sir,' she said.

Sanam nodded. 'Go home, Leander,' he said, standing up. 'You've done enough. And I'm sorry for it.'

'Go home?' I asked. 'Isn't there a whole gang out there that knows who I am? Aren't I in danger?'

'Kimber's operation is over,' he said. 'They're not in a position to be endangering anyone. The best thing that you can do is get some rest. So let Ms Vasari take you home.'

'I don't have a home!' I said, inciting myself to anger. 'You wanted me to be a weapon. You said I was a threat! And now I'm being dismissed? Fuck you! You don't even know who I am, do you? You didn't even fucking look me up. I'm in your database. You didn't even look me up. You've taken my DNA enough times to build a fucking twin. I have thousands of twins, anyway, thousands of girls and boys forgotten in the same backstreets, for the same reasons. Am I not worth searching for? Or was it all wiped clean when I turned eighteen? Was I just deleted again? Shoved off the end of the last waiting list, pushed across one too many state in-trays – until the ink was worn down and I was massaged out of the statistics. You didn't even look. I was thrown away! I was too young for your nets, that's why I fell through all of them – and that's how I learned to get away – you taught me – you've seen me so many times before, and you've forgotten, you'll keep forgetting, you'll always forget. I've seen you before – even though you had different names, and you had different faces – I've been abandoned before. But you should know who I am by now. I can't go home. I don't fucking have a home.'

'Stop shouting, Leander.'

'I don't want this. I don't want your forgiveness. I want a resolution! I want an ending!'

'We can speak again when you're sober.'

'Can I at least keep the snitch phone?' I asked, switching to comic plaintiveness.

'No, I'm afraid not. But Ms Vasari has my number if you wish to get hold of me.'

He ushered me out of the kitchen. I hugged him goodbye, he pushed me away. Past the huddle of cops, Iris was waiting – in a red wide-brimmed hat and darker red overcoat. I stumbled to her. Wordlessly she took my hand and pulled me towards the lift. Constable Carr followed us and forced a string-bag of satsumas into my hands.

'Stay safe Mock Turtle,' she said. 'I'm not forgetting you.'

I smiled as the lift closed, and rested my head on Iris' shoulder. Her coat smelt of shea butter. I gazed at her shoes – dark red leather with gold buckles. She hooked her arm around mine, steadying me down in silence. I heard no warble or cawing now – the drone in my head was neutral – and reflected nothing back at me. In my fatigue, I did not know whether my anger had been real or pretend.

The street was steeped in fog the colour of tea. As we walked towards a car whose lights answered Iris' key, we passed the bag I'd flung from the window. I retrieved it from beneath the bush.

Iris did not react, but as I fingered the Rockway's keys through its plastic, I began to feel apprehensive – as though everything was now more volatile. Nothing was resolved. There were threats without faces at the edges of my future. And the police had discarded me just as Francis had – into an unfinished crisis.

Iris helped me into the passenger seat – and as she rounded the bonnet for the driver's side, I lent back my head, alone – and inhaled slowly, to orient myself within my sloshing half-thoughts. Almost unknowingly, I was opening the bag in my lap – with a compulsion that felt the same as a suspicion – like I was completing a design that I'd been obeying for days, and that this was the final step – after which, it promised, I could attain my own kind of closure.

4.

Iris reversed from the tower.

'What's the time?' I asked.

'Nearly six.'

'How's it that late?'

'The hours had other things to do.'

My mind was ajar. The realisation that I had fooled the police – that it was over and I was getting away – was only slowly dawning upon me.

'Where are we going?' I asked.

'You know where we're going. Francis wants you to come home. Because contrary to your outburst in the kitchen, you do have a home. Francis wants you to come home – to him. Eva's there as well.'

The teal in her voice had an amphibian dampness now – and as I stared at the windshield, I imagined this colour stamping pentagrams on the glass.

'Francis thinks I'm disgusting,' I said. 'He doesn't want to see me.'

'He didn't know what he was saying,' Iris said. 'He didn't know what you'd been through. You didn't explain yourself. I had to show him the video of you on his doorstep. And he saw you were trying to get back to him. Eva could have turned him against you, but you've seduced her as well, haven't you? She was begging him to believe that you loved him. It was the most twisted emotional knot I've ever watched being tied. And you were the one tying it and you weren't even there.'

'I don't always have the energy to be in two places at once.'

'But I've seen you do it!' she said, ignoring my sarcasm. 'Like at the gallery. You were so upbeat with me there, you were so – there … but at the same time you were dealing with this whole other human trafficking counter-narrative. I'm impressed.'

'It wasn't a counter-narrative,' I said. 'It was the same narrative. Your industries are the same.'

She didn't reply. I tried to look out of the window – but it had thickened into the white walls of a gallery, the gallery of Iris' exhibition – and it was dimming upwards into the curve of a planetarium, with Saturn on the ceiling – and, as before, the projection became real – and we actually were on Saturn – and soot around us clumped into graphite which lightning turned to diamonds – and the diamonds were raining over us, as swift as bullets, riddling our bodies into mince – and I thought of how little I feared ageing, and how annoying I found those who did – and we were diamonds too – until Saturn became a car again.

'Can we drive somewhere else?' I asked. 'I have a meeting in Brixton. Francis doesn't want to see me. I've burnt that bridge – and burning bridges is only satisfying when you want to get back to the other side. And can't. He's seen what I am and he doesn't want it.'

'That's such bullshit. He's seen… ugh, whatever – I'm taking you to him and you're going to explain yourself. That's that. Who are you supposed to be meeting in Brixton?'

'I don't know,' I said. 'But just drive towards Brixton station. Please.'

'And then what?'

'And then you can do whatever you want to me.'

'Ok.' She moved into a lane that led to Lambeth Bridge. 'But then you're going home. You know… I should want to strangle you.'

'You should want – but you don't?' I smiled.

'I should, but I'm really just amazed. How did you manage to do all the ridiculous shit that you did while doing everything else?'

'What do you mean?' I asked innocently.

'You come onto my set and within days the police are shutting down my film – and my producer has her laptop seized as evidence relating to the same gang you and Francis were abducted by.'

I giggled at the colour-change in her voice – its teal was colder now, more reptilian, and stamping faster on the windshield.

'What wrong with a little police raid? Sounds exciting for you.'

'It delayed our shooting schedule.'

'So now you have more time to use me.'

'Why would I do that?'

'Did you not like my scene?' I asked, with an even more cloying innocence. 'Don't you think that you could get more out of me?'

'Your scene in the kitchen just now with the police was even better. I didn't realise you could do anger.'

'Give me the right room and I can do anything,' I said. 'I'm already in your film – I want to be in it more.'

'I know you do. But I don't like being manipulated.'

'You're not being manipulated, you're being seduced. This is what I told you I'd do.'

'Is that what that is? When my agent congratulates me for somehow getting the star of my film on the cover of i-D magazine? And my film isn't even half-finished? And he doesn't mean Eva – but he meant you! How are you the star?'

'Yes, that's being seduced. What a delightful surprise. And not the star yet – but you can make me one.'

'How do you even do that? Like what the fuck does that mean? Nikolas sent me an email saying he's done an interview with you. But he's not answering my calls. What did you do? This is so unnecessary. I hire people for their talent, not for their machinations. You can't change my mind with random disruptive acts.'

'My machinations are proof of my talent,' I said, with a grand hand gesture. 'The more unnecessary the better. And disruption is never random. I wanted to get your attention. I don't need to change your mind – you already want me – I wanted to extract your desires, and startle you with them.'

'By wrecking the lives of my co-workers?'

I let my eyelids close – and imagined we were driving through the suburbs of a different town – in Italy, say – after a storm had churned up the cemetery and turned loose its graves, into the summer heat – so that the streets hung with crematorium smoke and the odour of rotting bodies – and I knew that the sound of crying widows would follow us a long way out of town, until a sea wind cleaned the air – and recalled to me the scent of the hospitals of my childhood and the hate I felt only in summer.

'It was only one man,' I said, leaving my reverie. 'And Nikolas' life isn't wrecked. It's just going to be more complicated now. And Amélie was only a little shocked, she'll get her laptop back. Nothing that happened to them is as bad as what happened to me.'

'You're so ridiculous. Was this all planned? Was Francis a target to you? Am I just a target? And is being in my film even your endgame? Or am I another middle step in some insane staircase that only you can see?'

'You think I had a heart attack on purpose?' I asked, feigning anger. 'You think I got chained up and raped on purpose?'

'Is that… what happened?' she asked, her aggression instantly gone.

'That's part of what happened.'

'Is that what they found on Amélie's laptop?'

'Among other things,' I said. 'She should be happy to host some of my earliest video work. And your camera cares about similar things to Kimber's – the exploitation of youth and youthful sexuality. And anyway – I was high. Do you really think I put it on her laptop purposefully to get at you?'

The car crossed Lambeth Bridge – and with no buildings around us, the streetlights looked like upside-down narwhals, screwed into the stone by their horns, with the night sky as their bodies – or, reflected in the Thames, like blind whales' eyes – glossy and impalpable, with the memory of distant centuries. Lambeth suited the autumn best, since this was the season it seemed to have been built for and out of – and more so now that so many of its houses were ghost houses – sold off fast within a few years to foreign trusts, which kept them unoccupied until their value doubled and they could be sold on again.

I thought I saw a woman beside us in a dress of blue and white check, like an alpine milkmaid, with a sunbonnet and an apron – though in the cold darkness, her clothes seemed much sadder than mourning. She walked the other way.

'I don't know,' Iris said. 'The police explained some of this gang to us – but Francis isn't talking, and you're not a reliable narrator, so how am I supposed to know where my sympathies should be?'

I sighed insincerely. 'You're the one who made an exhibition called TRAUMA DREAM!'

'DREAM TRAUMA.'

'Whatever. I was traumatised. And you choose instead to imagine that I've been strategising my way into your film? I've been making the best out of a bad situation.'

'I didn't think that… I knew that you – I don't know. I'm sorry. There definitely would have been easier ways for you to get my attention.'

'Yeah,' I said. 'Though they wouldn't have been as exciting.

Just take it as another testament to my skills that I can make you believe that everything that happened to me was actually about you.'

'Alright!' Iris said softly, subdued but amused. 'But even if I do – why should I change my plans for you?'

'Your film is malleable. It's more malleable than before. You can make changes.'

'And how do you know my film won't be terrible?'

'I've seen your photos – you know how to extract a performance. I can modify your script. Come on. Let me win. Let the villain win.'

She laughed. 'You're so incoherent – you're claiming both no responsibility and full responsibility for ending up in this position.'

'Of course. Contradictions keep me alive. Life doesn't happen in tidy little diagrams. The diagrams come later, and they don't always overlap.'

'Then you need to draw a better diagram,' she said. 'How can you say you've burnt the bridge to Francis, but want to work with me? Those things overlap. What are the rules here?'

I paused a moment, allowing myself to lower into the opiate's ambience, until the motor throbbing below us sounded like a clock being unspun at the edge of a black hole.

'I want to be stimulated by people,' I said at last, with mock self-pity. 'But I never am. So I have to constantly replace them.'

'That's just narcissism,' she said. 'You could let yourself be loved. That would be harder, that would be more radical than this posturing.'

'I've done love. Love is just giving in to another perspective. I want the opposite, I want to find someone who's stuck in the same perspective as me – like a spider in a CCTV camera, forced to watch the world from high unpleasant corners – out of too many eyes, with static across the lens. Love is a shared self-absorption – I want something more mysterious.'

'You want yourself twice?' Iris asked. 'That's the standard autoerotic fantasy of the narcissist. That's not mysterious.'

'Yes it is. And it's not autoerotic – that's the whole point. I want to meet me-but-not-me. For most people that wouldn't be difficult – most people find their peers easily. But I can't.'

'You found us, you found friends.'

'That's just love again. All friendships are romances. I don't mean that.'

'So what do you mean?'

The green of twin traffic lights tripled the green in her eyes.

'I want to be beaten on my own terms,' I said. 'I want a psychological equal.'

'You haven't understood love if you think only an equal can beat you. And even if there is an equal waiting for you out there, he'd never satisfy you.'

'That might be true,' I said. 'But I'd rather find out for myself. I grew up alone for too long. I had to extract myself out of myself when I was a teenager – without anyone else there – and once you've warped into this kind of shape, you can't straighten out properly. Love can only take you so far. I want to meet someone else who had to be their own saviour – someone else who had to break into themselves when they were young and got wounded in the process.'

'You're sitting next to someone who did that. Most teenagers are lonely. It's not that rare. Your wounds don't have to be permanent. When I started taking female hormones, I didn't know they were going to make me sterile so fast. None of my sperm was saved. I was fifteen when I broke into myself, as you'd say – and it left me sterile. That's permanent. I had to extract myself out of myself for years. Imagine how much I had to say in my own head before I could say out loud to my parents – "Hi, I'm not a boy, I'm a girl, I'm not Lars, I'm

Iris, and I need surgery and this isn't a phase"? But I didn't romanticise myself into an island like you did. You should allow yourself more vulnerability, then you might find peace.'

'I don't want peace.'

'Stimulation, then. It's the same.'

I had no reply to this. So I leaned sideways into my window and gazed out at the amorphous landscapes around us – until I realised where we were.

'Can you take the second left?' I asked. 'That road – that one.'

She turned the car towards the road I was pointing at.

'I don't really believe you, by the way,' she said. 'I think you've already allowed yourself vulnerability. I think Francis means more to you than you want to admit.'

I smiled till my lips touched the glass. 'Sometimes the person you're manipulating gives in so easily that you begin to feel affection for them. That's all he was to me.'

'You mean "I don't love you but you make me cum"?' she said. 'I don't believe you. I think you are in love with him. I think all this shit about having no psychological equal is just a defence because he hurt you. You were wounded by his rejection yesterday. Which means you were beaten. What you've been claiming you long for – has already happened. I don't think you care about finding a double. You've found Francis. And you're vulnerable to him. That's stimulating. And you're trying to convince me – and really more trying to convince yourself – that you're the lonely villain and he means nothing. But this whole process, everything you've said out of denial, is a symptom of your failure – he means something. And you were beaten by him. Accept it.'

I laughed. 'Fine, I'm just trying to fend off Francis. I'm vulnerable to him. I accept it. He beat me.' I pointed to a parking space ahead. 'Can you stop here? You're actually right. Nothing I've said convinces me either.'

She parked the car in silence, annoyed by the readiness of my admission.

'But… we can fix that,' she said eventually. 'He's waiting for you. So why are we here?'

'I need to finish something. But you have to stay in the car.'

'No, I'm coming with you.'

'You can't,' I said. 'They'll only allow me in. You can do whatever you want with me afterwards.'

'How long will you take?'

'I dunno. Not that long. How long is an ending?'

I kissed her – and remembered our kiss in the kitchen, days ago, in the gallery, when there had still been a mayhem of futures before me. Again I saw a pond under mist – and lotus leaves, leaving, burning stacks of myrrh – but there was no more mayhem now, my future was simple.

I climbed out of the car in a drunken blood-rush, clutching the keys through the plastic bag. A street lamp walked into me. I felt oddly destabilised by Iris's perceptiveness. Not only had she persuaded me that I'd been beaten by Francis, but really, she'd beaten me herself. I shook my head. Perhaps she could have been my double – but it was too late for that now. I ran on towards the back entrance of the Rockway – ignoring my body, ignoring my affections – rousing my mind towards climax.

5.

My senses attuned to the dusk. Slowing my breathing, I sprinted past stacks of wet crates towards the Rockway's back door. It took three tries of Kimber's keys before it was unlocked. My skin felt like scum on a dead lake – but I loved the intoxication still – not just because it disguised me from myself, and not just because it took my thoughts down strange detours – but because I loved the feeling of being poisoned. Anything that betrays my body is my friend.

The emergency exit swung outwards and I stepped in. The kitchen hummed in a gloom illumined bluely by six strips of a fly-killing light. I would be an assassin too.

I ran past Kimber's cupboard of masks, past clean shelves and clean countertops – towards the interior door. Beyond it, I could hear the hubbub of waiting men. Their anxiety seemed to stretch beyond their social world, and out across the years behind them – until the sound of their speech seemed to me the sound of an entire millennium chastising itself. After two tests, I found the key that fitted this second door – and so locked myself into privacy, to cook undisturbed. This kitchen would always be mine.

The faces of Francis and Dawn floated towards me, with compassionate eyes – but I blinked them away. I would have no memories. I would have no music. Or, I would have only the music of fancy. My nerves could not risk kindness.

The steel surfaces implied themselves in the twilight. I paced around them, considering my ending. The fridges were empty and the larder's stock was low, but I did not need food. I needed fuel – so, first, I approached the propane canisters.

This scene could serve too as the climax of a coming-of-age arc, I supposed, since I was building a bomb out of the space my father owned and my mother had died in – although they were my parents only through the surrogacy of metaphor. I could also, then, call this a tomb, couldn't I? And as I carried the four canisters to the fan oven, I thought – hey, why not, let's call this a womb as well. A womb-tomb-bomb. I removed the oven's middle shelf and set its target heat to 240° Celsius.

I had, I supposed, fucked my father and killed my mother – and also, less interestingly, killed my father and fucked my mother. So what was there left for me to do, except become myself? Well, kill my brother too, of course – although perhaps Francis had been sufficiently transformed already. I untwisted the canisters' bleeder valves until their gas hissed softly out – and placed three of them on top of the oven – and one inside.

My body was unbalanced, long since past the last of its strength. I dialled all five of the hob's gas rings to maximum, lighting five automatic fires. But I did not want fire yet, so with the fire-blanket on the wall, I smothered their flames – until just the gas hissed out, unlit, to interfuse with the canisters' propane in the air – together waiting for a future spark. The oven felt like another body, a healthy body – a body I could climb on at night, threateningly, pressing and restricting, whispering 'Shut the fuck up, shut the fuck up,' too quietly for the parents sleeping down the hall to hear – until a voice dissociated from the body, whispering 'Please, please, please,' and I felt strong. I poured three bottles of oil into the chip fryer beside the hob, and switched it on.

I stepped back to admire my work. Soon, the chip oil would be hot enough to combust and so ignite the cloud of gases above it. The canisters' security valves would become fuses – and under the encouragement of heat, flame, and pressure, they would rupture. And their rupture would be a rapture. A fire would have been too slow – if I was to destroy my inheritance properly, then I required an explosion to claim whoever was gathered in the room on the other side of the wall. I doubted my text to Kimber's dozen contacts had summoned them all, but a few would be sufficient for an ending. And perhaps among them were my canal-side attackers – or the men they answered to.

I gazed around. There are no seasons in kitchens like this, I thought – here, men unyoke themselves from nature. This unyoking is only temporary, of course – the ice will melt and waves will cover London – and like every civilisation across the universe, we will make ourselves extinct before we find other life.

The scent of sunflower oil coiled around me, merging with the gases in my throat. The three formed a helmet of air, lowering over me, weighing my shoulders down. I sat. Soon too I crossed my legs and leant back my head. The vapours were leaking out faster than I'd anticipated. Or perhaps I'd hoped they would be this fast. I'd been a liar too long to know whether I was lying to myself or not anymore.

'Yes,' the gas whispered. 'You wished for this so your tricked yourself into staying here, here, yes, and yes this fire is for you.'

As I inhaled, the room softened. My eyes were drugged shut. The oil thickened into the smell of bubbling pig lard – and behind it was a history of other foods: the acorns of the oaks that the pig had been fattened on, the figs and groundnuts, the potatoes and sweet potatoes, the cabbages, the carrot peelings, the stale bread and stale butter, the turnips, the celeriac, the apples. The pig had been fattened until the moon was in the right quarter, in late October, four hundred years ago to the day. I was there.

At sunrise, we rose for his slaughter. The pig had been kept in a sty. I held him between my thighs. With a knife as long as my forearm, I slit his throat. The spurts of the carotid artery were caught in an iron pail and the blood was stirred before it cooled so that it would not coagulate. It was then thickened with breadcrumbs, chopped pork, pork fat, garlic, and cloves. Next – according to this fantasia my mind was tracing as it drifted further from the kitchen – this mixture was stuffed into the pig's washed intestines and boiled. Some of it would accompany beer; some would be poached in vegetable soup; some would be served with lentils, at New Year, for prosperity.

After the blood was drained, the pig was cooked in straw until his skin was hard and turned ivory with scrubbing. The joints and sides were carried to the loft to be smoked. Some cuts, I smelt, were salted into ham, others spiced into sausage. A few were stirred in with millet seed. The kidneys and liver were fried in sherry. But shouldn't that be madeira?

My body was fading into the gas – enhancing my dream-body's senses, so that soon inside my dream I began to see as well as smell. I ran out from the pig loft into fields. I was among sweating teenagers, centuries ago, gathered at the end of a day drilling winter wheat. They were tired, muscular, tanned – and happy, because they were together. And together, they walked back home between fields of rapeseed flowers. I and another boy parted from this pack, for a different track, across a river to the woods. There, we shared our first kiss. He was taller than me, and stronger, and better fed – and his lips tasted of red leaves.

'Kun-unun Nuogah!' a pheasant cried as we climbed the slope. 'Koo-unun Nuogu!'

In the woods, the boy found a pheasant feather – and poked it into my hair. We sat under a chestnut tree. As the gas thickened in the kitchen, the sky above my dream-body changed – from blue to lovat. The tops of the dream-trees were tweed – the air was shutting down. The peasant boy hugged me, with the same tightness as Francis did, nearly bruising me.

Among the tree roots there were conkers. The boy picked up

two and handed me one. The sky vanished. I leaned towards his mouth as if to kiss him, but then tacked away. His words were encrypting into the call of the pheasant, and the tree-trunks were disappearing, so that soon only the underbrush of fern and bramble would remain. As the dream-world dimmed, the scent of its soil brightened into a taste.

We had no strings to play the game, but we pretended. Holding the conkers between thumb and forefinger, we swung them at each other until they kissed. We both declared ourselves the loser; I insisted that his larger conker, if it had been on a string, would have shattered mine – and he insisted the same. But I threw my conker over his shoulder first, so forced him into victory. To confirm my defeat, he tapped his conker on the middle of my forehead.

The ferns left. We were alone on a circle of dirt. The conker in his hand shrivelled into a chestnut.

'Eat it, brother, eat it,' he whispered – and lifted it to my lips.

But as I ate it, I closed my dream-body's eyes – and lost the boy, and lost the woods. The call of the pheasant became the slur of a helicopter. Then, a lightning bolt returned me to the edge of the rapeseed fields. The workers had been replaced by tractors.

The bolt repeated into a flame and I was released more fully from the dream – into my body's present tense. I saw the kitchen, wavering in the gases' susurrating haze, but there was no flame. The sole illumination was still the blue of the fly-killing light. The oil had not yet heated itself alight.

The bolt repeated once more, and I realised I'd confused vision with sound – the bolt was a knock – someone knocking on the back door.

A fourth knock shocked me into movement. I crawled away from the oven. My breathing was shallow and my thoughts were in scraps – but I knew that I was changing my mind.

My movements became faster the further I crawled from the

envelope of gas. Its poison clotted my limbs into mindlessness, but something of myself persevered – outside of words – obeying a different plot. I stopped in front of Kimber's cupboard. The air around me looked like black whipped cream.

I took the riot cop uniform out of the cupboard and dressed in it. The heavy suit and flack jacket – both labelled 'POLICE' – fitted loosely over my clothes. I put on the balaclava, put on the helmet, put on the gloves, and took up the truncheon. I was suffocating into something cruder than a man – but inside this armour, I was re-energised.

And so I swam towards the back door – my sight limited by the misting visor – and before I could push it open, there was another knock. I fell out into Iris.

'No,' I slammed the door behind me. 'Get back in the car.'

The air snapped in half, the street's surfaces shrank.

'Why are you wearing that?' she asked. 'What's happening?'

'Nothing yet,' I said.

The gases' hiss was still in my blood – and the balaclava impeded my breathing – but I began to run. I ran through memories of tastes and touches: the stamp of cobalt trainers on my head, the canal's weary coolness, the jab of Kimber's gun into my wound, the wetness of the sink in Kimber's kitchen, the sangria-scent of my vomit this morning and the furriness of it in my throat as I threw it up. Francis hovered beside me as a perfume, of wheatgrass and coconut – and stupidly I smiled at it. I was running over a quilt of black and yellow squares, as though the pavement had closed its own eyes and was kneading them with its knuckles – externalising the interior landscape of a pressured optic nerve. The streetlamps glided by in bubbles.

As I rounded the corner, I split into four Leanders, in relay with myself, with the truncheon as our baton. We were racing each other towards the Rockway's front entrance, exchanging the baton at every step – finally as lithe and agile and nubile as I'd always longed to be, passing through myself towards myself beyond myself. There was nobody outside the bar except the steroidal doorman I'd confronted twice already. But I was no longer a lad – to him, now, I was a policeman.

So he backed inside, shutting the door before the four of me could reach him. I pulled off my glove with my teeth – barging into the other versions of myself – and retrieved the Rockway keys from the bag. With them, I double-locked the door from the outside – and so condemned all inside to the coming fire.

Iris's car drove up beside me – and the four Leanders simplified again into one. I climbed alone into the passenger side.

'What the fuck are you doing?'

'Just drive,' I said.

She drove. I removed the other glove and the helmet and the balaclava. With my freed hands, I ripped open the string-bag of satsumas.

'Wait – can you just stop at the top of the hill?' I asked, unpeeling the ripest fruit.

'Why?' she asked.

'Just please?'

She stopped the car. We were floating above South London like a pirate radio signal – crackling and spectral and degraded – a song for lonely bedrooms. I bit slowly into my first segment of satsuma, watching the Rockway in the wing-mirror. And before I had swallowed it – the kitchen exploded.

A belly of flame howled upwards towards us – and my signature was written across the sky.

'Fuck!' Iris shouted, and jerked the car forwards.

The fire kicked like a child forcing itself out of its mother – the brick façade imploded and scattered back upwards, borne by eager crimson cords. Smoke rose around it. The blaze's edges matched exactly the orange of my satsuma, though where the flame met smoke there were glimmers of viridian – like the neck of a pheasant whose plumage was the fire.

And as the Rockway shrunk in the mirror, the fire swelled – a roof collapsed, delighting the air with its dust – and I ate my satsuma, piece by piece, imagining the fists shrieking against the bar's locked doors. With each hit, I felt the keys in my pocket become vaguer, their teeth eroding into nubs that could unlock nothing now – until at last, I heard doors that had been locked all across my childhood burst open and open and open – as hundreds of younger Leanders walked out into sunlight.

To my intoxicated gaze, the building burning behind me seemed an image of my own body – so the ruined plasma of my blood was now copied by this ruin of lit stone, goaded by flames towards that other kind of plasma – the most universal state of matter, to which we all return.

The car came to a corner – and the fire left the mirror. I finished my satsuma. Nothing solid behind me remained.

6.

Iris yelled as I drifted along the borders of consciousness. The propane I'd inhaled mingled with the memory of paint thinner and heroin in my lungs. I let her yell until she exhausted herself. As we entered Francis' borough, she quietened, and I slipped lower into sleep.

She prodded my wound to wake me. We were parked by Francis' house, a few paces from where I'd crashed the police car. Its wreck had been towed away, but fragments of a shattered headlight glittered on the pavement still. Serenely I stepped into the evening – and was greeted by a weather equally serene. The storms of the week were spent, and now there hung instead a gibbous moon – alone, since London's light pollution had cancelled every star.

Iris walked me to Francis' door. At the ringing of his bell, I flinched – recalling my collapse here two days before and, with a curious anger, recalling the resolutions I'd offered up to the snow. Perhaps I was only now overhearing what I'd said then – and so was only now able to act upon those resolutions. I was angered by my old conception of myself, but this anger felt also like a longing – a longing to retire an ontology on a doorstep, so that when I was let indoors, my notion of selfhood would not come in with me, and I could begin to forge a new one.

Maybe my contradictions could not be resolved, but it seemed for the first time that I had another option besides revenge

– perhaps because I had exhausted revenge; it seemed that a new type of confession was available to me, which might at least lessen a little the burden of those contradictions. Francis probably knew more of me than I suspected – but I wanted now to tell him everything, and then to become someone else – or at least understand 'becoming' in a different way. I didn't want to 'seem to be' anyone before him – I wanted to forget the necessity of artifice completely, so that seeming and being were irrelevant – and that in his company, my mind simply was my body, and my act was simply the skin he was touching.

Eva opened the door to us. She smiled in confusion at my police uniform, and hugged me over the threshold.

'You look like you need a drink,' she said.

'I definitely do,' Iris said. 'Leander has outdone himself.'

Eva led us down the hall to the kitchen.

'Can we make mulled wine?' I asked.

'Sure. And I can cook you whatever you want as long as it's this exact omelette,' Eva pointed to a frying pan on the hob.

'I hate omelettes.' But as I said this, I remembered Dawn confusing the word 'omelette' for 'oubliette', and smiled. 'Or maybe I like them.'

'You can share it,' Eva said, halving it across two plates. 'And I'm only happy when I'm feeding you things you hate. If you upset me too much I'll make you drink more rice milk – I got another carton just in case. And there's spiced rum over there.' She gestured towards a bottle beside the radiator. 'It's basically hot enough to be like that German version of mulled wine. You're supposed to burn a sugar cube over it first. But you can do that in your imagination.'

Iris poured the rum out to the midpoint of two large tea-mugs – and handed me mine with religious sobriety. We drained them in tandem, meeting each other's eyes only as we slammed them emptied onto the granite.

'What are you celebrating?' Eva asked, alarmed by our speed.

'He just burnt a building down,' Iris said, coughing at the taste.

'No,' I said. 'I helped a building realise its potential.'

'What building?' Eva asked.

'My mother's tomb.'

'A bar in Brixton,' Iris said.

'It's called the Rockway,' I said. 'And it asked me to burn it down.'

'Why are you in a police uniform?' Eva asked.

'These were my robes,' I said. 'I wished to be disguised as authority.'

'I need to sit down,' Iris said.

She picked up her plate and carried it the table, shaking her head. And as she sat down, she smiled at us – as if she were on a train instead of a chair, leaving to somewhere else, and shouted, 'Long live decadence!'

I laughed, although I didn't understand the joke.

'Congratulations on your first magazine cover,' Eva said, leaning closer to me. 'I'm dying with jealousy.'

'It probably wasn't worth what I had to do to get it,' I said.

'Is Iris still pretending to be furious? She loved it. And Amélie keeps saying "he's perfect, he's perfect." She doesn't give a shit about her laptop. She couldn't be happier with you. She loved the magazine cover, she loved the police raid. Iris has been obsessively watching back the footage of you. You've saved us. And I've probably fallen in love with you as well, by the way, but I can't tell you that.'

'So you want me to be in more of the film?' I asked, with faux-naïvety.

'I require you to be in more of the film,' she smiled. 'You are the only person keeping things fun around here.'

'You're veering into hagiography...'

'It's the only way left to annoy you. But it's true. I've spoken to Francis – we're fine now. Everything's fine. We needed it...

we were stuck, it was pointless, I was in love with him, I still am, but he's not and it's pointless and now it's over. I'm old enough to forgive him, and he's young enough to… be discovering himself still. That's a better way of doing it. My friend's dad didn't act on any of his desires for men until he was like forty-four – and then he went off-piste, wrecked his marriage, fucked up his kids, got into debt, tripled their mortgage till they were evicted, spent ten years crawling down a line of exploitative boyfriends half his age, and then died of a stroke alone in a B&B. Fuck that.'

'Yeah,' I said. 'Always yield to your demon. The longer you wait the stronger it gets.'

'Except – in your case, you must yield to your angel. Me and Iris have decided that you're secretly a sweetheart – and it's time for you to come out the closet.'

'Ugh. Can I not keep some of my secrets to myself?'

'No. Now go upstairs and win back my boyfriend. He needs it. I can't do it. It's your turn to be the angel. Love him till he feels normal again.'

She lifted her chin like a ballet dancer, lengthening further her long neck – and I kissed it – and it still had the afterscent of her lily of the valley perfume.

'You used to think I was a paradox,' I complained as I kissed her.

'Aw, you still are, don't worry. But a paradox doesn't have to be an ambiguity. Sometimes – in art and life, and the art of life – ambiguity is essential. But sometimes it's cowardly. Choosing can be more difficult than implying. And you claim to prefer difficulty. So go upstairs and let everything be true, rather than nothing. Give in to your affection.'

'I was going to anyway,' I said sullenly.

She kissed me, smiling, and shoved me into the hall. 'Go.'

I obeyed. The walls and carpets were a swamp of carmine-red mud – in which, I could feel, hippopotamuses were hiding.

I ran upstairs, afraid of being sucked under – and knocked on Francis' door.

'It's me,' I said.

There was a shuffling in reply. I entered. The prick of an incense stick burnt through the darkness – and I imagined its tendrils assembling into a bdellium tree above me – which wept in a sunlight that I couldn't see, as its perfume was adulterated by lesser perfumes – and its branches grew white spots shaped like fingernails – and these fingernails all pointed at me – like I was the adulterer.

'Wake up,' I said, stumbling towards Francis' bedside.

He moaned, rolling away from me – releasing the bloom of a fever into the incense. I shook his shoulder.

'Francis!' I said. 'Francis.'

He elbowed me away – but then suddenly pushed himself up against the headboard, fully awake.

'I was just pretending,' he said.

I smiled, tiredly, unable to answer, perhaps about to cry – and handed him the bag of satsumas.

'What's this?' he asked.

'It's an elixir,' I said. 'A hero has to return from his journey with an elixir. Eat it and you'll be cured.'

'What's in it though?'

'It's either a satsuma or a tangerine or a clementine or a mandarin or an unshu mikan or a Christmas orange.'

'Relax.'

I smiled again, trying to summon the courage to speak to him properly. His silhouette picked out a satsuma and began to unpeel it. I took off my riot cop jacket.

'I wanted to say… sorry,' I said, forcing this out uncomfortably. 'I'm sorry. Everything I've done was… wrong. I wanted to tell you – everything about me. The… I was trying to act like I was strong. But you were right – I'm disgusting.'

'I didn't mean that,' he said, biting into a sliver of satsuma. 'I mean I meant it, but I didn't mean – I mean you was disgusting – you was covered in sick and white shit and there was blood everywhere. But you're alright now. I don't need to hear it. You're alright. I'm alright.'

'They said you were ill.'

'Not with you here.'

'I don't…' To my surprise, I was crying. 'You should be angry. I'm not ready for you to be kind to me. I'm… I fucked it up. You saw me… you saw what I'm like and you… I'm a psychopath – you can't love that.'

'Ah, shut up. Shut the fuck up. You sound like you're trying to convince yourself, but it's not working. Just sit down.' He pulled me onto the bed beside to him. 'Everything that happened – that weren't you – I know what's you. You got me out of there. This is you here, right here.'

I pulled away.

'I don't know how to be here, I'm never here.'

He pulled me back against him. 'What you mean?'

'Everything feels like it's separate from me,' I said, slowly, trying to confess. 'Like I'm living inside my own memoirs. I can't get in to the present – I'm watching myself after it's happened even when it's happening. The only time I ever felt like I was living in the present tense was after I died on your doorstep.'

'Fuck that. You're buying into this shit too much. You're not in a memoir. You're not in a film, you're not in a book. You're here.' He nudged me. 'See?'

'Ok,' I said.

He shifted to the right so I could climb in beside him.

'Tell me then,' he laughed. 'Let it out for once. What ain't you been telling me? When did this start?'

'What do you mean?' I asked.

I was intimidated by how straightforward we were being, but happy too – to be near him, to be listening. His words had the assurance of a shower of rain in May – and I imagined it washing over a field of wheat around us.

'The thing you're talking about,' he said. 'The feeling of not being here. When did that start?'

I stared into the darkness above us until the air turned ultramarine – as though the colour was gathering up my myalgia outside my body, beyond the heroin's defences – together waiting to be let back in.

'I dunno,' I said. 'Always. It got worse when my myalgia got worse – in puberty.'

'What's that? Myalgia?'

'It's pain – from a disease I've had for a decade. It's a constant pointless incurable muscle pain that blurs everything – it blurs days together, blurs the borders of your body, blurs your sense of yourself. You can't concentrate, you can't remember, you can't sleep – or if you sleep, you wake up worse. It broke me, and then I had to keep on going anyway. And that made me cruel, probably. I wanted to make other people feel what I had to feel… and I wanted… I dunno. Chronic pain isn't interesting – people can't relate to it.'

'What? You ain't told me this before. Why you ain't told me this before?' he asked – louder. 'You been like this for – you had… myalgia for a decade?'

'I didn't know you'd… believe me. And I didn't want you to pity me – I didn't want you to think I was… weak.'

'What did you just say?' He was nearly shouting. 'What did you say? That's the stupidest shit I ever heard out your mouth. What the fuck you on about?' He hit me in frustration. 'You was ill for ten years and you ain't told me before? You been in pain the whole time?'

'I don't tell people – because you can't see it, can you, I don't look that bad – it's invisible. Or… I kind of tell people – in a different way – that's how I… dealt with it. I thought, maybe if I made it into a metaphor… I could be understood. Everyone knows what a bad guy is. So I thought maybe if I told myself I was the villain – I could take back control from what was wrong with me. Being ill is so passive, and sickness and evil are so easily linked, so… "Carnivore" sounds better than "boy with unnamed chronic illness", doesn't it?' I laughed unhappily. 'But I realised – when I was on your doorstep, and you weren't there – carnivores don't have control either. They're bound to their condition, like I've always been, they can't control it.'

'Ah, shut up. Stop it. You're not a carnivore. You was joking when you was telling me about them. And now you're believing yourself! It means flesh-eater, yeah? So that's what your disease is, it sounds like – hurting you, eating you away – that's the carnivore, not you.'

I paused. 'Fuck, Francis, you actually are quite clever.'

He hit me again. I grinned.

'I always thought I was the cleverest person I knew,' I said. 'It's stupid, I need to grow out of it. But yeah maybe, maybe the disease can be the carnivore, not me, not us – it leaves no bite marks, but it's eating me alive.'

'But can it get better?' His concern still struggled with his anger. 'I can't believe you ain't… You should of said. I should know. You're a fucking weasel for that. It ain't – this ain't about pitying you – it's about… I'm supposed to be a support, you know? I want to be. It don't make you weak, it makes you – well,' he laughed, 'I mean it does make you weak probably, for your body and your mind yeah – but not your… I dunno, not your… not you.'

I grinned wider, and was pleased he couldn't see it in the darkness. 'It made me me,' I said, forcing myself to sound glum, hiding my joy at his words. 'For hours and months and years in bed – I had to go into myself alone – it taught me the world until the world was transparent and I could see through it and fly above it – because being in this much pain, being ill forever, with the years an amnesiac blur behind me, feels like flying

– over London's skyscrapers, reflecting the infected sky, in a sunset the colour of nectarines… I feel it all, hyper-keenly – but at a remove, synaesthetically – like I'm buzzing, at the wrong frequency to everyone else.'

'So how did you… get through school then? What did you…' He still sounded shocked.

Beneath my layers, my sweat had formed a film – so as I answered, I undressed – removing first the riot cop under-jacket, then Francis' two sweatshirts, then his shirt.

'That's what my last headmistress asked when I left,' I said. 'I changed schools twice, and then I left forever. I told her school felt like a garlic crusher – where you put in the garlic and press out all the flavour through a grid until only the dry dead strands are left behind. And I was the strands.'

'What'd she say to that?'

'She gave me quite good advice actually.' I pulled off my last top. 'She said – you're angry – you should use your anger, don't waste it – use it.' I rested back into him, my bare arm against his chest. 'But I didn't listen. I wasted it. And now look where I am.'

'Hey!' he elbowed me indignantly. 'Yeah – fucking look where you are! You're with me! You've made it up to the top!'

I laughed, but stayed still, not yet ready to respond to his touch. I wanted to say that living off disability benefits and hate and heroin and sex work didn't feel like living at the top – but that kind of wry remark didn't seem to suit me any more – and my mouth refused to say it. So instead I asked, 'What about your school?'

'School was shit,' he said. 'I only cared about fucking around. It was a waste of time. When you're talking about books they sound alright – but the books we had in our lessons was a fucking disaster. I seen scam emails trying to get my bank details that are better written than those fucking exam poems. My dad dropped out when he was sixteen so he didn't care if I did. And my mum weren't around, was she? We just went to the park and got drunk or got high. And then I got scouted to model, so it was fine. Don't need to read for that, do I?' he laughed, slightly bitterly.

I removed my socks – and wriggled out of the riot cop trousers, and then out of Francis' tracksuit bottoms – until, for the first time in a long time, I was no longer in any uniform.

'You stayed in school longer than me,' I said. 'I tried to study on my own – I went to the library – first because I was homeless and it was warm, and then I just went to read. I found books that weren't as shit as the ones we had to do at school. I grew up in them – and in hospitals – that was my friends. That was it, for years. Stories were the only things that stretched me out.'

Francis squirmed from his sitting position, pulling me with him, until we were lying, naked, our heads turned towards each other on the pillow.

'I liked history,' he said after a pause.

I turned my body inwards to his. 'Which bit?'

'They only teach you the Second World War, don't they? We did that every year for ten years.'

'It's the only time the English weren't the main bad guys.'

'But I liked some of it.'

'Which part?'

'I liked when they was sleeping in their horses,' he said. 'It was on a lake – it was Germans in Russia, maybe, and they had to escape and it was frozen so they had to kill their horses and cut out their stomachs and eat them and sleep inside them to get warm.'

'Oh that old trick. They did it in Napoleon's wars as well, but it was with French soldiers. Basically never try to invade Russia. You'll end up inside a horse.'

'I'll try to remember that.'

'Actually… you're the second person that's talked to me about horses today,' I said suspiciously. 'I was with a policewoman who said she cooked them. And I was speaking to Dawn about horses as well – I said being crushed by a horse was a good metaphor for… being crushed.'

He laughed. 'That does make some sense.'

'There are good novels about the Second World War.'

'Yeah? What's the top ten?'

He said this to annoy me – so I hit him. 'Top-ten lists are for boys with erectile dysfunction.'

'Ok but say one,' he said, his mouth closer to mine.

His skin smelt of peppermint – perhaps from an aftershave, since he was newly-shaved – so I kissed it.

'How about… *The Notebook* by Ágota Kristóf?' I said. 'It's about two brothers in the Second World War. Kind of an evil fairy tale. I like books that feel like they're poisoning you as you read them. At the end they trick their father into walking onto a minefield – so that he explodes, clearing the way for them. And they say, "Yes, there is a way to get across the frontier: it's to make someone else go first."'

'Did you just spoil the ending?' Francis whispered. 'You little cunt.'

He drifted his nose across my cheek. I smiled at the memory of the machines I'd dreamed of after my heart stopped – who'd called me a little cunt too and who'd said that everything was a surface. I pulled on Francis' arm until his body was over mine.

'Spoilers are for disposable stories,' I said. 'If the ending only affects you once, then it's a weak ending.'

'Yeah?' he said 'I'll tell you the end of your book – and then we'll see if you're still smiling.'

He kissed me and pressed his chest into mine. And with his arms around my neck, I thought of the necklace he'd given me a few days ago – the necklace that I'd thrown away. But this necklace here would last longer than that silver one with its tiny key – since this could be worn in a memory stronger than memory, stronger than flesh, long after he'd left and I was alone and wearing nothing.

'Ok but – before then, can you do me one tiny favour?' I asked, withdrawing slightly. 'You know it's my birthday today.'

'Is that true?' He bit on my lip to pull me back. 'Happy birthday.'

'Yeah – childhood's done. I'm a man now. And as my present – can you lie to the police?'

'No.'

'Ok but can you pervert the course of justice just a little bit?'

'No.'

'What about silence? You're a model – come on, you're a professional at having nothing to say. Can you just do silence, please?'

'Yeah. I can do silence.'

'No comment.'

'No comment,' he agreed.

'No memories.'

'Of what?'

I kissed him.

And, now reassured, my muscles lost their gravity. Lightened instead by dopamine, they craved only to be used.

My fingers across his back discovered a scar – and as I stroked it, I wondered how many hours ago he'd gained it, but didn't ask. His fingers found a matching one along my spine – and these mutual wounds did not seem signs of our vulnerability, but rather of our imperviousness to danger – since here we still were, despite them. Perhaps they allowed us a greater tenderness, even, since they remembered an opposite more extreme.

'You're my man now,' Francis said, folding himself into me. 'And I know you're here now, I can trust it. I want here to be your home. That's love. And that's what makes me so alright about everything, cos I've got you, you know what I mean? I know it sounds like… the words are dead cos they've been used too many times, but it's only cos of you that I'm… that I'm alright. Do you know what I mean? I thought you was going to die.'

'Not yet. I found a way out.'

'What's the way?' he asked – and kissed me, knowing any answer belonged beyond words.

All sex and storytelling ends beyond words, of course – but finding happiness beyond those words felt like my most audacious act of deviance yet. And so we fucked – and I smiled inwardly, my mind defenceless at last before itself and before his. And we curled into each other, and came, and uncurled out in silent laughter – towards an unshared meaningless dream.

Acknowledgements

Fibromyalgia, Myalgic Encephalomyletis, Lyme Disease, and Chronic Fatigue Syndrome – all are interchangeable names for the same hell – where I wrote this book. In doing so I hoped to make more visible an invisible epidemic. Despite the tens of millions of sufferers worldwide, there is no treatment or cure. Quack psychiatrists have done enough damage – we need real science to save us, otherwise hundreds of millions more will get sick.

Our healthcare systems need to realise that what they're doing isn't working for chronic disease.

I would like to say thank you to Zoe Ross for her supportive ear, Clio Cornish for her perceptive eye, Lisa Milton for her guiding hand, and Charlie Redmayne for his first bite. And to J most of all – for still listening – and maybe yeah I even still love you.

ONE PLACE. MANY STORIES

Bold, innovative and
empowering publishing.

FOLLOW US ON:

@HQStories